When a
Dragon Falls

Also by Kerrelyn Sparks:

How to Love Your Elf

The Siren and the Deep Blue Sea

When a Princess Proposes

When a Dragon Falls

kerrelyn SPARKS

KENSINGTON
PUBLISHING CORP.
www.kensingtonbooks.com

KENSINGTON BOOKS are published by

Kensington Publishing Corp.
119 West 40th Street
New York, NY 10018

All Kensington titles, imprints, and distributed lines are available at special quantity discounts for bulk purchases for sales promotion, premiums, fund-raising, educational, or institutional use.

This book is a work of fiction. Names, characters, businesses, organizations, places, events, and incidents either are the product of the author's imagination or are used fictitiously. Any resemblance to actual persons, living or dead, events, or locales is entirely coincidental.

To the extent that the image or images on the cover of this book depict a person or persons, such person or persons are merely models, and are not intended to portray any character or characters featured in the book.

Special book excerpts or customized printings can also be created to fit specific needs. For details, write or phone the office of the Kensington Sales Manager: Kensington Publishing Corp., 119 West 40th Street, New York, NY 10018. Attn. Sales Department. Phone: 1-800-221-2647.

The K with book logo Reg US Pat. & TM Off.

ISBN: 978-1-4967-3587-4 (ebook)

ISBN: 978-1-4967-3586-7

First Kensington Trade Paperback Printing: November 2023

10 9 8 7 6 5 4 3 2 1

Printed in the United States of America

With all my love to
my husband, hero, and best friend,
Don

ACKNOWLEDGMENTS

Over the last few years as my husband has battled stage-four cancer, my priorities have necessarily shifted from writing to helping my husband with his courageous fight for survival. So, I'd like to take this opportunity to thank my lovely readers for their patience over the long wait between books.

I'd also like to thank all the wonderful folks at Kensington Publishing for being so kind and supportive. I am blessed to have the best editor I've ever known, Alicia Condon. My thanks also to my agent, Michelle Grajkowski of Three Seas, for always being there for me.

Each day can be a struggle, so I am extremely grateful for my best friends and critique partners, MJ and Sandy, who keep me reasonably sane while they go over everything I write. They've been doing that for over twenty years now! Thank you, my dear friends.

And lastly, I want to thank my husband, who has always encouraged me and been proud of me. Keep fighting, my love. I will be there by your side.

Prologue

In another time on another world called Aerthlan, there are five kingdoms. Four of them extend across a vast continent, and the fifth, a kingdom of three islands, lies in the Great Western Ocean.

Twice a year, the two moons eclipse each other in an event called the Embrace. Any child born on those nights will be gifted with a magical power. Those children are known as the Embraced. Once feared by the people on the mainland, they are now widely accepted. After all, it was the Embraced kings and queens who defeated the worst danger ever to threaten Aerthlan—the Circle of Five.

But now, after twenty years of peace, a remnant of the circle called the Brotherhood of the Sun is threatening to destroy that hard-earned peace and kill the royal families in order to take over the five kingdoms of Aerthlan. The Seer, Queen Maeve, has dreamed of dark clouds spreading across the entire continent. Even though the headquarters of the Brotherhood was destroyed and the former Master killed, there are still members of the cult hiding and plotting in secret.

No one knows where the new Master may be hidden. No one knows how many followers he has or where they could strike next.

They only know the Embraced are in danger.

Chapter 1

Early spring, year 721
Lourdon Palace, Tourin

Princess Lenushka of Norveshka was tempted to breathe fire on one of the awful gowns and set it ablaze. Could she claim it was an accident? Brought on, perhaps, by an unfortunate hiccough. A touch of convenient heartburn.

Or could she be overreacting? After all, she wasn't accustomed to wearing a gown. Her years of military training had left her with a natural preference for breeches. Even now, she was wearing the dark green uniform that indicated her rank of captain in the Norveshki army. But it only took a quick glance at the stricken faces of her cousins, who were all habitual gown-wearers, to confirm that her first impression had been correct.

The bridesmaid gowns for Princess Roslyn's wedding were absolutely hideous.

Lennie sucked in a deep breath. What could she do? If she burned one gown to a crisp, the five other bridesmaids would be annoyed that she hadn't relieved them of their equally horrible gowns. Besides, she wasn't sure which one was actually hers.

Should she set them all ablaze? That would risk setting the room on fire, or even the entire palace, putting numerous people in danger. Not a great move the day before a big wedding. And she suspected none of her friends or family would believe it was an accident. They all knew how hard she had worked to gain complete control over her flying and fire-breathing capabilities.

As the first female dragon shifter in the world, Princess Lenushka was viewed by some as a miracle, but by others as a dreadful aberration. There were many Norveshki, mostly men, who were always watching for any sign that she was inferior and unworthy of being a dragon. And especially unworthy of inheriting the throne.

"Well, what do you think?" Roslyn asked, her face flushed with excitement, just a shade lighter than her carnation pink gown. "You seem quite speechless, so I can only assume that the gowns are as stunning as I planned them to be."

Lennie exchanged a wary glance with the other bridesmaids. Even though they referred to one another as cousins, Lennie was related to only two of them: Kendall and Glenda, the elfin princesses from Woodwyn. Lennie even resembled Glenda a bit, since they both had the white-blond hair of a River Elf, whereas Kendall's hair was dark red like a Wood Elf's.

Now that Lennie thought about it, there was another set of actual cousins in the room: Princess Julia of the Isles and Lady Faith. They looked quite similar with their black hair and blue eyes.

That left the last two young ladies present: Princess Roslyn of Tourin, who would be wed tomorrow, and Princess Eviana of Eberon, who had surprised everyone by suddenly getting married five months ago.

Related or not, all seven considered themselves cousins, and so, it had come as no surprise when eight months ago Princess Roslyn had asked the six of them to be her bridesmaids.

All the members of the royal families had originally intended to come to the wedding, but a month ago the Seer, Queen Maeve, had dreamed of an ominous cloud seeping out of Eberon to cast a dark shadow over the entire mainland. With this elevated threat of danger, each king had made plans to safeguard his country.

In Eberon, Prince Eric and General Nevis Harden had remained behind with the army on alert. In Norveshka, Lennie's father, King Silas, had left the capital in the hands of his cousin Annika and her husband, Dimitri, a powerful dragon shifter and general of the Norveshki army. Silas and his children, Lenushka and Pendras, were all dragon shifters, so if an emergency occurred, they could fly back to Norveshka in less than two hours.

That was not the case for the elfin kingdom of Woodwyn, from which the journey would take at least five days. So, King Brennan and his son had remained at Wyndelas Palace. Queen Sorcha and her daughters, Kendall and Glenda, had made the journey with three troops of soldiers and, guarding them from above, the dragon shifter Aleksi Marenko.

On the Isle of Moon, the crown prince had stayed behind while King Brodgar and his wife and daughter sailed across the Great Western Ocean to Tourin's capital, Lourdon, situated on the Loure River.

Tomorrow afternoon at Lourdon Cathedral, the big event would finally take place. Princess Roslyn would wed Earl Freydor, the owner of a huge estate that spanned several hundred miles of Tourin's northernmost mountainous area and jagged coastline.

From what Lennie had heard, the earl was not only young and handsome, but the wealthiest nobleman in the country thanks to the gold mine he owned. About nine months ago, he had journeyed to the royal court to beg King Ulfrid to rid his coastline of some pesky pirates who had been raiding his precious gold supply, and that was when he'd successfully courted the king's daughter.

But as far as Lennie could tell, Roslyn had not spent any time with the earl since that initial courtship, so she hardly knew him at all. She was much more interested in producing what she called the "wedding of the century" than in becoming better acquainted with the groom.

Lennie had hinted at her concern this morning over breakfast, but Roslyn had simply waved a dismissive hand, claiming that she and her future husband would have the rest of their lives to develop a closer relationship. After rushing all the bridesmaids through breakfast, Roslyn had whisked them off to the large parlor adjoining her bedchamber so each one could be fitted for her gown. The group had been happily chatting when they'd entered the room to find a line of six dressmaker dummies draped with white sheets, each with a maidservant standing nearby. With a dramatic wave of her hand, Roslyn had ordered the six servants to whip off the sheets all at once.

And the room had become deathly quiet. No one wanted to be the first to admit what they really thought.

The design for all the gowns was the same—an overabundance of lace, ruffles, fringe, flounces, and general puffiness—but each one was a different pastel color. Yellow, pale pink, rose, green, blue, and lavender. If that wasn't enough, each gown boasted a feathered bird in a matching color, perched on the right shoulder with its talons clamped onto a nest of sparkly ribbons.

Lennie suppressed a shudder. The wings of each bird were spread wide as if the creatures all intended to take flight, presumably in an attempt to escape the horrendous gowns that held them prisoner. From the way the birds' black eyes were glaring at her, she imagined they were even more revolted by the creations than she was.

"You may go now." Roslyn waved the servants off. "Bring

us some refreshments and tell the seamstress to come in case we need to make any adjustments. Oh, and let me know immediately if there's any news about my father."

"Aye, Your Highness." The maids curtsied and filed out of the room.

A befuddled expression came over Roslyn's face as the silence stretched out, and she nervously tucked her long blond hair behind one ear. Then, with a quick breath, she apparently reached some sort of conclusion for she gave them all an amused smile. "There's no need to look so shocked. I know the birds appear very lifelike, but they're not real. I can assure you that no animals were harmed in the making of these gowns."

"What a relief," Julia muttered.

"Indeed." Roslyn skipped over to the lavender gown and patted the hawk-like lavender bird on its feathered head. "But you must agree they *look* incredibly real. The artists who made them did a fabulous job."

Her smile faded as the room became silent once more. "Ah. I feared this would happen. You're all afraid you won't receive your favorite color." With a dramatic sigh, she sauntered down the row of gowns to the first one. "I can't tell you how many sleepless nights I endured, worried that you would end up in a terrible argument over who would wear which color. I finally decided that the most sensible course of action was to proceed according to age."

She stopped by the first gown and fondly stroked the oversized yellow canary perched on the shoulder. "That means this lovely yellow one belongs to the eldest, Eviana."

Lennie glanced at her best friend, Evie, whose pallor was rapidly becoming an even sicklier shade of yellow than her new gown.

"Of course, I'm the second eldest." Roslyn chuckled as she strolled toward the next gown. "But we have to skip me because I'm the bride."

Lennie tensed. *Goddesses, no. Not the pink.* The pink bird's beak was open as if it were laughing at her.

"The pale pink gown will go to the third eldest, Lenushka." Roslyn sighed as she fingered the pink lace. "How lucky you are, Lennie, to be wearing my absolute favorite color."

Lennie's hands curled into fists. She couldn't do this. Over the years, she'd endured far too many jests regarding the pinkish tint of her underbelly when in dragon form. *Girly scales,* her detractors called them. She'd also taken jabs over being smaller than the male dragons. *Size is important,* they would say, snickering at their not-so-subtle innuendo. More than once, she had been tempted to shorten the root of their masculine bravado with a not-so-subtle, well-aimed burst of fire.

"Relax," Kendall whispered in her ear. "There's smoke coming out your nose."

Lennie exhaled slowly to quell the heat simmering in her chest.

Oblivious, since her attention was focused entirely on the gowns, Roslyn continued down the line of dressmaker dummies. "Julia will wear the rose. Kendall, the green. Faith, the blue, and Glenda, the lavender. I do believe, Glenda, that this one will look fabulous with your lavender-colored eyes."

"How . . . convenient." Glenda's smile of gratitude looked more like a grimace. "Is there a reason why we have different colors?"

"And birds?" Eviana asked with a pained expression.

Lennie figured Evie was particularly uncomfortable at the prospect of wearing an ornamental bird since her newly wedded husband was an eagle shifter.

"Of course!" Roslyn grinned. "I was hoping you would ask. It all has to do with the theme of the wedding: A Most Glorious Day. My gown is a shimmering gold, so I will resemble the sun rising in the east as I walk down the aisle. And all of you will become my living rainbow." She waved a hand dramatically in the air as she gazed into the distance. "And just as the birds fly over the rainbow, I will take flight into my new and glorious future."

Eviana suddenly covered her mouth as if she were about to lose her breakfast.

"Are you all right?" Faith asked.

"Sorry." Eviana eased into a chair. "A bit of morning sickness."

"I feel the same way, and I'm not even expecting," Julia grumbled.

Roslyn huffed, frowning at Eviana. "I was quite shocked by your news, Evie. How could you even think about getting with child when you knew my wedding was just around the corner? I had everyone's gowns made according to the measurements you sent me four months ago. I'll be terribly upset if your gown no longer fits!"

"I'm sure it will," Eviana replied dryly. "I'm only six weeks pregnant."

"And I'm fairly certain you don't become that way by thinking about it," Julia added with a wry smile.

Lennie snorted. "True. You do realize, Roz, that after your wedding night, you might be with child, too?"

With a grimace, Roslyn shuddered. "Don't even say that. I refuse to have anything to do with such nonsense. Freydor will have to wait a few years before I'll feel like giving him an heir."

There was a collective gasp, and then Kendall asked, "You don't intend to sleep with your new husband?"

Roslyn huffed. "We're here to try on these beautiful gowns, not talk about nasty things."

Eviana sat back with a stunned look. "Why would you call it nast— You don't love him, do you?"

Roslyn shrugged. "I'm expected to marry, so I picked the best option available."

"Oh, *this* is romantic," Glenda muttered.

"I'm sure I'll love him with the passing of time," Roslyn protested. "He's young, handsome, and rich. What is there not to love? Besides, his estate has the best clay in the country. And he's promised to build me a marvelous studio where I can devote myself entirely to my pottery."

"So you're marrying him for his mud?" Lennie asked.

Roslyn's turquoise eyes flashed with anger. "Don't make light of my decision. I may not be Embraced or a shifter like most of you, but I do have a talent, and I intend to make the most of it." She turned away with an injured look on her face. "Do you think I enjoyed being the only princess at Benwick Academy who didn't have some sort of magical power? Whenever a new student arrived, I could hear the whispers: *Look! There's the powerless princess.*"

Lennie winced. Why had she never realized how difficult it must have been for Roslyn? *Because you were too focused on your own problem of being accepted as a female in a male dragon world.* "I'm sorry. I didn't mean to upset you."

Eviana sighed. "Honestly, Roz, there were many times when I was envious of you. I would have given anything not to have the terrible power I possess, and I would have loved to have attended Benwick with all of you."

Kendall nodded. "None of us can help the way we were born. And no one has ever thought any less of you, Roz."

"True," Glenda agreed. "Everyone thinks you're beautiful and clever."

"Very clever." Faith smiled. "There were many times when you had the highest score on the written exams."

"And you were the best on the archery field," Julia added.

"Because I practiced until my fingers bled, and I stayed up all night studying." Roslyn's eyes filled with tears. "I hated being called the ordinary one, the *normal* princess. So I always worked extra hard to stand out. And my wedding will be the same way. It will be the most stupendous ever."

"Aye, it will." Lennie exchanged a resigned look with her cousins. They would have to wear the hideous gowns. "I was just concerned that you were getting married for the wrong reasons."

Eviana nodded. "We want you to be happy."

"I *am* happy," Roslyn insisted. "I'm going to have the most fabulous wedding ever, and then I'm going to make the most marvelous pottery you've ever seen. Did you see the dishes I made for the wedding reception?"

"Yes, they're quite beautiful," Lennie conceded. Roslyn had designed the pattern to artfully merge the Tourinian royal colors of blue and gold with the earl's colors of maroon and gold. So why hadn't Roslyn's excellent taste extended to the bridesmaid gowns?

Roslyn gripped her hands together. "I've been working on the wedding for eight months now. I didn't even let Aunt Maeve's scary dream slow me down. I finished making all the dishes. The flowers and food are progressing on schedule. The musicians are here. The royal guests have come. The groom and his party arrived two nights ago, and he brought me those lovely flowers." She gestured impatiently to a nearby table where a large vase sat, filled with three dozen red roses.

"I haven't seen him since then because there's so much to do!" As Roslyn paced back and forth, her voice became louder and more and more shrill with agitation. "I have to make sure everything is perfect, but now it's all in jeopardy because of my father! The wedding is tomorrow, and we haven't heard from him in a week! How could he do this to me? What if he doesn't make it here in time? Surely, this is the most dreadful thing that could ever happen in the entire world. Do you think this is the reason for Aunt Maeve's terrible dream? *Is there a dark cloud of doom hanging over my wedding?*"

"No, no, of course not," all the bridesmaids assured her.

Roslyn's father, King Ulfrid, also known as Rupert, had taken a small fleet of ships to eradicate the pirates who had been attacking the northern coast. He'd left three weeks ago, expecting the mission to last only a week or so, but apparently something had gone wrong.

"Don't worry, Roz," Lennie told her. "My father and Aleksi left at the crack of dawn. I'm certain they'll locate your father. And they can contact me, my mother, and my brother telepathically, so we expect to hear from them any minute now."

"Aye." Kendall nodded. "Everything will be fine. Silas and Aleksi are two of the most powerful dragons in the world. I'm sure they can handle whatever problem may have occurred."

Roslyn wrung her hands. "I hope so. I'm not the only one upset. Mother is beside herself with worry."

"Don't forget your father has the power of the wind," Faith reminded her. "Even if he's out in the middle of the Great Western Ocean, he can blow himself here in a few hours."

Roslyn sighed. "You would think so, but—" She paused when a knock sounded at the door. "Come in!"

The seamstress, with her sewing basket in one hand, opened the door to let in two maids, who were carrying trays filled with a pot of hot tea, cheese, bread, and some of the new dishes Roslyn had made. The maids bobbed curtsies, then hurried over to the table to set up the refreshments around the vase of roses.

"Good morning, Your Highnesses," a lady-in-waiting said as she peeked into the room.

"Lady Milena." Roslyn greeted the pretty, dark-haired young woman who served her mother, Queen Brigitta. "Is there any news of my father?"

"Not yet, I'm afraid," Milena replied. "But your mother

sent me ahead to warn you that she's on her way here with Queen Luciana. They're very excited to finally see the bridesmaids'— *Gah!*" Milena's eyes widened as she finally spotted the dressmaker dummies. "I mean, the gowns."

"Your mother hasn't seen them yet?" Eviana asked Roslyn.

"No, I was keeping them a secret, so she wouldn't interfere with my plans. For months now, she's been looking for any excuse to call off my wedding." Roslyn heaved a weary sigh. "Mother can be overly dramatic."

Like mother, like daughter, Lennie thought.

"She keeps insisting that Freydor is hiding some sort of nefarious secret," Roslyn continued, her voice laced with annoyance. "And all because she happened to touch his hand briefly nine months ago when he first came here to the palace."

"Detecting hidden things is your mother's Embraced gift," Lennie reminded Roslyn. "If she saw something, you should believe her."

Roslyn scoffed. "I asked her to explain, but she said she only felt a hint of something wrong. Was I supposed to reject the earl over that? Don't we all have something in our past that we regret?"

As the cousins fell silent, Lennie wondered what each one of them was regretting. As for herself, her thoughts went back to that fateful night at Draven Castle when a group of stubborn old Norveshki noblemen had cornered her in a dark passageway to voice their objections and make their demands. Had she made the right decision then, or would she regret it for the rest of her life?

"Their Majesties are coming now." Lady Milena stepped back and bobbed a curtsy while the happily chatting queens, Brigitta and Luciana, sauntered into the room, followed by Luciana's lady-in-waiting, Lady Olana.

"I've been waiting for months to see these—" With a gasp, Brigitta jerked to a stop.

Luciana stepped back in shock and bumped into Lady Olana.

Lennie winced. Anyone who touched Lady Olana was compelled to blurt out the truth. The poor woman's Embraced gift had made her famous throughout Aerthlan as The Confessor.

"They're appalling," Luciana said, then slapped a hand over her mouth. "I meant—" She glanced at Brigitta for help. "They're . . . appealing?"

Brigitta winced. "You were right the first time."

"Mother!" Roslyn cried.

"Whatever were you thinking, my dear?" Brigitta asked her daughter. "These are far too . . . elaborate."

"That was the point!" Roslyn huffed. "For the most spectacular wedding of the century, everything must be extravagant. I want people to remember these gowns for years!"

"They certainly will," Julia muttered.

With a hand pressed to her chest, Brigitta heaved a sigh. "This is too much. First, your father has gone missing. And now, these awful gowns. I fear we must postpone the wedding."

"Don't say that!" Roslyn cried. "The wedding will be perfect. It has to be. I've worked on it for eight months!"

"I am sorry, my dear." Brigitta gave the young ladies in the room an apologetic look. "I seriously doubt your cousins want to be seen wearing these atrocities."

"To be honest," Lennie admitted, "I was contemplating setting them on fire."

"To be honest," Julia added, "we were hoping you would."

"*What?*" Roslyn's eyes widened with horror.

One of the maids stifled a giggle, while the other one fumbled, dropping a stack of dishes onto the small table. Roslyn's saucers remained intact, but a teacup fell over and rolled toward the table's edge.

"Careful." Lady Olana rushed over to keep the cup from plummeting to the floor. As the maid grabbed it, their hands collided.

"I slept with Earl Freydor last night," the maid confessed, then gasped, dropping the cup so that it shattered on the wooden floor. "Oh, I—" She stepped back, grimacing at the sound of gasps reverberating around the room.

"You *what?*" The second maid spun angrily toward her. "You slept with him, too?"

Another round of gasps circulated.

The first maid lifted her chin. "Why shouldn't I? He promised to take me to his castle, where I would never have to be a servant again!"

The second maid huffed. "That's what he promised me!"

"You can't have him! He's mine!" The first maid threw a saucer, but it bounced off the second maid's arm and fell to the floor, shattering into a dozen pieces.

"Not my dishes!" Roslyn cried.

"What about your groom?" Lennie asked.

"*Out!*" Queen Brigitta ordered the maids as she pointed to the door. "Go to your quarters. I will deal with you later."

The maids fled the room.

"Please go and don't speak of this to anyone," Brigitta told the seamstress, and the woman curtsied and dashed off.

Lennie exchanged a dubious look with her best friend, Eviana. There was no way to keep this sort of news from leaking out. The wedding of the century was rapidly turning into the scandal of the century.

Lady Milena closed the doors, then hurried over to Brigitta, who had collapsed in a chair. "Are you all right, Your Majesty?"

"No." Brigitta rubbed her brow. "I wish my husband was here. He would give that nasty earl the thrashing he deserves." She glanced sadly at her daughter. "I cannot have you marrying that scoundrel. The wedding is off."

Her face pale with shock, Roslyn swayed on her feet, then stumbled back a few steps. "N . . . no." Her voice was filled with anguish. "No."

Brigitta winced. "I am sorry, my dear."

"But . . ." Roslyn's gaze wandered aimlessly about the room, then finally settled on her broken dishes.

"Are you all right, Roz?" Lennie asked.

"The dark cloud of doom has destroyed my wedding," she whispered.

Lennie scoffed. "It wasn't a cloud of doom. It was the groom."

"Aye," Kendall agreed. "And it's better to find out now that he's an unfaithful dog."

"Don't even call him a dog," Julia grumbled. "It's an insult to canines."

Lennie nodded. Julia would feel that way since her shifter father, King Brodgar, had spent most of his youth as Brody, stuck in the form of a dog. "Aye, we can safely say the earl is a complete bastard. So, don't give him a second thought, Roz."

Roslyn staggered toward the table and dropped to her knees next to the shattered pottery on the floor. "Two hundred plates and soup bowls, two hundred saucers and teacups, all for nothing." Tears glistened in her eyes. "I might as well break them all. They're completely useless now."

"We could take them to Benwick to use for archery practice," Faith offered.

Kendall snorted. "I'd rather shoot at these birds."

A tear rolled down Roslyn's cheek, and her mother and everyone else rushed over to hug her. As they each attempted to comfort her, Lennie heard some words seep into her thoughts.

Gwennore, Lenushka, Pendras, do you hear me?

Aye, Silas. His wife, Gwennore, was the first to answer.

"Shh!" Lennie quickly hushed everyone at the sound of King Silas's voice. "My father is contacting me." *I hear you, Papa.*

Me, too. Pendras added.

As far as Lennie knew, her younger brother was spending the day in the library with Roslyn's older brother Prince Reynfrid; Julia's father, King Brodgar; and Evie's father, King Leo, her younger brother Prince Dominic, and her new husband, Quentin.

Did you find Rupert? Gwennore asked, calling King Ulfrid by the name his close friends preferred. She had remained in the breakfast room with Princess Elinor and the other queens, Sorcha and Maeve.

Yes, Silas replied. *You can assure his family that Rupert is safe and sound. A few nights ago, an armada of pirates made a sneak attack on him during the night. Some of his crewmen were paid handsomely in gold to betray him while he slept, so the pirates were able to take him prisoner. We have rescued him and will bring him home tomorrow.*

Thank the goddesses, Gwennore answered.

"King Ulfrid is fine, and my father will bring him home tomorrow," Lennie reported, and Brigitta's eyes filled with tears as she made the sign of the moons to give thanks to the moon goddesses.

We will remain here for now, so we can question the prisoners we've taken, Silas continued. *So far we have learned that it was the pirates who paid Rupert's crewmen to betray him. And the pirates were funded by the Brotherhood of the Sun.*

Lennie winced. "The pirates causing all this trouble were paid by the Brotherhood of the Sun."

A series of gasps echoed around the parlor.

"Is the Brotherhood attempting to take over my country?" Brigitta asked.

Luciana huffed. "They failed to destroy Eberon, so they moved on to Tourin?"

"This must be what caused my mother's bad dream," Julia added.

Lennie held up a hand to quiet all the comments so she could hear her father.

When we asked where the Brotherhood was getting the money to pay the pirates, we learned some disturbing news, Silas reported. *The one who financed this mission was Earl Freydor.*

With a gasp, Lennie staggered back a step.

"What's wrong?" Eviana asked.

You mean Roslyn's betrothed? Gwennore's telepathic voice sounded brittle from shock.

So this was an attempted coup? Pendras demanded.

Lennie swallowed hard when her father confirmed it. With a heavy heart, she turned toward Brigitta and Roslyn. "The pirates managed to take King Ulfrid prisoner for a while, and the one who paid them to do it was Earl Freydor."

Brigitta collapsed into a chair as everyone else stood still, shocked and speechless.

I'm with Reynfrid and the other men, Pendras reported. *We're going after Freydor.*

You need to catch him before he finds out that his plan failed, Silas warned.

We're headed to his bedchamber now, Pendras replied.

I'll alert the Captain of the Guard in case the earl tries to escape, Gwennore added.

As Roslyn snapped out of her shock, rage simmered in her eyes. "So my fiancé was behind the attack on my father?"

Lennie winced. "I'm afraid so."

"Then he's more than a bastard. He's a traitor." Roslyn leaned over to pick up a broken pottery shard with a pointed end. "This may not be so useless after all." As her hand curled around it in a tight grip, she appeared oblivious to the trickle of blood dripping from her palm. "It's sharp enough to kill, don't you think?"

Lennie stiffened. Who would reach the earl first, Roslyn or her brother Reynfrid? She wasn't sure, but a few things were for certain.

The wedding was off.

And the groom was about to die.

Chapter 2

"Let me kill him."

Bran winced inwardly at his younger brother's request. Not that long ago, seventeen-year-old Zane had been an innocent and kindhearted acolyte, who had lived his entire life at the Monastery of Light. He'd never uttered a harsh word against anyone, not even the vicious members of the Brotherhood of the Sun who had whipped him on the nights the moons embraced. But now, Zane's gentleness had changed into a grim resolve to gain vengeance.

As much as Bran hated what was happening to his brother, he could hardly object when he, himself, was obsessed with vengeance. Killing Greer was the reason he woke each morning. Staying strong enough to kill Greer was the reason he ate each meal. Praying that he could kill Greer was the only reason he had left to communicate with his god, the Light.

Greer was the assassin who had killed their brother, Arlo, so he had to die. But Bran had no idea where Greer had fled after the Monastery of Light had been seized. For the last five months he and his brother had been searching for Greer, and that quest had given them a purpose to go on living when it had become a struggle to find something to believe in. Everything they had been raised to accept as truth had turned out to be a stinking heap of lies.

As a raven shifter and spy for the Brotherhood, Bran had

been exposed to the world outside the monastery for over five years, so he'd had the advantage of slowly realizing the Brotherhood's true evil nature. But for Zane, the revelation had been brutally sudden, accompanied by the murder of their brother. His emotions were ravaged, leaving him prone to angry outbursts and fits of rage.

While Bran and Zane had traveled about, searching for the deadly assassin, they'd used every opportunity to destroy secondary targets: the monks who had molested their sisters years ago at the monastery. It had taken several weeks for Bran to convince his sister Vera to give him a list of the guilty bastards. And then, it had taken several months to locate the priests. After exposing the guilty men to their new communities, Bran had made sure they were all defrocked and shunned. And then, he and Zane had given each of them a thorough thrashing.

Bran wasn't sure he'd done the right thing by letting Zane take part in the beatings, but at the time, he'd thought it best to give the desperate young man an outlet for his rage. Too late, Bran realized he had enabled his brother's moral decline to the point that Zane was now insisting he should be the one to kill Greer. Deep down, Bran wanted to believe that Zane's inherent kindness would ultimately prevail. But only if Bran managed to keep his brother from falling deeper into depravity.

As for himself, Bran had long given up the hope that any trace of goodness remained in his soul. He was a lost cause, tainted with too many sins and too many unforgivable failures. He'd failed to rescue his younger brothers and sisters from the monastery. He'd failed to stop his closest friend, Father Saul, from committing the ritual suicide demanded by the Brotherhood. He'd failed to protect Arlo from the Brotherhood's assassin, Father Greer. And now he feared another failure: allowing his youngest brother to become a murderer.

"I will kill Greer myself," Bran said as they led their horses down a narrow cobblestone street that ran behind Lourdon Cathedral.

There were four men in their small group, all dressed in black, and the clip-clop noises made by their horses' hooves echoed around them, making their conversation inaudible to the occasional passerby. Zane was to Bran's left, while to his right, Father Bertram was walking quietly and leading his short, chubby monastery workhorse. Ahead of them, Father Sebastian, the head priest of the cathedral, was showing them the way to the tavern where Greer had reportedly taken a room.

When Zane looked ready to argue with him, Bran reaffirmed his stance. "I *have* to do the killing. I am the one who failed Arlo."

Zane's dark eyes flashed with anger. "I failed him, too. I should have realized when Greer and Horace didn't return to the monastery that they were going after Arlo. But I did *nothing*!"

Bran drew in a sharp breath as he felt the heat coming off his brother. Zane had the Embraced gift of being able to boil liquids with his touch, but whenever his emotions surged, his blood tended to run too hot. It was one of Bran's worst fears: that his brother would burn himself to death if his gift raged out of control.

"Calm down, Zane." Bran checked the dagger hidden in an inside pocket of his black woolen cloak. "Greer will die today by my hand. You will wait outside with Father Bertram and our horses so we can make a quick escape."

Beside him, Father Bertram let out a weary sigh.

"And what will you do if Greer uses his freezing power against you?" Zane demanded. "You need me."

Bran winced once again. He didn't want to admit it, but his brother was making a good point. Greer had used his Embraced power to freeze Arlo to death, and he would attempt the same maneuver on Bran.

"I may be the only one who *can* kill him," Zane protested. "So you have to let me do it."

Bran gritted his teeth. "I will allow you to come with me in case I need help. But *I* will do the killing."

Father Sebastian glanced back at them with a wry look. "As a priest, I feel obligated to remind you two that murder is considered a sin."

"Exactly," Father Bertram agreed. "I've been telling them that for weeks now, but they don't listen."

"We have to avenge Arlo," Zane insisted. "And Greer deserves to die. He's killed so many."

Bran nodded. "Arlo and Master Lorne, to name a few."

Father Sebastian sighed. "I agree with you that Greer is a vicious assassin who needs to be stopped, but—" The priest stopped in his tracks when Zane took a deep breath to launch a protest. "Hear me out. No matter what evil acts Greer has committed, it does not mean that either of you should become a murderer. Why not capture him and deliver him to the authorities? They'll see that he's executed for his crimes."

"But—" Zane started, hushing when Sebastian held up his hand.

"We'll be entering the town square soon," the head priest said. "There will be many of my flock there, so I suggest we limit our speech to peaceful, priestlike comments." His mouth twitched. "If you can manage it."

Zane huffed. "We will not be at peace until Greer is dead."

"May the Light in his benevolent mercy grant you that peace you so desire," Father Sebastian declared in a loud voice as he led them into the busy market square.

The roar of the crowd hit like a strong wave at the seashore, drowning out any further conversation. They weaved carefully through the throng of people who bustled around the stores that lined the square and the makeshift stalls that had been erected in rows. More vendors rolled carts up and down the rows, shouting to draw attention to their wares.

The smell of freshly baked bread made Bran's stomach rumble. He and his companions had left before dawn without breaking their fast so they could hasten to Lourdon as quickly as possible. After months of hunting for Greer, this had been the first reported sighting, and they didn't want to lose him.

"Father Sebastian!" A few vendors shouted a greeting to the head priest, and with a nod and a smile, he made a circular sign with his hands to represent the Light, the sun god that most Tourinians worshipped.

"May the Light shine his blessings upon you," Sebastian responded.

To Bran's surprise, a few vendors pressed free meat pies into his and his companions' hands. "Thank you. May the Light be with you." His chest tightened with conflicting emotions. He was touched by the people's respect for his priestly status, but also ashamed, for he knew good and well he didn't deserve anyone's respect. He was a fraud on his way to commit murder.

But he was also damned hungry. As he bit into his meat pie, he glanced over at his brother, who appeared equally uncomfortable with the generosity of strangers. It was not long ago that Zane had been taught only the Brotherhood was good and noble, while all outsiders were untrustworthy sinners.

They had arrived in Lourdon half an hour ago, and Bran had been shocked by the huge number of people in town. While they had let their horses rest and water, Sebastian had explained that hundreds of visitors from all over Tourin had flocked to the capital city in hopes of catching a glimpse of the royal princess and her groom as they traveled to and from the wedding ceremony at Lourdon Cathedral. The wedding was to take place tomorrow afternoon with Father Sebastian officiating. Why the hell Greer was in town at this time, Bran didn't know, but he was grateful that Sebastian had let him know Greer had been spotted.

Should they do as Sebastian suggested and simply capture the bastard and turn him over to authorities? Would that even work? Wouldn't Greer use his Embraced power to escape?

Bran glanced again at his younger brother, who was wolfing down a second meat pie. Would he be able to convince Zane to give up the only goal that had kept him grounded for the last five months? Now, when they were so close to their target?

Greer had managed to disappear before the Brotherhood's monastery in Eberon had been seized. But before fleeing, Greer had murdered Master Lorne, the head of the Brotherhood.

That had left Bran with the dubious honor of inheriting the title of Master of the Brotherhood. The prospect had sickened him at first. His uncle, Master Lorne, had been a perverse bastard who had set up a system in which all young acolytes were whipped twice a year and trained to be completely obedient to him. And once they became monks, they had to take on any mission the Master ordered and commit suicide if they failed.

Bran had wanted nothing more to do with the Brotherhood, its twisted customs, or its power-hungry, evil quest to eradicate the royal families and take over the world. But with the Eberoni army attempting to track him down, he had soon realized that his new title as Master enabled him to travel secretly around Aerthlan, because every village priest felt obliged to hide him and give him and Zane free room and board.

Slowly, as the months passed by and Bran grew better acquainted with those priests who simply wanted to minister to their flocks in a caring, compassionate manner, he began to realize that there was another goal he could strive for. A much worthier goal. He could use his position as the titular head of the Brotherhood to actually end the cult's mad quest for power and facilitate the dawning of an era of peace.

So now he felt torn between two goals. Vengeance or peace? The latter was much nobler, but with his tainted soul, he still refused to give up his quest to kill Greer.

As they traveled about, he had sounded out each priest to see where he stood. A few priests were still hopeful that the Brotherhood intended to murder the royal families and take over the world. That, in turn, would enable them to fulfill the ultimate quest: cleansing Aerthlan of those monstrous people who were Embraced or worshipped the false moon goddesses. The vindictive priests had exploded with rage when Bran had told them that he no longer wanted to pursue that goal. In fact, a few had declared him a traitor and had announced their intent to follow Father Greer as the true Master of the Brotherhood since the assassin held fast to their beliefs.

Fortunately, most of the priests had welcomed Bran's suggestion of a future that eschewed hatred and violence, and they had readily joined his new secret network. A month ago, Bran and Zane had taken residence at Father Bertram's small monastery and orphanage only about ten miles east of the Tourinian capital. From there, they could reach out to all the priests in their network and receive their reports.

Of all the monks at the old Monastery of Light, Bertram had been the most like a father to Bran and his brothers. But when Bran was twelve years old, Master Lorne had suddenly kicked Bertram out of the monastery. Bran had never known what had caused Bertram to fall out of favor, but he suspected it had something to do with Bertram's Embraced gift.

It was an unusual power. Suddenly, without notice, Bertram would stop, his gaze would cloud over, and he would make a prediction. When he came to, he would have no memory of what he had said and no clue as to how to interpret it. He wasn't exactly a Seer, because he never saw the big picture. His gift of foresight was narrow, usually focused on one person and on something that would happen to that person quite soon.

After leaving the Monastery of Light, Bertram had traveled to Tourin to ask King Ulfrid and Queen Brigitta to help him establish a monastery and orphanage that would minister to anyone in the country who was homeless or in need. The king and queen had funded his request and, by doing so, had earned his loyalty. And so, Bertram had no desire to harm the royal family or rule the world. Instead, he reigned over the Monastery of Mercy with kindness and compassion.

Bran had been delighted to find Bertram, and the kindly older priest had insisted on Bran and Zane making their home with him. Yesterday evening, when they had received notice that Greer had been spotted, they'd immediately made plans to leave before dawn.

The last bite of meat pie stuck in Bran's throat. Would he be able to commit murder? That question had haunted him the last few months, but he'd always brushed it aside, convincing himself what he planned to do wasn't murder. Greer would fight back, so that made it self-defense, didn't it?

Stop obsessing, he chided himself. He was already a lost cause, and Greer deserved to die.

A loud shout, followed by frantic cries, whipped him out of his thoughts, and he turned to see that a commotion had started in the town square. Men on horseback had charged into the square, barely slowing down, causing people to cry out as they scattered to keep from being mowed down.

"Make way!" the lead horseman yelled. He and three of the riders were dressed in maroon-and-gold uniforms. Guards, Bran assumed, since they were all armed. A fifth man, in the center of the group, rode a white horse, draped in maroon-and-gold silk. His breeches were expensive leather dyed a dark red and his silk tunic and cap were embroidered with gold thread and pearls. A cape of rich maroon velvet was attached to his shoulders with golden clasps.

Bran and his companions quickly pulled their horses to the side as the crowd around them parted to make a wide path.

"Mama!" a little boy cried, making a dash across the path to join his mother, who had her arms full with a newborn and bags of produce.

Just as the mother screamed, Bran grabbed the boy and leaped to the side. With the boy in his arms, he spun around a second before the group of horsemen thundered past him.

As soon as the horsemen had passed by, the mother ran toward Bran.

"Here." Bran set the stunned boy on the ground. "He's fine."

"Thank you!" The mother burst into tears. "Oh, thank you, Father!"

"May the Light be with you," Bran grumbled, then grabbed his horse's reins to leave.

The mother nudged her son, and he tugged on Bran's black cloak. "Thank you, Father!"

Bran nodded, then mumbled, "Be a good boy." He looked away and winced when he noticed Bertram and Sebastian exchanging amused glances. *Dammit.* He led his horse toward the edge of the square and noted that the group of five horsemen had disappeared down a narrow road that led toward the eastern side of town.

"Don't tell me you're embarrassed at being caught doing something good," Father Bertram teased as the others joined him.

"It was nothing," Bran muttered. "But I would like to know who those assholes were."

"Earl Freydor and his guards," Father Sebastian replied.

"Freydor owns a huge estate and a gold mine in the far north, making him the wealthiest nobleman in the country. He's the groom at tomorrow's wedding."

Bertram wrinkled his nose. "That ill-mannered lout is marrying the princess?"

Sebastian sighed. "I'm afraid so." He led the group onto the same road that the earl and his guards had taken.

Bran narrowed his eyes, watching the group of horsemen far ahead of them.

When the group made a sudden left turn, headed north onto a narrow crossroad, Sebastian paused briefly, then resumed walking. "Well, that's strange."

"What is?" Zane asked.

"The earl seems to be headed in the same direction as we are." Sebastian pointed ahead. "We'll be turning there, too."

As they walked their three horses down the road, Bran noticed that the buildings were becoming shabbier and more rubbish had been left in smelly piles on the cobblestones. Grungy, moth-eaten laundry flapped from open windows. Apparently Greer was staying in one of the cheaper inns in Lourdon. But why would Freydor, the wealthiest nobleman in Tourin, venture into this part of town?

And why was Sebastian leading them so slowly through town? Was he trying to buy time in hopes that Bran would reconsider committing murder? Bran smoothed a hand over his cloak, feeling the outline of the dagger hidden inside. *Dammit.* He had to do this. For Arlo. And for Zane, to keep him from doing it.

When they turned left into the crossroad, Father Bertram came to a sudden halt and gazed up at the cloudy sky with a blank expression.

Bran and the others stopped and waited to hear what the priest would say. Over the last few weeks, Bran had learned that this sort of behavior meant Father Bertram's Embraced gift was about to manifest itself.

"Greer will not be the one to die today," Bertram murmured.

"What?" Zane stepped toward the older priest. "Are you saying Greer will escape?"

Bran tensed as he reconsidered the older priest's words. "You mean someone else will die?" *Dear god of Light, don't let any harm come to my brother.*

Father Bertram turned toward Bran, his eyes still vacant as he continued. "Beware, my son. The woman will not be who she claims to be. She will bring you to despair, causing you to tear at your hair and suffer great gnashing of teeth."

Bran blinked. "What?"

The older priest blinked, too, as he came out of his brief trance. "What did I say?"

Bran gave him an incredulous look. "You . . . never mind." He didn't even want to talk about the unknown woman Father Bertram had mentioned. Besides, the prediction about Greer seemed much more important. If Greer wasn't going to die, then who was?

Sebastian's mouth twitched with amusement. "Apparently there is a woman who will cause Bran to tear his hair and gnash his teeth."

Bran groaned inwardly while his younger brother stifled a laugh.

"I think you must have it backward, Father Bertram," Zane said with a grin. "There's a much greater likelihood that any woman who meets my brother will want to tear *her* hair and gnash *her* teeth."

Bran shot his younger brother an annoyed look, even though his heart had tightened in his chest. How long had it been since he'd seen his brother smile? Zane looked so much like his old self right now. *I have to keep him innocent. And safe. Even if it costs me my own soul.*

"I said something about a woman?" Father Bertram turned toward Bran. "What woman?"

"How would I know?" Bran growled. "I live in a bloody monastery."

Bertram huffed. "There is no reason to speak poorly of my establishment, young man."

Bran's clenched jaw shifted. "I apologize. Zane and I are truly happy to have found a home with you."

The older man's eyes softened and he patted Bran on the back. "I am happy to have you."

"There are some women living outside the monastery—homeless women and their children." Zane gave Father Bertram a pointed look. "Perhaps you were referring to one of them?"

"I've had nothing to do with them," Bran protested before the priest could answer. "Can we please be on our way?" *I have someone I need to kill.* He bit his lip to keep from saying the words out loud. By the Light, no woman in her right mind would want anything to do with him and his tainted soul.

Father Sebastian chuckled. "He hasn't even met her yet, and he's already gnashing his teeth."

"I am not," Bran grumbled. His only experience with women had occurred five years ago, and that disaster had made him vow never to look at another woman again. But then . . . *she* had happened. Before he could mentally block it, the image of that mysterious woman sneaked into his thoughts, the most beautiful woman he had ever seen.

It had been five months ago when he'd spotted her asleep amongst the Eberoni army troops who had escorted Queen Luciana south to Vindalyn. Ever since then, he had wondered about her, even dreamed about her, not just because her beauty was astounding, but because she presented a puzzle he could not solve.

Her white-blond hair and slightly pointed ears seemed to indicate that she was an elf, so why wasn't she in Woodwyn with the other elves? What was she doing with the Eberoni army? And why would the most beautiful woman in the world be dressed as a soldier? There had been nothing war-like about her. In her peaceful slumber, she had radiated an innocence and purity that had made his wretched heart ache and yearn for something more. Something impossible.

Don't go there, he chided himself. She was only a dream, a beautiful dream that had no place in his bleak, sordid reality. The only purpose of his existence was to commit murder.

"Maybe Father Bertram meant our sisters?" Zane asked as they resumed their journey down the narrow crossroad. "They certainly made us grind our teeth."

Bran shook his head. "That was months ago." Father Bertram's words always referred to the future, not the past.

But Zane was right that Bran had been furious when Vera had confessed what had happened to her and her younger sister years ago at the Monastery of Light. That asshole Master Lorne had encouraged the monks to molest them. Lessons in seduction, Lorne had called them, so the young girls would have the knowledge and skills to target any man Lorne ordered them to.

Vera had been placed in Ebton Palace five years ago to spy on the royal family, but over time her loyalty had switched to Queen Luciana, who had always treated her with kindness and respect. Now, Vera felt safe and happy in her position as one of Luciana's ladies-in-waiting.

"How is Milena doing?" Bran asked, referring to their other sister, who had been sent to the royal Tourinian court. She'd started off as a lady-in-waiting to the princess, but a year ago, she'd been promoted to serve Queen Brigitta.

"She seems well enough," Sebastian replied. "It is Milena whom we have to thank for finding Greer. She was running errands for the queen in the marketplace yesterday morning when she spotted him. She was afraid he would recognize her, so she rushed over to the cathedral to find me. I followed him so I could discover where he had taken a room. And then I sent the message to you at Bertram's monastery."

Bran nodded. "That's good." Milena would have certainly avoided meeting Greer. He had enjoyed frightening her as a young child by freezing small animals to death. Bran could only hope that Milena had found happiness after leaving the monastery. Perhaps, like Vera, her loyalty now lay with the kindhearted queen she served.

As they continued down the narrow road in silence, Father Sebastian once more taking the lead, Bran noticed that the earl and his guards were no longer visible. They must have turned onto the wider street he spotted ahead.

"Is that the King's Way up there?" Father Bertram asked, and when Father Sebastian agreed, Bertram explained to Bran, "That is the road we came in on this morning."

When they reached the wide thoroughfare, Sebastian turned right, then jumped back into the road and pressed against the rickety wooden building with a stunned look on his face.

"Is something wrong?" Bran stepped closer and peeked around the building.

"Aye." Sebastian pulled him back. "This is quite . . . alarming."

The glimpse Bran had taken had revealed enough. Earl Freydor's four guards had dismounted and were lurking around the entrance to a three-story ramshackle inn. The earl's horse was tied to an iron hitching post close to the door. He had apparently gone inside.

"What is it?" Zane moved forward to take a peek, but Bran stopped him.

"Is that the inn where Greer is staying?" Bran asked the head priest.

"It is," Sebastian replied, his forehead creased with worry. "The Fox and Hound. But why would Freydor go there?"

Bran thought a moment as he came up with a plan. "Is there a back door to the inn?"

"Aye, it opens onto a back alley." Sebastian gestured to a narrow lane across the busy street. "We can access it from there."

Bran tilted his head to take a quick glance up the King's Way. "There are some handcarts and a horse-drawn wagon coming this way. Wait for them to pass by. They will provide cover for you to sneak across unnoticed."

Sebastian nodded. "I understand."

Bran pulled off his black cloak with the hidden knife and handed it to Father Bertram. "Take my clothes and the horses with you."

"What are you doing?" Zane demanded.

"What I usually do," Bran replied as he tugged off his boots. "Spy."

Zane scowled at the prospect of being left out. "We don't need to know what Freydor is up to. We just need to kill Greer."

Bran unbuttoned his black robe. "We do need to know. If the richest man in Tourin is meeting with an assassin, then they're up to something evil." He removed the robe and handed it to his brother. "Wait for me at the back door in case we need to make a quick escape."

"But you need me so we can kill Greer," Zane protested as Bran shifted into a raven. "Dammit!"

Dammit was right, Bran thought as he flew toward the inn. If Earl Freydor and Greer were hatching some sort of nefarious plan, he wanted to know exactly what it was.

And then, he would kill Greer.

Greer will not be the one to die today. Bertram's words echoed in Bran's head as he landed on a windowsill of the top floor and peered through the glass. The room was empty.

Did that mean . . . ? *No*, Bran assured himself as he flew to the next window. He couldn't be the one to die, not when Bertram had predicted a mysterious woman in his future who would make him tear his hair and gnash his teeth. And Bran had purposely left his brother behind so Zane would be safe.

Then who was dying today?

Chapter 3

Lennie was itching to go after Earl Freydor, not just because she wanted to catch the traitor, but because she was eager to escape the chaos that had ensued in Roslyn's parlor.

Brigitta had taken one look at her daughter's bloody hand and had slumped onto the floor in a near-swoon. Her lady-in-waiting was helping her back into a chair, while Luciana was warning her that she needed to brace herself. Tourin was in trouble and would need a strong queen.

Meanwhile, Eviana had succumbed to a wave of nausea and was losing her breakfast in a nearby chamber pot, painted white with pink butterflies flitting around darker pink coneflowers—one of Roslyn's creations, Lennie assumed. Lady Olana was holding Evie's hair out of the way and rubbing her back. Olana's touch had caused Evie to confess, between heaves, that her bridesmaid's gown was the ugliest thing she had ever seen, and that had made Roslyn burst into tears.

Princess Elinor and the other queens, Sorcha and Maeve, had rushed into the parlor, presumably to be supportive, but they had only contributed to the madness. Elinor had tossed the earl's three dozen roses out the window. Sorcha had announced she would hunt down "Earl Traitor" and use her Embraced gift to set him on fire, while Maeve had argued that, as a sea witch, she should put a spell on him and turn him into a sea slug. Their daughters had tried to convince them that it would be better to make the earl stand trial, but Sorcha and Maeve insisted he could still be tried as a slightly crispy slug.

Lennie groaned. Were these people really her friends and family?

Faith ripped a lavender ruffle off the nearest gown, then smoothed it out flat. "Stop your crying, Roz. The earl will not escape. There are two kings, two princes, and an eagle shifter pursuing him."

Roslyn used her good hand to wipe her cheeks. "Why would I waste a tear over that traitorous weasel? The reason I'm crying is because my perfect wedding has been destroyed!" She sniffled. "And none of you like the gowns I designed for you."

"The dishes were beautiful, though. I think it is always best for us to stick to our true talents, don't you?" Faith pressed her palm against Roslyn's bleeding hand.

Was that a glow emanating from their joined hands? Lennie stepped closer to look, but stopped when she heard Pendras's voice in her head.

"Quiet, please!" Lennie exclaimed. "I can't hear my brother." Everyone hushed and turned anxiously toward her, except for Faith, who was busily binding Roslyn's hand with the lavender ruffle. *Pendras, what did you say?*

Freydor was not in his room, Pendras repeated. *The servants say he left the palace with his personal guard. We're on our way to the courtyard.*

Be quick, Silas urged his son.

I just spoke to the Captain of the Guard, Gwennore reported. *He said the earl charged out the main gate a few minutes ago, headed toward the town square. I'll order the horses made ready so you can follow him.*

I wonder if he knows we have found him out? Lennie asked.

We can't be sure until he's caught and questioned, Silas answered.

I'm going to shift so I can spot him from the air, Pendras announced. *The other men will follow.*

By the time Lennie related the news to the women in the parlor, Pendras was flying toward the town square and the men were saddling up.

I'm going, too, Gwennore declared.

What? Silas's mental voice vibrated with tension. *Gwennie, you mustn't endanger yourself.*

Don't worry, Gwennore replied gently to her husband. *A troop of soldiers is accompanying us. I'll simply follow along behind so I can tell you what is happening.*

I'll shift, too, Lennie offered. *It'll be easier to spot Freydor if there are two dragons looking for him.* Lennie repeated her plans as she strode toward Roslyn's bedchamber to undress. "Do you mind if I use your room, Roz? I can launch from your balcony."

"Yes, of course," Roslyn agreed.

"I'll help you." Eviana joined Lennie and together they swung open the double doors to Roslyn's bedchamber.

Lennie froze for a second, taken aback by the sight before her. Pink walls, a pink rug, a pink-and-white silk coverlet on the four-poster bed with a lacy pink canopy overhead, and chairs padded with pink velvet pillows.

"Oh, my," Eviana breathed.

"Are you all right, Evie?" Lennie asked her, worried that the décor might induce another wave of nausea.

She gave her a wry smile. "For the moment, I'm fine. I just wish I could go with you."

"That's what *I* should do." Roslyn strode toward them. "I'm going with you. Milena, will you help me change clothes?"

"I . . ." Milena gave Roslyn's mother a questioning look, but Brigitta simply stared back, too stunned to answer. "I'm coming." The lady-in-waiting followed Roslyn into the bed-chamber.

Standing next to the four-poster bed, Lennie unbelted her dark green tunic, then quickly undid the brass buttons. She passed the tunic to Evie, who folded it neatly on top of the silk coverlet, while Lennie proceeded to pull off her black boots.

Brigitta came to her senses and marched into the bed-chamber, followed by the other queens, who lurked around the entrance. "Roslyn, what are you doing?"

Roslyn had kicked off her pink satin shoes while Milena was untying the laces of her carnation pink gown. "You heard me. I'm going with Lennie. If I wear my uniform from Benwick Academy, I'll be able to ride fast enough to keep up with her."

"But why?" Brigitta glanced at Lennie, then back to Roslyn. "Your brothers can take care of this. There's no need—"

"There is every need." Roslyn's gown and petticoats pooled at her feet, and she kicked them aside. "I'm the one who insisted on marrying that traitorous weasel. I'm the one who endangered my father." She yanked at the pink satin draw-string that gathered the neckline of her white linen shift. "So I should be the one to capture the bastard!"

"Well said," Eviana murmured as she set Lennie's black boots on the pink rug beside the bed.

Lennie removed her dark green breeches, leaving her in a white cotton camisole, smallpants, and stockings.

Frowning, Brigitta paced across the room. "This goes far beyond a ruined wedding. Earl Freydor and the Brotherhood are guilty of insurrection. That makes it a matter for the crown prince and our soldiers—"

"I'm going!" Roslyn pulled on the dark blue breeches and tunic that comprised the Benwick Academy uniform. "How can I stay here and do nothing? How can I stomach the looks of pity or resentment that the servants and courtiers will aim in my direction? How will I ever have anyone's respect if I don't take care of this mess myself?"

Lennie paused in the middle of taking off her stockings. All the annoyance she had felt over the hideous gowns was now replaced with admiration for Roslyn's brave stance. "Roz, can you follow me? I'll find the earl and lead you straight to him."

"Great! Let's do it." Roslyn sat on the pink tufted bench in front of her dressing table to pull on a pair of sturdy black boots.

Brigitta gave Lennie an exasperated look. "You shouldn't encourage her. She's not a soldier like you."

"Mother, I trained for this at Benwick." Roslyn fastened a belt around her waist and slid sharp daggers into the two leather sheaths.

"This is not the same as a training exercise!" Brigitta argued. "The earl has his personal guard with him. They will fight to the death to protect him. They'll fight *you* to the death."

"Brigitta." Queen Luciana stepped into the room. "The men will be there, along with a troop of soldiers. All fully armed."

"Even my mother is going," Lennie added.

"We each had an adventure when we were young," Queen Sorcha reminded her.

"And we each came close to dying," Brigitta muttered.

"We were naïve and unprepared for danger," Queen Maeve protested. "But our daughters have the confidence and training that we lacked."

Luciana nodded. "We should trust the girls to be capable."

"Exactly," Evie agreed, then gave Lennie and Roslyn an encouraging smile. "I believe in you."

"So do we!" the other princesses yelled from the parlor.

Brigitta heaved a sigh. "Very well, but you must both be careful. Your brothers are already headed into danger. It is not wise for all the heirs to be at risk at the same time." Tears filled her eyes. "Not to mention how it would break my heart if anything happened to any of you."

"I understand." Roz gave her mother an encouraging smile. "We'll be fine."

I've located Freydor's guards, Pendras reported. *They're in front of an inn called the Fox and Hound.*

Lennie repeated the news.

"The Fox and Hound?" Roslyn shouldered her quiver of arrows. "I've never heard of it."

"I know where it is." Milena handed her the bow. "Northeast of the town square."

"I'll join my brother there," Lennie said. "You can spot us in the air and head toward us."

Roslyn nodded. "All right."

"Can you bring my uniform with you?" Lennie motioned to the folded army uniform on the bed. "In case I need to shift."

"Of course." Roslyn hurried over with a canvas bag, then she and Evie stuffed Lennie's boots and uniform inside. "I'll add your smallclothes as soon as you shift."

Brigitta shook her head. "This day just keeps getting worse."

Lennie snorted. "It's about to get even worse for Earl Freydor."

Bran heard voices emanating from the third and last window—two voices, male, and one sounded like Greer. He landed on the windowsill and peered through the dingy gray lace curtains that fluttered in the breeze and kept him somewhat hidden. Greer was inside, seated on a rickety chair by a battered table that had a wooden slat wedged under one of the uneven legs to keep it from wobbling. On top of the table sat two dented pewter goblets, a container of cheap wine, and a wood-handled dagger.

Greer had always been slim, but he appeared even thinner since Bran had last seen him. The result made Greer's beaklike nose more prominent and his beady eyes more sunken—he had the look of a vulture hunting for his next meal. He was dressed all in black, but not the black robes of a priest. His breeches and shirt were threadbare; his boots and the hem of his long, hooded cloak were caked with mud.

In sharp contrast, the earl was resplendent in his extravagant clothes, embroidered with golden thread and pearls. The gold chain around his neck displayed a pendant engraved with his family's crest. The same crest decorated his gold signet ring and the sheath that housed his gold-handled dagger.

Freydor paced across the small room, then pivoted, causing his velvet cape to swoosh around him. "Is that all you have to drink around here?" He reached into a velvet pouch hanging from his belt, pulled out a gold coin, then tossed it onto the table. "Order the best they have."

Greer didn't move, other than his beady eyes narrowing a bit. "I've already given my orders. I told you to leave."

With a snort, Freydor resumed his pacing. "I have every right to be involved in each step of the plan. I'm the one paying for it, remember?"

Greer rose slowly to his feet. "The more involved you get, the more you screw it up."

"I haven't screwed up anything! I'm following the plan. My pirates captured the king—"

"Too early!" Greer growled. "You were supposed to marry the bitch *before* attacking her family."

"Can I help it if the king sailed up north before the wedding? I asked him to come a few weeks from now, but he—"

"You fool," Greer hissed as he strode toward the earl.

"How many times did I tell you to bide your time and wait for the right moment? There would have been other chances to attack the king. If you kill him now, he won't be here for the wedding, and the queen might call it off."

"I'm not a fool!" Freydor insisted. "I told my men not to kill Ulfrid until after the wedding. And besides, the princess *will* marry me. The stupid girl will do whatever I tell her." He jabbed a finger in Greer's direction. "You had better uphold your end of the bargain. I expect you to get rid of the queen and prince right after the wedding. Then my men will kill the king, and as Roslyn's husband, I can take the throne."

Bran dug his talons into the wooden windowsill. So Greer was using this rich nobleman to take over Tourin.

Greer halted a few feet in front of the earl. "When you rush through the plan, you make it too damned obvious. You think your new bride won't suspect anything when her whole family is dead within days of the wedding?"

Freydor shrugged. "She'll be too distraught with grief to think clearly. And I'll be very supportive and sympathetic."

"And if she accuses you of murder?"

"Then she'll have to die. But not until the throne is securely in my hands." Freydor poked a finger at Greer's chest. "I'm warning you. You had better do your part. If you fail, I'll tell everyone that you were behind Ulfrid's death."

Greer shoved the earl's hand aside. "Are you threatening me?"

Freydor snorted. "I'm paying you. If you don't deliver, I can do whatever I—" He gasped when Greer suddenly grasped him by the neck and rammed him against the wall.

"You're forgetting who's in charge," Greer growled. "Fortunately, that is me, for *you* are too great a fool to be king."

Freydor shivered, and Bran suspected Greer had activated his freezing power.

"St-st-stop!" Freydor stuttered, his teeth chattering. "We-we need to work to-together."

"We are." Greer sneered at him. "While your men were busy taking King Ulfrid prisoner, my men took over your gold mine."

"*What?* Y-you bastard!" Freydor whipped out his gold-handled dagger, but Greer caught his wrist and pinned it to the wall next to the earl's head. Freydor's hand turned blue, and the dagger tumbled to the floor.

"Had enough?" Greer released his hold on Freydor, and the earl shuddered as he gasped for air.

"I-I'll do whatever you say," Freydor said, his voice hoarse and his half-frozen hand cradled against his chest.

"That you will." Greer pulled off the earl's signet ring and the gold chain with the family crest.

"What are you doing?"

"Do you think I went to all this trouble to put *you* on the throne?" With a smirk, Greer stuffed the stolen items into an inner pocket of his cape. "I'm taking the gold, your estate, and the throne."

"No!" The earl lifted a fist to clobber Greer, but was shoved back against the wall when Greer planted both hands on his chest. "N-no." The earl shuddered, his face turning blue. He clawed at Greer's hands, but Bran knew from experience that it was like trying to grab hold of blocks of ice.

You need to kill Greer now, Bran told himself, but he hesitated, shaken to the core by the horrified expression on the earl's face as he realized he was going to die. *Had Arlo looked the same way? Was this how he had suffered?*

Bran's heart tightened in his chest. *Arlo, forgive me for not protecting you.* He glanced at the table, where the dagger lay. All he had to do was jump into the room, shift, and take his brother's murderer by surprise. He could succeed in gaining vengeance for Arlo, but with a gut-twisting realization, he knew it would not do a damned thing to ease the guilt he felt for failing his brother. That would haunt him forever.

A roar overhead distracted him enough to glance up. *A dragon?* What the hell was it doing here? It circled the inn, huffing smoke from its nostrils. Down below, Freydor's guards tried to slip away down the street, but the dragon responded with a burst of fire that hit the cobblestones a few yards from their feet. With a yelp, they huddled in front of the inn.

The clatter of hooves grew louder, and a group of horsemen rounded a corner and pulled up before the inn. Bran recognized a few of them: King Leofric of Eberon and his son Dominic, King Brodgar of the Isles, Prince Reynfrid of Tourin, and the eagle shifter Quentin. They were accompanied by a troop of soldiers, who started arresting Freydor's guards.

Bran was further distracted when an elfin woman, richly dressed, dismounted from her horse. For a heart-pounding second, he thought she was the mysterious woman he'd seen in Eberon, but he quickly realized this woman was older. Still beautiful, though, and quite similar to the one who haunted his dreams.

When Leo and the other men dashed into the inn, Bran realized he needed to act quickly if he was going to kill Greer. He jumped into the room, shifted, and grabbed the dagger from the table. Freydor had slumped to the floor, his skin a clammy bluish-white, his hair sparkling with ice crystals. Meanwhile, Greer was confiscating the man's pouch of gold coins. As Bran sprinted toward him, his dagger raised, Greer spotted him and raised a hand, palm facing outward.

A blast of cold air knocked Bran back onto his rump. *What the hell?*

With a smirk, Greer rose to his feet. "So you finally found me. But you'll never be able to defeat me. As you can see, my powers have grown." He darted out the door.

With the dagger still in hand, Bran chased after him. Shouts sounded on the floor beneath them as the Eberoni king and his companions searched the bedchambers for Freydor. The clomp of heavy boots echoed in the stairwell.

"Damn," Greer growled, realizing he could no longer flee down the stairs. He wrenched open the door to a room facing the back of the inn, and a woman cried in alarm as he barged in.

Bran followed him, and the woman squealed, pulling her bedsheet up to her chin. Damn, he'd forgotten he was naked. "Ah, begging your pardon, madam."

Idiot, he chided himself. Why was he bothering with good manners when he was about to kill someone? He turned his attention to Greer, who was frantically scrabbling at a window latch that had rusted shut.

Lifting his dagger, Bran ran toward him.

Greer thrust his hand toward Bran, palm outward, and once again a blast of icy air knocked him back onto his rear. Then Greer wrenched open the window, climbed onto the windowsill, and jumped.

With a shudder, Bran scrambled back onto his feet.

"Brr." The woman in bed shivered. Her gaze drifted over Bran, then, with a gleam in her eyes, she patted the bed beside her. "Would you like me to warm you up, love?"

Bran blinked. "No, thank you." He ran to the window and peered out. Zane, Sebastian, and Bertram were waiting in the alley with the three horses. Greer had managed to land on a large pile of refuse to cushion his fall. As he limped toward the horses, Zane charged toward him, and Greer blasted him back.

As Fathers Sebastian and Bertram ran over to check on Zane, Greer jumped onto Bran's untethered horse and took off.

"Go after him!" Bran yelled, and his brother leaped on his horse and charged after Greer. The two priests clambered onto the short, chubby workhorse and gave chase.

Male voices shouted from the hallway.

"I found Freydor! He's dead!"

Bran dropped his dagger, planning to shift and fly after Greer.

"Halt!"

He glanced back to find Prince Reynfrid standing in the open doorway.

"Who are you?" The prince drew his sword. "Did you kill Freydor?"

Another man peered over the prince's shoulder. "Bran?"

It was Quentin, the eagle shifter. Bran gave him a quick nod. "Greer's the one we need to catch. He froze the earl, then escaped."

"Who is Greer?" the prince demanded, but Bran ignored him, shifted, and flew out the window.

Dressed only in her smallclothes, Lennie opened the doors to Roslyn's balcony. As she loosened the drawstring to her camisole, her mother's words filtered into her mind.

I have gone inside the inn to see what is happening, Gwennore reported.

Gwennie! Silas sounded alarmed. *Don't endanger yourself.*

The danger has passed, Gwennore replied. *According to Leo, the earl was dead when Quentin found him. Reynfrid believes he spotted the killer, but Quentin disagrees.*

Wait! Pendras shouted mentally. *I see a bird flying out a back window. It's the Raven!*

Lennie gasped. *Isn't he the one who kidnapped Evie? And Luciana?*

"What's wrong?" Eviana asked her. "What happened?"

"The earl is dead," Lennie announced. "Murdered."

"*What?*" Roslyn strode toward her. "We're too late?"

"Who killed him?" Luciana asked.

The Raven, Lennie thought to herself. He must have done

it. After all, he was now the Master of the Brotherhood, and they were the ones who had conspired with Earl Freydor to take over Tourin.

Her hands clenched as she recalled the one time she had seen the Raven in human form. It was five months ago, right after Evie had used her Embraced power to put everyone at the Monastery of Light into a deep sleep, so that her mother, Queen Luciana, could be rescued. Evie's gift didn't work on shifters who were in animal form, so Lennie's dragon and Quentin's eagle had been able to fly unhindered into the monastery's courtyard.

Surrounded by unconscious monks, Lennie had been shocked when one young priest had calmly exited the door of the Great Hall, carrying a sleeping young man in his arms. She'd known instantly he had to be the Raven. He must have been in bird form when Evie had activated her power. And now, the bastard was trying to escape.

She'd stepped toward him, letting the fire swell in her chest. He'd glanced up, freezing in place at the sight of her. She'd frozen, too, for a few seconds, taken aback by how handsome he was. Blast. Weren't villains supposed to be ugly? Wasn't there some unwritten law that his face was supposed to match the wretched ugliness of his evil soul? How dare this foul priest kidnap her friend, Evie, and Evie's mother!

With fire crackling inside her that demanded to be released, she'd stepped toward him, steam puffing from her nostrils. But instead of cowering, the bastard had just stared back at her, as if he were daring her to fry him.

She was ashamed now to admit that she'd hesitated. Whether it was a response to his bravery or his handsome face she wasn't sure, but she'd let the fire inside her dwindle.

Then Quentin had yelled at her to stop, and while she'd hesitated, the Raven had escaped. She'd never gotten a chance to ask Quentin why he had stopped her. Soon after that, he'd flown to Vindemar Castle to be with Eviana, and they had married. Lennie hadn't seen them again until two days ago.

"Lennie!" Evie yelled, pulling her from her thoughts. "How did the earl die?"

"The Raven must have killed him," Lennie replied, feeling another spurt of shame. Why had she let him escape five months ago? If she had done her job, today's terrible events might not have ever happened. "Pendras saw him flying from the inn."

"Bran?" Evie frowned with a doubtful look. "Why would he be there?"

"He wouldn't have been there if I'd burned his ass five months ago," Lennie grumbled. "This time I won't let him get away from me."

With a gasp, Milena snatched a second Benwick Academy uniform from Roslyn's wardrobe.

"Lennie." Evie stepped closer. "He's not as bad as you think. He helped Quentin rescue me."

Lennie scoffed. "He wouldn't have had to do that if he hadn't kidnapped you in the first place! And he kidnapped your mother, didn't he? Now the bastard's here, trying to take over Tourin. He deserves to die."

"No!" Milena cried; then her eyes widened as everyone turned to stare at her. "I mean . . ." She quickly pulled on a pair of Benwick Academy breeches underneath her petti-coats. "This is not something you should do alone. I'll go with you."

"Why would you?" Roslyn asked. "This isn't your fight."

"I-I want to help. I know where the Fox and Hound is. I can lead you there." Milena glanced at Queen Brigitta. "Please allow me to go. I'll watch over your daughter to keep her safe."

Brigitta blinked, completely dumbfounded. "I-I suppose that would be all right."

"You'll have to catch up with me." Lennie pulled off her camisole and smallpants, then dashed toward the balcony, shifting into a dragon. She leaped over the balustrade and spread her wings.

She flew northeast at top speed, headed toward her brother. This time no one was going to stop her. That accursed Raven had come close to causing Evie to die. Evie's mother, too. And as the new head of the Brotherhood, he had to be behind the plot to take over Tourin.

Damn him. He must have planned to murder Roslyn's entire family. And he wouldn't stop there. The Brotherhood's goal was to eliminate all the royal families so they could take over the world.

Blast. She'd never had to kill anyone before. Could she do it? *You have to. Why else did you train all those years with the army?* As the future queen of Norveshka, she had to prove she was capable of protecting her country and her family. When it came to the Raven, there was only one course of action. It didn't matter how brave or handsome he was.

She had to incinerate him.

Chapter 4

Flying as fast as he could, the Raven quickly passed the two priests. Their short and stout workhorse noisily clip-clopped on the cobblestones, but Zane's faster steed had already reached the edge of town, where the road's surface changed to dirt. About a week ago, the early spring snowmelt had turned the road into a ribbon of mud, but now, after a few sunny days, the surface had dried to form a crackly crust, furrowed with deep ruts from supply wagons. Greer was farther ahead, his horse galloping at full speed and kicking up small clumps of mud.

Bran recalled coming into town on this same road. It was called the King's Way, since it connected the royal capital of Lourdon to the rest of the country to the north. For now, the road was headed in a northeastern direction toward Tourin's central plain. From there, it veered straight north across fertile farmland, then rose into the Highlands, weaving through increasingly taller mountains before coming to an abrupt end at the coast, where the high cliffs of the North Cape butted against the raging Northern Sea.

Father Bertram's monastery was in central Tourin, located just a mile east of the King's Way. Farther east, the central plain gave way to foothills, then those hills became larger and more rugged, eventually rising into the mountains that marked the border with Norveshka.

After catching a warm current of air coming off the west

coast, Bran coasted a few minutes to rest his wings while he ruminated over how, once again, Father Bertram's prediction had come true. Greer had not been the one to die. True to form, the assassin had been the one committing murder. His victim, Earl Freydor, owned an estate in the north, and since Greer had boasted about taking the earl's land and gold mine, Bran suspected the bastard was headed there now to establish his control.

He will never arrive, Bran vowed to himself. He and his brother would capture him and . . . Father Bertram's exact words came back to mind: *Greer will not be the one to die today*. Damn. Did that mean any plan to kill him today was doomed to failure?

Behind Bran, a loud screech erupted. He immediately angled to the left, so he could glance back. *Dammit!* The dragon from the inn was following him. With its enormous wings, the dragon could catch up to him fairly quickly, but strangely, it seemed to be biding its time. An answering screech responded, and Bran was stunned to see a second dragon flying toward him at top speed. Apparently, the first dragon was waiting for it and for the group of men on the road to catch up.

Bran swooped back toward the right to catch another glimpse at the road behind him. The kings Leo and Brodgar had caught up with the priests, and Sebastian was answering their questions. Behind them a troop of soldiers had slowed their speed to keep pace with the kings, and even farther behind them, another small group, led by a female, was quickly advancing. The younger men—Quentin, Prince Dominic, and Prince Reynfrid—charged ahead, urging their horses into a full gallop.

No doubt, those three would try to stop Bran and Zane. If Bran was going to catch up with Greer, he needed to do it fast. Flapping hard, he zoomed past his younger brother, who was galloping below him on the ground.

"Bran!" Zane yelled up at him. "Wait for me!"

Reaching his top speed, Bran drew closer and closer to Greer. They had reached a section of the King's Way that was flanked by an old forest—the enormous oak trees budding with the bright green leaves of early spring. Alongside the road, the yellowed grass of winter was turning green, and sun-loving wildflowers bobbed in the breeze. In the forest, bluebells carpeted the ground, interspersed with the occasional clump of yellow daffodils.

It was a beautiful day, Bran realized with a sense of dread. And here he was, rushing as fast as he could to commit a murder that, according to Bertram, wouldn't even happen. But was the old man right all of the time? How could Bran let the priest's mumblings deter him from what needed to be done?

Even so, Bran had to admit the old man had a point. How could he kill anyone while in raven form? He had no weapon on him, and, even though his beak was sharp, he could hardly peck the man to death. Perhaps he could spook the horse enough that it would rear up and throw Greer? And while Greer lay stunned on the ground, Bran could shift, steal the man's dagger, and then stab him through his cold heart.

As Bran approached, focusing on his target, he willed the hot rage that had burned inside him after Arlo's death to flare up again, to consume him so that he would be eager to kill in order to quench the fire once and for all.

But the rage fizzled, dampened by other emotions that had recently settled in his heart like heavy lumps of coal. Dread. Weariness. Disillusionment. It was so damned tiring to live only for hate.

You have to do this, he argued with himself. *For Arlo. For Zane.*

But Arlo had been such a kindhearted, compassionate

soul. Would he have truly wanted his brothers to become murderers?

A flash of dragon fire shot past Bran close enough he could feel the heat singeing the feathers of his left wing. The fire struck the ground, blasting a small hole in the road. As clumps of mud flew into the air, Bran swerved back and forth to avoid being hit.

Greer glanced back with a frantic look, then steered his horse northward into the forest.

Bran veered to the left, catching a glimpse of the dragon who had breathed fire at him and Greer. The second dragon shot a column of fire that hit the ground close to Zane.

Those damned dragons! The terrified look on Zane's face ignited the rage that Bran had been searching for. So help him, he would never allow anyone to harm his younger brother. He swooped around, then crossed the road in front of his brother, giving him a squawk as he flew into the forest. Luckily, Zane understood and followed him.

Bran landed beside a thick oak tree, shifted, and called to his brother.

Zane pulled his horse to a stop and glanced up at the sky. "Those dragons are trying to kill us!"

"I'll stop them," Bran said quickly. "For now, I want you to follow Greer. He's taken to the forest on this side of the road. Don't lose him. I'll lead the dragons off your trail, then join you later."

Zane gave him a worried look. "You're no match for a pair of dragons. They're faster than you. And they can burn you to a crisp!"

"Don't worry. I'm smaller, so I can weave through trees better than they can. And I doubt they'll risk setting an entire forest on fire. Now, hurry! Don't lose Greer. He'll be headed north." Bran grasped his brother's arm. "And swear to me, you won't attack until I'm there."

Zane's frown deepened. "Bran—"

"Swear!"

"Fine, I swear!" Zane's eyes glistened. "But you swear to me that you won't get yourself killed!"

"I won't. Go!" Bran slapped the horse's rear, and Zane charged away.

Bran shifted back into raven form and took off. As he flew across the road, he noted with alarm how close the dragons were. He gave a loud squawk to get their attention, then zoomed into the forest on the south side of the road.

Lennie huffed, a puff of smoke emerging from her nostrils. Did the silly bird think she'd fall for this trick? *Pendras, follow the younger brother. I'll go after the Raven.*

She veered to the right, keeping the black bird in her sights. A few feet underneath the canopy, he zigzagged through the old oak trees at breakneck speed, remaining just visible enough that she could follow him. And that was exactly what he wanted, damn him.

Conflicting emotions swelled inside her, inciting another huff of smoke. Part of her was amazed by the remarkable skill he was displaying. If she ever attempted some of his maneuvers, she would probably crash. Even so, her reluctant admiration was greatly overshadowed by the annoying fact that he was deliberately trying to steer her off course. She was tempted to reward his efforts with a blast of fire, but the scoundrel had probably guessed she would be reluctant to start a forest fire. All she could do was stay on his trail, and eventually, there would be a big enough clearing for her to make her move.

During her flight from Lourdon Palace, she'd reconsidered her initial decision to destroy the Raven. For months she had loathed him for his part in the kidnapping of Eviana and Queen Luciana, but now she realized something was off about that whole narrative. If the Raven was guilty, why did Eviana defend him? Shouldn't she hate him even more than Lennie? And she had to admit it was wrong to react in a hasty, emotional manner. As the future ruler of Norveshka, she needed to think more strategically and act in the manner that her father would.

And so, she had decided to capture the Raven and haul him back to Lourdon Palace. There, Lady Olana could make him reveal the Brotherhood's nefarious plans, along with the identities of its allies. Then the threat of the Brotherhood could be eliminated once and for all.

It was a good plan. She felt confident in her decision, but a tiny inner voice nagged at her, reminding her that this was the way it would be from now on. Every decision she made for the rest of her life would be based entirely on what was best for her country and countrymen. There would be no room for anything else.

For a dragon accustomed to the freedom of the open skies, she was becoming increasingly aware that her future felt as if there were iron walls closing in. *No whining,* she reminded herself. Her parents had dealt with the responsibility of ruling Norveshka for years, and they had remained strong and vigilant. It was her duty, her honor, to do no less. While many Norveshki noblemen doubted she was up to the task and wanted her younger brother to inherit the throne, Lennie's parents had declared her the next ruler. They believed in her. She would not let them down.

Down below, the Raven curved into a more easterly direction to make his trajectory parallel to the road. No doubt he was reluctant to get too far away from his brother.

She glanced to the left. Pendras was far ahead of her now, following the road on the northern side. Apparently the Raven's younger brother was moving fast and had stayed close to the road. The three horsemen—Quentin, Dominic, and Reynfrid—were close on Pendras's tail, while Roslyn and Milena, determined not to be left out, had passed the kings, who were deep in conversation with the priests. The young women were not far behind Lennie.

Ahead in the distance, she spotted an area on the south side of the road where the forest gave way to a large green pasture. A herd of sheep was lazily munching on the new spring grass. As Pendras zoomed past them, the sheep panicked. Bleating frantically, they scrambled to a far corner of the field and huddled against the stone wall.

Lennie's nerves tensed. The pasture would be the perfect place for her to make her move. She increased her speed, keeping a close watch on her prey.

After a few minutes, the Raven emerged from the forest into the clear sky above the pasture. Lennie inhaled deeply to feed oxygen to the simmering fire in her chest. But before she could release it, the Raven suddenly veered left, screeching as he flew straight for Pendras. He must have noticed how close the dragon was to his brother.

The idiot will get himself killed! Lennie thought as she swerved to keep up with him. Her brother could blast fire at him or swat him with his tail as if the Raven were nothing more than a pesky insect. The silly bird had to know that, so why was he flying straight into danger? She could only conclude that his desperation was a sign of how deeply he loved his brother.

He is fiercely loyal to those he loves. As soon as the thought entered her mind, Lennie chastised herself. Why should she care about the Raven's feelings? Or his safety? *I'm not worried about him!* She simply wanted to keep him alive so she could have him interrogated. This was strategy, not sympathy.

And now, it was time to take him captive.

She zoomed around to his left side and blew a warning blast of fire, hitting the road to his left. The Raven immediately veered right, away from Pendras and back toward the pasture. Good. She was herding him; now she needed to force him to land.

Her second shot of fire came close enough to singe his tail feathers, but instead of dropping to the ground in surrender, he raced in the direction of the forest on the other side of the pasture.

With a burst of speed, she caught up with him and loomed directly overhead. Then she slowly lowered her altitude in a maneuver designed to force him to land. He spotted her above him and dropped lower. An arrow zinged past him, grazing his belly. Instantly, he jerked up, coming within inches of Lennie's talons. She made a grab for him, but he rolled over, managing to fly upside down for a few seconds before righting himself. And he never even slowed down. What incredible skill!

And what a great shot! Lennie glanced back to see Roslyn at the edge of the pasture, her horse standing still as she nocked another arrow to her bow. With an angry shout, Milena spurred her horse into the pasture.

Lennie raced in front of the Raven and blasted a column of fire in front of him to force him to halt. He skirted it at great speed, waffling in the air, nearly out of control. She winced. *He's going to enter the forest too fast. Why won't he just stop?*

He was a few feet from the tree line when Roslyn's second arrow hit a tree trunk just inches below him. He jerked upward.

Oh, no. Lennie watched with dismay. He was entering the forest in the midst of a thick and treacherous canopy.

She flew just above the trees, watching. He managed to avoid the first couple of branches, but after swooping around the wide trunk of a huge oak tree, he clipped a wing against a smaller tree that had been hidden behind it. Losing his balance, he flipped over and knocked a wing hard on a thick branch.

Lennie grimaced as he collapsed into a freefall, tumbling and crashing through smaller branches until he hit the ground hard. Unconscious, his body shifted back into human form.

Don't feel guilty, she told herself as she searched for an opening large enough to make a landing. Any sensible man would have admitted he was overpowered and surrendered. And she really had no choice but to take him captive. He was the head of the Brotherhood, a kidnapper, and, perhaps, even a murderer.

She lowered herself into a small opening in the canopy, then folded her wings to drop to the ground. As she lumbered around an oak tree, he came into view. Crumpled on the ground. Motionless. *Please be alive.*

Since every other dragon shifter in the world was male, Lennie had experienced the dubious honor, over the years, of seeing more male body parts than she cared to admit. Her female cousins enjoyed teasing her about the dreaded "hardship" she had to endure. In truth, what they didn't understand was that, most of the time, it was simply awkward.

The male dragon shifters were so accustomed to shedding their clothes to shift that they never thought twice about it. But the sudden addition of a twelve-year-old female shifter had thrown centuries of custom out the window.

At first, she'd tried taking flight lessons with the other young dragons close to her age, Sergei and Anton. That had been a disaster. The two young males had dared each other to strip in front of her, and Sergei had done it, getting a thrill out of shocking the young, innocent princess. Anton had tried his best to see her naked, which had embarrassed her and infuriated her father. Silas had ended up giving her private lessons and banning any other dragon from being in the vicinity when it was time for her to shift.

During her years of military training, she'd managed to guard her privacy fairly well. But, of course, the male dragons shifted whenever and wherever they needed to. After all, that was their duty, and they took it seriously.

Gradually, she'd become accustomed to those flashes of nudity before the men could take dragon form, and her cousins, who asked curious questions about godlike, heavenly bodies, were not far from the truth. The men were tall and radiated excellent health and vitality. Their smooth, tanned skin displayed an abundance of muscles. They each had a healthy head of hair, dark and shoulder-length. And their eyes tended to be a vibrant green like her father's. To be honest, they were gorgeous.

To be blunt, some of them knew it too well.

And so, the first glimpse of the Raven's naked body was not at all shocking. The fact that he was not moving was worrisome. But what stopped her in her tracks were the scars.

She nearly choked on her own smoke as she inhaled sharply. The skin on his legs and buttocks was smooth and golden, but his back . . . good goddesses, the number of red welts that crisscrossed his back could only mean years, many years, of severe whipping. Flogging harshly enough to tear his skin, over and over.

Her talons dug into the ground. The man appeared young, not much more than her own twenty years. He must have been a child when this had started. What kind of monster would do this to a child? How had this Raven even survived his childhood?

Perhaps he hadn't. It was quite possible that his mind and soul were as scarred as his body. Was he a victim, or had his mind been twisted enough to turn him into a villain?

She stepped closer. He was lying on his side, his back to her. One of his arms was bent oddly. A broken arm. A twinge of guilt needled her. It would be a while before the Raven could fly again. But the harsh reality of her military training reminded her it would now be easier to hold him prisoner.

Horse hooves pounded against the ground as Milena's mount charged into the forest. She spotted Lennie and the Raven and pulled her horse to a stop.

"Oh, dear Light." She ran toward him. Kneeling beside him, she let out a sigh of relief. "He's still breathing."

Thank the Light and goddesses. Lennie exhaled slowly.

Milena removed her cloak and draped it over the Raven's hips. "But he's bleeding."

Lennie shifted into human form and stepped closer. "He's wounded? Where?"

"His stomach. The arrow must have grazed him." Milena lifted her skirt to rip off the lower section of her white cotton petticoat. In her haste to leave the palace, she'd simply pulled on a pair of breeches underneath her gown and petticoat. She folded up some of the white cotton and pressed it against the Raven's torso.

When he moaned, Lennie glanced at his face. Damn, he was every bit as handsome as she had remembered. But instead of glaring at her fiercely, he now looked . . . vulnerable. Almost innocent. His skin was pale against the midnight black of his hair. And his dark eyebrows were drawn tight in pain.

"How is he?" Roslyn yelled as she rode up to them.

"His arm is broken, and he's bleeding." Milena shot her an annoyed look. "Were you trying to kill him?"

"No!" Roslyn quickly dismounted. "I didn't mean to hit him. I aimed for about a foot beneath him, but he suddenly dropped lower just as the arrow was passing."

Lennie winced. "He dropped to escape me."

Milena sighed. "We need to take him back to Lourdon Palace to be treated, but I don't see how he can ride a horse."

"I can carry him while I fly," Lennie offered.

The Raven moved his head and moaned.

Was he waking? Not wanting him to see her naked, Lennie stepped back and quickly shifted.

"Bran? Can you hear me?" Milena brushed his hair away from his face.

She knew his name? Lennie thought back. Eviana must have mentioned it earlier. Even so, Milena seemed a bit too familiar with him, the way she was stroking his hair. Or was she simply reacting to his blasted good looks?

"Oh, no." Milena grimaced at the sight of blood on her hand. "His head is bleeding, too."

"Damned dragon," the Raven muttered, his eyes still closed. "That creature from hell tried to kill me."

With a silent groan, Lennie retreated and slipped behind some trees where she could still see. Milena ripped off another strip of petticoat. As she wrapped it around the Raven's head, the sound of male voices came from the nearby pasture.

"Where is he?" the first voice bellowed.

"In the forest, I believe," another man replied. "Look! There's an arrow in that tree. We'll go in there."

"We'd better find him quick," the first man warned. "That crazy woman could be shooting him full of arrows right now!"

Roslyn gasped with indignation as a short, stubby horse crashed through the underbrush.

It was the two priests who had been conversing with the kings, Leo and Brodgar.

"There he is!" The younger of the two priests pulled the horse to a stop while the older one plummeted to the ground in his haste to dismount. "Bertram, are you all right?"

"Aye." The older priest scrambled toward the Raven. "Bran! My dear boy, are you all right?"

The younger priest dismounted, gave Roslyn a quick bow and Lennie a wary glance, then hurried over to the Raven. "How is he?"

Lennie watched, a bit surprised by how much the two priests obviously cared for the Raven.

"He has stomach and head wounds, plus a broken arm," Milena reported as she pressed a clean wad of petticoat against the Raven's stomach. "The bleeding has slowed down."

"Praise the Light. Thank you." The older priest gave her a curious look. "And you are . . . ?"

"Lady Milena from Lourdon Palace."

"Oh!" The older priest's eyes widened. "Then you're Br—"

"Brigitta's lady-in-waiting," the younger priest quickly interrupted as he gave the older man a pointed look. "I am acquainted with her since she often relays messages to me from the queen."

As the two priests exchanged furtive looks with each other and Lady Milena, Lennie suspected something was being left unsaid.

"I see." The older priest nodded at Milena. "It's a pleasure to meet you. I'm Father Bertram."

"Father . . ." the Raven mumbled.

"Don't worry, dear boy." Bertram patted his cheek. "We'll take good care of you."

"Bran?" The younger priest leaned over him. "This is Father Sebastian. Do you think you can ride a horse?"

The Raven moaned.

"The poor boy is in pain." With an angry huff, Bertram scrambled to his feet and glared at Roslyn, who still had a quiver slung over her back. "You! With the arrows. How dare you shoot at a defenseless bird!"

Roslyn looked too shocked to reply.

"Bertram," Father Sebastian muttered. "You shouldn't—"

"I'll have you know," Bertram growled, "that I am well acquainted with King Ulfrid and Queen Brigitta. I plan on reporting you, young lady, for assault and attempted mur—"

"Bertram!" Sebastian yelled, then lowered his voice. "You have the honor of meeting Princess Roslyn."

Bertram blinked. "What?"

"Ulfrid and Brigitta's daughter," Sebastian mumbled as he bowed once again to the princess. "Your Highness."

"Oh." Bertram made a quick bow. "Begging your pardon." He gave her a confused look. "I thought you were getting married."

Roslyn winced. "The wedding is off. The groom is dead."

"Oh, right, the man who was murdered." Bertram nodded. "All the same, I cannot, for the life of me, fathom why you would gallivant across the countryside to shoot down a defenseless bird!"

Roslyn gritted her teeth. "Isn't he the head of the Brotherhood? Was he not conspiring with Earl Freydor to kill my father and take over my country?"

Father Bertram scoffed. "Bran would never do something that evil! He's a good lad!"

The Raven's eyes fluttered open briefly. "I'm going to find that dragon—"

"Dragon?" Bertram noticed Lennie lurking behind the trees and jumped back. "Holy Light! The dragon is here!"

"—and rip its bloody wings off," the Raven finished.

Bertram winced, giving Lennie an apologetic look. "He doesn't mean it. He's just upset. Understandably so. He was attacked for no good reason."

"Then why was he running away from the inn where Freydor was murdered?" Roslyn asked.

"We explained the situation to the kings," Father Sebastian said. "The earl was murdered by a nasty fellow named Greer. Bran and his brother were chasing him down to capture him."

"That's right!" Bertram nodded. "They only wanted to bring the murderer to justice. Bran's a good lad, I tell you. He wouldn't harm a fly!"

"I'm going to ram a hot knife through Greer's cold heart," the Raven mumbled.

"He doesn't mean it!" Bertram knelt beside the Raven. "Hush now," he whispered. "Save your energy so you recover."

"So I can kill Greer," the Raven muttered. "After I destroy that damned dragon."

"Shh." Bertram shot Lennie a wary look. "It's just the pain talking."

Milena handed him a strip of cotton. "Maybe we should gag him."

"Or knock him out," Father Sebastian muttered.

Just then, the two kings and Lennie's mother, Gwennore, rode up, followed by a small troop of soldiers. Leo instructed the soldiers to wait in the nearby pasture.

Gwennore hurried over to Lennie. *Are you all right, dear?*

Aye, Lennie replied telepathically. *I didn't mean to make the Raven crash. I only wanted him to stop.*

Gwennore repeated her words to the priests.

"Well, he certainly succeeded in stopping the poor boy," Bertram grumbled, making the usual assumption that the dragon was male.

Leo looked the Raven over. "We should take him back to Lourdon Palace so the physician can take care of him."

Roslyn motioned to Lennie. "The dragon has offered to carry him there."

"No, no," Father Bertram objected. "We should take him home to the Monastery of Mercy. It's just a few miles from here. And we have excellent healers."

Leo frowned. "I would like to have a talk with him."

"You are welcome to come with us," Father Bertram offered.

Leo hesitated, then nodded his head. "Very well, we'll go with you."

Mother, Lennie said telepathically. *I can carry him to the monastery.*

Gwennore relayed her message to the others.

Bertram scowled at the dragon. "How can we trust that dragon? He's the one who made Bran crash."

Mother, Lennie began, *please assure them I will not harm—*

I've spotted the fellow the younger brother is following, Pendras cut into their thoughts. *He has entered a pasture north of the King's Way, and he's meeting two men there. Both dressed in black. Priests, I think. One middle-aged, one young.*

Can you capture them? Silas asked.

Aye, Pendras replied. *No problem. We outnumber them. Reynfrid, Dominic, and Quentin are right behind me, and a dozen soldiers behind them.*

How is it going there, Silas? Gwennore asked.

It's quiet—wait. Some horns have sounded over the hill.

Something is wrong here, Pendras reported. *The three men seem to be waiting for us.*

A trap? Lennie asked.

One of the men has raised his arms. He— Agh! Pendras broke off with a garbled sound.

Pendras, what's wrong? Silas demanded.

Gwennore waved Leo and Brody over. "Something has happened to Pendras."

"I could shift and fly over to see," Brody offered, since he could shift into an eagle.

I'm all right, Pendras reported. *One of the men blasted us back with a burst of freezing-cold air. The soldiers were knocked off their horses. I think Quentin's horse is injured. Quentin is throwing off his clothes, must be planning to shift.*

When Gwennore explained what had happened, Father Sebastian told them, "That was Greer who shot the blast of cold air. His Embraced power allows him to freeze things to death.

He's a vicious assassin who wants to complete the Brother-hood's evil quest. He even calls himself the new Master."

So it wasn't the Raven who had conspired to take over Tourin, Lennie thought as she glanced toward him. The Raven's eyes were open now, and he was glaring at her. *Pen-dras, capture Greer and his companions. Father, it was Greer who allied with Freydor to capture King Ulfrid.* When there was no response, she repeated, *Father?*

We're under attack! There must be several hundred.

Lennie exchanged a stunned look with her mother.

Silas, be careful—Gwennore began, but her husband inter-rupted.

Aleksi is down! He's been shot!

Lennie dug her talons into the ground as Gwennore quickly told the kings what was happening.

I'm drawing near to Greer and his companions, Pendras reported. *The youngest one has raised his arms toward the sky. The air is shimmering. I don't know what . . . Argh!*

Pendras! Lennie called mentally. *What happened?*

No answer.

Pendras! Gwennore yelled. Still no answer. *Silas?* No reply. She gave Lennie a frantic look.

Papa? Lennie cried. *Papa, please answer.* Nothing but a terrifying silence.

"Gwen, you're shaking." Brody stepped toward her. "What's wrong?"

She reached a trembling hand to rest on Lennie's wing. "Silas and Pendras are unable to respond."

"I can check on Pendras." Brody headed into the woods to strip and shift, but before he could do so, Quentin landed be-side him in eagle form. He shifted, hidden behind a large oak, and Brody handed him his cloak.

"Pendras and Reynfrid have been captured," Quentin an-nounced as he wrapped the cloak around his waist.

"How is that possible?" Leo asked. "How can three men capture a dragon?"

"One of the men has an Embraced gift I've never seen before," Quentin explained. "He made an invisible wall around the three of them, and when Pendras flew into it, he crashed as if he'd flown into a brick wall. Reynfrid's horse rode into it. It broke its neck and fell on top of Reynfrid. Pendras hit the ground so hard, he was unconscious and shifted back to human form. Dominic tried to reach them, but the Embraced man had moved the wall to encompass the two princes. Dominic and his soldiers banged on the invisible wall, but couldn't get through. I flew here to tell you what had happened."

"And Dominic is still there?" Leo asked.

"Aye," Quentin replied. "The last glimpse I had of them, Dominic and his troop were outside the invisible wall. The priests inside had tied up Reynfrid and Pendras and hefted them onto their horses."

While Quentin was making his report, Lennie repeated it telepathically in case her father could hear it. *Papa, did you hear that? Pendras and Reynfrid have been taken prisoner.*

Still no response from Silas.

Lenushka, a male voice answered. It was Dimitri Tolenko, the Norveshki general who had been left in charge of the capital with his wife, Annika. *I am dispatching two dragons to help you rescue your brother. You will be in charge of the mission.*

Aye, General, Lennie responded, accepting the order.

Gwennore, Dimitri continued, *I'm sending four more dragons for Silas.*

There would be only a few dragons left in Norveshka, Lennie thought. This was a dangerous situation for everyone.

Thank you, Gwennore replied to Dimitri. Quickly, her voice trembling, she explained the situation to Kings Leo and Brody.

Leo's gloved hands clenched. "Brody and I will take this troop of soldiers back to Lourdon Palace. There, we'll request the aid of the Tourinian army. Gwen, can you come with us to communicate with the dragons coming to help us?"

"Aye, I will." Gwennore nodded, then turned to Lennie with tears in her eyes. "I'm counting on you to save Pendras."

I won't let you down, Lennie replied.

"I'll do everything I can to help." Roslyn stepped toward them. "I have to save Reynfrid."

Quentin motioned toward the Raven, who was watching them with narrowed eyes. "His brother was captured, too."

"What?" The Raven struggled to sit up and fell back with a grimace. "I have to go. Zane needs me."

Leo glanced at him, then faced the entire group. "This is the plan. Brody, Gwen, and I will rescue the kings. You all"—he looked at Lennie, Roslyn, Milena, Quentin, and Bran—"will rescue the brothers with the help of Dominic and his troop."

Lennie nodded her head. *Mother.* She stretched out a wing to envelop Gwennore. *Be careful.*

You, too. A tear rolled down Gwennore's cheek. *Save your brother. I'll save your father.* She hurried off with the kings to ride back to Lourdon Palace.

"I'll go back to Dominic to see what's happening there," Quentin said. "Shall I find you this evening to give a report?"

Lennie nodded her head.

"Good luck to you all." Quentin stepped behind a tree and tossed out the cloak he'd used. Within seconds, a large eagle took off into the sky.

Lennie glanced at the Raven, who was glowering at her.

"If any harm comes to my brother," he hissed, "I will scale you like a fish—"

"Shh." Bertram hushed him. "We need the dragon, so he can carry you back to the monastery."

"He will not!" the Raven protested. His dark eyes flashed with anger as Lennie slowly moved toward him. "Back off, you flying snake!"

Snake? Lennie huffed a puff of smoke from her nostrils.

"Bran!" Father Sebastian fussed at him. "We need to work with this dragon and Princess—"

"They're the ones who made me crash," the Raven growled. "Just get me a damned horse! I'm going after Greer now. I know where he's headed." He struggled to get to his feet, then tumbled over, hitting his broken arm. With a yelp of pain, he fell unconscious.

"Thank the Light for small mercies," Milena muttered as she tucked her cloak around him.

Lennie sighed as she approached the Raven. She was going to have to work with this angry bird. Even though he hated her. Even though she detested him. And his handsome face. Blast him.

She was tempted to leave him behind, but he'd just admitted he knew where Greer was going. She needed him if she was going to rescue her brother, Pendras, and Reynfrid, the crown prince of Tourin.

To save them, she would ally herself with the devil, himself. As she gingerly scooped the Raven into her forearms, she wondered if that was exactly what she was doing.

Chapter 5

It was not long before Lennie spotted the Monastery of Mercy from the air. Just as Father Bertram had described, it was nearby, located east of the King's Way after the road curved in a northerly direction. Behind her, the priests were on the road, riding alongside Roslyn and Milena.

Lennie had kept her flight as smooth as possible in order not to jar her unconscious passenger. Her wings might be working calmly and steadily, but her mind was racing so fast, she had to warn herself not to succumb to panic. What was happening right now to her father? To Pendras? If Greer meant to accomplish the Brotherhood's evil quest of conquering the world, then eliminating the royal families would be part of his plan. Rupert, Silas, Reynfrid, Pendras: they were all in terrible danger.

Pendras? She tried once again to contact him, but there was no reply. Was he already— *No, he's not dead!* She tamped down the terror that threatened to consume her once again. She would rescue her brother. She had to. How could she live with herself if she failed?

Calm yourself. She breathed in and out slowly to steady her nerves. *You were trained to handle missions. There is always a path to success, no matter how hard it might seem. Think it through and you will come up with a plan.*

The more she thought about it, the more she realized the key to her success was lying unconscious in her arms. The

Raven knew where Greer was headed. Could she convince him to work with her even though he hated her and Roslyn for injuring him? She recalled his threat: *If any harm comes to my brother, I will scale you like a fish.*

How could she blame him? The thought of any harm coming to *her* brother had her ready to explode, too.

So, how could she make the Raven cooperate? Appeal to his common sense? He, Lennie, and Roslyn all shared the same goal: the rescue of their three brothers.

Still, she suspected he would want to go after his brother alone. How could she gain his trust when he hated her?

Of course! The solution came in a flash, causing her breath to catch in her throat. It was so simple! All she had to do was approach him in human form. He'd never met her before as Princess Lenushka of Norveshka, so he would have no reason to resent her.

But what if he'd been raised by the Brotherhood to hate royalty? In that case, she should probably present herself as Captain Dravenko, her title in the Norveshki army. Yes, she nodded to herself. That would be the best strategy. As soon as possible, she would have to warn Roslyn and Milena to keep her dragon and princess identity a secret.

But was that a lie of omission? *It doesn't matter*, she told herself. Rescuing the three captives had to be her first priority. Pendras would be the future general of the Norveshki army and Lord Protector of the Realm. Reynfrid was the crown prince of Tourin. She had to do everything in her power to liberate them as quickly as possible. And after she'd helped the Raven rescue his brother, he would be so grateful, he wouldn't care if he found out she was the dragon that caused him to crash. Besides, once the mission was over, there would be no reason for her ever to see him again.

His body gave a small jerk as he regained consciousness. "What the hell?"

Was the grouch going to struggle against her hold and risk

falling? Luckily, Milena's cloak was wrapped around him securely enough to keep him from moving too much. She tightened her grip, pressing him more firmly against her chest.

"You," he muttered, his voice full of disdain. "You've absconded with me against my will."

She ignored him.

His head shifted against her chest, but she refused to think about how soft his hair was. "I've seen you before. You're the dragon with the pink belly."

Her talons flinched, but she forced them to relax.

"Ouch." He sounded more amused than in pain. "Did I hit a nerve? Do the other dragons tease you about your pink belly?"

The monastery was less than a mile away now. She was tempted to fly over it and let him drop. On his handsome head.

"You were in Eberon, weren't you? At the Monastery of Light when I was escaping."

So he remembered her. She snorted, releasing a puff of smoke.

"You wanted to kill me then."

Still do, she thought, recalling how he'd kidnapped Eviana and her mother.

Princess Lenushka, a male dragon's voice called to her. *This is Sergei.*

Anton, here, another dragon added. *Never fear, Your Highness. We're on our way to help!*

Aye, we'll rescue Pendras for you. No need for Your Highness to worry. Even in telepathic form, Sergei's voice was laced with arrogant condescension. Lennie gritted her teeth. If he were standing next to her in person, he would probably be patting her on the shoulder. After he'd flipped back his silky mane of shoulder-length black hair.

You can count on me! Anton boasted. *You know I would do anything for you, right?*

Lennie shuddered, not answering because she wasn't sure she could do it without screaming. Dammit! There were a dozen dragons in the Norveshki army, so why the hell was Dimitri sending these two? Of course, they had probably volunteered as soon as the news broke that she was in charge of Pendras's rescue. Sergei and Anton never missed a chance to try to impress her. They would view this mission as the ultimate competition, each vying to outperform the other.

And the ultimate prize would not be rescuing Pendras. It would be her. Not that Sergei or Anton was actually smitten with her. What they craved most was the benefit marriage to her would bring them—the chance at becoming the next king of Norveshka.

The iron walls kept closing in.

"Hey!" the Raven hollered. "Are you still trying to kill me? You're squeezing me to death."

Oops. She relaxed her hold. Damn, she'd let those two jerks upset her. Now the Raven would be more convinced than ever that she wished him harm. She would definitely have to keep her dragon identity a secret. *Sergei and Anton, please join our rescue team at the Monastery of Mercy in central Tourin.*

On our way! Anton replied.

See you soon! Sergei added.

When you see me, refer to me as Captain Dravenko, Lennie told them. *This is a military mission, and the general has put me in charge.*

Aye, Captain!

Were they even needed? Lennie wondered to herself. Dominic was an excellent soldier and had a troop of twelve men at his command. And then there was Quentin. Lennie and her brother had grown up with Quentin at Draven Castle and completely trusted him. As an eagle shifter, he could spy on Greer and his companions while drawing little to no attention. Two dragons, though, were an entirely different matter. If Greer spotted dragons overhead, he might feel compelled to take drastic measures, which would put the three prisoners in even more danger. She would have to be very careful how she used the dragons.

With the monastery drawing nigh, she slowed and lowered her altitude. The place was larger than she'd anticipated. More like a village than a religious retreat. There were outlying fields where two monks were guiding mule-drawn plows in straight furrows. She figured wheat, barley, or corn would soon be planted. Another field, surrounded by a stone wall, held a few cows, sheep, and goats. Close to the barns, there was an assortment of wooden buildings—what looked like cottages, workhouses, and a small school. Beyond that was a large kitchen garden, and then a rectangular enclosure made of stone.

That had to be the heart of the monastery, where the monks lived and prayed. At one short end, there was a wide wooden gate and at the other, a large stone church. Two stone buildings stretched along the longer sides of the rectangle. Lennie figured they housed dormitories, storerooms, or offices. Along the front of each building ran an arched colonnade that looked out over the grassy lawn in the center. Close to the church, a stone basin rested in front of a metal pump to give the monks a ready source of water.

As Lennie passed over the fields, one of the monks sighted her and ran to a nearby post to ring a warning bell. People emerged from the workhouses, homes, and school. To her surprise, they were all women and children. Most of them gawked at her. A few screamed.

"The dragon will burn our homes to the ground!" an older woman yelled.

"And then he'll eat us!" a young redhead shrieked.

"No, the dragon will kidnap the children!" a third one screamed.

"And eat them!" the redhead added.

With that brilliant announcement, the children began to wail and cling to their mothers.

"Have no fear!" the Raven yelled down at them. "The dragon comes in peace! He will not harm you. He's only bringing me home."

What? Lennie blinked in surprise. Was the Raven admitting she was an ally? Somehow, she doubted that. More likely, he was simply trying to avoid terrifying the women and children. Grudgingly, she had to admit it was kind of him to calm their fears.

Despite his reassurance, the women below were taking no chances. They quickly herded the children into the school building. The redhead made a sign at Lennie, designed to ward off evil.

Lennie let out a puff of smoke. She could hardly blame them. The old legend about dragons kidnapping young children was unfortunately based on fact. Her uncle, King Petras, had swooped down to capture a number of young children, including Eviana, when she was only three. At the time, Norveshka had been hit hard with a plague for several generations, making it nearly impossible for the Norveshki people to have children. In their desperation, they had resorted to kidnapping children from neighboring countries. Their criminal actions had incited so much horror, it was little wonder that a rumor had started about the dragons actually eating children.

Twenty years ago, Lennie's mother, Gwennore, had ended the plague and made a medicine to heal the Norveshki people. Silas had become king and outlawed the kidnapping of children. But the old stories had continued, making many people outside of Norveshka fearful of dragons.

"I'm not the only one who distrusts you," the Raven muttered.

Was she close enough to the ground that he would survive if she dropped him? She huffed. It wasn't like her to be petty and spiteful, but it was hard to ignore the fact that this man had kidnapped Eviana and held Queen Luciana prisoner at the Brotherhood's monastery. No doubt he found it equally hard to ignore the fact that she had injured him, making it more difficult for him to rescue his younger brother.

And yet, they needed to work together. Normally, she would take the time as a dragon to earn his trust and respect, but in this situation, there simply was no time. And so, she had to stick to her decision to keep her true identity a secret.

"Set me down on the green in front of the church."

Now he was issuing orders? She poked him with a talon.

"I felt that."

Below, in the grassy area, a small group of monks were gathering. A soldier, equipped with sword, bow, and arrow, ran toward them, urging them to step back into the shaded colonnade that ran along the front of the dormitory. With the lawn clear, Lennie landed on her hind legs, then gently placed the Raven on the grass. She stepped back, folding her wings.

The soldier approached, his sword drawn, then stiffened with recognition. "Your—"

With a grunt, Lennie shook her head. She recognized him, too. Terrance had been the archery instructor at Benwick Academy. As one of the children from the Isle of Secrets, he'd eventually ended up at Benwick, where he could be trained to use his Embraced gift. After graduating, he'd had no home to return to, so he'd stayed on at the academy as an instructor. But two years ago, he'd suddenly left.

Had it been some sort of scandal? Lennie had heard rumors to that effect but wasn't really sure, since his departure had occurred during a summer break when she'd gone home to train with the Norveshki army.

Terrance narrowed his eyes, no doubt wondering why she didn't want to be identified. But then he turned his attention to the man on the ground, struggling with his one good arm to disengage himself from the cloak wrapped around him.

"Bran!" Terrance rushed toward him, then motioned to the group of monks. "He's been injured. Let's get him to his room."

As Terrance helped the Raven to his feet, the cloak fell to the ground and, once again, Lennie saw the scars crisscrossing his back. Her talons dug into the grass. As much as she despised the Raven, she detested even more the way he'd been treated as a child.

Terrance glanced at her, knowing she was female, and quickly draped the cloak around the Raven's shoulders. Meanwhile, two monks inched forward, casting fearful glances at Lennie.

"I know this dragon," Terrance told them. "You need not be afraid."

The monks rushed forward and one of them quickly examined the Raven. "We'll need to set his arm and stitch these wounds. Brother Timothy, please bring the supplies we'll need."

"Aye, Brother Jerome." As Timothy scurried off, another monk joined him.

Lennie watched as Terrance and Jerome guided the unsteady Raven to his room and carefully noted which room it was. The building on the left side of the church, four doors from the right. There were still three monks gathered in the colonnade, and they each made the circular sign of the sun god and murmured a blessing as the Raven stumbled past them and into his room.

As the door shut, the three monks aimed suspicious looks at Lennie. No doubt they were wondering if she'd saved the Raven or been the cause of his injuries. With an inward groan, she settled on the grass. She couldn't do anything until Roslyn arrived with her clothes.

Brother Timothy and his companion hurried back, their arms laden with medical supplies. One of the monks opened the Raven's door to let them in. Meanwhile, a few young women had gathered by the monastery gate to peek inside. After spotting Lennie, they quickly retreated behind the six-foot-high stone wall. When they called out greetings, Lennie realized the priests, Bertram and Sebastian, were finally arriving.

The priests rode through the gate on their stocky little horse, followed by Roslyn and Milena on their sleek mares from the stables of Lourdon Palace.

Bertram scrambled off the horse. "Where is Bran? Is he all right?"

"Terrance and Brother Jerome took him to his room," one of the monks in the colonnade replied. "Brothers Timothy and Sean brought in supplies."

"That's good." Bertram turned to Father Sebastian, who was dismounting. "Bran is in excellent hands. We have the best healers in the country."

A yelp of pain erupted from Bran's room.

Sebastian slanted a wary glance toward the dormitory. "Are you sure they know what they're doing?"

Bertram winced. "I believe so. They're the—"

A loud litany of colorful curses followed, and the priests in the colonnade exchanged shocked looks.

Sebastian's eyes widened. "Where did Bran learn words like that?"

"Not here!" Bertram protested. "It's just the pain talking. He's a good lad."

"We'd better see what's happening." Sebastian dashed toward the room with Father Bertram on his heels.

"I want to help," Milena offered as she followed them.

Once again, Lennie wondered why Milena seemed so interested in the Raven's welfare.

Roslyn brought Lennie the canvas sack containing her boots and uniform. "Here you go." She looked around the monastery. "But I'm not sure where you can change."

Lennie grabbed the bag with the talons of her right foreleg.

Most probably she would have to fly to the nearest bunch of trees—

Roslyn's gasp interrupted her thoughts. Terrance had just emerged from the Raven's room and was holding the door while the priests and Milena filed inside.

"Don't worry, he's fine," Terrance told them. "They just reset his arm. They gave him a potion for the pain, but it hasn't quite taken effect yet."

"Master Terrance?" Roslyn whispered in a stunned voice.

He glanced their way and his jaw dropped. He blinked a few times, as if he didn't believe what he saw, then slowly walked toward them.

Why was he staring at Roslyn? Lennie wondered as she glanced at the princess beside her. And why was Roslyn suddenly blushing and smoothing back her hair?

"Your Highness," Terrance greeted her with a bow.

"She's a princess?" one of the monks asked.

"Aye." Terrance glanced back at the three monks. "Could you see to the horses and prepare the guestroom?"

"Of course." Two of the priests scurried toward the horses and led them through the gate, while the other priest rushed down the colonnade to the last room.

Meanwhile, Terrance stopped in front of Roslyn, watching her intently, while her gaze flitted nervously about before finally resting on him.

"Master Terrance." She gave him a tight smile. "What an unexpected surprise."

"I could say the same thing." He took a deep breath. "I cannot believe you are here. I thought you were getting married tomorrow?"

She shrugged. "That's been canceled. The groom is dead."

"Oh, good. I mean—" He grimaced. "My condolences."

"No need to feel sorry." She waved a dismissive hand. "And why are you here?"

He rested a hand on the hilt of his sword. "I am in charge of security."

"Oh, good. I mean—" She winced. "I am glad you found employment after the scandal—"

"There was no scandal," he interrupted, his brown eyes flashing with annoyance.

"Oh, I thought . . ." Roslyn hesitated. "I wasn't sure why you left the academy so suddenly."

His jaw shifted. "It's a long story." He motioned to the quiver on her back. "Does Your Highness still shoot?"

Roslyn's blush crept back. "Yes."

Lennie rolled her eyes. Had these two forgotten there was a dragon standing next to them? And several kidnapped men to rescue? Although, to give him credit, Terrance might not have heard the news yet. She gritted her teeth. At this rate, he might never hear it.

Terrance suddenly stiffened. "Wait a minute. Bran said his stomach wound was caused by an arrow. Are you the one who shot him?"

Roslyn winced. "Well, about that . . . He was a bird at the time, and we thought he was escaping a crime—"

"You struck him while he was flying?" Terrance's eyes widened. "That's amazing."

Roslyn's cheeks grew bright pink as she gave him a shy smile. "Well, I had an amazing instructor."

Now Terrance blushed. "You were the one who worked so hard, practicing till your fingers bled—"

She gasped. "You knew?"

"Of course I knew."

Enough! Lennie huffed, emitting a puff of smoke.

"Oh, Lennie." Roslyn glanced at her as if she'd suddenly appeared. "You remember Master Terrance from Benwick?"

With an impatient grunt, she lifted the canvas sack containing her clothes.

"Right, you need to get dressed." Roslyn turned to Terrance. "Did you say you were having a room prepared for us?"

"She won't fit through the door," Terrance murmured as he glanced around the monastery. "I know! There's a walled-in garden behind the church. This way."

Lennie lumbered after them as they walked briskly around the stone church.

"Oh." Terrance shot her an apologetic look. "Sorry. The garden gate is too narrow."

She suppressed a growl, annoyed at being made to feel enormous when in reality, as far as dragons went, she was rather petite. But the garden did look like an excellent place to shift. The stone walls were six feet high, connecting the back of the church to the stone enclosure. The garden inside wouldn't be huge, but certainly big enough for her.

With a flap of her wings, she rose up and over the wall, then dropped down beside a stone bench. She looked around. It was a beautiful oasis of blooming flowers, sheltered from the wind and cold by the four walls. Complete privacy, although she could still hear Terrance and Roslyn talking on the other side of the gate. At last, Roslyn was finally explaining what had happened.

Lennie pivoted toward the bench to drop her sack on top, then winced as she realized she'd just swished her tail along the ground, effectively mowing down half a flowerbed. Damn. Whenever she was in flight, she felt strong and powerful, as if she ruled the sky, but on the ground, she felt more like a clumsy beached whale. Actually, now that she'd seen the amazing agility the Raven had displayed while in flight, she realized there were limitations to what she could do there, too.

Most of her training in the army had been focused on how to repel and defeat an attacking military force. But this upcoming mission was not two armies clashing on the field.

This was a mission that would require stealth and strategy. She could do strategy, but stealth? She needed Dominic and Quentin for that. And, whether she liked it or not, she needed the Raven.

"Pendras was captured?" Terrance's shocked voice rose in volume. "How could three men capture a dragon?"

Roslyn quickly explained what they had learned from Quentin. "My brother Reynfrid was taken prisoner, too, along with the Raven's brother."

"Zane?" Terrance huffed. "He's one of the inhabitants here I have sworn to protect. I must assist Your Highness with this mission."

"Oh, Master Terrance!" Roslyn exclaimed. "Could you?"

"Of course." While he went on to explain that he was Tourinian by birth and therefore had an additional obligation to rescue Prince Reynfrid and assist the royal princess in her endeavors, Lennie shifted and pulled on her small-clothes.

"Thank you, Terrance," she called to him over the wall. "We can use all the help we can get."

"He's more than mere help," Roslyn protested. "He's the best archer in the world! And excellent with a spear, too, I might add."

"Your Highness, you honor me too much," Terrance murmured.

In the privacy of the garden, Lennie made a face as if she were gagging. Had Roslyn always gushed over the former archery instructor like this? Lennie had no idea. And that was not good.

When she'd turned sixteen, her parents had decided to name her the heir to the throne, instead of her younger brother. The announcement had roused an onslaught of protest from noblemen all over the country. She'd been so stressed over it she'd spent the last four years entirely absorbed with the need to prove herself worthy. But now, she realized that had to change. She would never make a good monarch if she was oblivious to what was going on around her.

"Terrance," she called to him as she pulled on her Norveshki army uniform. "I would like to leave as soon as possible. Could you have a supply wagon and horses made ready?"

There was a pause, and then Terrance mumbled, "I apologize, Your Highness, but this is a poor establishment. Other than my horse, there are only two mules and the workhorse Father Bertram was riding. We have no wagon, only a farm cart with two wheels."

"Oh, dear," Roslyn murmured. "At least we have the two horses that Milena and I brought."

But they would need two more for the dragon shifters, Lennie thought as she fastened the brass buttons on her dark green tunic. And one for her, even though she might end up driving the wagon. "I'll take care of it." *Sergei and Anton, where are you?*

We've crossed the border into Tourin, Sergei replied.

We'll be there soon! Anton added.

I have new orders for you, Lennie told them mentally. *Go to Lourdon Palace and request three fast horses, plus a wagon with supplies and weapons. I'll also need an official travel badge so we can change horses along the King's Way. Bring everything here to the monastery. We will leave as soon as you arrive.*

Why bother with horses? Sergei protested. *We can fly faster than we can ride.*

Lennie gritted her teeth. As usual, Sergei implied he knew better than she. *I will not have you fly anywhere near the villains who have kidnapped Pendras. The sight of two dragons could cause them to panic and that would put the prisoners at greater risk.*

You are right, of course. Brilliant, as always, Anton responded with his usual unctuous tone.

We'll take care of everything and see you in a few hours, Sergei replied.

Lennie stifled a groan. One of them thought he'd win her over by showing how tough and smart he was, while the other had decided that flattery was the way to her heart. Did neither of them realize she saw right through their tactics?

Lenushka, Gwennore called to her. *I will tell Brigitta of your request, and she will have everything ready for the dragons when they arrive.*

Thank you, Mother. Lennie sat on the bench to pull on her boots. *Have you arrived at Lourdon Palace?*

Yes, Gwennore replied. *Brigitta has given Leo and Brody authority to command the Tourinian army until Rupert can be rescued. Leo is leaving now with several troops. Brody and I will be taking his ship, transporting supplies and more soldiers. Admiral Darroc is coming with two more ships, and he'll use his wind power to blow us north.*

Lennie recalled what she'd heard of Darroc. Like Terrance, he had been one of the Embraced orphans from the Isle of Secrets. Darroc's gift had been wind sorcery, the same as King Ulfrid, or Rupert as his close friends called him. After the final battle, Rupert had taken Darroc back to Tourin to train him to be a naval officer. About five years ago, Darroc had been promoted to the rank of admiral.

Take care, dear heart, Gwennore told her.

You, too, Mama. A surge of frustration swept over Lennie. Darroc would be able to move the ships north in just a few hours, but here she was, unable to even start her mission until the horses and wagon arrived. But what choice did she have? They needed weapons. And the wagon, since she doubted the Raven could even sit a horse in his current condition.

With a sigh, she stood, folded up the canvas bag, and stuffed it into a tunic pocket. "It's all set. Sergei and Anton will bring horses and a supply wagon from Lourdon Palace. We will leave as soon as they arrive."

"Excellent," Terrance called to her.

"Who are Sergei and Anton?" Roslyn asked.

The bane of my existence, Lennie almost said aloud, but while she hesitated, Terrance answered for her.

"Dragons," he told Roslyn. "They spent only one year at the academy. I believe it was your first year, so you may not remember them."

"Then they are older than us?" Roslyn asked.

"Us?" He chuckled. "Have you forgotten I'm five years older than you?"

Roslyn scoffed. "That's nothing."

"Sergei and Anton are both twenty-one," Lennie said as she opened the gate.

"I see." Roslyn gave her a curious look. "I heard there were two dragon shifters courting you. Are they the ones?"

"Yes." Lennie slammed the gate behind her with more force than necessary. "But I'd rather not talk about it."

"Oh, my!" Roslyn's eyes lit up. "This is so exciting!"

Lennie gritted her teeth. "I have instructed them to call me Captain Dravenko. I would like you to do the same."

"Why?" Roslyn asked.

"Because we need the Raven's help," Lennie explained. "He knows where Greer is headed, but I doubt he'll want to confide in me if he knows I'm the dragon who made him crash."

"Oh, dear." Roslyn made a face. "He's not going to trust me, either."

"I could talk to him," Terrance offered.

"I believe the easiest solution is for me to become Captain Dravenko." Lennie braided her long hair. "He's never met this version of me before."

Roslyn's eyes widened. "How exciting! It will be like play-acting."

Lennie gave her a wry look. "I *am* Captain Dravenko."

Terrance nodded. "I should warn you, Captain, that Bran will insist on rescuing Zane himself. He and his brother are extremely close."

Lennie pulled a leather thong from her pocket. The Raven's fierce loyalty toward his brother should work in her favor. "I'll convince him to join us. We have three brothers to save, so it makes sense for us to work together."

"Exactly!" Roslyn nodded enthusiastically. "What can I do to help?"

Lennie used the thong to tie off the end of her braid. "Conserve your energy. Get some rest. We'll be leaving soon."

"I can show you to your room." Terrance offered an arm to Roslyn. "Or take you to the dining hall, if you prefer."

"The dining hall would be lovely." Roslyn smiled as she took his arm.

"What is this?" Terrance took her bandaged hand in his. "You were injured?"

Roslyn shrugged. "It's nothing, really. A small cut."

Lennie snorted, recalling how Roslyn had squeezed a shard of broken pottery in her hand, claiming she would use it to kill the traitorous groom.

With a frown, Terrance examined the spot of blood on the bandage. "You need a new bandage. And some of the excellent salve that Brother Jerome makes. May I?" When Roslyn nodded, he untied the knot to unwind the bandage.

Roslyn's cheeks grew pink once again.

Terrance's eyes narrowed as he studied the streak of blood on her palm. "This is odd. Come this way." He led her over to the well next to the church.

Lennie followed since it was on the way to the Raven's room.

At the well, Terrance pumped some water over Roslyn's hand, and the blood washed away. "Where is the cut?"

Roslyn ran a thumb over the palm of her hand. "I don't know. It—it's gone."

"Gone?" Lennie took a look at Roslyn's hand. Sure enough, her skin was smooth, as if the cut had never happened.

Roslyn frowned at her hand. "It must not have been as bad as I thought."

"No, it was bleeding," Lennie said. "I saw it." And she'd seen Faith press her hand against it. And then a glow? Did Faith have the power to heal? Is so, she had to be Embraced.

Terrance shrugged. "It makes no sense, but I suppose we should thank the Light that Your Highness has recovered."

Lennie opened her mouth to explain about Faith, then closed it. If Faith was Embraced and healing was her gift, then why had her parents always kept it a secret? They must have had a good reason, one that Lennie ought to respect. She caught Terrance watching her intently. Did he suspect she knew what had happened?

"Well, I am famished," Roslyn said, attempting to change the subject. "I hardly ate at all this morning. And it seems like ages ago, doesn't it, Lennie?"

Lennie nodded. So much had happened, and it was barely past noon.

"Then I will take Your Highness to the dining hall." Terrance offered his arm once again.

"Thank you. And please, since we're all going to be working together, you should call me Roslyn."

"Very well." He smiled as he led her across the lawn. "Roslyn."

Lennie rolled her eyes. As far as she could tell, Roslyn had completely recovered from the disappointment of her ruined wedding. But maybe that was easy to do when she'd never loved the groom. And he had turned out to be a cheating, traitorous bastard.

Roslyn glanced up at Terrance and smiled.

How could it be so easy? Lennie wondered with a twinge of annoyance. She had two handsome young dragons courting her, but she never blushed or smiled at either of them. *Because you don't love them.* The walls crept in closer around her. *And you never will.*

She took a deep breath and mentally shoved the walls back. Feelings were a luxury she didn't have time for, especially negative ones like despair. Nothing could get in the way of her successfully completing this mission.

And the first step was winning over the Raven.

Chapter 6

Bran was soaring through the sky, delighting in the freedom to go wherever he wanted. Below him, the green patchwork quilt of rich farmland spread as far as he could see. Above him, the sun's rays brightened the sky to a pale blue and warmed his soul. Veering to the right, he swooped into a puffy cloud and reveled at the feel of the cool vapor sifting through his feathers. Life was good.

Somewhere in the back of his mind, a slight twinge reminded him that this wasn't real. Something was actually terribly wrong, but he couldn't remember what. The notion drifted away from him like the wisp of a cloud, impossible to grasp.

Floating higher and higher, he was filled with an overwhelming sense of peace. Surely this flight was leading him to heaven.

In the distance, he heard a muffled noise. A knocking? How could that be when he was surrounded by sky? Ah, of course. Someone was knocking on the gate of heaven, so he could enter. How thoughtful. A voice followed, a woman's voice, so soft and sweet it had to belong to an angel.

"Welcome," Father Bertram greeted her. "I don't believe we have met."

Father Sebastian introduced himself and Bertram. "And you are . . . ?"

Bran heard the beautiful voice answer, though the words

were muddled. Why couldn't the priests recognize an angel when they saw one?

"How is he?" the angel asked as she approached.

Ah, his angel was worried about him. Bran managed to open his eyes for a glimpse of her before his eyelids drooped shut once more. His angel was beautiful. More sweet and pure of heart than any mortal could ever be.

A conversation ensued between his angel and the priests. They were asking too many questions, Bran thought. It wasn't polite to interrogate an angel like that.

"Stop," he murmured. "No ques . . ." With great effort, he forced his eyes to open.

The priests were to his left, gazing down at him with worried expressions, while the angel had taken a seat on the stool at the foot of his bed.

She blurred before his eyes, and he struggled to make his eyes and mouth work. "My angel. You are so beautiful."

She looked over her shoulder as if he were talking to someone else.

Did she not realize how lovely she was? His sweet angel was so adorably modest. He wanted to touch her. Lay his head on her breast and feel the sweet warmth of her light and goodness radiate into his dark and tainted soul. "Father Bertr . . ." His tongue got in the way, and he stopped to regain control.

"Yes, my son." Bertram leaned over him.

"Is it a sin to want to kiss an angel?"

With a small gasp, Bertram stiffened. Sebastian frowned. The angel sprang to her feet.

"Don't mind him," Bertram quickly told her. "He doesn't mean it. It's the pain talking."

"More likely, it's Brother Jerome's Special Potion of Peaceful Repose that's talking." Sebastian leaned over Bran. "How are you feeling?"

"I'm peaceful. And reposed."

"He's soused," Sebastian muttered to the other priest. "What is in that potion?"

"*Special* potion," Bran corrected him, then smiled. "Would you like some? It could make you more peaceful."

Sebastian scoffed. "I prefer to keep my wits about me."

"Father Sebash . . ." Bran bit his lip to get some feeling back. "You should always try to be peaceful in the presence of an angel." He attempted to motion toward her, but for some strange reason, his right arm was stuck and couldn't move. All he could do was lift a forefinger and point. "Do not be distracted by her beauty. At any minute, she could unleash her heavenly wrath upon you and thoroughly smite you."

The angel cleared her throat. "I don't intend to smite anyone."

"Too late for me," Bran muttered. "I'm a lost cause. The minute I was born, the Holy Light smited . . . smit . . . smote me . . . however the hell you say it."

"Now, now, that's not true." Bertram gave the angel an apologetic smile. "He doesn't usually talk like this. He's a good lad."

"Noooo." Bran tried to shake his head, but that made the room spin. "I could never be good enough for an angel."

With a sigh, the angel sat back on the stool. "Since you are somewhat lucid at the moment, I should introduce myself. I am Captain Dravenko of the Norveshki army."

That made no sense whatsoever. Why would an angel be in an army? And why from Norveshka? That was where those damned dragons lived. Bran frowned, attempting to burrow through the thick fog in his head. It was sadly true that he could never be good enough for an angel. That meant the likelihood of one showing up for a friendly visit was nil. And that could only mean this visitor wasn't an angel, after all.

How could she be human? How could any human be that beautiful? He narrowed his eyes, forcing himself to refocus more clearly on her. What he'd thought was a white, glowing nimbus radiating from her head was the white-blond hair of an elf. Her ears were slightly pointed, her face heart-shaped, her eyes a vibrant green, and her delicate eyebrows a startling black against her smooth white brow. She looked familiar somehow . . .

Holy Light! The shock reverberated through him.

"Bran!" Father Bertram touched his shoulder. "What's wrong?"

"This . . . this can't be real." How could the woman he'd spotted five months ago at the Eberoni army camp be here in his room? The woman whom he'd dreamed about over and over again?

He was still in a dream. That had to be it. Reality could never be this good, but the Light was merciful, allowing him to take refuge in this beautiful dream. With a sigh of relief he closed his eyes and let the tendrils of Brother Jerome's special potion wrap around him and drag him under.

"Bran?" Father Bertram called to him. "The captain needs to talk to you."

"She's no captain."

The woman cleared her throat. "On the contrary, I—"

"She is the woman who haunts my dreams." Bran drifted off, succumbing to oblivion.

Lennie slathered butter over a slice of freshly baked bread as she considered her options concerning the Raven. How could she talk to him when he was delusional? The woman who haunts his dreams? An angel he wanted to kiss? What nonsense!

Pay him no mind. She'd seen enough drunken soldiers on leave to know how ridiculous they could be. But she'd also noticed that an inebriated man tended to be embarrassingly honest. So had the Raven spoken the truth?

You are so beautiful.

Ha! His outrageous statements were bad enough, but her

reaction had been even worse. Even now, just recalling his words made her heart flutter in her chest.

Dear goddesses, what was wrong with her? She didn't normally become a mindless idiot when confronted with a handsome face. Sergei and Anton certainly had no effect on her, so why did the Raven muddle her thoughts? He'd done it before five months ago, and now, he was doing it again, blast him. How could she forget he was the one who had kidnapped Eviana and her mother? She would not forgive him for that.

But it seemed as if Eviana had forgiven him. Once again, Lennie was pricked with a suspicion that there was a part of her that wanted the Raven to be found innocent and good. Was it simply because she found him handsome, brave, and loyal? Or was it because she suspected there was more to his story than she'd been told? Why had the Raven called himself a lost cause? Did he really believe he'd been born that way? The minute he'd said that, she'd recalled the scars on his back. Had he been whipped so often as a child that he had come to believe he deserved to be abused? Had the Brotherhood taken an innocent child and convinced him he was evil?

Rage flared up inside her, and she felt a swell of fire in her chest. Was there anything more monstrous than torturing children and stealing their innocence?

She slammed her butter knife down and ripped off a hunk of bread with her teeth.

Across from her, Father Bertram's eyes widened. "Oh, dear. Is the food not to your liking?"

She chewed quickly, tamping down her anger as the two priests across the table regarded her in silence. After Bran had fallen into a deep sleep, they had shown her to the dining hall while they remained outside, huddled together for a quick conference.

When Lennie had spotted the table where Roslyn, Terrance, and Milena were eating, she had hurried over so she could remind the lady-in-waiting to refer to her as Captain Dravenko.

Earlier, when she'd first approached the Raven's door, the physicians had exited with their tools, headed toward the well to give them a wash. Milena had left the room with them, and Lennie had quickly introduced herself as Captain Dravenko and suggested she find Roslyn in the dining room.

Lennie had planned on joining her companions at their table, but the two priests had rushed over to insist she sit with them. Some monks had quickly brought them trays of food, along with three wooden cups and a jug of watered-down wine. The fare had been simple: lentil stew with fresh bread and butter.

She swallowed and gave the two priests a smile. "The food is delicious. Thank you. I'm afraid I'm somewhat nervous about the mission. I do hope Bran will agree to join us."

"I'm sure he will." Father Bertram's eyes glinted with excitement. "In fact, Father Sebastian and I have decided that we must go, too."

Lennie hesitated with her slice of bread halfway to her mouth. "I'm not sure that is wise. The men we are pursuing are extremely dangerous."

"Aye," Father Sebastian agreed. "We know all about Father Greer. He was Master Lorne's favorite assassin."

Bertram nodded. "And he's already committed murder today."

She dropped her bread onto her wooden tray, her appetite gone. The thought of Pendras being abused or tortured while she sat here eating was too much. "I want to leave now, this instant, but I don't know where to go until Bran tells us. I only know the three captives are in grave danger."

"Don't worry." Bertram reached across the table to pat her hand. "I saw only one death for today. The men will be fine."

She blinked. "You *saw*?"

"Aye." Bertram tapped a finger to his temple. "My Embraced gift is foresight—one of the reasons you should allow us to accompany you. My gift might come in handy."

"And our knowledge of the Brotherhood might be helpful, too," Sebastian added.

"Aye." Bertram nodded. "And we must be there for Zane. He's like a son to us."

She hesitated, not sure if the two priests could keep pace. "We'll be moving quickly."

"We can keep up," Bertram insisted.

Lennie's first thought had been that a smaller group could move faster. That was important since they'd lost so much valuable time. But now, she could see an advantage to a larger group. It would discourage any brigands looking for someone to rob. And if the priests came, Bran would most likely join them. "Very well. I will appreciate your company."

"Excellent!" Bertram lifted his wooden cup and drained it.

Lennie considered asking Sergei and Anton to bring more horses, then decided against it. One of the priests could ride in the wagon, and once she had her royal travel badge, she could always order more horses at the next posting station. The badge would mean she was on a mission for the king and allow her and her team to have free food, lodging, and fresh horses at any of the official stations along the King's Way. Even though it was frustrating to have to wait here, once she had the travel pass, she would be able to move quickly.

Sebastian looked at her curiously. "You said there are two dragon shifters bringing us horses and supplies?"

"Yes," Lennie replied. "Anton and Sergei from the Norveshki army."

"I mean no offense . . ." Sebastian started, and Lennie mentally prepared herself for what would most likely be offensive. "But I am wondering why you were put in charge of the rescue, when there are two dragons coming who are also trained soldiers."

"I outrank them." She avoided any reference to being the crown princess and popped a bite of bread into her mouth.

"How interesting." Sebastian poured more wine into his and Bertram's cups. "Here in Tourin, there are no females in the army."

"True." Lennie glanced across the dining hall to where her friends were eating. "But Princess Roslyn is as skilled as any man with the bow and arrow."

Bertram huffed. "Aye, I thought she was going to kill our dear Bran."

"She actually aimed to miss him," Lennie assured the priests, not wanting them to hold a grudge against Roslyn. "Bran was only wounded because he dropped unexpectedly."

Bertram scowled. "Aye, to escape that horrible dragon."

Lennie winced inwardly. They definitely held a grudge against her dragon.

Sebastian's eyes narrowed. "Where did the dragon go?"

She quickly took a sip of wine. "It left."

"Good riddance," Bertram muttered.

Sebastian ran a fingertip along the rim of his cup. "King Silas is in the north, far away from us. How was he able to assign you the mission?"

The younger priest was not nearly as trusting as Father Bertram, Lennie thought. Not that Sebastian was all that young. She estimated he was in his late thirties. He had been suspicious of her ever since she'd entered Bran's room. He'd asked her several questions then, such as how an elfin woman had become a soldier for the Norveshki army. Now, he had more. All she could do was be as honest as possible. "It was the Norveshki Lord Protector, General Tolenko, who gave me the order."

"And he gave you the order in the Norveshki capital?" Sebastian asked.

Another trap, she thought. There was no way that a normal human being could travel from Draven Castle to the monastery as quickly as she had. "I am from the Dravenko clan, one of the three clans in Norveshka that give birth to the dragon shifters. I was born with the gift of being able to communicate telepathically with the dragons. That is how General Tolenko was able to give me the order."

"Ah." Sebastian nodded slowly. "How interesting."

"I am also in communication with the two dragons who are bringing us horses and supplies from Lourdon Palace," she continued. "And hopefully, Pendras will be able to reach me soon."

"Pendras?" Bertram asked.

"The dragon who was captured." She hesitated, then decided to risk a bit more honesty. "He is my brother."

"Ah." Sebastian's eyes widened. "No wonder you were chosen to lead the mission. Still . . ." He leaned forward. "You arrived here at the monastery not too long after we did. How was that possible?"

Lennie had been expecting this question, so she was ready for it. She motioned for Roslyn and her companions to join her. "I was on my way to Lourdon and Princess Roslyn's wedding. We're old friends from Benwick Academy, right?"

"Exactly!" With a grin, Roslyn slipped into the chair next to Lennie. "I've known the captain for years. And Master Terrance knew us there. He was our archery instructor."

Lennie bowed her head to Milena. "It is good to see you again, my lady."

Milena glanced at the two priests, then back at Lennie and gave her a strained smile. "Always a pleasure, Captain."

"We're all going on the mission together!" Bertram announced with a smile.

Terrance gave the older priest a worried look. "Are you sure you're up to it, Father?"

"Of course," Bertram insisted. "We can't leave our poor Zane in the hands of those villains!"

Roslyn nodded. "I am determined, as well, to rescue my brother Reynfrid."

"And I will do everything in my power to assist you," Terrance told the princess.

"As will I," Lady Milena added quietly.

Roslyn gave her a curious look. "You are going far beyond the call of duty, my lady. Could it be"—her eyes glinted with mischief—"perhaps you harbor more than the usual concern for my brother?"

Milena's face turned pink. "No, not at all! I mean, I am concerned for His Highness, of course, as any loyal subject would be. I-I admit we were friends once, but I hardly speak to him anymore." She dunked her head. "I know my place."

Roslyn frowned at her. "You must not know Reynfrid well, after all, if you believe he selects his friends according to rank."

Milena nodded. "He is a good man." She winced, her face flushing darker. "I—I think I should rest for a while. Is there a room for us?"

"I'll show you," Terrance offered.

"I should rest, too." Roslyn bowed her head to the priests. "Thank you for your hospitality. We will see you soon."

As Terrance strolled out the door with the two women, Lennie wondered if there was any truth to Roslyn's teasing. Had Milena's offer to accompany them on this mission been motivated by secret feelings for Prince Reynfrid? But if that was so, why was she showing so much concern for the Raven?

She glanced through the dining hall window at the Raven's room. Would he be awake now? "If you don't mind, I would like to see how Bran is doing."

"We'll go with you." Bertram headed for the door with her, followed by Sebastian.

Out on the green, Sebastian pivoted as he scanned the monastery. "I would like to look around a bit if you don't mind. This is my first time here."

"Be my guest, old friend." Bertram clapped him on the shoulder, then headed toward Bran's room with Lennie.

When she entered the room, Lennie's gaze went first to Bran. He was on his back, sound asleep on a narrow bed against the left side of the room. His right forearm had been splinted and bandaged tightly, then strapped down to keep him from moving it in his sleep. Extra pillows had been stuffed between his injured arm and the wall. Milena's cloak had been tossed aside and lay in a heap at the foot of his bed. To give the healers access to his injured arm and stomach, his blanket had been pulled up only to his waist. Other than the bandages around his arm and stomach, his torso was bare.

Lennie had seen many masculine chests during her years in the army, but she had to admit, the Raven's was exceptional. Whereas dragons had powerful wings attached to their strong backs, their forelegs didn't contribute anything to their flight. That meant the dragon shifters had to lift weights while in human form, so they would have the necessary strength to wield a sword. But the Raven . . . his arms became his wings, and years of flight had given him wide, powerful shoulders and muscular arms.

It was a phenomenon she'd seen before in Quentin, the eagle shifter. The dragons, of course, saw themselves as vastly superior to mere birds, but when it came to shoulders, she had to admit, the birds ruled the roost.

She pulled her gaze away from him so Father Bertram wouldn't catch her admiring the handsome scoundrel. It was terribly annoying the way her gaze was immediately drawn to him, but in her defense, the room was so plain, there was nothing else to look at. The whitewashed walls were empty except for a few wooden pegs to hold clothes. Beneath them, a small trunk was pushed against the wall. Between the two narrow cots sat a small table topped with a lone candlestick. And then there was the one stool she had sat on before.

"It may be a while before he wakes," Bertram murmured quietly as he motioned for her to take the stool.

She sat at the foot of the Raven's bed and gestured toward the other cot. "Please rest yourself, Father."

"I *am* tired." He hesitated, then took a seat on the other bed. With a sad expression, he smoothed a hand over the coarse blanket. "This is Zane's bed, the poor lad."

"You seem very close to the brothers."

"Aye. I've known them since they were babes." He glanced at Bran and smiled. "I even knew the first Father Bran. He was like a father to me."

"The first?"

Bertram yawned, his eyes watering. "Aye. That was many years ago. And a long story."

"I'm not going anywhere."

Bertram's mouth twitched. "Very well, then. Father Bran was the youngest son of the Duke of Southwood, who owns the land between Lourdon and the Eberoni border. Bran went into the priesthood and eventually became the head priest of Lourdon Cathedral and the palace, the position that Father Sebastian holds today. In fact, it was Father Bran who conducted the wedding of Ulfrid and Brigitta."

"I see." Lennie glanced at the Bran next to her. Still asleep. Still bare-chested. Still annoying, blast him.

"After the elder brother became duke, he had a son, whom he doted upon, and a daughter, whom he ignored. But she, Lady Beatrice, was quite fond of her Uncle Bran." Bertram smiled with a faraway look. "I was already living there in Father Bran's household. I was an Embraced orphan he was hiding from the authorities who wanted to do away with Embraced children. Father Bran taught me to read and write, and he taught Lady Beatrice, too. She grew into a lovely and intelligent young lady."

Bertram's smile faded. "But then came that fateful day when Lord Morris came to visit. He fell for Beatrice and asked to marry her. I suppose poor Beatrice was eager to leave her father's dreary home, so she agreed and married Lord Morris. She went with him to Ebton Palace, where he was King Frederic's chief counsel."

Lennie winced. "Morris was also one of the Circle of Five."

"Exactly." Bertram yawned. "When Beatrice learned what he was up to, she fled back to Father Bran in Lourdon. That is where she gave birth to Morris's son. She named him Bran after the uncle who meant so much to her."

Lennie glanced at the man on the cot. So he was actually the legitimate son of an Eberoni earl and grandson of a Tourinian duke. His future should have been one of ease and comfort, but instead he had been whipped and abused.

"Beatrice died a month later." Bertram sighed. "I believe from a broken heart. When Morris learned of her death, he was devastated. What small amount of sanity he had left, shattered. He became fanatical to the point that, soon after, he committed suicide for his ill-fated cause. But before that, he ordered me to take his son to his home in Eberon, the castle that his brother, Master Lorne, turned into the Monastery of Light."

Bertram's face crumpled. "If only I had disobeyed! I never should have taken a poor innocent child to that evil place."

Lennie's heart ached at the sight of this kindhearted monk suffering for what had been the crimes of other men. "I'm sure you didn't know how evil it would be."

He wiped a tear from his face. "At first it wasn't too bad. I stayed in the nursery and taught Bran and his younger brothers."

"How could Bran have younger brothers if his father was dead?" Lennie asked.

"Ah." Bertram sighed. "Morris had become obsessed with

the idea of having Embraced children. Before his death, he fathered Arlo with another woman. Then Morris's brother, Master Lorne, took up the perverse quest and fathered Zane with Arlo's mother."

"Then Bran and Zane are actually cousins?"

Bertram nodded. "Aye, though they have always considered themselves brothers since Arlo was a brother to them both."

Lennie tried to imagine how strange it must have been to grow up in a monastery that Bertram had called evil.

Bertram gazed sadly at Bran. "On the night of the Spring Embrace when Bran turned ten, Lorne had him whipped. The other orphans his age received fifteen lashings, but because Bran was Embraced, he was given thirty."

Lennie shuddered. It was amazing the young Bran had survived.

"Greer was an orphan there, too, the same age as Bran, and he was also given thirty. The floggings happened twice a year when the moons embraced." Bertram grimaced. "I believe that is what twisted Greer into the murderer he is today. Thank the Light, Bran managed to stay good."

Good? Lennie nearly scoffed but remained quiet. Kidnapping women was not her idea of good.

"I begged Master Lorne to whip me instead, for I was Embraced, too." Bertram's shoulders hunched over. "I was flogged, but even then, Lorne insisted on whipping Bran. I knew, in time, Bran's younger brothers would also be abused, so I planned to escape and take them with me." His breath caught, and more tears ran down his face. "My plan was discovered, and I was ejected from the monastery. Those poor boys were left there all alone."

She winced. Damn, but she was starting to feel a great deal of sympathy toward this priest. And Bran.

Bertram wiped away his tears. "It was all my fault. If I had gotten the boys away from there, Arlo would still be alive."

He sniffed and glanced at Bran. "And this poor boy wouldn't be torturing himself, taking the blame for Arlo's death."

"I am so sorry," she murmured.

Bertram drew in a deep shaky breath. "Now, perhaps, you will understand why I must be there to save Zane."

"We will rescue him, Father."

Bertram gave her a wobbly smile. "You are a good person, I can tell. Please don't let Sebastian's nosy questions upset you. It is my fault he is like that, I'm afraid."

"Why do you think that?"

"Because of the prediction I made earlier today." Bertram shrugged. "I can never remember afterward what I've said, but apparently, I warned Bran about a woman, and Sebastian suspects that woman is you."

Lennie sat back on the hard stool. "What was the gist of this warning?"

"Hmm." Bertram narrowed his eyes as he tried to recall. "Something about a woman not being who she claims to be."

Damn. She winced. That hit close to home.

"Oh, and there's more." Bertram motioned toward Bran. "She will bring the poor lad to despair, make him tear his hair and gnash his teeth."

Her mouth fell open. *I will not!* She cleared her throat. "That seems rather harsh. No doubt he would have a similar effect on her."

Bertram yawned again. "Perhaps so."

"You can barely stay awake, Father." She suspected the poor man was also emotionally drained. "There's no need to keep me company if you would prefer to go to your room to rest."

He shook his head. "This is a monastery. I cannot leave you alone here with a young man."

She scoffed. The young man in question was drugged and injured, entirely incapable of molesting her. Did they think she would molest him? She glanced at the Raven, her gaze once more falling on the black curls in the center of his wide muscular chest. *Dammit.* Villains were not supposed to be that gorgeous.

Taking a deep breath, she gestured toward Zane's bed. "Then lie down there. When Bran wakes, I'll let you know."

"Very well." Bertram collapsed onto the thin pillow, and within seconds, he was sound asleep.

Time dragged by, and the stool became more and more uncomfortable. Lennie propped her elbows on the foot of Bran's bed and leaned forward. When his leg moved underneath the blanket, she sat up with a jerk and glanced at his face. Still asleep.

Pendras? She tried calling her brother and then her father. No response from either of them.

Your Highness, Sergei butted in. *We have left Lourdon Palace. We will see you in an hour or so.*

All right, Lennie replied. She glanced down and found her hands fisted around Milena's cloak. Relaxing her grip, she wondered why such a simple conversation had irritated her so much. *It's not the conversation,* she thought with a sense of dread. It was the fact that she was being pushed into accepting either Sergei or Anton as her future husband.

Her thoughts went back to that fateful night when a group of Norveshki noblemen had cornered her in a dark hallway at Draven Castle. Marry a dragon, they had demanded, or they would never accept her as the next ruler.

A knock sounded on the door, interrupting her thoughts, and she pivoted on the stool as a young woman entered with a tray. It was the redhead who had claimed earlier that Lennie would eat the children.

"Oh." The redhead gaped at Lennie. "Where did you come from?"

"I am Captain Dravenko of the Norveshki army. And you are . . . ?"

"I'm Joanna." The lanky young woman lurched into the room, her gaze riveted on Bran's handsome face as she strode by him to place her tray on the table next to his bed. "I brought some porridge for Father Bran. I made it myself!"

"He's asleep."

"Well, he'll wake up soon and be hungry, won't he?" Joanna's gaze wandered to Bran's bare chest, and her thin shoulders drooped as she let out a dreamy sigh.

Lennie was suddenly tempted to pull the blanket up to his chin. "If you're done—"

"Why are you here?" Joanna shot an annoyed glance in Lennie's direction before resuming her wistful adoration of Bran's handsome face.

"I have business with him," Lennie ground out.

Joanna huffed. "So do I. Bran saved my life, so I am morally bound to him."

Lennie scoffed.

"It is true!" Joanna lifted her pointy chin. "A week ago, my brother tried to auction me off in the village green to pay off his gambling debts. Praise the Light that Bran and his brother happened to be riding through. Bran punched my brother in the face and put me on his horse. Then he and Zane brought me here, where I would be safe."

Lennie grew still, not sure what to think. On one hand, a case could be made that Bran had kidnapped another woman. Joanna's brother would certainly think so. But on the other hand, Joanna had been thrust into a desperate and dangerous situation, and Bran had not hesitated to save her. It was no wonder she was practically drooling on him.

But how dare this scoundrel play the hero! He had kidnapped Eviana and her mother against their will. Even so, Evie insisted he'd helped Quentin rescue her later. Dammit, if the man was going to be evil, he should at least have the decency to be consistent about it.

"When Father Bran wakes up, please tell him that it was

me, Joanna, who brought him the porridge," the young woman insisted as she strode toward the door.

"I will." When the door shut, Lennie glanced at the sleeping man. Good or bad? Hero or villain? The only thing she was certain of was that the man was terribly annoying. And confusing. And dreadfully handsome, blast him. Never before had a man so thoroughly intrigued her.

She wandered over to the bowl of porridge. Joanna had topped it with some raisins, laid out in the shape of a heart. Some monastery this was, when young women could chase after the priests. Lennie grabbed the spoon and stirred the raisins into the mix.

"It's for your own protection," she muttered to Bran. She glanced over at Father Bertram. He was still asleep.

Another knock on the door. Another young woman rushed inside, this one very pretty, with golden blond hair and a curvy figure. "Oh, hello." She barely glanced at Lennie before her gaze landed on the bare-chested Bran. "Oh, my."

Lennie sighed. She might get rich if she charged admission to see the man's chest. "And you are . . . ?"

"Justina. Oh goodness, I came just in time." She scurried to Bran's bedside and draped a thick woolen scarf over his neck and chest. "We mustn't let our dear Father Bran catch a cold."

"Winter is over."

"The nights can still be chilly." Justina adjusted the scarf, then gave it a proud pat. "I knitted it myself. It was the least I could do after Father Bran saved me."

"Ah. You, too?"

Justina nodded, then finally turned to talk to Lennie. "My daughter, also. After my husband died, his brother took over the estate and kicked me and little Amelia out. We were on the side of the road with nowhere to go, when Father Bran and his brother rode by. They put us on their horses and walked us here."

Even though Lennie wanted to stay annoyed, she couldn't help but empathize with these women. The world could be harsh to women. Her mother, Gwennore, had taken a strong stance in Norveshka to give women equal rights, and Lennie was determined to continue the work when she became queen. "I am glad you are safe now."

Justina smiled. "Thank you. I would stay to chat, but I must hurry back to the school. I'm the teacher there." She rushed out the door and closed it behind her.

Lennie let out a slow breath. At this rate, she was going to think the blasted Raven was a candidate for sainthood. "I don't know what to think of you," she muttered as she removed the knitted scarf and set it on the table next to the tray.

Before any more women could come in and ogle his chest, she leaned over to tug the blanket up to his neck. Damn, but he was handsome. Dark whiskers shaded his chin and sharp jawline. His mouth was wide and beautifully shaped. Had he really wanted to kiss her earlier?

What was she thinking? She turned away abruptly, and her long braid of hair slipped over her shoulder, the tip falling onto the blanket. When she attempted to straighten, she couldn't. Her hair had caught on something.

She glanced down and let out a small gasp. Her braid was grasped firmly in a strong fist. She yanked it free and gave Bran a wary look.

His eyes were open, and he was staring at her.

She opened her mouth to speak, but no words came out. The fluttering in her chest came back, and all she could think about was that his eyes were not as dark as she had originally thought. She'd figured they were as black as his evil soul. But they were actually a light brown, edged with green. And they were watching her, drinking her in as if he was dying of thirst.

"You're still with me," he said, his voice deep and soft. A corner of his mouth lifted, and the glint in his eyes made her suspect he was not thinking priestly thoughts.

The soft fluttering of butterflies in her chest shifted into the pounding of horses in full stampede, and she suddenly knew exactly what he was. Not a hero. Not a villain.

Dear goddesses, the man was trouble.

Chapter 7

The woman was a blessing, Bran thought, as he looked her over. Not only beautiful, but resourceful and kind. Here he was, down and injured, and not only had she managed to find him, but she was staying by his side to nurse him. The woman of his dreams was both human and angel. Kind and compassionate.

A sliver of uncertainty sifted through the drugged haze that still clouded his brain. How could the woman he'd seen five months ago be here now? Sadly, this had to be a dream.

"If only you could be real," he murmured. "You have haunted my dreams since the night I first saw you."

Her eyebrows lifted slightly. "We have not met before."

"We have." He smiled. This was an excellent dream. She was actually talking to him. "Or, I should say that I met you. You were asleep at the time. I was flying over the camp to make sure everyone was knocked out, and there you were. The most beautiful wom—"

"When was this?"

A small trigger of alarm reverberated in his fuzzy brain. There was something wrong with this dream. Her voice had suddenly grown harsh and her lovely green eyes sharp with suspicion. Where had the kindly angel gone?

He smiled again, willing her to come back. "I saw you five months ago, and ever since then, I have dreamed of you. And thought of you. You were a mystery I could never solve. Why was a beautiful elfin woman traveling with the Eberoni army?"

Her eyes narrowed. "Five months ago, Queen Luciana was taken from an Eberoni army encampment while we all slept, drugged by tainted wine. Are you admitting you were there?"

"Aye, I was." The drugged wine had been Arlo's idea, and a damned good one, Bran thought. A sharp jab of pain struck his chest, and he closed his eyes as another wave of grief rolled over him. *Holy Light, forgive me.* That was the night he'd lost Arlo. The night Greer had murdered him. *Forgive me, Arlo, for failing you.*

"Bastard," the woman hissed, and he opened his eyes to find her glaring at him.

She didn't seem at all dreamy right now. Or angelic. Either this was real, or his dream had become a nightmare. *You fool, ever since Arlo died, your reality is a nightmare.*

The woman's hands curled into fists. "Do you admit to taking part in Queen Luciana's kidnapping?"

His heart sank. He should have known this would happen. His sins had caught up with him, and now, the most beautiful woman in the world despised him. "It was my idea."

She gritted her teeth, her eyes flashing with anger. "Do you also admit to kidnapping Princess Eviana?"

"Aye."

"You—" She lifted a hand to point at him, then curled it into a fist as she strode toward the corner by the window. With a huff, she hit her fist on the wall.

The ache in his heart deepened. There was no reprieve from the crimes he'd committed, no escape from the stain upon his soul. It was only right that he should suffer, but it hurt even worse to see the woman of his dreams suffering because of him. But the worst torment of all was the realization that she would never care for him. There would be no kindness. No compassion. No love.

The hunger in his soul would never be quenched. The longing in his heart would wither away, leaving him a hollow shell kept alive only by regret.

The door opened and Father Sebastian strolled inside. "Bran, you're awake. Excellent." As he approached, his smile faded. "Why are you gnashing your teeth?"

"I'm not," Bran growled, then dragged his left hand through his hair.

"And you're tearing . . ." Sebastian glanced around and saw the woman in the corner, her hands still fisted and pressed against the wall. "Ah. So it has begun."

The woman took a deep breath and turned to face them. "I am prepared to work with him, even if he is the scoundrel who kidnapped my best friend, Princess Eviana, and her mother, Queen Luciana."

Father Sebastian winced. "I assure you, we feel great remorse for what happened in Eberon. Bran was caught in a desperate and cruel situation—"

"*That is no excuse!*" she shouted.

"What?" Father Bertram asked, causing Bran to stiffen with surprise. He hadn't known the priest was even in the room.

Bertram sat up, rubbing his eyes. "Is it time to go?"

What was the priest doing in Zane's bed? *Zane.* The fog in Bran's head quickly dispersed as if a strong wind whooshed right through his skull, leaving in its wake the vivid memory of what had happened earlier. "I have to save Zane!"

He struggled to a sitting position, ignoring the dull pain of his wounded stomach, head, and broken arm. Stars floated before his eyes, and he squeezed his lids shut, then reopened them, hoping for a better result. No such luck. "I'm leaving now. Get my hor—" *Crap!* Greer had stolen his horse.

"Do you plan on walking?" the woman asked in a wry tone.

He scowled at her.

Father Sebastian sidled over to Bertram and whispered, "Now you see what I mean? He's gnashing his teeth."

"I am not!" Bran growled. "I'm leaving now, even if I have to ride a damned donkey." He planted his feet on the floor and tossed his blanket aside. *Damn!* He snatched the blanket back. He'd forgotten he was naked.

He glanced at his dream girl, who now hated him. She'd turned her face away, although he suspected her pink cheeks meant she'd seen more than she wanted.

"Oh, dear." Bertram made the sign of the Light, and Bran snorted. A prayer to the sun god wasn't going to erase what had just happened.

"Bran." Father Sebastian gave him a stern look. "We all want to rescue Zane, but you need to face the facts right now. You can't fly. You can't wield a sword. I highly doubt you can sit a horse, even if you had one."

"You expect me to give up?" He curled his fist, gripping the blanket covering his lap. "I will not."

"You don't have to." Sebastian motioned to the woman. "Captain Dravenko has kindly arranged for us to have horses and a wagon, along with supplies and weapons. Bertram and I will be traveling with her, and we expect you to join us."

Bran glanced once again at the woman, who was staring at a wall, refusing to look at him. "She's a captain?"

She bowed her head. "Captain Dravenko of the Norveshki army."

Norveshki? Bran vaguely remembered hearing something like that before. "I thought you would be from Woodwyn."

She gave him a brief glance. "I am one-quarter elf. I grew up in Norveshka, where my parents live."

The land of the damned dragons. Bran narrowed his eyes.

"Why the bloody hell would a Norveshki help us save Zane?"

"Language," Bertram whispered to him.

She turned toward him. "I know you don't trust me. I certainly don't trust you. But we need to work together to rescue the three men who were captured. I will supply the horses and so forth, and you—"

"Are the horses here?" he interrupted. "If so, we need to stop jabbering and go."

Her green eyes flashed with annoyance. "If they were here, I would have already thrown you into a wagon and left."

He snorted. "Why would *you* be in such a hurry?"

A pained look crossed her face, but she quickly squelched it. "One of the captives is my brother."

Bran stiffened, wincing at the pull of stitches across his stomach. No wonder she seemed on edge. She had as much to lose as he did. He thought back, trying to remember what Quentin had said earlier about the captured men. One was Zane. Another was the Tourinian prince. "Who is your brother?"

"Pendras." She paused. "A dragon shifter."

Crap! His dream girl was a dragon's sister? Bran shook his head. "I want nothing to do with him. If you'll let me borrow a horse, I'll—"

"You won't last an hour on your own!" Sebastian exclaimed.

Bran glared back. "Have you forgotten it was a dragon who attacked me?"

"That wasn't Pendras." The woman came quickly to her brother's defense.

"So he was the one attacking Zane?" Bran scoffed. "Oh, that makes it all better now."

She gritted her teeth. "He thought he was tracking a criminal, but that is beside the point now. Our priority has to be rescuing our brothers. I have put together a team. Two of my soldiers are bringing the horses and supplies, and I expect them to arrive shortly."

"*Norveshki* soldiers?" Bran asked in a wry tone.

She gave him a wry look back. "Yes. And they happen to be dragon shifters."

"No." Bran shook his head. "I don't want to be anywhere near them. One of them could be the dragon who attacked me!"

"They're not," the woman muttered. "Also on our team, we have Terrance, an excellent archer, and Princess Roslyn."

"Hell, no," Bran growled. "That's the daft woman who attacked me!"

"Get over it!" the woman yelled, then winced and looked away.

Bran ground his teeth as he glowered at her. Did she think he was whining for no good reason? "If I hadn't been attacked by that damned dragon and pesky princess, I could have flown straight to my brother, and he would not be in the danger he is now."

She looked at him askance. "You would have defeated three villains on your own with no weapon?"

He hissed in a breath. She had a point, but he'd never admit it.

Bertram cleared his throat. "Now, now, I'm sure if we put our minds to it, we can all get along."

Sebastian's mouth twitched. "Perhaps I should add that Lady Milena is coming with us."

"What?" Bran briefly forgot that he was pissed at the beautiful but annoying captain from Dragon Land. His brother was already in danger. He couldn't allow the same fate to befall his sister. "No. She should stay here, where it's safe."

"You know her?" the annoying captain asked, her green eyes round with curiosity.

Crap. Now he was close to blowing his sister's cover. Bran motioned to Sebastian. "He called her a lady. I just assumed she was not trained for a rescue mission."

From the way the annoying captain narrowed her eyes, he suspected she wasn't buying his explanation. To change the subject, he quickly added, "You have convinced me. I will join your team."

Caught by surprise, she reacted with a sudden grin, and for a few seconds, he thought his heart was going to burst. All the beauty in the world had been captured and put on glorious display with that one heavenly smile.

"Thank you." She took a deep breath. "I have no doubt you are as eager to save your brother as I am mine. As long as we focus on the goal we have in common, I am sure we will succeed."

How could he have ever been annoyed with her? She was strong and decisive. Intelligent and well spoken. Beautiful and . . . Dammit, he needed to stop this madness. How could he fall for a woman who despised him?

"We will leave as soon as my men arrive with the horses," she continued. "I know you are injured, so I will do my best to make the journey as comfortable as possible for you."

He stiffened. Was her opinion of him so low that she intended to treat him like a baby? "I am not a weakling. I know how to handle pain."

Her eyes glinted with some strong emotion, he wasn't sure what. "You have already suffered more pain than anyone should. I . . . I am sorry you are now dealing with more." She turned abruptly and hurried out the door as if the room had suddenly caught fire.

Had she just apologized for the attack on him? And how would she know anything about the pain he'd suffered?

"Excellent!" Father Sebastian clapped his hands together. "We should pack a few clothes, some food and water, and then we'll be ready to go." He strode toward the pegs on the wall and selected a black robe. "First, we need to get Bran dressed."

He shook his head. "I can't wear a robe with my arm in this sling."

"You have to wear something." Sebastian's mouth twitched. "Unless you're planning on shocking more young ladies?"

"Holy Light forbid," Bertram muttered.

Bran glowered at the priests. "I can wear breeches. Boots. A cloak. Oh, my boots." He winced. He'd taken them off in Lourdon and given them to his brother. They were probably still in a horse's saddlebags somewhere.

Sebastian found a pair of sandals on the floor. "You can wear these instead."

Bran tossed his blanket aside, trying not to remember the last time he'd done that, then slowly rose to his feet. *Damn.* The stars were back, and his whole body ached. How many branches had he collided with while plummeting to the ground? "I need to piss."

"No problem." Bertram dragged out the chamber pot from beneath Zane's bed, then went over to help Sebastian rummage through the small trunk of clothes.

Bran took a step and the stars whooshed around his head. *Dammit.* Sebastian was right. He'd probably fall off a horse. Hell, he wasn't sure he could even get onto a horse. And the ride would be agony.

He frowned at his tightly bandaged right arm. It would be weeks before he could fly. And for now, he would have to use his left hand for everything. Even to take a piss. He glanced at the two priests, who were cleverly keeping their backs to him so they wouldn't have to witness his less than stellar, left-handed aim at the chamber pot.

"I'm so glad you're joining us, Bran," Bertram said as he shook out a pair of black breeches. "I was afraid you'd refuse."

Sebastian waited till Bran was finished, then handed him a pair of white linen smallclothes. "What convinced you to come with us?"

The image of the captain's beautiful face flitted through his mind, but Bran ignored it as he eased back onto the bed. "I was trying to protect Milena." Damn, but it was hard to get his feet through the right holes. "And since you two foolishly decided to go, I need to be there to protect you as well."

"Ah." Sebastian nodded as Bran stood and awkwardly dragged the underpants past his hips. "You're watching out for us."

"Exactly." He fumbled with the button at his waist, trying to do it with one hand. The button popped from his grip, and the smallclothes fell to his knees. "Dammit." He winced with pain as he reached for them.

"Allow me." Bertram quickly jerked the underpants up and buttoned them. "I think *we'll* be watching out for *you*, dear boy. Now let us get these breeches on you."

With a frustrated sigh, Bran allowed the two priests to dress him as if he were a small child. "I hate being so damned helpless. Especially when Zane needs me."

"He needs all of us." Sebastian fastened the sandals on Bran's feet. "You're not in this alone, you know. You have me, your sister, and Bertram."

Without warning, tears came to Bran's eyes, and he quickly blinked them away. *Dammit.* Ever since Arlo's death, he'd had this problem, and he hated how weak it made him feel. He'd endured floggings without shedding a tear, so why did he have such lousy control now?

"I should eat before we go." He needed to be strong. Zane needed him.

Bertram tutted as he eyed the bowl of porridge on the small table. "This is cold. I'll bring you some hot food." He grabbed the tray and rushed out the door.

Sebastian folded his arms over his chest and eyed Bran. "So, what do you think?"

"Of what?" Bran sat on his bed and loosened some of the linen strips that anchored his arm to his chest. His forearm was tightly splinted and would remain so, but he wanted to be able to move his shoulder. "The rescue plan?"

"The woman in charge, Captain Dravenko."

Bran snorted. "Who chose her? And why?"

"A Norveshki general made the decision. Apparently, she has the gift of being able to communicate telepathically with the dragons. That, and the fact that her brother was captured, are the reasons she was put in charge. Once her brother regains consciousness, he should be able to contact her and let us know where they are."

A surge of hope filled Bran's heart. Even though he had hated the thought of his dream woman being related to dragons, he found himself quite willing to set aside that prejudice if it made it easier and faster to rescue Zane. Besides, it wasn't as if she could choose the family into which she'd been born.

He understood that all too well. His father, Lord Morris, had been a murderous traitor, and his uncle, Master Lorne, had taken the family's maniacal quest for world domination to even greater heights. Bran was simply not in any position to judge, and, to be honest, now that he'd recovered from his initial shock over the captain's dragon connection, he found himself reluctant to persist with any ill thoughts toward her. He much preferred to perpetuate his five-month-long belief that she was the perfect dream girl, now made even more perfectly glorious by her ability to help him locate Zane. "But she hasn't heard from her brother yet? Shouldn't he be conscious by now?"

Sebastian winced. "You would think so."

Were the captives already dead? Bran shoved that thought away. No. If Greer had wanted them dead, he would have killed them right away. He wouldn't have bothered to take them with him.

Sebastian took a seat on Zane's bed. "Are you going to be all right traveling with the captain?"

Bran shrugged his left shoulder. "Why wouldn't I be?"

"You seem to have some past history with her." Sebastian gave him a pointed look. "I heard the way you talked to her when you were drugged."

Bran winced. "What did I— Never mind, I don't want to know."

"Have you actually been dreaming about her?"

"Don't want to talk about it." Bran glanced at the knitted scarf on his table. Where the hell had that come from?

"I believe she is the woman Bertram referred to in his prediction. That means she may not be who she claims to be."

Bran tensed. He wouldn't believe it. His dream woman was not a liar. "Why would she lie about being a captain? Or a Norveshki?"

"It's what she doesn't tell us that has me concerned."

Bran shook his head. "She knows how I feel about dragons, yet she still admitted her brother is one."

"How did she get here?"

Bran gave the priest a wry look. "No doubt she was born like everyone else. Unless the dragon families hatch their young from eggs."

Sebastian rolled his eyes. "I meant how did she arrive here at the monastery? While you were asleep, I snooped around and asked if anyone had seen her arrival. Not a single person had."

That was odd, Bran had to admit. The women who lived nearby tended to be very nosy. "Was there a new horse in the barn?"

"No. It's as if she dropped out of the sky."

One of those damned dragons must have dropped her off, Bran thought, clenching his jaw. "So you think she can't be trusted?"

"You're doing it again. She's causing you to gnash your—"

"It's *you* doing that," Bran growled. "She's willing to help us rescue Zane, so I don't give a damn if she's keeping a few secrets. We all have secrets."

Sebastian arched a brow. "You seem intent on defending her. You *have* been dreaming about her, haven't—"

"There is nothing between us." Bran looked away to hide the pain of knowing she despised him. "She is willing to work with me in order to save her brother, but she will always see me as a criminal."

Sebastian sighed. "I know your life has been difficult up to this point, but there is no reason why you cannot live a full life, a happy life—"

"I lost Arlo. How can I live at all if I lose Zane?"

Sebastian winced. "You won't lose him. And Bertram and I refuse to lose you."

The unwanted tears threatened to come back. Even when they found Zane, he feared he would never stop feeling like a failure. He'd failed his best friend, Father Saul, and his brother, Arlo. As for the woman of his dreams . . . although he didn't actually know her, he'd loved taking refuge in his dreams of her. He'd loved the hope that had come from dreaming of her. But now, the sad truth was bearing down hard on his heart. Because of his crimes, he'd failed her before she'd even had a chance to meet him.

Sebastian leaned toward him. "There is always hope, Bran. As long as the sun rises every day, there is hope."

He blinked back his tears. Deep inside, he knew Sebastian was right. He could choose between despair and hope. The words of the young woman he'd kidnapped came back to him. Princess Eviana had told him there was always a choice. He'd made the right choice then. He needed to do it again.

Taking a deep breath, he realized he'd already made the choice. The second he'd agreed to go with Captain Dravenko, the die had been cast. In that moment, without realizing it, he'd committed himself to following her. To trusting her.

How could he do otherwise? He had dreamed of her for too long. Her mere presence in the world had given him comfort. And now, he had a chance to actually get to know her. Even though his soul was tainted, even though she despised him, he could not give up this chance. May the Light forgive him for having the sheer audacity to desire more than he deserved, but his decision was made.

He was going to pursue her.

Pendras slowly opened his eyes to darkness. And a headache. Where was he? What time was it? As more and more questions crowded into his throbbing head, he realized with a small sense of alarm that he was blindfolded, gagged painfully, and tied up. It would be damned difficult for him to answer any of his own questions.

Still, he had to try. Steeling his nerves, he addressed the first one.

And failed. He had no idea where he was.

Next question. What time was it? There was a sliver of light along the edges of his blindfold, so it was still day. The sun was warm on his back, so it was probably afternoon.

Could he escape? He tried to move his arms and legs. Damn, whoever had tied him up had trussed him like a goose. *To keep you from shifting.* The gag in his mouth tasted of olive oil. His captors must have doused the linen with oil. *To keep you from breathing fire.* If he tried to burn the gag away, he'd end up setting his own face on fire.

He closed his eyes and focused on what he could feel and hear. The steady clop of horse hooves, the slight bounce of movement, the heat of a horse beneath his belly, the ache of too much blood in his head. Clearly, he'd been slung over a horse and tied in place.

Something hard was pressed against his left side. A saddle? It creaked as someone shifted their weight. He listened closely and detected the sound of a person breathing. One of the captors must be sitting in the saddle, and he had been tied down behind him like a pair of saddlebags.

Was Reynfrid nearby, also tied up? Pendras considered moaning to see if Reynfrid would answer but decided it would be best for now to let his captors think he was still unconscious.

Father? Mother? No answer. *Lennie?*

Dammit! His nerves tensed. How could this be? He'd been able to communicate telepathically with his sister and other dragons since he was a babe. He'd never been cut off like this before.

Calm yourself. There has to be a reason. He thought back to what had happened. He had been advancing on the three priests, when the air in front of him had shimmered strangely, light dappling as if it were glistening off a still lake. Then wham! He'd struck what had felt like a stone wall. No wonder his head and neck still hurt.

The hit had rendered him unconscious. He must have fallen to the ground and shifted. And they'd tied him up. Had the slam to his skull caused his inability to communicate? Or was the invisible wall still surrounding them and blocking his messages?

Lennie, do you hear me? He tried once again. No answer.

He closed his eyes to concentrate better on listening. The clop of horse hooves, the creak of saddles, the sound of men and horses breathing. But where was the sound of birds? Or the wind rustling the trees? If the invisible wall was around them, it might be blocking any sounds from coming in. And that meant Lennie could have been calling him and he'd failed to hear her.

He stifled a groan of frustration. No communication with the dragons, or with his fellow captives, assuming they were here. He couldn't shift. He couldn't move. He couldn't even see their location. All he could do was listen.

A moan sounded nearby. So he wasn't the only captive,

Pendras thought. He didn't recognize the voice, but then, a moan wasn't much to go on.

"I think they're waking up," a man's voice grumbled. He was located to the right of the horse Pendras was tied to.

"It's not a problem," a voice answered sharply.

The second speaker was farther ahead, leading the group, Pendras thought. Probably the man in charge. Most likely the priest called Greer.

"They can't move," the leader continued. "And even if they could, they can't escape, not with the shield in place. It's still intact, isn't it, Kasper?"

"Yes, Master." The younger-sounding voice came from the saddle next to Pendras.

"The boy can't keep the wall up for—"

"Hush, Roland," Greer snapped. "If they're awake, then they can hear."

"Why are we even keeping them?" Roland whispered, and Pendras strained to hear. "They're slowing us down."

"Once we kill them, we can no longer use them," Greer replied. "I want to keep all my options open."

They stopped talking, but Pendras stayed on alert for any sound that would give him additional information. There was clearly more than one captive, so he had to assume Reynfrid was nearby. Apparently, the young man in front of him was Kasper, who possessed the unusual Embraced gift of putting an invisible shield around them. But, according to the priest called Roland, this Kasper fellow would not be able to keep up the wall indefinitely. Most probably, it would disappear when the young man fell asleep for the night.

Then, Pendras would be able to tell his family everything he'd learned. And then, the Light willing, they would be able to find him and Reynfrid.

Chapter 8

Lennie waved when she finally spotted them on the horizon: one man on horseback leading two more horses, plus a wagon drawn by two others. They were advancing at a steady pace, not too fast to keep from tiring the animals. One of the men, the one driving the wagon, waved back with great enthusiasm. That was probably Anton. The other one, Sergei, was too busy looking manly atop his noble steed. He acknowledged her wave with a slight lift of his chin.

Good goddesses, it would be torture having to travel with these two men. At least she would not be alone with them. Yet another good reason, she thought, for allowing so many people to come on this journey. With the recent addition of the two priests, her team had grown to a total of nine members. *I should have asked for more horses.*

"Who are those men?" a woman behind her demanded.

Lennie glanced back. It was Joanna. The young redhead was lurking close to the monastery gate with a group of nosy women.

After Sergei and Anton had sent Lennie a mental message that they would be arriving soon, she had passed through the gate and walked down the road a short way so she could meet them. It hadn't taken long for the group of women to approach her. After introducing themselves, they had proceeded to hound her with questions. How was Father Bran doing? Who was she? Why was a newcomer like her allowed to watch over Father Bran, while they were not?

Lennie had refrained from mentioning just how much her watchful eyes had seen. And goddesses help her, there was no way she could unsee it. Even now, the memory made her cheeks flush with heat. One thing was certain from the small glimpse (or rather large glimpse) she'd gotten: these women had definitely selected a candidate who was worthy of their devotion.

"Who are they?" Joanna repeated, causing Lennie to wince with embarrassment at the realization her thoughts had once again wandered to a certain man's anatomy. Joanna lifted her chin defiantly. "We don't like strange men coming here."

The other women murmured in agreement.

Lennie could understand their unease; after all, most of them had been abused in some manner by men. "They are soldiers under my command, so there is no reason to be concerned. We will be leaving shortly."

"To rescue Zane?" another woman asked. Dorothy, if Lennie remembered correctly.

"Yes." She nodded. "My brother, also, and Reynfrid, the prince of Tourin."

"The prince?" A young woman named Stella clasped her hands together and sighed. "He must be wonderfully handsome."

Joanna huffed. "No one can be as handsome as Father Bran!"

All the women rushed to agree, leaving poor Stella to hang her head in shame for committing what was obviously an act of sacrilege.

With a sigh, Lennie turned back to face the incoming soldiers. Anton and Sergei were close enough now that she could see they were dressed as lieutenants of the Tourinian army.

After landing and shifting at Lourdon Palace, they must have been given these uniforms, matching their rank in the Norveshki army.

"They're not nearly as handsome as Father Bran," Stella announced, and the other women agreed.

Lennie hid a smile at Stella's attempt to regain favor with the group of Raven worshippers. The young woman was right, though. The courtiers at Draven Castle considered Anton and Sergei quite handsome, and the men knew it, Lennie thought wryly. But even so, they could not compare to that blasted Bran.

One of the monks working in the fields rang the bell to alert the others to the incoming visitors. Two other monks, who had been tending livestock in the barn, hurried out to watch the arrival.

"At last!" Terrance called out as he strode toward Lennie. Milena and Roslyn were not far behind. "Now, we can leave soon."

"Yes," Lennie agreed, relieved to see the two ladies awake and ready to go. She'd checked on them earlier and they'd both been sound asleep.

Roslyn held up a hand to shield her eyes from the sun as she studied the approaching men. "I don't remember them well from the academy. Which one is which?"

"Anton is driving the wagon, and Sergei is riding," Lennie explained.

"They definitely look like dragon shifters." Roslyn slanted a teasing smile at her. "So which one of your handsome suitors has taken the lead?"

Lennie shrugged. "Does it matter?"

Roslyn exchanged a worried glance with Milena. "I have to say, Lennie, you don't sound very thrilled . . ."

She wasn't. The irony of the situation didn't escape

Lennie. This morning she had questioned Roslyn's method of choosing a husband, when, honestly, her situation was just as bad. Even worse, perhaps, since she wasn't being given much of a choice at all. Either Sergei or Anton.

The walls closed in tighter, along with the now familiar gnawing in her gut, but she shoved it all aside. "The rescue of the three captives is our top priority and the sole purpose of this mission," she announced. "There will be no time for courtship."

"Oh." Roslyn's gaze slipped over to Terrance; then she turned away, her shoulders slumping. But Lennie spotted a glint of determination in Terrance's eyes. Milena must have seen it, too, for she covered her mouth to hide a smile.

Dust clouded the air as the wagon and horses pulled to a stop. Anton jumped down from the driver's bench just as Sergei dismounted. They both rushed forward to greet Lennie.

Anton leaped in front, then bowed. "Your High—"

"She's a captain, you idiot." Sergei pushed Anton aside before giving Lennie a salute. "Lieutenant Sergei Tolenko reporting for duty."

Lennie returned the salute. Thank the goddesses the two men had been speaking in Norveshki. Roslyn, as a well-educated princess, knew all four Aerthlan languages, but fortunately, the others in the vicinity would not have caught Anton's mistake.

Switching to the Tourinian language, which was closely related to Eberoni, Lennie told the soldiers, "We'll be leaving soon. Which one of you has the travel badge?"

"I do." A slight look of annoyance passed over Sergei's face before he squelched it. He reached into an inner jacket pocket and retrieved a round wooden disk wound with an attached red ribbon. "Here you go, Captain." With a charming smile that didn't reach his eyes, he handed it to her.

"Thank you." As Lennie unwound the ribbon, she suspected Sergei had hoped to keep the badge, himself, which would have effectively put him in charge of the mission.

Anton stepped closer and lowered his voice to a conspiratorial whisper. "Queen Brigitta left a stash of coins for you in the wagon, hidden in the base of a lantern."

"Thank you." Right on cue, Anton was pretending to be her new best friend. Lennie noted the wooden disk was carved with the Tourinian royal coat of arms. She slipped the ribbon over her head like a necklace, then tucked the badge beneath her jacket. "Terrance, would you take my men to the dining hall so they can eat before we go?"

"Of course." Terrance motioned for them to follow him. "This way."

"I'll go, too," Roslyn offered. "I could pack some food for the journey." She rushed off to join Terrance, while Milena remained close by.

As Sergei strolled past Lennie, he flipped his long black hair over a shoulder, then gave her a rakish grin and a wink. He strode past the gate, his self-assured swagger making it clear he thought he'd left her melting into a pool of desire.

Goddesses help me. She might have announced there would be no place for courtship on this mission, but, clearly, the dragons saw this as the perfect opportunity to make their move.

Anton lurched toward her, grabbing her hand in both of his. "My poor dear, having both your father and brother captured on the same day! This must be terribly stressful for you."

She withdrew her hand. "I will manage."

"So brave in the face of despair!" Anton gazed at her with tremulous adoration. "Still, it grieves me to see you suffer so."

Goddesses, no. Was he trying to squeeze out a tear?

He pressed a hand to his heart. "Please rest assured, my dear, that I will do everything in my power to assist you."

"Thank you, Lieutenant." Lennie motioned for him to follow the others, and he bowed, then ran after them.

She took a deep breath, then turned toward the supply wagon. Thankfully, the two monks had already unhitched the horses and were leading them to the barn, where they could be fed and watered along with the other new horses.

"Those are your suitors?" Milena asked quietly.

"Aye." Lennie noted the faint look of disapproval on the lady's face. "They're considered quite the catch in Norveshka. You don't agree?"

Milena paused, then murmured, "Physically, they seem quite fit."

"What do you really think?"

Milena winced. "I saw a scoundrel and a sycophant."

Lennie sucked in a breath. "Is it that obvious?"

"Perhaps not to everyone." Milena gave her a small smile. "It is part of my job to be more observant than most."

Did she mean as a lady-in-waiting? Lennie wondered. It would come in handy for a queen to have someone this observant by her side. "I can see why Brigitta values your company."

Milena's smile widened. "Her Majesty has been very kind to me."

There was something familiar about her smile, Lennie thought. And her brown eyes. "Well, shall we see what kind of supplies Brigitta packed for us?"

They clambered into the wagon bed and discovered four crates. One long box contained bows and arrows; its twin, swords and daggers. A square box was filled with three lanterns and a flask of oil to refill them. *Excellent*, Lennie thought as she located two poles to hang the lanterns. The lanterns would allow them to travel once the sun went down.

It was easy to tell which lantern held the hidden coins, because it weighed more than the others. Lennie slid the bottom open an inch, spotted the velvet pouch, then closed it again. She peeked underneath an oilcloth and found a stack of blankets and three bedrolls.

Meanwhile, Milena had opened the last crate. Two jugs of water, a jug of cider, dried beef, and crackers. Army rations. She sighed. "Thank the Light the monastery can give us some fresh food."

"Aye." Lennie examined the wagon bed. Somehow, she needed to make a comfortable place for Bran. "I saw only three bedrolls. Were there more packed on the horses?"

"I'll go look." Milena climbed onto the driver's bench, then jumped to the ground.

"If you find any, bring them here." Lennie went to work, shoving the crates against the backboard until she'd cleared a narrow space behind the driver's bench. She could stick the Raven there, and then, while she drove the wagon, he could give her directions.

"I found three," Milena announced as she exited the barn with her arms full. "Each horse had one attached to the back of the saddle."

"Wonderful." Lennie unrolled the three bedrolls already in the wagon, then spread them out in the spot she had made.

"There were saddlebags, too," Milena reported. "Filled with things like smallclothes, socks, and toothbrushes."

"Excellent." Lennie kneeled down to test the thickness of the pallet she'd made. It would do.

"What are you doing?" Milena asked as she set her three bedrolls on the driver's bench.

Lennie took two more and set them, still rolled, along one side of the wagon. They would cushion Bran's back so he could sit up a bit. "I'm trying to make a comfortable place for Bran."

"Oh." Milena hefted herself up onto the driver's bench for a better view. "That's very thoughtful of you. I'm sure he'll appreciate it."

"It's partly for convenience," Lennie admitted as she retrieved a few blankets. "I intend to drive, and I'll need him close by to give me directions."

"I see." Milena spread out the last bedroll and folded it lengthwise to make a cushion for the driver's bench. "This should make it more comfortable for you, too."

"Thank you." Lennie folded up one of the blankets and placed it on top of the bedrolls to make a pillow for Bran's injured head.

"Feeling guilty?" Milena asked softly.

At first, Lennie felt annoyed by the question, but then she realized her irritation was only because it was true. "I really didn't mean for him to crash."

Milena nodded with a small smile. "That's what I thought."

Lennie gave her a curious look. "You seem quite interested in him."

Milena's eyes widened. "Well, I . . ." She scoffed. "I certainly have no romantic interest in him!"

"So you're interested in someone else?" Lennie asked, recalling how Roslyn had teased her about Prince Reynfrid. And, she realized, the crafty lady-in-waiting had expertly dodged the original question. Before she could inquire further, the two monks strolled through the gate, calling out their greetings.

She noticed the baskets they were carrying, but wondered why Bran wasn't with them.

"Father Bertram." Joanna stopped the priests and motioned over her shoulder to Lennie and Milena. "Why are those two women allowed to travel with Father Bran? You should be taking me, instead!"

"Me, too!" Dorothy and the others joined in.

Father Sebastian gave them a disapproving frown, but Father Bertram merely smiled.

"Now, now, dear ladies," the elderly priest replied in a soothing tone. "No one knows better than you how to keep the monastery going in my absence. Brother Jerome will be in charge, but the poor man is over his head. I'm counting on you all to give him the utmost support."

"We will, Father," they quickly vowed.

"Please take good care of Father Bran," Justina pleaded.

"We will. May the Light be with you all." Still smiling, Father Bertram proceeded toward the wagon.

Frowning, Sebastian followed him. When they reached the wagon, Lennie helped them stow the baskets. One was filled with food, the other with male clothing and extra bandages and medications for Bran.

"I have to say, Bertram," Sebastian whispered, glancing back at the group of women who were still lingering at the gate in hopes of seeing Bran, "having so many single women living on the monastery grounds does not make for an ideal situation."

"I understand your concern," Bertram replied, "but Ulfrid and Brigitta gave me this land and financed the buildings with a royal charter that does not allow me to turn away any person in need."

Sebastian sighed. "I suppose it is a sad sign of our times that it is the women and children who are most in need."

Bertram nodded. "The queen does her best to find good employment and lodging for the young women, but some of them prefer to stay here and help in the kitchen or garden."

"Are there never any men?" Lennie asked.

"Yes, indeed, there are, but they rarely stay for very long," Bertram admitted. "They're expected to live as monks inside the walls, and some find our rules too confining. Others, like Brother Timothy, decide to join us." The priest smiled. "A few have fallen in love with women here, and it has been my pleasure to officiate at their weddings. For example, Brother Allen and his wife now own the nearby dairy farm and supply us with butter and cheese."

Lennie lowered her voice. "There was no problem with the priests breaking their vows?"

"No." Bertram smiled at her. "You see, my dear, very few priests are like myself and Sebastian, who take our vows for life. Most of the priests here, and especially the young ones, pledge themselves for only five years. That gives them time to mature in a stable, nurturing environment, where they can learn a skill or trade while they do good works and grow spiritually. And then, when their time is up, they are better prepared for marriage and raising a family."

"I see." Lennie nodded, although she couldn't help but wonder if Father Bran was on the five-year plan.

"You're doing excellent work here, Bertram; I have no doubt of that." Sebastian glanced back at the group of women. "But I'm afraid you could have a problem when all the women start competing for the same man."

"Ah, yes." Bertram nodded. "Bran's arrival has caused quite a stir."

Sebastian lowered his voice. "You're aware of it, then?"

"How can I not be?" Bertram smiled. "Even Zane has noticed. But thankfully, the young man in question seems completely oblivious."

Lennie had serious doubts about that. How could any man not notice he had a gaggle of not-so-secret admirers? And where was he anyway? "He is coming, isn't he?"

"I'll see how he's doing." Sebastian hurried back through the gate.

"I've made a comfortable place for Bran." Lennie showed Father Bertram the padded spot in the wagon. "At least I hope it will be."

"How kind of you!" Bertram grinned at her. "I'm sure he'll greatly appreciate it."

"And we have three horses from Lourdon Palace," Lennie continued. "You may have your pick—"

"Oh, no!" Bertram shook his head with a horrified look. "I could never ride one of those huge monstrosities. Daffy is the only horse for me." He rushed toward the barn. "I'll get my sweet Daffy ready to go!"

Daffy must be the workhorse with the short, stubby legs, Lennie thought. Inside the barn, Bertram apparently told the two monks they were ready to go, for the men led out two horses and hitched them to the wagon.

Terrance and Roslyn arrived with another basket of food, along with their bows and quivers of arrows. After depositing everything in the back of the wagon, they went to the barn with Milena to collect their horses.

It was almost time to go, Lennie thought with a great sense of relief. *Hold on, Pendras!* He didn't answer, but she refused to let that cause her any distress. She would remain calm and in control. No matter what.

Her heart gave a quick lurch when she spotted Bran. Damn, so much for remaining calm. Willing her pulse to settle into a steady beat, she watched as he slowly crossed the green, headed for the gate. His face was pale, his jaw clenched, his eyes focused on the ground ahead of him. Clearly in pain but determined to walk the distance on his own. Father Sebastian stayed next to him, ready to grab him if he stumbled.

A collective sigh emerged from the group of women. Then whispers, slowly growing in volume till Lennie could hear them.

"He's in so much pain, the dear man!"

"But so brave and strong!"

"We should wallop whoever hurt him!" That declaration came from Joanna, and the others agreed.

Father Sebastian shook his head at them, frowning, and they lowered their voices once again.

Lennie spotted Sergei and Anton in the distance as they left the dining hall and strode across the green lawn. When they approached the gate, they found themselves behind Bran and Sebastian, whose slow progress was causing a bottleneck. The two dragon shifters shuffled from side to side, looking for enough space to pass by, clearly annoyed at being forced to wait.

"Oh, he's wearing the scarf I made him!" Justina cried as Bran plodded through the gate.

Lennie gritted her teeth. Indeed, he *was* wearing the scarf. He had on a pair of black breeches and leather sandals, but nothing on top but a black hooded cloak tied at his neck. The scarf had been looped around his neck in a vain attempt to cover his bare chest.

As another collective sigh came from the ladies, it became all too apparent that the scarf had not hidden enough. She glanced at Bran's face to see if he was, as Bertram had claimed, completely oblivious.

He was looking at her.

Her heart squeezed, and she immediately chastised herself for reacting. Was she no better than his gaggle of hero worshippers?

"So handsome!"

"Magnificent!"

"May the Light shine on you always!"

The women called out to him, but Bran didn't seem to notice. His gaze remained fixed on her as he slowly approached. And her heart continued to pound.

"Why, thank you, ladies." Sergei flipped his long black hair over his shoulder.

"You are too kind." Anton flashed them a brilliant smile.

Lennie groaned inwardly. Of all the dragons she knew, only two were vain and self-absorbed. The two courting her. "Lieutenants, ready your horses. We will leave shortly."

Anton answered with a formal salute, whereas Sergei simply nodded; then they both strode toward the barn.

Lennie greeted Father Sebastian as he approached. "We have a spare horse for you, if you prefer to ride."

"And one for me?" Bran asked.

Sebastian leaned close to him and muttered, "We've been over that. You can't manage it."

Bran let out a frustrated sigh, then nodded. "Very well. I'll drive the wagon, then."

"I was planning on doing that," Lennie said quietly as they stopped in front of her. "But I would be willing to take turns with you, if you're up to it."

Bran replied, "I am," at the same time Sebastian grumbled, "He isn't," then shot a peeved look at the older priest.

Lennie suspected they were about to launch into an argument when there really wasn't time for it, so she jumped in. "The journey could go on for days. Perhaps Bran will be able to drive tomorrow. Or the next day."

"I doubt it," Sebastian muttered.

Bran lifted his chin. "I will wait till tomorrow, then."

At least she'd delayed the argument by one day, Lennie thought. From the corner of her eye, she spotted Terrance, Roslyn, and Milena leading out their saddled horses. "Father Sebastian, if you could make ready—"

"Of course!" He darted toward the barn, leaving her alone with Bran.

She gave him a quick smile and motioned toward the padded cocoon she'd made for him. "I have endeavored to make the journey as comfortable as possible for you."

His dark brows lifted; then he sidled over to the wagon and peered inside. Instantly, his face darkened. "No. Hell, no."

She blinked. Hadn't Father Bertram and Milena both insisted he would appreciate it? "But it looks quite comfy."

"Then you enjoy it. I'll sit on the driver's bench."

She huffed. "There's nothing wrong with the pallet I made—"

"Pallets are for babies."

She gave him a pointed look to indicate he was behaving like one.

He clenched his jaw. "I will not be treated like a pathetic weakling."

Lennie planted her fists on her hips. "You were severely injured. A weaker man would lie in bed for a fortnight, making some poor nurse spoon-feed him gruel and wipe his chin. Only a strong man such as yourself would ignore the pain to undertake this mission. So stop complaining. Are you a raven or a grouse?"

His brown eyes had widened with shock at her tirade, but now, the corner of his mouth twitched, and he broke into a full smile that made her heart skip a beat.

Blast him. She should be able to stay annoyed with the dreadful man for longer than this.

His eyes twinkled. "At least you didn't call me a chicken."

A smile tugged at her lips. "That was next on the list."

"Ha!" He glanced once again at the pallet and winced. "I admit it does look comfortable, and I appreciate your efforts . . ."

"But . . . ?"

He sighed. "To be honest, I hate feeling useless."

She blinked. "Are you serious? You're the most useful person on the team." When he gave her a dubious look, she continued, "Allow me to be honest, too." Or as honest as she could afford to be. "I thought, by making you as comfortable as possible, it would serve to build a bond of trust between us."

He scoffed. "You'll never trust me. You consider me a criminal."

"I'm trying not to think about that."

"That's big of you."

She shot him an exasperated look. "We both want to save our brothers, so we should put the past behind us. I'll stop thinking of you as a kidnapper of defenseless women."

"I'll stop thinking of you as a dragon's bossy sister."

Bossy? Well, she was in charge, whether he liked it or not. "Instead of arguing, I suggest we get on with this mission."

"Agreed."

She stepped closer, lowering her voice. "The problem is, I have no idea where to go, other than north. I heard you know where Greer is headed."

"I heard you can communicate with the dragons telepathically, so your brother should be able to tell you where to go." Bran eyed her closely. "Have you not heard from him?"

"No." As tears threatened her eyes, she blinked and looked away. "I can only assume he is unconscious . . . or asleep . . ." She wouldn't say *dead*. She wouldn't believe it.

"They'll be all right," Bran whispered. "Our brothers will be fine."

She nodded, then gave him a quick smile. "Yes. So, you see, my only source of information at this time is you. That's why I consider you the most valuable member of the team. I need you."

Something fierce glinted in his eyes, and she swallowed hard.

"I will do everything in my power to help you." He extended his left hand toward her. "I give you my word. Together, we will find them. And rescue them."

His words hit her heart as true. She'd doubted his character before; she'd considered him a criminal, but she'd also seen firsthand how fiercely he had sought to protect his brother. The Raven was brave and loyal, a man who didn't hesitate to risk his life for those he cared about. And now he was extending that gift of loyalty to her.

Her heart filled with relief and gratitude, and she took his hand. "We'll do it. Together."

As his fingers curled around her palm in a light squeeze, she felt a tug in her heart. Dear goddesses, what was wrong with her? She glanced up to meet his intense brown-eyed gaze, and a peculiar, disorienting feeling swept over her, as if she were slipping . . . falling into the unknown.

An inner alarm caused her to flinch, and, stepping back, she withdrew her hand. How on Aerthlan would she be able to save anyone if she allowed herself to become completely lost?

Chapter 9

As much as Bran hated feeling useless, he hated being helpless even more. He'd had so much trouble hefting himself up onto the driver's seat that Terrance and Milena had rushed over. Terrance had climbed onto the driver's bench from the other side so he could grab onto Bran's left arm to haul him up, and Milena had stayed on the ground behind him to shove his arse.

Damn, this was embarrassing. Finally seated on the bench, he glanced over at his dream girl, who had thankfully missed his shameful performance. Her back was to him as she quietly gave orders in Norveshki to the two soldiers, and they, in turn, eyed her as if she was dragon bait and they each wanted a nibble.

With a groan, he swung his legs over the bench to face the back of the wagon. The bedroll on the bench twisted underneath him, turning sideways and making him look like an even clumsier oaf. Dammit, how could he court his dream girl when she barely tolerated him? He'd thought his heart would burst when he'd held her hand, but she'd flinched and moved away.

"Will you be all right?" Terrance asked, then noticed the Tourinian princess fetching her bow and quiver of arrows from the back of the wagon. As she strode toward her horse, Terrance jumped off the wagon and ran after her, forgetting all about Bran.

With a shake of his head, Bran watched. The vicious woman had wounded him for no good reason, and now, she was fluttering her eyelashes and gifting Terrance with a sweet, innocent smile. She even blushed as he assisted her onto her horse. "I should warn Terrance to stay away from her. At least half a mile. She has excellent aim."

Milena smiled as she adjusted the makeshift pillow on the humiliating pallet. "Leave them be."

Bran huffed. "Wasn't she supposed to get married tomorrow?"

"The wedding of the century was canceled. Thankfully."

"Right." Bran recalled the dead earl covered with ice particles. He smirked. "You could say the groom got cold feet."

Milena nodded with a wry look. "Greer made sure of that."

Terrance continued to fuss ridiculously over the princess, and Bran grimaced. He'd known the man a month now, and he'd never seemed the foolish romantic type before. But then, the princess was gazing at him with such adoring puppy eyes, how could the poor man resist? "She's lost no time targeting a new victim. Or groom, I should say."

"Don't be such a cynic, Bran," his sister muttered. "Roslyn has known Terrance for years from her time at Benwick Academy. As far as I can tell, this attraction between them is not new."

"Then why has nothing come of it?"

Milena sighed. "How could it? He's a poor orphan and she's a princess."

"Now *you* sound like the cynic."

A pained look crossed Milena's pretty face. "I just know reality when I see it."

Was she referring to herself? Bran wondered. He glanced over at his dream girl. At least she wasn't royalty. He might have a chance with her. He dropped down into the padded hole, then attempted to sit with his back against the stacked bedrolls on one side.

"Comfy?" his sister asked, but he ignored her. She looked far too amused by his floundering about with only one good arm.

"Dammit," he muttered when his cloak got pinned beneath his rump and his jerking movement to release it caused the stack of bedrolls to fall over.

Taking pity on him, she reached into the wagon to put things right. Soon he was leaning against the bedrolls, and she gave him a pat on the head. "You make a grumpy patient, Bran."

A grouse, he thought, remembering his dream girl's fussing. "I hate feeling useless and helpless." He glanced over at the captain, who was still talking to the two soldiers. They were young, strong, and standing much too close to her. "If those are the Norveshki dragons, why are they dressed as Tourinians?"

Milena had hefted herself up onto the driver's bench so she could adjust the bedroll cushion he'd messed up. "I assume they flew into Lourdon Palace, and after they shifted, they were given those uniforms to keep them from prancing about the countryside naked."

"Is one of them the dragon who made me crash?"

Milena's eyes widened, but she didn't answer. Instead, she scrambled down from the driver's bench.

He glanced over his shoulder at her. "Am I right, then? Which one of them attacked me?"

She chewed on her bottom lip, giving the three Norveshki a worried look.

"Tell me what you know, Milena."

She took a deep breath. "The men are called Sergei and Anton. Sergei is the one who's a bit taller."

"Was it him?"

Milena winced and lowered her voice to a whisper. "I don't like either of them. They . . ."

"What?" Bran tensed. "Have the bastards been rude to you?"

"They don't know I exist." She glanced back at them and muttered, "They're both courting her."

Bran stiffened. *Dammit.* He narrowed his eyes on the two bastards—healthy, handsome, and fit while he was sprawled here on a baby pallet like an oversized toddler.

Dragons. No doubt every young woman in Norveshka had been raised with the belief that a dragon was the ultimate catch. Who would want a scrawny black bird with a broken wing when a fire-breathing dragon was available? Not just one, dammit, but two of the flying snakes were homing in on his dream girl. "I don't like them, either," he growled.

"The captain deserves better."

Did she mean him? Bran turned his head toward Milena, but before he could ask, she strode toward her horse and mounted up. Fathers Sebastian and Bertram rode their horses out of the barn, and his dream girl climbed onto the driver's bench and took the reins.

The armed dragon shifters mounted as well and led the way down the short dirt road to the King's Way. The captain followed them, driving the wagon with a baby on board, Bran thought wryly. The two priests and Milena rode behind the wagon, while Terrance and Roslyn, both armed, made up the rear guard.

There were shouts from the monks and women, wishing them safe travels, and Bertram and Sebastian waved and called out blessings, but it was all noise to Bran when he realized his position was not only fairly comfortable but also afforded him a lovely view of the driver. She sat upright but managed to look more graceful than stiff. Her long, braided hair swayed gently against her back, the tip sometimes catching in the woolen fabric of her dark green uniform. The color was perfect for her, making the green of her eyes almost dazzling in their intensity.

She glanced back at him briefly. "Doing all right?"

"Yes. Enjoying the lovely view."

She glanced again, then did a double take when she realized his view was fixed on her. With a slight blush on her cheeks, she focused on the road in front of her. "I take it we should turn right onto the King's Way and head north?"

"Yes."

She glanced back again. "How far north?"

"As far as you can go. Earl Freydor's land."

Her eyes widened. "That could take several days."

"At least."

"And we would have to cross mountains."

"Aye."

She stiffened as she turned to face the road. "We'll have to move quickly so we can catch them before they reach the mountains."

Bran nodded. "That would be for the best."

"If I might ask, how do you know where Greer is headed?" She glanced back. "Not that I'm doubting you. I'm just curious."

"While I was in raven form, I listened in on Greer's conversation with Freydor at the inn. Freydor was boasting how he should be making the decisions since he was financing everything, and Greer mocked him, telling him he had taken over the earl's gold mine."

The captain looked back at him, her green eyes sharp as she considered the ramifications. "If that is true, then Greer has his own group of thugs working for him. And the pirates must be working for him, too."

"What pirates?"

"The ones who attacked my—the kings Silas and Ulfrid along the coast of Freydor's land."

Bran's mouth fell open. "The kings have been attacked?"

"You didn't know?" Her eyes narrowed. "But you were there when King Leo was discussing it."

"After I crashed?" Bran could only dimly recall the Eberoni king. "I remember being angry at a certain dragon, but everything else is a blur." And how did the captain know what had happened then?

With a wince, she faced the road once again. "Well, to be brief, King Ulfrid sailed up north to get rid of some pirates who were plaguing Earl Freydor's coast; then he disappeared. We know now, of course, that it was a trap set by Freydor and Greer. King Silas and Aleksi, both dragons, flew there this morning, and then they were all attacked by pirates." A pained look crossed her face. "I am unable to communicate now with Silas or Aleksi."

"Or your brother."

"Aye." Her hands gripped the reins so hard, her knuckles whitened.

He was tempted to offer her some kind words of reassurance, but he knew she'd see the gesture as pointless. With both the king and crown prince of Tourin now captured, the country was on the verge of collapse. And with King Silas also captured, Norveshka would be next. If Greer had taken over a gold mine, he could pay a large army of thugs to do his bidding. It looked like the bastard's dream of taking over the world might actually come to pass.

"King Leo is marching the Tourinian army north along the coast," she said softly. "And King Brodgar is taking the navy up the coast. They will rescue the kings."

"And we'll save the others," Bran said, and she nodded.

"Our team will be larger once we reach Dominic and his troop of soldiers." She pulled the wagon to a stop just as they reached the King's Way.

The two dragon shifters dismounted and ran toward the nearest grove of trees.

"What are they doing?" Bran asked.

"One will shift, while the other brings back his clothes," the captain explained. "A dragon escort will enable us to travel more quickly without fear of being set upon by brigands."

"Makes sense," Bran grumbled, not looking forward to seeing one of the damned dragons.

The captain shifted on the bench to give him an intense look. "My first thought was that I didn't want either of them to shift. I feared the sight of a dragon would incite Greer to violence against the captives. But we are hours behind them at this point, so I believe it is a safe decision for now."

"I think you're right." Bran's heart warmed that she would discuss her decisions with him. And when his agreement eased the tension in her face, his heart nearly melted.

A dragon took off from the nearby grove and shot up into the sky. Bran watched as it dipped back down, veering right to circle over them. *Show-off,* he thought with a snort. His raven could do that stunt upside down.

The shorter soldier ran back to the horses and stuffed the dragon's discarded clothes into his saddlebags. Then he tied the horse to his, mounted, and turned onto the King's Way.

With a cluck at the horses, the captain started the wagon, and the whole train settled into a brisk walking pace. The dragon flew overhead, guarding them from above. Bran winced as the wagon bounced over a rut and jostled him hard enough to tug at his stitches.

The pain from all his wounds was creeping back, but he would need to bear it. The alternative was another swig of Brother Jerome's special potion, and only the Light knew what ridiculous things he might say under the influence.

To make himself feel better, he settled back and let the miles go by while he watched his dream girl. She was alert, watching the road and the forest in case any highwaymen were lurking behind the trees. Not really necessary this close to the monastery. Terrance had been keeping the area safe. Once the word had spread about his Embraced gift, no brigand in his right mind would come within five miles of the monastery.

A loud squawk sounded overhead, and he glanced up to find the dragon glaring down at him. So, the flying snake had caught him admiring the captain. Too bad. With his left hand, he gave the dragon a sign to encourage him to get lost. With a huff of smoke, the dragon flew on ahead.

"Behave," Father Bertram admonished him softly.

His dream girl glanced back at him, and he gave her an innocent look.

"He's not the one," Bran announced.

"What do you mean?" she asked, her beautiful eyes wide.

"He's not the one who attacked me." Bran motioned toward the dragon. "His belly is more of a purplish green. He's bigger. Meaner looking. Ugly as a slug."

She frowned at him. "You think dragons are ugly?"

"When they're attacking me, yes. So I guess *he's* the one who did it." Bran pointed at the shorter soldier, who was riding in front. "Anton, right?"

With a wince, she faced the road.

"Tell me, does Anton have a pink belly? He's a little bit shorter, so I guess he makes a smaller dragon?"

"He's the same size as Sergei."

"Then where is the little one?"

"It's not that little," she grumbled.

Bran chuckled. "Compared to the behemoth above us, it was practically cute and cuddly. It must have been the runt of the litter."

"*Runt?*" She shot him an incredulous look.

He nodded. "Leave it to a runt to pick on a little bird. Probably made him feel big."

With a huff, she turned away.

She was beautiful when she was angry, Bran thought, although he felt guilty and stupid for letting his resentment get the better of him. Insulting dragons was clearly not the way to win her heart. Still, he was a bit surprised that she had taken it so personally. Did this mean she was already attached to one of those damned dragon suitors?

He watched to see if her gaze lifted often to the dragon overhead, but it didn't. Wasn't that a good sign? Was the pink tint of her cheeks due to anger or was she being exposed to too much sun?

It was late afternoon now, and the heat of the day was at its peak. The woolen scarf around his neck was becoming unbearable. He never would have worn the silly thing, but Sebastian had insisted he do something to cover up his naked chest. Apparently the wound on his stomach was too frightful for anyone to see. As he unwound the scarf, a jab of pain made him grit his teeth.

The captain muttered something about a *runt* under her breath.

So she was still peeved about his dragon comments, Bran thought with an inward groan. "I heard the two dragons are courting you," he grumbled.

"That's none of your business." She shot him an annoyed look, then her eyes widened with shock at the sight of his exposed chest.

"Sorry." He pulled the edge of his cloak over to cover up the wound. "I know these stitches are hideous to look at."

"It's not the—" She looked away. "I've seen wounds before."

She glanced at him again, keeping her gaze on his face. "Don't you like the scarf?"

"It's too hot." He tossed it aside and it landed in one of the food baskets.

"I told her it would be," the captain muttered.

"Who?"

"Justina."

He scoured his memory but couldn't recall which of the women went by that name.

The captain gave him a frustrated look. "She's the pretty blonde who knitted the scarf for you."

He frowned. "Why would she do that?"

"Because she and her daughter were ejected from their home, and you rescued them."

He shook his head. "I don't rescue anyone. Father Bertram does that." He glanced over at the priest and smiled. "He rescues people all the time. Including Zane and me."

The captain narrowed her eyes. "Did you eat the porridge?"

"What porridge?"

"The porridge Joanna made for you."

"Who?"

"Joanna!" The captain huffed. "Are you seriously that blind?"

"My eyesight is better than normal. I'm a raven, you know."

She scoffed. "And you're supposed to be a spy?"

"I'm an excellent spy." He gave her a wry look. "What is your job in the military? Interrogation?"

She shook her head. "Oblivious. I can't believe it."

"Oblivious to what? I assure you, I am exceedingly aware of anything and anyone I deem important." He focused on her intently. "I am painfully aware of my faults, my feelings, and my most urgent desires."

Her cheeks turned pink. "And the feelings of others?"

"I am aware of those, too. I know you can barely tolerate me, but I hope that will change—"

"Not me! I'm talking about the herd of women drooling over you as if you were some sort of demigod."

He snorted, then rested a hand against his stitches. "Ow. Don't make me laugh."

"You think I'm jesting? There are ten of them. Joanna,

Justina, Dorothy, Stella, Winifred, Karena, Amanda . . ." She paused, wincing as she struggled to remember. "Daphne?"

His mouth twitched. "Daphne is Bertram's horse. But Daffy is rather fond of me. Anyway, that's only eight."

She glowered at him, then lifted her chin to announce, "Lulabelle and Constanza."

"I don't recall anyone with those names."

She shrugged. "I made them up. But there really are ten!"

He laughed, pressing his hand against his wound. "Ow! You're doing this on purpose, aren't you? To cause me pain?"

"No!"

He realized, by the hurt look on her face, that she meant it. "Then why are you telling me such a silly story?"

"It's not silly. You really do have a group of admirers who are completely devoted to you."

He blinked. "Why would that be?"

"Well . . ." Her gaze dropped to his chest, then back to his face, before moving away. "I suppose they figure you are not bad to look at."

He frowned. "Surely they realize I'm a priest?"

"That doesn't make you less handsome." She winced, her cheeks turning a brighter pink. "In fact, being forbidden probably makes you even more attractive."

He scoffed, not sure if he should believe this nonsense. But he did wonder what his dream girl thought. Had she just admitted she found him attractive?

"And then," she continued, "there is the fact that you rescued the ladies and brought them to the monastery."

"Not all of them. I've been there only a month."

"You rescued enough of them for the women to decide you're a hero."

That was laughable. "Then they really don't know me, do they?"

She glanced back, regarding him curiously. "You don't see your actions as heroic?"

He shrugged. "I do what needs to be done at the time." He gave her a wry look. "Even if it makes certain people see me as a criminal."

She tilted her head, watching him. "Am I wrong to think that? I've been asking myself whether you're a hero or a villain. What am I to think of you?"

His heart grew still. She was giving him a chance to make his case, to explain what horrible events had forced him to kidnap a queen and a princess, to swear that he never would have allowed any harm to come to them. This was his chance to make his vow that his feelings for her were true, that they would remain steadfast. If she allowed it, he would follow her to the ends of the earth and never let her down.

But though he willed the words to come out, he couldn't bring himself to speak them. Tears came to his eyes, and he blinked them away. He'd failed too many people to be considered a hero. What had possessed him to think he could ever be worthy of this beautiful woman? "There is no need to wonder about me. I am a lost cause."

She slowly turned to face the road, and a long pause stretched between them.

Bran slumped against the bedrolls. He'd done the best he could for his dream girl. He'd chased her off.

Her voice was soft as a whisper. "But I still wonder."

Eventually, Pendras's head was throbbing too much for him to hear the conversations of his captors. They had kept him slung over the back of the horse with his head down for what felt like hours. It was hard to tell the time with the blindfold on, but as the air grew cooler, he figured it must be dusk.

They slowed to a stop, and the young man in the saddle next to him dismounted. He heard doors creaking open. The horses ambled inside, then stopped again. The smell of old straw, dust, and animals made his nose itch. An abandoned barn?

He was dragged off the horse and dropped onto a thin pile of straw. Still trussed up and blindfolded, he landed hard and managed to turn his head at the last minute to keep from breaking his nose. A rush of blood surged through his body, quickly followed by an onslaught of pain.

Lennie? Father? Anyone? He called out telepathically, but there was no answer. There hadn't been any answer for hours. The only reason he could think of was the shield that Kasper had erected.

"Sit up!" A man, Roland he suspected, grabbed him by his shoulder-length hair and yanked him into a sitting position. Then his head was pulled back, and a sharp blade was pressed against his exposed throat.

"You bastard," Reynfrid growled.

"One wrong move and we slaughter the dragon," Greer announced. "Now take a piss or whatever you need. Quickly."

Pendras couldn't see, but he assumed they had untied Reynfrid. They'd certainly taken his blindfold and gag off, since he could see and talk.

"You won't get away with this," Reynfrid grumbled.

Greer scoffed. "You think I'm worried about that puny troop of soldiers following us? Our shield has pushed them back so far, they've lost track of us." He chuckled. "Done? Go sit over there, your back against that post."

Pendras heard some scuffling noises, then a jangling metallic sound as if chains were being moved around.

"Your turn, Zane," Greer announced. "Behave or we'll kill the other two."

Zane? Pendras thought back. This had to be the Raven's younger brother, the one he had followed.

"Go ahead," Zane growled as he passed by Pendras. "They mean nothing to me!"

Great, Pendras thought.

After a short while, Zane was told where to sit, and the clanking sound of more chains soon followed.

"Don't try any of your boiling hot tricks," Greer warned the young man. "It won't work on these chains. You'll just burn yourself. And if you set the straw on fire, the whole barn will burn down with you trapped inside."

What was his boiling hot trick? Pendras wondered. Was it his Embraced power?

"Your turn, dragon," Roland hissed, removing the blade from his throat. He sawed through the ropes binding him, doing it in a careless manner that left Pendras with a multitude of small cuts.

Pendras winced, more from frustration than pain. As long as the oil-soaked gag was covering his mouth, he didn't dare attempt to breathe fire.

"Careful, he's the most dangerous of the three," Greer muttered, then raised his voice. "Did you hear what I told Zane? If you try breathing fire, you'll set this barn ablaze. Your fellow captives are chained to posts, and I'll be hiding the key. You won't be able to get them out before they burn to death. Understand?"

Pendras nodded his head. The blindfold was whisked off, and the gag untied. He shifted his jaw and blinked as he grew accustomed to the light, even though it was only one oil lamp and some moonlight gleaming through the open doors.

His assumptions had been correct. They were in an old barn. He was sitting on a low pile of straw, naked except for a scratchy horse blanket that had been tossed across his lap. There were no animals in the barn other than the three horses that had brought them here. Reynfrid sat across from him and gave him a resigned nod. The other one, Zane, was to his left, glowering at everyone. Kasper, the shield-maker, was nowhere in sight.

Greer grasped him by the shoulder and an icy blast shot painfully into his bones. "See how easy it would be for me to kill you?"

Pendras was tempted to knock the man's arm aside and punch him in his smirking face, but Roland had an arrow nocked and ready to fire into Reynfrid's chest.

"One wrong move and the prince dies," Greer warned him as he stepped back. "Now do your business."

Pendras stood up, letting the blanket fall to the ground. He strode to the open door as if he were leaving.

"Halt!" Greer grabbed his arm, letting a freezing cold jab stab at his bicep.

"You want to watch?" Pendras sneered at him, and Greer stepped back.

After emptying his bladder, Pendras returned to the blanket and adjusted it so he could sit on one end and fold the other end over his lap. Greer locked a leg iron around his right ankle, then wound the attached chain around a post before snapping the end manacle around his left wrist.

Pendras exchanged a look with Reynfrid, and the prince shrugged slightly as if admitting there wasn't a hell of a lot they could do. Starting a fire was out of the question. Pendras couldn't shift with these chains locked around an ankle and wrist. And even if he could, where would he fly as long as the shield was in place?

Kasper sauntered through the door with a basket of food.

"The shield is still up?" Greer asked as he removed one of the loaves of bread from the basket.

"Aye, Master," Kasper replied. "No one can come within a mile of us."

"Excellent," Greer replied with his usual smirk. "They will never find us."

Not really, Pendras thought wryly. If Dominic or one of his soldiers bumped into the wall during their search, they wouldn't be able to penetrate it, but it would roughly reveal Greer's location. Then they would only have to wait for the wall to fall to make their move. Surely, the young Kasper couldn't keep the wall up while he slept.

Greer ripped the loaf into three parts and handed them out to his prisoners. "There's no point in trying to escape. Even if you leave the barn, you can't get through the shield." He chuckled. "Eat and go to sleep while we decide what to do with you."

Roland flung a wineskin at Pendras's feet, then joined his cohorts by the door. Pendras pulled out the cork and took a sip. Water. It tasted all right. He took a longer drink, then tossed it over to Reynfrid.

"Thank you." Reynfrid drank a little, then winced as he shifted on his patch of straw.

"Are you injured?" Pendras asked quietly.

Reynfrid shook his head. "Bruised a bit when my horse fell on me."

Pendras suspected the Tourinian prince was hurt more than he was admitting.

He tossed the waterskin to Zane. "You must be the Raven's younger brother. I'm Reynfrid and this is Pendras."

Zane took a drink, then gnawed on his hunk of bread, ignoring them.

Pendras ripped off a piece of bread and chewed on it while he watched Greer and his two cohorts close the door and slide a thick bolt in place. The interior of the barn grew darker, but he could still see them leading their horses into three stalls.

"We should cooperate with one another since we're all—" Reynfrid whispered but was interrupted.

"I wouldn't have been captured if that dragon hadn't chased me down." Zane glowered angrily at Pendras.

"I assure you we mean you no harm," Reynfrid said, but the young man scoffed.

"The dragons were breathing fire on me and my brother!" Pendras winced. "I apologize."

"As if that'll help," Zane mumbled, then stuffed more bread into his mouth.

"It was a misunderstanding," Reynfrid said in a soothing voice, and Pendras could see how he would make a good king someday. If they got out of this alive.

"Since you were a member of the Brotherhood, we thought you were in league with . . ." Reynfrid motioned with his head toward Greer.

Zane grimaced. "That bastard killed my brother. The only *cooperation* I need from you two clowns is for you to stay the hell away from me when I kill him."

"Ha!" Greer sneered at him as he strolled out of a stall. "You're no match for me, boy, and you know it. You and Bran are a pair of weaklings. That's why I had to take over the Brotherhood. And why I'll be the one to take over the world!"

"Oh!" Pendras pretended to be impressed. "One country is not enough for this daring priest. He needs to rule the entire world! Such a sane and healthy ambition—"

"Shut it, dragon," Greer growled at him. "Killing you would just make it easier for me to take your country."

"Then why are we keeping them alive?" Roland hissed from the adjoining stall, and Greer strode over to him. Pendras had to strain to hear the rest of the conversation.

"I told you they might come in handy," Greer hissed. "If King Ulfrid manages to escape from my pirates, we can use his son as a hostage."

Good thing they don't realize I'm also a prince, Pendras thought, or they would try to use him to control Silas.

"And the others?" Roland whined. "It's too hard to keep all three under control. And they're slowing us down. At this rate, it'll take a week to reach the gold—"

"Shh." Greer hushed him. "We'll manage. As long as we have this dragon, we can use him to keep the other dragons at bay. And if we have Zane, we can control Bran."

"If you say so . . ." Roland grumbled.

"I do," Greer snapped in a sharp tone to emphasize he was in charge. "But don't worry, the minute I decide they are worthless, we'll kill them."

Chapter 10

Fool, Bran chided himself. The miles had stretched on and on, and he'd kept his mouth shut, even though he knew the captain was willing to hear his story. Of course she was willing. The woman had the heart of an angel. And that, unfortunately, made him long for her even more.

Still, he had remained silent. It was easy enough to clench his jaw shut, for the pain of his injuries had come back with a vengeance. Just what he deserved for being such a fool.

The sun had lowered toward the top of the forest, and since he was facing west, the glare had slammed him right in the face. He'd turned his head away, closing his eyes, no longer admiring his beautiful dream girl, no longer attempting to talk to her. Hopefully, she would think him asleep and leave him alone.

Father Bertram had set a container of Brother Jerome's Special Potion of Peaceful Repose within reach of his left hand, but he refused to take a swig. Better to be in pain than soused to the point that he made lurid confessions of love and devotion to a girl who considered him a criminal.

But if he explained what had happened that fateful night, would she be able to forgive him? She might pity him, and that seemed even worse.

The wagon jolted over a rut in the road, and he gritted his teeth, squeezing his eyes shut.

"Sorry," she whispered.

He wondered if she was peering at him, but kept his eyes shut. Eventually, the glare of the sun against his eyelids lessened as twilight fell and the temperature dropped. He almost wished he had the silly scarf back, but he'd tossed it out of reach.

A male voice, probably Anton's, yelled out that they'd arrived at a posting station, and soon, the captain slowed the wagon to a stop. People started talking, horses snorted and stomped their hooves, bridles jangled, and females groaned as they dismounted.

"Bran," the captain whispered. "Are you still asleep?"

Still a fool, he thought, frowning with his eyes closed. *Still in pain.*

"Bran?" she spoke a little louder. "We've stopped to get new horses. Would you like something to eat?"

He opened his eyes, and to his surprise, she was leaning over him, peering at him with a worried look.

She frowned as she studied his eyes. "Are you in pain?"

He nodded.

"Did you take more of the special potion?"

He shook his head.

She gave him an exasperated look. "Why not?"

"I might say something I regret."

She scoffed. "I'd rather you say silly things than be in pain. I feel guilty enough . . . Here, let me." She reached across him for the container, then teetered on the edge of the driver's bench. The loose bedroll she was sitting on started to slide off the bench. "Agh!"

Quickly, wincing against a jab of pain, he sat up and lifted his broken right arm out of the way. The bedroll slipped off, taking her with it. At least the bedroll cushioned her fall as she landed on her back, sprawled across his thighs with her booted feet up in the air.

With his left hand, he cradled the back of her head to keep

her from knocking it against anything. He leaned forward, looking her over. "Are you all right?"

"Yes." Her eyes met his, then she hastily looked away, her cheeks growing pink. "No. I'm mortified. I'm not usually so clumsy." She grimaced. "I just fell on a wounded man."

"It's all right." He gave her a small smile. "Feel free to fall on me whenever you like."

Her eyes widened; then she glanced at his broken arm and the bandages across his stomach. "Are you sure I didn't hurt you?"

"Actually, you've helped take my mind off the pain." In fact, with her lovely body on top of him, his groin was starting to demand more attention than his wounds.

She glanced once again at his broken arm, now resting on the wooden driver's bench. "I'm so sorry you're suffering like this."

"Angel, it's not your fault."

She winced. "Let me see if I can move off you." She planted her boots against the edge of the bench and lifted her hips a bit, trying to rotate her body. "This is awkward. Perhaps it would help if you lie back."

"All right." He leaned back and winced as she squirmed on top of him. Slowly, she twisted around until her head was resting against his chest and her legs were on top of his. Unfortunately, all the movement against his groin was giving rise to a different sort of problem. "Just be still for a moment."

"Am I causing you pain?"

More like a cheap thrill, he thought with an increasing fear of finding himself in an embarrassing situation.

"Could you spread your legs a bit?" she asked.

Wasn't that his line? With a snort, he complied.

She planted a foot between his knees, then pushed against the wagon bed to roll off of him. "There." She crawled toward him in the narrow space between him and the boxes and baskets. "Not much room here. Let me get this bedroll off you."

After grabbing the bedroll, she leaned over him to toss it back onto the driver's bench. In danger of losing her balance once again, she planted a hand against his chest to steady herself. "Oh, sorry." She lifted her hand. "Did I hurt you?"

"No, my chest is fine."

"Yes, it is." With a wince, she looked away. "Here." She seized the container of potion and offered it to him. "Please take the potion from now on. I don't care if you say silly things."

After all the effort she'd put into retrieving the container, he couldn't bring himself to disappoint her, so he accepted it. "And what if I say silly things about you?"

She gave him a sad look. "I'm not the angel you think I am."

"Perhaps not, but the thought of you has given me comfort for the past five months, and I am grateful for that."

She scoffed. "I didn't do anything. I was asleep."

He nodded. "While I was kidnapping the queen."

Anger flashed in her brilliant green eyes. "Do you want me to hate you?"

"It would be safer for you if you did."

Her eyes narrowed. "I'm more interested in the truth than in feeling safe."

"Continue to hate me, angel." His gaze lowered to her mouth. "For the truth right now is I find you extremely hard to resist."

Her mouth fell open, then shut firmly as she swallowed hard.

"Bran, dear boy, are you all right?" Father Bertram had dismounted and now stood beside the wagon, peering at them with curiousity.

"I'll be going now." She stood up. "I was trying to encourage Bran to take some of the special potion for his pain." She stepped carefully between his legs to get back to the bench.

"Here, let me help you." Father Sebastian climbed onto the driver's bench and grabbed the captain's hand to assist her.

Bran resisted the urge to give her a boost from behind. He figured she wouldn't enjoy his hand on her lovely rump nearly as much as he would.

"Oh, dear." Bertram clucked his tongue. "Bran, have you not been taking your tonic?"

"I'll take some after we eat," Bran promised as he watched the captain scramble over the driver's bench. She jumped to the ground, and then, without a backward glance, rushed into the posting station with Terrance and Princess Roslyn.

Milena opened the backboard of the wagon and dug into a basket containing food from the monastery.

Meanwhile, the two dragon shifters had emerged from the forest. Apparently, as soon as the captain had stopped, Sergei had shifted in the woods and Anton had delivered his clothes to him. Now, by the way they were glaring at him, he figured they'd seen the captain sprawled on top of him.

Yes, you flying snakes, Bran thought, lifting an eyebrow at them. *You have competition.*

With a haughty sniff, they turned away as if to say a one-armed raven could never pose a threat to a mighty dragon.

Unfortunately, they could be right, Bran thought as he struggled awkwardly to get to his feet.

"Let me help you," Sebastian said, offering Bran a hand.

By the time Bran had managed to set his feet on the ground, workers from the posting station had unhitched the horses and taken them into the stable, along with the other horses. More stable hands brought out fresh saddled horses, while boys transferred the saddlebags to the new horses.

"We're not spending the night here?" Bertram asked.

"No," Sergei replied shortly as he retrieved the lantern poles from the back of the wagon. "We need to press on."

"Captain's orders," Anton said, and Sergei shot him an annoyed look as if he would have preferred that everyone think it was his idea. "The captain is hoping that Greer will stop when it gets dark. If we keep going, we can make up for the hours we lost and catch up with them, hopefully by tomorrow."

"Isn't it dangerous to travel in the dark?" Milena asked. She had quickly arranged a platter of bread, butter, cheese, and apples onto a tablecloth she'd spread across the tailgate.

"I'll be flying overhead for protection," Anton boasted. "And we'll use these to light the way." He pulled out a lantern, opened the glass door, then lit the wick with a quick burst of fire.

Bran stiffened. He hadn't known the dragons could breathe fire while in human form.

"Holy Light," Bertram whispered.

Anton gave them a smirk, then fastened the lantern over the hook of a pole. Sergei slid the pole into a bracket on the side of the wagon. Soon, they had a second lantern lighting the other side.

The captain, Terrance, and Roslyn emerged from the tavern portion of the posting station with two jugs, a stack of cups, and a platter of sliced roast beef.

"Eat quickly so we can get back on the road," the captain told them as she set the platter next to the one Milena had prepared.

Terrance and Roslyn set the cups and jugs of cider down, and everyone started helping themselves.

"Oh, no!" Bertram scurried over to his stubby horse when a stable hand approached her. "My sweet Daffy must stay with me. I can't leave her here with strangers. It will frighten her too much."

Bran snorted. Daffy had wandered off to leisurely munch on the green grass beside the road. During his time at the monastery, he'd never seen the little horse get excited or frightened. When Bertram wrapped his arms around her neck, she gave him a bland look, then went back to eating.

"She needs to rest, Bertram," Sebastian told him, then eyed the older priest. "I think you should rest, too."

The old man did look exhausted, Bran thought as he finished a slice of beef. "Father Bertram can use the pallet. I'll sit on the bench for a while."

"Won't that be painful for you?" the captain asked.

"I'll be all right once I take some of the potion." Bran gave her a small smile. "You don't mind sharing the bench?"

She shrugged. "It's fine with me." She poured a cup full of cider, then handed it to him.

"Thank you."

With a slight blush, she turned away to pour herself a cup. As Bran drank, he noticed the two dragons still glaring at him.

Bertram approached, leading his little horse by the reins. He grabbed an apple off the tailgate and fed it to her. "What about Daffy?"

The captain smiled at him. "We can tie her to the back of the wagon while you rest on the pallet."

"Excellent." Now happy, the priest helped himself to some food.

Soon, everyone had eaten their fill. Bran followed up his meal with a quick swig from the bottle of potion. The men relieved themselves in the woods, while the women used the facilities in the tavern. Anton shifted, and Sergei put the discarded clothes in Anton's saddlebags, then tied the horse to his. He lit the third lantern, and when Anton lifted off the ground, he grabbed the ring with one of his talons. He took off, flying low to the road with the lantern to help light their way.

Bran narrowed his eyes, watching the dragon carefully. Anton was a large dragon with the same purplish-green belly that Sergei possessed. Neither of them was the one who had made him crash. So where had that dragon gone? And why would it leave when the captain's brother was in danger?

After Father Bertram was happily settled on the pallet, Bran struggled to climb onto the driver's bench, insisting he could manage it himself. Finally, he was seated on the cushion next to his dream girl.

With Anton flying ahead to light the way, Sergei followed on horseback, followed by the wagon with its three occupants and a tethered Daffy, Sebastian and Milena on horseback, and, bringing up the rear, Terrance and Princess Roslyn on their horses. As they left the well-lit posting station behind, it grew much darker. Only the stars, the twin moons, and their three lanterns illuminated the road. On either side, the forest loomed, black and forbidding.

They hadn't traveled very long when Bran heard Bertram snoring behind him. He glanced back just as the captain did, and their gazes met. He smiled, but she ducked her head with a shy look before focusing on the road.

As time passed by, he felt an awkward silence hovering over them. Had he gone too far admitting he found her hard to resist? Or perhaps her silence was nothing more than weariness after hours of travel.

"You must be tired," he whispered.

"A little." She paused, then slanted him a quick look. "You must be in pain."

"A little."

A corner of her mouth lifted as if she knew he was downplaying the truth. "I realize our progress is slow in the dark, but this is the only way we can catch up with Greer. We have to make up for the time we lost."

"I agree." He glanced up at the twin moons, both half full. "I can hold the reins for a while if your hands are tired."

"I'm fine. But thank you for the offer."

He sighed. Was it his imagination or was she being overly formal? Perhaps, after sitting on his lap, she was now trying to put some distance between them. "Have you heard from your brother yet?"

Her hands tightened on the reins. "No."

"He'll be all right. All three of them will be."

She nodded.

Another pause stretched out as they slowly traveled along the King's Way. Her hands were still tense, so he tried to think of something entertaining to say that would take her mind off her missing brother. Unfortunately, he'd spent most of the past five years as a bird and a spy, and that had not helped his conversational skills. Even at the Monastery of Light, where he'd grown up, the dismal atmosphere had not been conducive to light banter. The only time those bastard monks had gotten excited was when the moons embraced and they got to whip the young boys who lived there or molest the young girls. Vera, the older of his sisters, had been tormented by no fewer than seven perverted monks. Milena, as far as he knew, had managed to avoid the bastards because she was four years younger.

"How old were you when you joined the army?" he asked the captain.

She glanced at him. "Fourteen."

"That young?" He gave her an incredulous look.

She shrugged. "My father was a general. My brother joined at the same time. He's eighteen months younger than I am."

"You must be very close."

She nodded. "We are. Ever since we could form words, we could hear each other's thoughts." She gave him a small smile. "Eventually we learned how to keep our thoughts private."

"Does he look like you?"

Her smile widened. "No. He has my father's black hair and my mother's elfin eyes. Meaning they're lavender-blue."

"So your green eyes are not elfin?"

"No." She gave him a curious look. "You must be close to your brother, too."

He frowned. "I was close to both of my brothers."

"You lost one?"

He nodded. "The night I first saw you."

She paused for a moment, then shifted slightly closer on the bench. "Can you tell me what really happened?"

His frown deepened. Wasn't he in enough pain already? But sometimes it helped to talk about his brother. And the more time he spent with his dream girl, the more he wanted to open his heart to her. "Arlo had a special Embraced gift. He could make people believe whatever he told them, no matter how preposterous."

"That sounds dangerous."

Bran nodded. "Aye, but Arlo was always determined to use his gift for good. All he ever wanted was to be a priest in a small community where he could help people believe in themselves and succeed in becoming the best they could be."

"He was a kind soul."

"Aye." Once again, Bran felt the weight of his grief push down on him as if it would grind him to dust. His eyes filled with tears, and he blinked them away. Damn, he didn't want to appear a weakling. "It was because of Arlo and Zane that I knew the monks were lying to us. They always said we were evil because we'd been born Embraced, but there was never anything evil about my brothers."

"How did your brother die?" she asked softly.

Bran took a deep breath. Yes, vengeance was the answer. It never failed to give him purpose and strength. "Greer killed him. That's why Zane and I have been hunting him for these past five months."

"Greer killed him on the night of the kidnappings?"

"I never should have left him alone." Bran slumped. "He'd wanted to go with me, but I thought he'd slow me down."

"Where were you going?"

"To kidnap the Eberoni princess."

The captain hissed in a breath.

"I don't blame you for hating me." Bran snorted. "I hate myself."

"Then why did you do it?" she ground out between clenched teeth.

Her anger and his own self-recrimination stabbed at him till he couldn't bear it anymore. He opened his mouth, and the words rushed out as if a floodgate had been opened. "Do you know how missions worked at the Monastery of Light? If you failed, you had to kill yourself. Master Lorne made sure every priest had a nice silver ring filled with poison. My friend, Father Saul, was first tasked with kidnapping the princess while she was on a barge. When he failed, I was there. I had to sit by and watch my best friend die. And that bastard Greer was there, too. If Saul hadn't taken the poison, Greer would have killed him."

The captain's eyes had widened with a stunned look. Bran knew he should shut the hell up, that he was appalling her, but all the wretched feelings he had kept bottled up were breaking free.

"Greer had always hated me and my brothers since we had the unfortunate privilege of actually being related to those bastard brothers, Lord Morris and Master Lorne." Bran scoffed harshly. "As if I wanted to inherit that godforsaken hellhole. Greer wanted to get rid of me, so he convinced Master Lorne to give me the task of kidnapping the princess. I knew what her power was, and I had told Master Lorne it was impossible. Greer was counting on that, so I would fail and have to kill myself."

The captain sucked in a breath.

"But before the Master could give me the job, Arlo volunteered." Tears came to Bran's eyes once again. "He only did it to save me. I was so afraid he would have to take the poison that I took his place."

"That's why you kidnapped Eviana? To save your brother?"

He nodded. "While I was away doing it, Greer found my brother and froze him to death." He blinked away the tears. "After that, I let the princess escape, but Greer caught her."

"And that's when you helped Quentin rescue her?"

"Aye."

The captain turned to face the road and was silent for a while before speaking again. "I am sorry for your loss."

Bran took a deep breath, still in shock that he'd spilled his guts like that. The little bit of potion he'd taken must have loosened his tongue.

"I am sorry you had to grow up in such a horrific place." She grimaced. "I saw the scars on your back. I'm so sorry—"

"Don't," he growled. "Don't turn me into some sort of pathetic, pitiful creature—"

"I'm not!" She glanced at him. "I just wanted to understand—"

"You can understand this. I knew that monastery was evil. I knew my brothers and my sisters were good, kindhearted souls, who were being tortured, and I did nothing. I should have rescued them, but I did *nothing*. That makes me every bit as evil as—"

"Stop it!" Bertram cried.

Bran glanced back to find the old man in tears.

"You were a child," Bertram whimpered. "A brainwashed child raised in torment and fear. What could you have done? Where could you have gone? It was *my* fault. I failed you all."

Bran blinked. "What do you mean? Master Lorne kicked you out."

"Aye." Bertram wiped his face. "I was planning to rescue you, but he found out and evicted me. Still, I should have found some way to save you."

"I thought he turned on you because of your gift," Bran said.

Bertram shrugged. "He was mad about that, too. After he gave the order for my eviction, I was so distraught I went into a trance and gave him one last prediction. That made him so furious, he tossed me out without a penny."

"What did you predict?"

Bertram winced. "It doesn't bear repeating."

"Give it a rest," Father Sebastian told them, having spurred his horse to catch up with them and keep pace alongside the wagon. "We can hear you, and it's breaking our hearts."

Bran glanced back to see Milena wiping tears from her face. "I'm sorry."

"No one blames you for what happened," Father Sebastian declared. "Stop being so harsh on yourself."

With a sigh, Bran turned to face the road.

"Father Sebastian is right," the captain whispered. "The blame should always fall on those who actually commit the crime. You were just as much a victim as your brothers and sisters."

"I'm the eldest," he grumbled. "I'll always feel responsible for them."

She nodded slowly. "I can understand that. I'm the eldest, too—everyone expects so much of me." She winced. "It can be hard to live up to."

"What is expected of you?"

One corner of her mouth curled up as she gave him a wry look. "Perfection."

"A tall order, but if anyone can do it, you can."

Her eyes softened and she rested her palm on his left hand. "We'll save your brother."

He clasped her hand with his. "We'll save yours, too."

She glanced at him, and their gazes met. And held. She was so beautiful and looking right at him as if she were searching for his soul.

He squeezed her hand and whispered, "Do you still hate me?"

"No." Her eyes glinted with emotion. "Do you still hate yourself?"

"I'm learning not to." He gave her a small smile, and she smiled back. "Will you tell me your name?"

She hesitated, then Father Sebastian interrupted with a sharp voice.

"Bertram! Are you all right?"

Bran released her hand and shifted on the bench to look behind him at the elderly priest. Bertram's eyes had glazed over.

"He's about to make another prediction," Bran said, his nerves growing tense. He seriously doubted this would be good news.

The captain glanced back with a curious look.

Bertram's face paled as his unfocused gaze wandered up to the stars. "Just after midnight, three men will die."

Chapter 11

Lennie flinched. Was Father Bertram referring to the captives? *Pendras!* she screamed mentally, but there was no reply.

The horses whinnied as they came to an abrupt halt, and she realized she had jerked hard on the reins, pulling them to her chest as if she could stop her heart from ripping apart.

Three men will die. The words repeated over and over in her mind. Agitated voices rose around her, but she barely heard them. *Three men will die.*

Bran said something as he pried the reins from her tight grip and looped them around a ring on the wagon.

Her vision blurred, the stars in the sky growing dull and gray. With a groan, she leaned over, her head in her lap. Was Pendras going to die? Reynfrid and Zane?

Stop it! she yelled at herself mentally. She was in charge here. She had to be strong. She had to do something. What if she shifted and flew north? But she didn't know where the captives were.

She sat up abruptly. "What time is it?"

Bran glanced up at the sky. "I figure we have about two hours until midnight."

She hissed in a breath. "We can't ride there in time."

"No." His jaw was set as if he refused to be battered by harsh news, but the pain glimmering in his eyes brought tears to her own. "If only I could fly."

That hit her like a stab in the heart. How would he ever forgive her if he knew she was the dragon who had caused his broken arm? With a wince, she glanced back at Bertram. He'd come out of his trance, and, apparently, he'd been told what he'd said, for now he was curled up on the pallet, covering his face with his hands. Terrance, Roslyn, and Milena had gathered close to the wagon and Father Sebastian. By the looks on their stricken faces, they'd also heard the news.

"Reynfrid!" Roslyn cried, teetering precariously on her saddle. Terrance leaped off his horse and caught her in his arms.

Milena doubled over, whimpering as she pressed a hand to her heart.

"Zane, our poor Zane," Bertram moaned.

"Enough!" Sebastian exclaimed, his own face tense with emotion. "Bertram said three men. We don't know for sure that he meant the captives."

"Why are we stopping?" Sergei demanded as his horse galloped back toward the wagon. Anton landed on the road but remained in dragon form.

"Father Bertram made a prediction," Terrance said softly as he set Roslyn on her feet. "He said three men will die."

"Oh, Zane," Bertram moaned. "My poor boy."

Sergei scoffed. "We stopped because of an old man's ramblings?" He looked askance at Lennie. "Don't tell me you believe this nonsense?"

She gritted her teeth. "Father Bertram, how often do your predictions come true?"

He wiped tears from his face. "Always."

Lennie's heart sank. *Pendras! Do you hear me?* No answer. Surely he would have regained consciousness by now? But it wasn't midnight yet. He had to be alive. For now.

Milena pressed a hand to her mouth as a sob escaped.

The lady-in-waiting must have strong feelings for Reynfrid, Lennie thought. She glanced over at Bran and winced at how pale his face looked against his black hair.

"While it is true that Bertram's predictions always come true," Bran said softly, "they often happen in an unexpected way."

"Exactly," Father Sebastian agreed. "That's what I was saying. Three men could mean any three men in the world."

Lennie stiffened at the thought of another three captives. "King Silas, King Ulfrid, and Aleksi."

Roslyn gasped. "Papa!" Her body crumpled, and Terrance supported her to keep her from collapsing. "Either my brother or my father?" With tears in her eyes, she looked at Lennie, who was in the same terrible situation. "What do we do?"

Papa? Silas, do you hear me? Lennie called, but there was no answer. Instead, Lennie's mother responded.

My dear, why are you distraught? Gwennore asked. *What has happened?*

Lennie quickly explained Father Bertram's prediction. *If he's referring to the princes, we're too far away to help them. And if he's referring to the kings . . .*

I understand. Gwennore's mental voice sounded faint with shock. *We must trust them to stay alive. They are not defenseless. Prince Dominic and his soldiers should be close by, searching for the princes. And we are drawing near to Freydor's port. The additional dragons are here. And Brody. They will scour the countryside until we find the kings. Their powers will keep them safe. We have to believe that.*

Yes, Mama. Lennie took a deep breath to steady her nerves. *I will keep you updated.*

And I will do the same. You will do well, Lenushka. Your father and I have always believed in you.

Thank you. Lennie blinked away her tears and told everyone what her mother had said.

A squawk sounded overhead, and she glanced up to see an eagle circling overhead. "Quentin!"

He landed on the road, close to the dragon, while Terrance dashed toward him with a blanket. He held it out, and Quentin shifted behind it, then wrapped the blanket around his waist.

Quentin gave Terrance a light slap on the shoulder. "It's good to see you again." His smile faded as he noticed everyone's grim expressions.

Meanwhile, Lennie had scrambled off the wagon with Bran close behind her. Those still on horses dismounted, and they all gathered around the eagle shifter.

"Were you able to see the captives?" Lennie asked. "Are they all right?"

"Aye," Quentin replied. "The young Embraced priest who makes the invisible wall kept enlarging it until we were pushed nearly a mile away from them. When we could no longer see them, I took to the air to spot them. I tried getting through the shield from above, but it covers them completely like an inverted bowl. After watching them for a while, I realized there was no sound coming from them. And when I made a loud squawk, no one looked up. I don't believe they heard me."

Lennie drew in a sharp breath. This could explain why she was unable to contact Pendras. But why wasn't her father answering?

"How are the captives?" Bran asked.

Quentin gave the other bird shifter a quick nod. "I saw your brother, Bran, and the others. All three were tied to the backs of horses. They're gagged, but I saw them moving a bit."

"When was this?" Lennie asked.

"Shortly before sunset. Roughly two hours ago." Quentin glanced around at the dark woods surrounding them. "I thought I'd find you at a posting station. You've come farther than I expected."

"We're hoping to catch up with Dominic by tomorrow," Lennie said.

Quentin nodded. "Dominic asked me to inform you of his plan. He's hoping the shield will fall some time tonight, and then he and his men can move in and rescue the prisoners."

"That makes sense," Terrance said. "Whenever the Embraced priest falls asleep, his power should abate."

"Exactly," Quentin agreed. "I need to hurry back so I can assist with the rescue."

"Take Anton with you." Lennie motioned to the dragon sitting close by on the road. "He'll help you and keep us informed, so you won't have to keep flying back and forth. And as we draw closer, he can give us directions to find you."

Quentin glanced at the unarmed priests and lady-in-waiting. "Are you sure you don't need the dragon here for protection?"

"I'm a dragon, too!" Sergei pushed his way toward Lennie. "I can protect the princess."

Lennie winced and gave him a pointed look.

"Oh." Sergei's eyes widened, and then he pointed at Roslyn. "I meant her. She's the princess."

"Oh, right! That's me." Roslyn rushed over and grabbed Lennie's arm. "And this is Captain Dravenko."

Lennie suppressed a groan. Roslyn was only making the situation worse.

Quentin looked back and forth between them with a confused look, while Sebastian narrowed his eyes with suspicion.

"There is another matter that has us greatly concerned," Lennie said quickly, and she related the news about Bertram's prediction.

Quentin paled. "If that is true, we need to leave immediately. If we fly back at top speed, we might arrive before midnight." He circled behind Anton, shifted, and flew north.

"Keep me informed," Lennie ordered Anton, and he nodded.

Sergei took the lantern Anton had been holding and handed him the saddlebags containing his clothes.

Anton cradled the leather bags against his chest with his forelegs, then pushed off from the ground, his great wings flapping. He quickly caught up with Quentin.

Lennie pressed a hand to her mouth. Had she made a terrible mistake by not accompanying them?

"Mount up!" Sergei ordered. "Let's get going!"

As everyone moved about, Lennie stood alone, watching the form of Anton silhouetted against the larger of the two moons.

"Captain?" Bran peered at her closely.

"I should have gone with them," she whispered.

"You mean hitching a ride on Anton?"

No, she meant flying herself, but because she was hiding her true identity, she let Bran believe he was right about her meaning. "If something happens to Pendras, I'll never forgive myself."

"Don't say that." When she trembled, he took hold of her arm. "Remember what you told me: The only ones you should blame for a crime are the ones who committed it."

Tears came to her eyes. "But I can blame myself for not being there to stop the crime from ever happening."

"There is no guarantee that the prediction referred to your brother," Bran insisted. "Nor is there a guarantee that Anton can arrive before midnight. Or be able to find the captives."

"But we certainly can't ride there in time. We're moving much more slowly than a dragon. It might take four, maybe five hours—"

"I know." He gave her arm a light squeeze. "And if we push ourselves to get there, we'll be too exhausted to be of any use when we arrive. I know this is damned hard to accept, but sometimes things are out of our control. I have struggled, too, thinking that I was responsible for everything that happens, but it isn't true. We have to trust that our loved ones will be as brave and resourceful as we know they are. They can handle this. All we can do is pray and have faith."

She blinked away her tears and gave him a shaky smile. "Right now, you actually sound like a priest."

He winced. "Heaven forbid. The Light knows I'm not worthy."

Oh, but he was, she thought. He was a much better man than he realized. Kind, brave, loyal, strong, and smart. When he'd told her about his horrific past, her heart had ached for him. Yes, she'd felt some pity, but also a great deal of amazement. He'd survived abuse without losing the goodness in his heart and soul. He still knew how to love and how to give. The women at the monastery were right to admire him. And if she wasn't careful, she would end up falling for him just as they had.

"What are you waiting for?" Sergei yelled back at them. "Let's go!"

As Bran hefted himself onto the driver's bench, Lennie realized the others had readied themselves for departure while she and Bran had been talking. Somehow, he had become a confidant. Perhaps that wasn't so strange, she thought as she climbed onto the bench next to him. He was understanding and supportive, definitely easier to talk to than Sergei. She glanced at the dragon shifter, who was glowering at her. His idea of a conversation would be his dictating and her listening. And then obeying.

Oh, dear goddesses, she needed her father and brother with her in Norveshka. Without them, she would be surrounded by men who only wanted to use her.

She flicked the reins and the horses perked up.

"Hee-yah, Lulabelle and Constanza!" Bran yelled at them, and they lurched forward into a brisk pace.

She shot him an incredulous look. "What was that?"

He shrugged. "I liked those names so much I gave them to the horses."

She found herself smiling for a brief moment before reality came back. Shortly after midnight she could lose her father or her brother. Should she have gone with Anton? What if she shifted right now and took off? She shook her head. If she spent the next two hours playing "what if" scenarios in her mind, she would end up in a panic. Already, panic was lurking at the edges of her consciousness, searching for a foothold to breach her defenses.

Dominic was a formidable warrior, she reminded herself. He was being trained to be the next general and Lord Protector of the Realm in Eberon. Pendras was slated to hold the same office in Norveshka, so he and Dominic had spent years together under General Nevis's relentless tutelage. Being trained together had led them to become best friends. If anyone could save Pendras, it would be Dominic. She would have to trust him.

Behind her, she could hear Father Bertram, Sebastian, and Milena murmuring prayers for the captives. "Goddesses, please protect them," she whispered, glancing up at the moons, Luna and Lessa.

Beside her, Bran flinched with surprise. "You . . . you're praying to the goddesses?"

"Why not?" She noted his shocked expression and smiled. No doubt, having grown up in the Monastery of Light, he'd been trained to think only the sun god was legitimate. "My mother was raised on the Isle of Moon, where they worship the moons. But my father comes from Norveshka, where they worship the sun."

"And that never caused any discord in their marriage?" Bran asked.

"No." Lennie's smile widened. "They respect each other too much. And love each other so much." Her smile faded as she watched Sergei riding ahead. Did her parents not realize the weight of the burden they'd placed on her? By declaring her the heir to the throne, they'd made it extremely difficult for her ever to find a suitable mate. How could she marry any man that her countrymen couldn't accept as king? And the nobles had made it clear that they would accept no less than a dragon. With no real choice in the matter, she highly doubted she could ever have the happy sort of marriage that her parents enjoyed. If she married Sergei, she would not only be a miserable wife, but also a miserable queen, because he would be constantly trying to take over.

Bran lifted his head to gaze at the twin moons. "I was raised to believe the goddesses are evil, as they're the ones who cause children to be Embraced."

Lennie shook her head. "There's nothing wrong with being born Embraced. What matters is that you use your gift for good. The moons, themselves, do no evil. They give us light in the darkness and guide us with their stars."

"But the sun gives us life."

"And the moons give us rest. Both are needed, don't you think?" Lennie glanced at him. He was easy to talk to, and she was grateful to have something other than her personal problems to think about. "Have you ever heard of the great philosopher Tedric?"

"No. Where does he live?"

"He doesn't. He's a ghost." She smiled at Bran's stunned expression.

"Are you jesting with me?" When she shook her head, he scoffed. "I assume the man was alive at some point?"

"Yes, but his most brilliant philosophical observations happened after he died."

"Better late than never." Bran gave her a wry look. "But how did he share his brilliance with the world when he was dead?"

"Queen Luciana's Embraced gift enables her to see and talk to ghosts. Tedric was actually Leo's cousin, and he had a marriage of sorts—"

"You *are* fooling with me." Bran's mouth twitched. "Why would a woman agree to marry a ghost?"

"Luciana's sister did. I believe she fell for his brilliant mind."

"That may be all he had to offer. But I didn't think the queen had a sister."

"She did. Tatiana died over twenty years ago."

"Oh, she's a ghost, too." Bran snorted. "Might as well keep all the spooks in the family."

"Yes." Lennie grinned. "Luciana's mother is also a ghost."

"Ah, poor Tedric! Even in death, he can't escape the nosy mother-in-law."

"Well, he did, actually. About six years ago, Tedric declared that he'd made all the observations he could and that the only way to further his knowledge would be to embark on that great journey into the Realm of the Heavens."

Bran's eyes widened. "So he left?"

Lennie nodded. "And Tatiana went with him. Even though she was afraid, she said she couldn't bear eternity without him and that she loved him enough to follow him into the Great Unknown."

"Impressive."

"Exactly!" Lennie smiled. "I remember Eviana telling me all about it. She thought it was wonderfully romantic."

"And did you agree?"

Lennie sighed. She'd thought so, too, six years ago, but

now she didn't even want to think about romance. Not when it could never happen for her. The walls kept closing . . . She shook those thoughts away. "So do you want to hear what Tedric had to say?"

"I'm dying to hear it."

She snorted. "Very well. According to Tedric, the sun didn't magically appear one day. It was created. The moons, too. The stars in the heavens. The earth and sea and all the people and creatures that inhabit it. So this Creator is the one we should be worshipping, not his creations. What do you think?"

Bran sat back. "His theory has . . . a simple beauty to it that rings true. I'll have to think about it."

Lennie nodded. "Personally, I think Tedric was right. I also think good and evil both exist, and we have to make a choice. That is what really matters: which one you decide to keep in your heart."

He took a deep breath. "But what makes a person go one way or the other? I have tried for years to understand it. I always knew my siblings were good, no matter what the priests said. I knew the Brotherhood had to be evil for the way they treated innocent children. What amazed me the most, though, was that no matter how much they tormented us, we stayed strong. Our love for each other, our bond seemed to protect us, to keep us from being twisted or broken."

"Families are a blessing that way," Lennie admitted. "They give us strength. Friends, too. My mother was raised an orphan, but she and her friends became sisters, as close as any family could be. Did Greer grow up without family or friends? Or was it the whippings that twisted his mind?"

"He had friends, or I should say other children who let him use them." Bran shook his head. "There was always a strange anger in him. His Embraced gift came to him early, at the age of seven, but the power never seemed to give him any comfort. It only made his anger grow. He used to freeze small animals to death for entertainment. And that was before the whippings began."

Lennie shuddered. "He was already evil."

Bran nodded. "Aye. It is hard to know where evil begins."

Or where it would end, Lennie thought. Was Greer planning the murder of her father or brother right now? She shoved that thought aside. It would only cause panic that would weaken her defenses.

At least she wasn't alone. She glanced at Bran. Was it only this morning that she had hated him? So much had changed. Now she was grateful to have him for an ally. "I'm glad you survived with your heart and mind intact."

His mouth twitched. "That's still up for debate."

With a smile, she shook her head. "There's nothing evil about you."

"Even though I have failed those I love? And done things I regret?"

"We all do that." She thought back to her agreement to placate the Norveshki noblemen. "But you feel love. And guilt. You've tormented yourself over the bad things you were forced to do."

"As you said earlier, there is no excuse."

"No, but you acknowledge your guilt, and you suffer for it. When you helped Quentin rescue Eviana, you risked your life to make amends. Evil people don't do that, Bran. They don't care what's right or wrong. I doubt they even define those things the same way we do. They only care about winning or achieving their ends. If Greer kills a thousand people in his quest to take over the world, he will not bat an eye."

"Then it can be an act of goodness to destroy that which is evil?" When Lennie nodded, he regarded her with wonder. "Now I know why I have dreamed of you. You've confirmed everything I most needed to hear. For months, I have searched for Greer with the intent to kill him, but I've been afraid that when the moment came, I wouldn't be able to do it, that it would constitute an act of evil that would condemn me forever."

"That very fear means you are a good man." Lennie felt the warmth of a blush creeping into her face. He had dreamed about her. And he held her in deep respect; she could feel it. Would he still feel that way if he learned the truth about her, that she was the dragon who had broken his arm?

The thought that he might eventually reject her hurt. In the brief time she'd known him, she'd found it incredibly easy to discuss all sorts of things with him. She couldn't imagine talking like this to Sergei or Anton.

How could she feel so close to Bran so quickly? Was it simply because they were in a dire situation together, in which they shared the same fear over the fate of their brothers? If that was so, when this ordeal was resolved, she would leave and never have reason to see him again.

That thought caused a pang in her chest. But it was sadly true that she would part ways with him. She shouldn't allow herself to become attached. And most definitely, she should not fall for him.

But was it already happening? Was that why the thought of parting with him made her heart ache?

Her hands tightened on the reins. How else could she explain her annoyance when other women fawned over him? The sad truth was she found him every bit as handsome and tragically heroic as that gaggle of women. But somehow, miraculously, he didn't even see them. He only saw her.

Good goddesses, how could she resist such single-minded attention?

"Relax," he whispered to her. "You're clenching the reins so tightly, you'll end up with muscle cramps. Here, I'll drive for a while." He moved closer and took the reins from her.

When his hand brushed over hers, her heart leaped in her

chest. Oh dear, how far had she fallen? She couldn't let this happen. Any hint of a scandal would give her opponents the excuse they needed to ensure she never inherited the throne. And no Norveshki nobleman would ever accept the Raven as her mate.

She gasped. How could she even think of him that way? For Light's sake, she'd known the man one day. The most he could ever be was a friend. Nothing more.

"What's wrong?" He looked at her closely. "Did you hear from your brother?"

She shook her head.

Sergei cleared his throat as he glared at them over his shoulder.

Did the dragon shifter think he owned her? Lennie felt a surge of rebelliousness and lifted her chin. "Don't mind us. I consider Bran a good friend."

With a huff, Sergei yanked at his horse's reins, then charged away at a gallop.

When she glanced at Bran, he was watching her intently. Warmth invaded her cheeks. "Of course, I'll completely understand if you'd rather not accept my offer of friendship—"

"I want it."

The determined glint in his eyes brought more heat to her face. "Very well, then." She should draw away from him, she knew it, but dammit, why *couldn't* she have a friend who was supportive and easy to talk to? And handsome as hell. Goddesses help her, she wanted it, too. "My name is Lennie."

His mouth curled up with a slow smile. "It suits you."

Her heart tightened in her chest. Dear goddesses, she *was* falling for this man. She needed to stop it but wasn't sure how.

Oh, you do know how. All she had to do was tell him she was the dragon who had caused him to crash, or that she was a princess who would never be allowed to marry a man whose father and uncle had caused death and destruction in their twisted attempt to take over the world. Whatever she was feeling or suspected he was feeling, whatever this strange sensation that kept tugging them closer together, she could put a stop to it here and now.

All she had to do was open her mouth and speak the truth. She could doom their relationship.

Or she could stay silent and let it grow.

Chapter 12

They were being awfully quiet, Bran thought wryly, for a pair of newfound friends. As time slowly trickled by, an awkward silence had fallen over him and his dream girl. *Lennie.*

He glanced at her. She was focused on the road in front of them, a frown causing a slight crease between her dark brows. No doubt she was worried about her brother and the Norveshki king. Bran understood that too well. His own worry for Zane had left him tense and frustrated.

Glancing up at the sky, he estimated it was near midnight now. Somewhere soon, three men would die. Behind him, in the wagon bed, Bertram had prayed until he'd worn himself out. He now slept, an occasional moan escaping his lips.

Terrance and Sergei were managing to stay alert, but Sebastian and the two women were drooping on their mounts. Even their horses looked half asleep.

Beside him, Lennie shifted once more on the bench. He was still sitting close to her to hold the reins, so every time she moved, he felt it. Even the slightest brush against his arm or shoulder caused a crackle of energy to sizzle through him, and that left him feeling sharply alive and singed with an ever-increasing need for . . . something. For *her*, he realized with gritted teeth. It was odd, but the more worried he became over their brothers, the more intensely aware he became of her. Her every movement, her every sigh, even her breathing incited his longing for her. His ache for her.

Being friends would never be enough.

His feelings were far ahead of hers, he realized. He'd had five months to dream about her. In his dreams, she'd been a kind, angelic force that had given him support and comfort. Now, in real life, she'd wakened a strong physical desire.

But desire was only the beginning. A powerful need was surging inside him, a need to care for her and protect her. After all the support and comfort she'd given him, it was now his turn to give it back.

A loud bellowing noise jerked him fully awake and caused Lennie to gasp. A small group of men wearing dark clothes and feathered caps poured onto the road to form a semicircle about thirty yards in front of them. Each one had nocked an arrow into his longbow, all pointed at Bran and his companions.

He pulled the wagon to a stop.

Sergei, still on horseback, whipped out his sword.

"You'll be dead before you can use that," warned the man with the longest feather in his cap.

He must be the leader of these highwaymen, Bran thought. He stood in the center of their line with three men to each side.

"We are on business for the king," Lennie announced in a strong voice, pulling out her royal travel pass. "I suggest you leave now before you pay the consequences."

The leader guffawed, and his companions joined in. "Oh, I'm so afraid!" the leader sneered. "The pretty lady is threatening us with . . . consequences!"

"Not the dreaded consequences!"

"I'm shaking in my boots!"

"Ha! I've got a big consequence for her." One of the highwaymen rubbed an arrow against his breeches.

The men continued to laugh, then abruptly hushed when the leader lifted his hand.

He narrowed his eyes. "Don't let our jolliness fool you. If you don't hand over your wagon and horses, we will kill each and every one of you."

"Captain," one of his men whined, "we could use some new women in our camp."

"Those are the prettiest womenfolk I've seen in ages," lisped another who was missing half his teeth.

Bertram scrambled to his feet in the wagon bed. "You should be ashamed of yourself!"

The leader simply aimed his arrow at the priest while the other men chuckled.

Bran rose to his feet to block any arrows meant for Bertram. When Lennie stood beside him, he glanced at her, then noted at the edge of his vision that Terrance was using their cover to dismount and nock an arrow into his bow.

"We're on an important mission," Bran told the highwaymen, attempting to keep their attention focused on him. "If you cooperate, the king will see fit to offer you—"

Terrance ran to the side of their group and let his arrow fly. It zinged toward the men at lightning speed, pierced right through the first man's cap, then the second one, and on down the line, curving neatly around the semicircle until all seven caps had been skewered on the wooden shaft. Then with a motion of his hand, Terrance brought the arrow back to him and nabbed it.

The seven highwaymen stared at him, dumbfounded. A few even patted the top of their heads as if they couldn't believe he'd just scalped them all with one arrow.

Terrance dropped the cap-laden arrow at his feet and nocked a new one. "This time I'll aim about ten inches lower."

The leader gasped. "Kill him!"

One of the highwaymen turned to aim at Terrance, but

Sergei blew a blast of fire at him, incinerating his bow and arrow.

"Run away!" The highwaymen scattered in all directions, bumping into one another and dropping their weapons in their haste to escape.

Sergei charged after them, breathing fire.

"Oh, my biscuits are burning!" One of the thieves swatted at his breeches to put out the flames.

They disappeared deep into the woods.

Bran turned to give Terrance a grin. He'd always wanted to see the man's Embraced power in action. Terrance's skill was well known around the monastery, so no one ever tried anything criminal there.

Roslyn clasped her hands together. "You were magnificent!"

"Why, thank you." Sergei flipped his hair over his shoulder as he rode back to the wagon.

Lennie snorted.

So she wasn't impressed by her dragon suitor, Bran thought with a sigh of relief. With his broken arm, he'd felt humiliated by his inability to protect anyone. Thank the Light Sergei and Terrance had been with them.

Terrance leaned over to pick up the arrow full of caps. "We should clean up the mess they made."

Everyone dismounted and added the highwaymen's discarded weapons to their own stash in the wagon. Terrance made sure the woods alongside the road were safe; then the women slipped in to relieve themselves. When it was the men's turn, Bran was further embarrassed that he needed Father Bertram's help to rebutton his breeches.

A feminine shout caused them all to dash back to the wagon.

"What's wrong?" Bran demanded when he saw Lennie's pale face.

"King Silas has contacted her," Roslyn whispered.

Sergei shook back his long mane of black hair. "Of course, I can hear him, too."

"Is the king all right?" Terrance asked.

"What's happening?" Sebastian asked.

Sergei lifted a hand to halt the questions, then in a smug tone said, "Later. Right now, I need to listen."

Bran suppressed an urge to wipe the dragon's arrogant smirk off his face. "Lennie will tell us when she's able."

Sergei's eyes narrowed. "Who told you her name?"

"She did." Ignoring the dragon's glare, Bran walked over to Lennie.

She was standing still, her hands clenched, her green eyes wide and appearing almost black in the heavy darkness surrounding them. The three lanterns had run low on oil, one of them guttering so much it cast ominous flashes of light and shadow across everyone's faces. Terrance and Milena went to work, quietly refilling the lanterns with oil. And still, Lennie was quiet, her gaze unfocused as if she were miles away.

Then she blinked and took a deep breath. Everyone gathered around to hear the news.

She gave them a quick smile that didn't reach her eyes. "The kings Silas and Ulfrid, along with a wounded Aleksi, were taken prisoner by some pirates. They were heavily drugged, which is why the dragons couldn't communicate. When they woke up, they managed to escape. Ulfrid and Aleksi are onboard the ship with Gwennore. Silas and the other dragons are flying about, breathing fire on any pirate ships they can find. When Leo arrives with the army tomorrow, they will hunt down any pirates on land."

"So my father is safe?" Roslyn asked.

Lennie nodded. "The kings are all right, but . . ." She looked away, her eyes glistening with tears.

"But not the princes," Terrance whispered.

"Reynfrid?" Roslyn stumbled back and Terrance grabbed on to her.

"Zane," Bertram whispered, and Milena's knees gave out as she slumped onto the ground.

Bran closed his eyes as the harsh truth hit him. With the three older captives safe, it became more likely that the brothers were the ones doomed to die.

A soft hand enveloped his, and he opened his eyes to find Lennie watching him sadly.

He gave her hand a squeeze. "Let's get back onto the road."

She nodded. "Yes."

They kept traveling, worn and weary. Lennie knew they wouldn't make it in time, but she couldn't bring herself to order a halt for the night. Rolling themselves up all warm and cozy in blankets and bedrolls seemed heartless when their loved ones could be dying. She and the others were exhausted, but their frazzled nerves were keeping them awake.

She brushed away a mosquito that buzzed by her ear. The lanterns were lighting their way, but unfortunately attracting insects. Bran was still seated beside her, taking turns handling the reins. He didn't say much. What could anyone say? She glanced once again at the night sky.

"It must be past midnight," Bran said softly.

She nodded. "I—" She stiffened when she heard a voice in her head.

Your Highness, we have arrived at Dominic's camp.

"Your brother?" Bran asked, taking the reins from her so she could focus.

She shook her head. "Anton." *What news do you have?*

Dominic sent his men out to search for the shield. When several didn't return, they went looking for them. Three of his soldiers are dead. Frozen to death.

Lennie gasped and reached to the side, her hand landing on Bran's thigh. He stiffened, his eyes growing wide with alarm. In her shock, she struggled to make sense of Anton's words. So the three soldiers were the ones doomed by Father Bertram's prediction? *Any news of the captives?*

No. We can't find them. Can't find the shield, either. Quentin and I are flying about, but we can't see anything in the dark. We believe the captives are well. Dominic thinks that if Greer had killed them, he would have left them for us to find, as he did with the soldiers.

I understand. Thank you, Anton. Keep me updated.

A pleasure to serve, Your Highness.

"Is it bad news?" Bran's voice was low and tense.

"We think the brothers are all right." Relief flooded his face, and Lennie raised her voice so everyone could hear. "I just heard from Anton. We believe the brothers are safe."

Gasps and cries of relief circled their small group. Bran pulled the wagon to a stop, and everyone drew close.

"I guess the priest was wrong, then." Sergei cast Father Bertram an annoyed look. "We were worried for nothing."

"He wasn't wrong," Lennie muttered. "You heard Anton, too."

"Are you sure Reynfrid is all right?" Roslyn asked.

"And Zane?" Milena added.

Lennie glanced at Father Bertram, whose face was still solemn as if he knew bad news was coming. "You said only three, right?" She winced at how heartless it sounded. When the priest nodded, she confessed, "We're assuming the captives are alive because three others have died. Dominic's soldiers. Frozen to death."

Everyone gasped again.

"Greer, again," Bran grumbled.

"Those poor boys." Bertram made the sign of the Light. "They had parents, perhaps even wives and children."

"Oh, this is terrible," Roslyn whispered.

Silence fell over the group as they all wrestled with the fact that three innocent men had died. And there was something else wrong, Lennie thought, though as emotionally and physically exhausted as she was, she couldn't quite grasp it.

"Let's find a place to stop for the night," Bran suggested, and everyone agreed.

As Bran drove the wagon, he glanced over at Lennie. "You're still worried about your brother, aren't you?"

She nodded, and then the problem suddenly became clear. "The shield. It kept the soldiers out, but it also kept Greer inside."

"Ah. So the shield had to be lowered for Greer to kill those three soldiers."

"Right." The fear she'd been dealing with for hours flared back to life. "If the shield is down, why doesn't Pendras contact me?"

"I'm sure he's all right, Lennie. There could be many reasons for his silence. He might have been drugged as the kings were. Or maybe the shield went back up right after the men were murdered."

She bit her lip. "I hope you're right."

The hooves of Sergei's horse made a clattering noise as he passed over a wooden bridge.

"There's a stream up ahead," Bran said. "That will make a good place to stop."

After crossing the bridge, Bran pulled the wagon into a small pasture. Everyone dismounted and took care of the horses. Terrance suggested they remove the crates from the wagon and let the women sleep there while the men camped out on the ground.

Everyone agreed and began the process of unloading the wagon. The baskets of food were fairly light, but the two long crates containing weapons were heavy. When Terrance hefted one over his shoulder, Roslyn gasped.

"Oh, my! You're so strong!" She followed him to where he set it down.

"That's nothing." Sergei seized the second crate and pumped it into the air over his head as he gave Lennie a knowing smirk. "Light as a feather."

Lennie refrained from mentioning the sweat beading his brow or the red color infusing his cheeks. She was not in the mood to be impressed. The hours of weary travel coupled with the almost unbearable tension of worrying if her father or brother would die tonight, or if she and her companions would die at the hands of highwaymen, only to find herself shamefully relieved when three other innocent men were killed—it was all too much.

"I'm going to the stream to wash up," Lennie said, blinking back tears that suddenly wanted to break loose. "Please continue to set up camp. Get some sleep. Terrance, will you take the first watch?"

"Aye, Captain."

"Do you need company?" Milena asked her.

"No." Lennie shook her head. "I wish to be alone." As she rushed through the woods, the tears began to fall. Thank the Light, her father had escaped. And her brother had to be all right. But three other men had died. She pressed a hand to her mouth to suppress a sob. What a terrible world was this when she had to celebrate her brother's survival at the cost of another man's life.

She reached the stream and leaned over to splash cold water on her face. The world had goodness in it, too. She had to remember that. Goodness and love. She sent up a prayer for the families of the three who had died.

Settling on top of a knee-high boulder, she took a deep breath and watched the moons and stars. She couldn't give up. As long as evil roamed the world of Aerthlan, she would fight it. Sometimes the cost would seem too high. The valleys too deep. The fear too vast. But giving up was never an option.

The sound of a twig snapping made her jump to her feet.

"Relax," Sergei said in Norveshki. "It's just me."

With a sigh, she sat back down. "I made it clear I wanted to be alone."

"You're upset—I can understand that." Sergei approached slowly. "I was tense, too, worrying about Silas and Pendras. It must have been even harder for you."

Lennie groaned inwardly. Listening to Sergei's attempt to be sensitive was awkward. "I'm fine. Go get some sleep. You'll have the second watch."

"Actually . . ." He came closer and planted a boot on a two-foot-high boulder, presumably to display a thickly muscled thigh. He lifted his chin, gifting her with the full view of his stunning profile. "I thought you might appreciate some assistance in releasing the tremendous amount of tension you must be feeling."

He'd assumed an impressive pose, Lennie thought, but he wasn't making any sense. "I'm not following."

"Of course not." He crossed his arms over his massive chest while he gave her an amused, indulgent look. "You're still an innocent maid."

"I'm only a year younger than you."

"But years behind in experience." He smirked. "I say that in all fondness of you, my dear. I wouldn't have you any other way."

Lennie gritted her teeth. "And you have years of experience?"

"Of course. I had to make sure I could bring a high level of expertise to our marriage bed. I'm sure you'll thank me someday."

"I have never agreed to marry you."

He waved a dismissive hand. "Never fear, you will. But now, my sweet, I humbly offer you my services. I know certain methods that will greatly alleviate the tension you are currently experiencing."

"You wish to fornicate in the mud along this stream?"

He stiffened. "Holy Light, no!"

"On the rocks, then?"

He sputtered. "I don't intend to take you until we are married. I meant . . . other ways of bringing you pleasure."

"Ah." Lennie nodded knowingly, although she had no idea what he meant. "I think I will do something to please myself."

His eyes lit up. "Really? Can I watch?"

"No. What will please me is for you to leave."

He scoffed. "I should have known you were jesting. An innocent like you would never know—"

"Leave!" Lennie rose to her feet.

"Oh, Lennie!" Roslyn called from the nearby trees. "Do you mind if we join you?"

Milena emerged from the trees first, carrying a set of saddlebags. "We wanted to wash up before going to sleep."

"Indeed." Roslyn stepped out and gave Sergei a dismissive look. "We need to be alone to attend to our needs."

Sergei's jaw shifted. "Of course." He bowed, then strode back toward camp.

Roslyn dashed over to Lennie's side. "Are you all right?"

"Of course." Lennie glanced at the woods to make sure Sergei was gone.

Milena set the saddlebags on the boulder formerly graced with Sergei's boot and opened one of the pouches. "There are washcloths and toothbrushes here."

"Excellent!" Roslyn headed for some nearby bushes. "I'll be right back."

Milena handed Lennie a wood-handled toothbrush. "We were going to leave you alone and wash up a bit downstream, but Bran begged us to check on you. He saw Sergei follow you and was worried. Are you truly all right?"

"Yes." Lennie glanced toward the camp. Bran had worried about her?

"You and Bran seem to get along remarkably well."

"I suppose." Lennie stuck the toothbrush in her mouth so she wouldn't be expected to say more.

"I am exhausted!" Roslyn announced as she emerged from the bushes. "I don't think I've ever ridden so long." She washed her hands, then waggled a washcloth in the stream. "I feel like I have a pound of grit on my face."

Lennie finished brushing and rinsed out her mouth.

"So much excitement, though," Roslyn continued as she scrubbed her face. "Wasn't it amazing how Terrance handled those awful highwaymen?"

"It certainly was," Milena agreed as she washed her face. "I had no idea Terrance had such a formidable gift."

"I know!" Roslyn stuck a toothbrush in her mouth.

Lennie took the last washcloth to clean her face. "Why did he leave Benwick Academy? He was such a good instructor."

Roslyn plucked the toothbrush from her mouth. "I don't know. I'm dying to find out."

"Then ask him." Lennie scrubbed her face and neck.

"Shall I?" Roslyn glanced toward the camp.

Milena smiled. "You're obviously taken with him."

"Who, me?" Roslyn looked indignant, and Milena snickered as she brushed her teeth.

"Why would I—" Roslyn started, then halted with a grimace. "All right, I admit it. I've been smitten with him for years. It broke my heart when I returned to Benwick and he wasn't there."

"So you went home and got engaged to someone else?" Lennie asked.

"Not immediately," Roslyn muttered as she returned her toiletry items to the saddlebag. "It took about a year." She heaved a sigh. "I tried to forget about him, but I couldn't."

"Thank the Light the wedding didn't happen." Lennie shoved her items into the saddlebag.

"True." Roslyn's shoulders slumped. "I feel so stupid. How could Terrance ever like someone like me?"

"Are you jesting?" Lennie gave her an incredulous look. "The man practically worships you."

Roslyn's eyes lit up. "Do you think so? Do you think my father could accept him?"

That might be a problem, Lennie thought. "Well, he's helping us rescue the crown prince, so that should bring him favor."

"Quite frankly, I believe his gift is being underused at the monastery," Milena remarked. "He would make an excellent captain of the guard at Lourdon Palace. When we return, I shall plead his case to the queen."

"Oh, thank you!" Roslyn gave her a quick hug. "And what about you, Milena? You must truly care for my brother if you're going through all this hardship."

Milena's mouth dropped open. "Well . . ."

"Come now." Roslyn grinned and nudged her with an elbow. "I know for a fact that Reynfrid used to take a new bouquet of roses to his bedchamber every day. I teased him about it unmercifully, accusing him of studying flower arrangement instead of swordsmanship. He finally admitted the roses were merely an excuse. He was going to the garden every day because he knew you were there."

Milena's cheeks blushed. "He . . . he said that?"

"Yes! He was terribly fond of you." Roslyn's grin faded. "But then you stopped going to the garden. You didn't even answer his letters."

Milena winced. "I had no wish to hurt his feelings."

"Then you do care for him?" Roslyn asked.

"My feelings don't matter." Milena picked up the saddlebags. "I'm a servant. An orphan. I'm entirely unsuitable and you know it." She strode back toward the camp.

"Wait!" Roslyn waved good-bye at Lennie, then darted after Milena.

Lennie heaved a sigh. She hated to admit it, but Milena was right. There would be many Tourinians, perhaps even the king, who would oppose the crown prince's interest in her. Whoever Reynfrid married would become the next queen. It was much like Lennie's own situation. For hundreds of years, the Norveshki people had always been ruled by a dragon shifter. Whenever she married, her groom would have to be a dragon. Her people would never accept anything else.

But how could she accept Sergei or Anton? The walls kept closing in, making her feel thoroughly trapped. There weren't that many dragons to begin with, and unfortunately, Sergei and Anton were the only ones who were single and available. She had to marry one or the other.

Or neither, she thought with a growing surge of rebelliousness. She could remain single, and Pendras would be her heir. For now, it was the only escape route she could think of. But it also meant she would be doomed to a life of loneliness. No husband and no children.

That wasn't an escape. It was just a different sort of prison.

With a groan, she headed back to camp.

Chapter 13

Bran hadn't been able to help very much with only one working arm, but soon, the men had the camp set up. Two bedrolls had been spread in the wagon bed for the women to sleep on, with blankets for warmth. On the ground, the oil-cloth tarp had been staked, then the remaining four bedrolls placed upon the dry surface.

The lamps had been put out and the food baskets covered. Fully armed, Terrance began his watch by marching around the perimeter of the meadow. After spotting Sergei slinking off into the woods in the same direction Lennie had gone, Bran had asked Roslyn and Milena to make sure she was all right.

Father Bertram had settled into a bedroll and fallen fast asleep, but Sebastian drew Bran aside for a quiet talk.

"Did you see what happened when Quentin came?" Sebastian whispered. "Sergei made some sort of mistake, and Princess Roslyn tried to cover for him."

Bran groaned. "I don't remember that. My mind was on Zane."

Sebastian snorted. "As far as I can tell, your mind is mostly focused on the Norveshki captain."

Bran gritted his teeth. "So?"

"Now you're gnashing your teeth again."

"Because I'm annoyed!"

"You're not the only one." Sebastian leaned closer. "I'm telling you there is more to her than we know."

"Fine. And I'm telling you that what I do know about her is all good."

Sebastian frowned. "She's keeping secrets."

"If she is, it's probably for the usual reason—she has something embarrassing to hide. But I don't care."

"You should. I'm worried about you."

"Save your worry for Zane. And get some sleep."

Sebastian sighed. "You, too. You must be in pain from sitting up for so long."

Bran shrugged. He *was* in pain, but he wasn't going to lie down until he knew Lennie was safe. "Go ahead, Father. I'll be along soon."

"Very well." Sebastian patted him on the back, then trudged over to the bedrolls to sleep next to Bertram.

Sergei returned with a sour look on his face, which Bran interpreted as good news. Hopefully, Lennie had told him to get lost. The dragon shifter took the bedroll on the far end of the tarp.

Bran wandered toward the edge of the woods and found a large oak tree to lean against. In the distance he could hear an owl hooting, then the sound of female voices. After a short wait, Milena and Roslyn passed by as they returned to camp. In the dark, they didn't see him, so he stepped into their view.

"Oh, goodness!" Roslyn pressed a hand to her chest. "You gave me a start."

"I apologize." He gave the princess a small bow. "Did you see the captain?"

"Yes, indeed." Roslyn sidled up close and lowered her voice. "You were right to send us. They were speaking in Norveshki, but I could understand it." She aimed a disgusted look at the sleeping Sergei. "He was behaving like an arse."

Bran's jaw clenched.

"The captain handled it well," Milena added. She motioned toward the wagon. "Go ahead, Your Highness. I'll be along soon."

Roslyn yawned. "Good night." With a wave of her hand, she trudged toward the wagon.

Milena dropped the saddlebags she was carrying onto the ground, then drew him into the woods a short distance so they could speak in private. "How are you feeling? Should I change your bandages? Or give you more of that potion?"

Bran smiled. "You don't need to mother me." He glanced toward the stream. "You left her there alone?"

"She wanted to be alone." Milena tilted her head, attempting to study him in the dark. "Do you truly care about her?"

He dragged a hand through his hair, then admitted, "Yes."

Milena took a deep breath that ended with a frown.

"Is there something you need to tell me?" Bran grumbled. "Sebastian keeps warning me about her."

"What does he say?"

"Nothing. He's suspicious for no good reason."

"There must be a reason—"

"Bertram made a prediction about a mystery woman who would be more than she claimed to be or some such nonsense. It has Sebastian imagining that Lennie is hiding some dark, nefarious secret."

Milena paused, then asked, "You call her by her name now?"

He noticed his sister didn't deny there was a secret. That was annoying. "Why shouldn't I? We've become good friends."

Milena was silent, frowning at a nearby tree. She knew something, Bran thought, so why wouldn't she tell him?

Footsteps sounded nearby, and Bran, with his superior raven eyes, spotted Lennie headed their way. "She's coming."

Milena turned as the captain emerged into view. "Ah, there you are. I'll head off for bed now. Good night." She strode through the narrow stretch of woods to reach the meadow.

"How are you feeling now?" Bran asked.

"I'm fine." Lennie watched as Milena retrieved the saddlebags, then headed toward the wagon. "You two seem to know each other."

He shrugged in a nonchalant manner. "We're all getting to know each other on this trip." Hopefully, no one would ever know that Milena had originally been planted in Lourdon Palace as a spy for the Brotherhood. With the death of her father, Master Lorne, her spying days were thankfully over, but still, if the truth ever came out, it would put her in danger. "Lady Milena and I have found something we agree about."

Lennie's eyes narrowed. "What is that?"

"We don't like your dragon suitors. We think you deserve better."

She scoffed. "There is no need for you to discuss my personal life."

"But didn't we decide to be friends?"

She gave him a frustrated look. "True, but even so, we just met in person yesterday."

"I met you five months ago."

"You saw me asleep. That hardly constitutes—"

"I held you close to my heart all that time. So when I see two clowns trying to win your affections, I find it hard to like them. More importantly, I don't think you like them, either."

She snorted. "I never said that."

"You say it with every annoyed look you give them, with every irritated sigh or groan. Even now, at the mere thought of them, you are grinding your teeth."

She opened her mouth, then closed it with a wince.

"If you don't like them, Lennie, reject them."

"It's not that simple."

"It should be. Can you love one of them? Respect him? See yourself happy living with him?"

She closed her eyes briefly, then shook her head. "No."

"Then tell them that. No."

"There are other factors—"

"More important than your happiness?"

"It's complicated. I have duty, responsibility, and honor to consider, and part of my happiness is tied to those virtues. If I choose a dishonorable path in order to pursue my personal happiness, I will end up with neither joy nor honor."

Did she truly feel that trapped? Bran wondered. What could be so important that it would force her to marry a man she didn't like? "Lennie, I don't know all the circumstances involved, but I can tell you what it is like to live your life with a shroud of despair weighing down on you. I would never wish that kind of misery on anyone, especially you."

Her eyes softened. "That part of your life is over now. You shouldn't ever be miserable again. You should be happy."

"You should be happy, too." He gave her a teasing smile. "If you find the man you want, you should grab him."

She laughed. "Are you suggesting I pounce on some poor unsuspecting man and take him against his will?"

"Ha! If he's that easily subdued, then he's not worthy of you." His smile faded. "Though he might gladly surrender if he is willing."

Her face sobered as the air around them grew thick with tension. The owl in the distance stopped hooting. Even the wind died off, no longer rustling leaves and branches. A still-ness fell around them as if they were alone in the world with nothing but forest around them and the stars and moons overhead.

She gave him a quick, nervous glance. "How can a woman know if a man is willing?"

"There are signs." He took a step toward her, and her eyes widened. "He will try to be close to her."

She lowered her gaze to his chest, then looked away. "Wouldn't it be simpler if he just confessed?"

"Perhaps, but I think he will wait."

"Why?"

"To see if she is willing."

She scoffed. "The two will reach an impasse if neither one is daring enough to take action."

His mouth twitched. "Your military training is showing." When she shrugged, he added, "Then maybe she should be daring and pounce on him after all."

"Ha!" Her chin lifted. "Maybe you should follow your own advice. If you see the woman you want, *you* should grab her."

"I intend to." He moved closer until he was only inches away. "But first I need to ask: Are you willing?"

She blinked, then retreated a step. "I-I have to think about this."

"What is there to think about? Unless you're trying to come up with reasons why you should not follow your heart."

"It's not that simple."

"It *is* simple. You either feel the same sort of deep, irreversible longing that I am feeling, or you do not."

Her eyes glistened as a tear threatened to escape. "Is that a confession?"

"It is. Lennie, I can't see you without wanting to touch you." He brushed a thumb across her cheekbone to catch the tear. "And I can't touch you without wanting to kiss you."

She searched his eyes, then flung an arm around his neck and pressed her mouth against his.

His heart soared. His angel was kissing him. She'd followed her heart and pounced. But far too quickly she broke the kiss and released him.

"I shouldn't have—" she began, but he pulled her close with his left arm.

"No regrets." He gave her a quick kiss, then drew back only slightly, hovering over her mouth, longing for her to respond.

Their breaths mingled. He moved in slowly and her mouth opened to meet his. *Yes.* He kissed her slowly, languidly, tenderly. She reached for him, her arms slipping beneath his cloak so her hands glided over his bare flesh. When her fingers encountered the scarred skin on his back, she groaned against his mouth.

"Lennie." He planted kisses along her jaw, then nipped at her ear.

With a gasp, she stiffened and pulled back.

A frisson of alarm shot through him. "Did I hurt you? Holy Light, I—"

"It's Pendras!"

"Your brother's talking to you? Is he all right? What about Zane?"

She nodded. "They're fine." She lifted a hand to halt his questions, and her brow puckered as she concentrated on her brother's voice.

Bran took her hand to lead her through the trees to the meadow. She moved alongside him as if in a trance, her gaze unfocused. When they reached the meadow, he stopped. Moonlight filtered down on her face, pale and ghostly as if her spirit was miles away.

Bertram and Sebastian were sound asleep, but Sergei had sat up. No doubt he was listening in. The women in the wagon seemed to be asleep. Bran motioned for Terrance to join them.

"What is it?" Terrance asked as he noted the glazed look on Lennie's face. "She's talking to someone?"

"Her brother," Bran whispered.

"*He was asleep?*" Sergei shouted as he rose to his feet. "Of all the idiotic . . ."

Lennie blinked, taking note of Sergei's angry outburst. "Pendras was pretending to sleep while he waited for the shield to fall. He had to wait so long, he dozed off for a little while. No harm was done."

Bran nodded. "I'm sure he was exhausted."

"It was dereliction of duty," Sergei snarled.

"Enough!" Lennie glared at the dragon shifter. "Be quiet so I can listen." She glanced at Bran and Terrance. "The captives are fine. Pendras is giving a full report to my father—"

"Your father?" Bran asked. "Then he's a dragon, too?"

Her eyes widened with alarm.

Sergei scoffed. "You've done it now."

She gritted her teeth. "I'll explain everything later. I need to listen for now." She turned away, frowning.

Sergei plunked down on his bedroll and aimed a smirk at Bran.

What the hell was this about? Bran wondered. Had Lennie come close to revealing her secret? Not much of a secret if it was just that her father was a dragon. Her brother was one, and as far as Bran knew, all dragon shifters inherited the gift from their fathers. Why bother to keep something so obvious a secret?

"Shall we wake everyone up so they can hear the latest news?" Terrance asked.

Bran shook his head as he looked around the camp. "They fell asleep believing the captives were safe. That has not changed, so let them rest while they can. Dawn will break in just a few hours."

He glanced at Lennie. Just moments ago, she'd been in his arms, kissing him, and he'd thought they'd reached an understanding. But now, he wondered about the things he didn't know. What was she keeping secret? Was it powerful enough to break the connection between them?

*   *   *

Hours later, Pendras woke with a start when cold water was dumped on his head.

"Wake up, dragon!" Roland tossed a piece of bread at him.

Pendras sat up, pretending to be bleary-eyed while he quickly took note of his surroundings. He was still fettered at one wrist and ankle. Reynfrid and Zane were, too. They were awake and eating. The barn doors were open, and the sky had lightened to murky, predawn gray.

He wiped the straw and dust from his piece of stale bread and tore off a bite. As he chewed, he glanced at their captors. They were busy saddling their horses, paying him no mind. He sat up when he noticed three more horses just outside the door.

Had three more villains come? He glanced around quickly, but saw only Greer, Roland, and Kasper.

Father? Lennie? No answer, so he figured Kasper had the shield up again.

Another prick of guilt needled him and he tore off a second bit of bread with more force than necessary. *Dammit.* He still felt ashamed about dozing off last night.

He groaned inwardly. He had deserved a much harsher reprimand than he'd received. His parents and Lennie were so happy to hear he was all right, they'd hardly fussed at all. But he knew it was inexcusable. No wonder his parents had decided that Lennie should inherit the throne. She never made mistakes like this.

A few noblemen had approached him after his parents' decision to see if he planned on accepting their decree. They seemed disappointed that he had. He had thought them ridiculous. Had they really thought he would defy his parents, betray his sister, and plunge the country into turmoil, even civil war, over a bruised ego? The truth was, no matter how disappointed he might be, he still loved his sister. He was proud of her. She was the first female dragon ever. She was brave and clever. And right now, she was proving herself the better choice.

After making a full report, Pendras had been relieved to hear that his father had escaped. As far as he knew, Greer was not aware that the kings were safe and that the dragons had burned every pirate ship in sight. Later today, King Leo would be arriving with the Tourinian army to destroy the rest of the pirates.

Lennie had told him of her progress and that she planned to meet up with Dominic today. Anton had confirmed that Dominic had lost three soldiers last night. Greer had frozen them to death.

Pendras glanced again at the three new horses. Yes, the saddles and saddlebags looked like standard issue from the Tourinian army. Greer had killed the three soldiers for their horses.

Damn it to hell. Those men had died just so Greer would find it easier to transport his prisoners. Pendras caught Reynfrid's eyes and motioned with his head toward the horses. Reynfrid nodded, anger simmering in his eyes.

The young one, Zane, was eating his bread and ignoring them.

"Let's go," Greer ordered.

Kasper nocked an arrow and pointed it at Reynfrid's chest while Roland approached Pendras with a long rag that stank of rancid oil.

"Be a good little dragon or the prince dies," Roland snarled as he unlocked the fetters binding Pendras's wrist. He tied Pendras's hands together behind his back, then looped the oily rag around his neck, stuffing the ends in his mouth. "That'll keep you from breathing fire."

"The shield is in place," Greer warned them. "So even if you break free, you can't escape. I killed three last night. I have no problem killing three more."

All they could do, Pendras thought, was bide their time and wait for the right opportunity.

Soon, the villains had their captives seated on the three new horses, their hands bound to the saddle horn and their feet to the stirrups. The reins of each new horse were tied to a horse being ridden by one of the captors.

At least he could see today, Pendras thought as they headed across the hilly countryside. No road in sight, but Greer seemed to know where they were going. The first golden rays of the sun burst over the horizon to his right, a confirmation that they were traveling north. To Earl Freydor's land, Lennie had told him. The hills would increase in size as the day went on until they reached the mountains.

Lennie's last words came back to him now. *Stay alive,* she had told him. *Make yourself too valuable for Greer to kill.*

He had all day to figure out a plan.

Chapter 14

"You heard from Pendras?" Roslyn's excited voice rose in volume, waking Lennie from a deep slumber. "When was this? Where are they? How is Reynfrid?"

Still blurry-eyed, Lennie pushed herself to a sitting position in the wagon bed. Everyone seemed to be awake and gathered around the food baskets breaking their fast as they listened to Sergei.

"Pendras contacted us a few hours ago," he reported quietly. "The captives are fine. They spent the night in an abandoned barn."

Lennie blinked. Why was Sergei giving the report? That was her job. With a gasp, she realized the sun was up. "We should be on the road by now!"

"Oh, you're up." Roslyn gave her an injured look. "You should have wakened us when Pendras contacted you."

"It's *his* fault." Sergei pointed at Bran, who was still fast asleep on the ground. "He insisted on letting everyone sleep."

"And he was right." Milena shot Sergei an annoyed look. "We already knew the captives were safe, so being well rested was more important."

"I agree," Lennie muttered, noting that Sergei was eager to disparage Bran while Milena was quick to defend him. Whatever was motivating them, she would deal with it later. For now, they needed to get moving.

She suppressed a rush of anger as she pulled on her boots. If Sergei had wakened her as he'd been ordered to, they wouldn't be running late now. This delay might mean they would not catch up with Dominic by nightfall. "We should have left over an hour ago. Everyone, finish eating and prepare for departure. As soon as we're on the road, I'll tell you everything Pendras said."

As her companions darted busily about, Lennie slipped off the wagon and strode toward Sergei. "I told you I had the last watch. You were supposed to wake me up."

He gave her a small, patronizing smile. "My dear, it would have been too cruel to wake you when you were so exhausted. I thought it best to—"

"That was not your decision," she snapped.

"Come now." He continued to smile, but there was a glint of hardness in his eyes. "You know once we are married, we will naturally share the burden of decision-making."

Lennie's jaw clenched. He had every intention of taking over, she knew it. And if he couldn't coax her into compliance, he would eventually resort to harsher methods. She stepped close and lowered her voice so no one else could hear. "I am not marrying you."

He hissed in a breath, his smile vanishing and his eyes growing cold. "I sacrificed my own sleep for you. You should appreciate it."

"You should have followed orders."

"You *will* marry me. I'm your only real choice, so get over your childish dreams and accept it."

She moved closer, looking him in the eyes. "I'm being considerate now, keeping this private. Don't make me reject you in public. You will find it humiliating."

Anger seethed in his eyes, and he motioned angrily toward Bran. "Is it because of him? The lazy oaf hasn't even gotten up yet."

"It's not him," Lennie ground out. "It's you. I'd rather live my life single and childless than marry you."

A low growl reverberated in his throat and his hands curled into fists.

"Try it," Lennie hissed. "Try hitting a superior officer. Even your distant relative, General Dimitri Tolenko, will refuse to help you."

Sergei smirked. "I have more support than you know."

"Are you threatening to cause civil strife? I suggest you shut your mouth now before I report you to the king." With her heart pounding, she strode into the forest before the situation could escalate. *Calm down. He's not a real threat. He's a loyal soldier. He's just reacting poorly because he was rejected.*

She drew in a deep breath. *Remember your priorities.* First, she had to rescue her brother, along with Reynfrid and Zane. Greer and his cohorts needed to be captured or killed. For now, she needed Sergei on her side. She would have to make a better effort at getting along with him.

After relieving herself, she washed up in the stream and splashed cold water on her face. Good goddesses, she was so tired, and there was another long day of travel ahead. The mistake she'd made the night before came back to mind, and she winced. Exhaustion coupled with angry frustration had made her more susceptible to error. She'd come close to exposing her father as the Norveshki king.

She strode back toward the camp, but her steps slowed to a stop when she realized she was in the vicinity where Bran had kissed her. *Oh, admit it, you kissed him first.* She must have been out of her mind. No, she had been following her heart. And it had been glorious.

A few seconds was all she could spare, but she took them and let the memory wash over her: the heat of his body, the taste of his lips, and the touch of his hand. The intoxicating war between fear and pleasure, hesitancy and boldness, gentleness and heated passion.

How could she have let it happen? How could she have refrained after his sweet confession? The man intrigued her, attracted her, enticed her, causing all sorts of emotional reactions, ranging from anger to outright desire.

And what should she do now? If she truly cared about him, didn't she owe him the truth? But wouldn't the truth destroy them?

There was no future for them, it pained her to admit. But how could she tell him that when it would hurt him? Hadn't the poor man suffered enough? Feeling the ridges and damaged skin of his scars had made her heart ache. She'd wanted to hold him and kiss all the scars until he understood they were nothing to be ashamed of. They were a testament to his strength, a sign of his victory over the evil men who had stolen his childhood and tried to destroy him.

No future. It hurt her, too. More than she would have ever expected, and that could only mean she did truly care for him. How could she have fallen for him so quickly?

Because it felt so right. The strong attraction had been there from the second she'd laid eyes on him. She couldn't look at him without feeling that attraction reverberate right through her. She was constantly aware of him, his every movement, his every expression. It all drew her in, making her long to be close to him. But as powerful as that longing was, it was only the beginning. Everything they talked about, every decision they made, every emotion they shared, they were in agreement. In harmony with each other, not just in words or thoughts, but in their souls. It felt as if she'd always known him; she'd just been waiting for his arrival.

In her heart, she recognized that this was a rare phenomenon. A precious one, not likely ever to happen again. So how could she let him slip away?

Tears crowded her eyes, but she blinked them away and squared her shoulders. She'd take care of the mission first. Then she would tend to her heart.

She strode back into the meadow. The wagon had been loaded, the horses hitched. She glanced over at the oilcloth tarp. One bedroll remained on top with Bran still sound asleep in it. Father Bertram was standing over him. Her mouth curled up. How was Bran able to sleep through all this commotion? Her smile faded. Was he unconscious? Or worse? Had he been in so much pain, he'd swallowed too much of the special potion?

Her heart clenched in her chest, and she ran toward him.

Father Bertram leaned over to nudge Bran's shoulder. With a gasp, he drew his hand back. "He's burning up!"

A fever? Lennie fell to her knees beside him. Good goddesses, she could feel the heat radiating off him.

Father Sebastian and Milena had rushed over, and she rested a palm against Bran's brow.

"Oh!" Milena lifted her hand. "His fever is dangerously high."

Lennie tamped down a surge of panic. "His wound could be infected. He could . . ." No, she would not let him die. She squeezed his hand, wincing at the heat. "Bran, we'll take care of you. You'll get better. Do you hear me?"

He moaned, his dark brows drawing together.

"Did you bring any medicine that would lower a fever?" Milena asked the priests.

Sebastian shook his head. "Just the special potion, a salve for his stomach wound, and some clean bandages."

Sergei strode toward them, frowning. "We don't have time for this. We can toss him into the wagon and drop him off at the next posting station. They can take care-"

"No." Lennie glared at him. "He stays with us. His brother is one of the captives."

"My angel," Bran moaned. "So beautiful and fearless."

Lennie's heart tightened. Even in pain, he could only say good things about her.

Bertram gave her an apologetic look. "Don't mind him. It's the fever talking."

With a huff, Sergei stalked off.

Lennie's mind raced. Her mother was an excellent healer. What would Gwennore do? "We need fresh water to wash the wound and cool him down. And I think there was a willow tree close to the stream. The bark will alleviate the fever."

"Of course." Milena dashed back to the wagon.

"I'll go to the stream." Roslyn dug into the food basket and found a copper bowl filled with apples. She dumped the apples into the basket. Then, taking the bowl, she and Terrance ran toward the stream.

Milena pulled out her cotton petticoat and tore off more strips. Then she brought them over with a jug of water.

"We need to check his wound." Lennie pulled the knife from her boot. *And pray that it's not infected.* She gently sliced through the knot where the bandages had been tied off.

Meanwhile, Milena drenched a pad of cotton with water and placed it on Bran's brow. He moaned.

She brushed his sweat-dampened hair back from his brow. "Feel better?"

"Milena," he whispered.

"Yes, Bran, I'm here."

They definitely know each other, Lennie thought. *And know each other well.* There was no mistaking the loving touch Milena used as she wiped his face with the cool wet cloth. Gritting her teeth, Lennie slid the knife back into her boot. Bran needed her help now, not a stupid bout of jealousy.

She peeled back the bandage, wincing at the heat coming from his body in waves. "I need him lifted a bit."

Sebastian slipped an arm beneath Bran's shoulders to raise him enough that Lennie could unwrap the bandage. The heat radiating from his body singed the tips of her fingers and made the priest's robe smell like burnt wool. She worked quickly so Sebastian could lower Bran and withdraw his arm. When he did, his wide bell-shaped sleeve fell back, revealing red skin.

Father Bertram clucked. "You may have to put some salve on your arm."

"Oh, dear Light," Lennie whispered in shock.

Bertram sighed. "I know. I've never seen a fever this bad."

"No. Look." Lennie pointed at Bran's wound. Or what should have been the wound. The skin was an angry red, but the edges of the cut had already grown back together so well she could hardly tell where the wound had been. "It looks . . . healed."

"Holy Light! It does," Milena exclaimed.

Bertram gasped. "It's a miracle! Praise the Light!"

"A miracle, yes," Bran mumbled. "She kissed me."

Lennie winced.

"What was that?" Bertram asked, leaning closer.

"My angel kissed me."

Bertram scoffed, then sat back, shaking his head. "The poor boy is delirious."

Milena bit her lip as if she were trying not to smile.

Sebastian glanced at Lennie, and she shrugged as if she were clueless. "Well." He leaned over for a closer look at the wound. "This is astounding. Has Bran always been able to heal this quickly?"

"I don't know." Bertram glanced at Bran. "I've never seen him injured before. Bran?" He leaned closer. "Do you have a special power we don't know about?"

"I can fly."

"Yes, yes, we know that, but can you—"

"I can fall . . ."

"Well, yes," Bertram murmured. "The crash was unfortu—"

". . . in love."

Lennie's breath caught.

Bertram shook his head. "The fever has him completely addled."

Lennie changed the subject. "The fast rate of healing may be part of being a shifter. Dragons are known to recover quickly as well."

"Do they run a fever like this?" Sebastian asked.

"No, but dragons are naturally hot inside because of their fire-breathing capabilities." Lennie tilted her head, studying Bran. "It could be that the fever is part of his healing process."

Sebastian nodded. "Perhaps, but since this wound has already healed, I think we should try to lower the fever."

"I agree." Milena prepared another wet cloth and pressed it against Bran's brow. "I wonder if his broken arm has mended."

Lennie touched his bandaged forearm. The splints were still in place. "I think we should wait a few days. We wouldn't want him to attempt flying too early. The risk of falling—"

"In love," Bran mumbled. "I'm falling in love."

"Oh!" Lennie jumped to her feet. "Here comes the water."

Terrance approached with the copper bowl full of water. He set it on the ground next to Bran, and Milena dumped a few cotton strips into it.

"Here." Roslyn passed Lennie a damp handkerchief folded up like an envelope to hold something. "I peeled off some willow bark and washed it in the stream. Shall we start a fire so you can brew it?"

"I know a faster way." Lennie jammed the handkerchief in a pocket, then ran to the wagon to retrieve a blanket and a pewter tankard from the food basket. Then she sprinted to the stream, filled the tankard with water, dumped in the willow bark, and breathed fire until the tankard was red hot and the water boiling.

Using the blanket to insulate her hands, she carried the hot tankard of willow bark tea back to the meadow.

In her absence, Terrance and Sebastian had carried Bran to the wagon and deposited him on the pallet behind the driver's bench. Milena had covered him with strips of cotton, drenched with cold water from the stream.

Lennie set the blanket-covered tankard close to Bran. "This should steep for a while and cool down before Bran drinks it."

"I'll make sure he takes it," Father Bertram announced as he wedged himself into the narrow space beside Bran. "I'll take care of him while we travel."

Lennie climbed onto the driver's bench and took the reins, while the rest of the group mounted up. Soon, they were back on the King's Way.

They'd come a long distance the night before in the dark, Lennie realized. Now, in daylight, she could see the hills surrounding them and the outline of mountains farther to the north.

She glanced over her shoulder. Father Bertram was placing a freshly wetted cloth on Bran's brow.

I'm falling in love.

Her heart tightened at the recollection of Bran's words. Did she feel the same way? Goddesses help her, she was afraid she did. The panic she had felt at the thought of losing him had been real. She didn't want to live without him.

But she would have to.

With a silent groan, she turned back to face the road ahead of her. The King's Way. It was too reminiscent of her life. She was expected to follow the royal path set out for her. Duty and honor would not allow her to stray from it.

But first, the mission. *Anton,* she called. *Give me a report.*

Yes, Your Highness, he replied right away. *A short while ago, we stopped at the posting station by the village of Green Hill. Dominic arranged for a wagon and driver to take the three dead soldiers back to Lourdon Palace. They'll be traveling south on the King's Way and will pass by you at some point.*

Any news of the captives? Lennie asked. *Or the captors?*

I'm afraid we have lost sight of them, Anton confessed. *Quentin has flown ahead searching for them. I'll let you know what he reports.*

Yes, thank you. Lennie raised her voice to gather everyone around. Terrance and Roslyn guided their horses to the left side of the wagon, while Sebastian and Milena were to the right. Sergei was ahead of them, but slowed his horse so he would be close enough to hear.

Lennie told them what Anton had reported. She glanced over her shoulder to see how Bran was doing. The priest had propped him up so he could drizzle some of the willow bark tea down the patient's throat. Bran swallowed a bit, then lay back down. The fever must be going down, Lennie thought, if Bertram was handling him that easily.

"You were going to tell us about Pendras?" Roslyn prompted.

"Oh, right." Lennie nodded. "Pendras was able to talk to the other two captives last night. He believes Reynfrid might be a bit sore from his horse falling on him, but he refuses to admit it."

"Sounds like my brother," Roslyn muttered.

"And Zane?" Bertram asked.

"He was fine," Lennie said. "Although he was angry at being captured. He told Pendras and Reynfrid to stay out of his way when he kills Greer."

"Sounds like Zane," Sebastian muttered.

"Did he say anything about his captors?" Terrance asked. "How are they keeping the prisoners from escaping?"

Lennie sighed. "Pendras said they were tied up, blind-folded, and tossed over the back of horses all day. So, unfortunately, he couldn't see anything. They keep an oil-soaked gag around him to keep him from breathing fire."

Sergei snorted. "He would end up setting himself ablaze."

Lennie nodded. "And with the shield in place, the prisoners can't really escape. Pendras said the young man who raises the shield is called Kasper. Have you ever heard of him?" she asked Bertram and Sebastian.

"No." They shook their heads.

"Greer is the one in charge, of course," Lennie continued. "The third captor has no special powers other than a propensity for being incredibly rude. His name is Roland."

Milena stiffened in her saddle with a gasp. Her hand flew to her mouth, then she squeezed her eyes shut, leaning forward with a muffled groan.

"Milena!" Sebastian edged his horse closer to hers. "Whatever is wrong?"

"Oh, dear." Bertram gave her a worried look.

How did these priests know her so well? Lennie thought. Bran, too, seemed quite friendly with her. And what had caused her extreme reaction to the mention of Roland?

"I-I'm all right," Milena mumbled, slowly straightening in her saddle. "Something from breakfast didn't agree with me."

She's lying, Lennie thought. Milena was pale, her eyes downcast, her mouth drawn into a tight line. She appeared distraught now, but Lennie had seen her when she'd first reacted. It hadn't been a case of discomfort. Her eyes had been filled with horror.

Silence fell over the group as everyone cast furtive looks at Milena.

Maybe Father Bertram's prediction actually referred to Milena? Lennie wondered. It seemed that the lady-in-waiting was not exactly who she claimed to be.

Sebastian cleared his throat. "Roland used to be the head

priest at the church in Ebton. He's been friends with Greer for years."

"Has Pendras contacted you today?" Terrance asked, drawing her attention to the other side of the wagon. "Can he give us any idea of their current location?"

Lennie shook her head. "I can't communicate with him when the shield is up. Tonight, when Kasper falls asleep, I should hear from my brother again."

"If he can manage to stay awake," Sergei snarled.

Lennie bristled. "He was starved and abused all day. If he succumbed to sleep for an hour or so, it is understandable."

Sergei scoffed, then spurred his horse ahead of the group a short way.

Terrance moved his horse closer to the wagon. "Does he not get along with your brother?"

Lennie shrugged. "They were never close. Pendras is best friends with Dominic." The two princes were both destined to become generals and Lord Protectors of their respective countries.

But Sergei had hopes of becoming king. If he planned on taking over and pushing Lennie into a subservient role, her brother would object and side with her.

Lennie's breath caught. Did Sergei see her brother as a threat? Was this why he was pushing the idea that Pendras was guilty of neglecting his duty? Had Sergei purposely made sure they were late to get started this morning?

Her hands tightened on the reins. She and her team were tasked with the rescue of the captives, but what if Sergei wanted them to fail?

Chapter 15

The second day of travel was proving to be long, weary, and uneventful, Lennie thought. She hated to admit it, but the hours seemed to creep by at a snail's pace without Bran to keep her company. Behind her, Bertram continued to pray and place cool compresses on Bran's brow.

By midmorning, the wagon carrying the three dead soldiers passed by. She called a short halt to their journey so they could pay their respects and offer prayers as the wagon lumbered past. Around noontime, they reached the posting station at Green Hill that Anton had mentioned earlier. After acquiring fresh horses and a quick lunch, they continued north on the King's Way. The hills grew steeper and more numerous, the air increasingly chilly. On the higher hills, small patches of snow had survived in hollows or beneath a grove of trees.

Now in the afternoon, Bertram declared Bran's fever had finally broken. He was sleeping peacefully on the pallet. Whenever Lennie glanced back at him, her heart squeezed. How could he look so wickedly attractive and innocent at the same time? She was torn between the desire to embrace him and the cruel reality that she must never do it again.

Your Highness, Anton called to her. *Quentin has located Greer and the captives.*

Excellent! she replied. *Where are they?*

Since we couldn't find them on the King's Way, we figured

they must have gone off road. Quentin scoured the country-side for hours. He finally spotted them on a small road, hardly more than a footpath, that is headed northwest.

Toward Earl Freydor's land? Lennie asked.

Yes. We just left the posting station in the village of Trey Falls. It's located at the junction of the King's Way and the Coastal Road that heads straight east toward the coast. To the west is the Trey River with the falls. It's a busy place—people are arriving for some sort of celebration. You'll want to stop there for fresh horses and a local guide.

A guide? Lennie asked. *Why?*

According to the stationmaster, once you leave the road, the land is treacherous with cliffs, ravines, and bogs that will swallow you whole. He lent us a guide, so we're headed across the countryside to the path that Greer is on. It winds in a northwesterly direction through a narrow mountain pass that only locals know about. The gorge forms the border be-tween Freydor's land and that belonging to the Duke of Trevelyan.

Lennie considered this, then gave Anton a warning. *Greer could be joined by more men once he reaches Freydor's land. If you follow him into the narrow pass, you run the risk of an ambush.*

That is what Dominic believes, Anton confirmed. *What Greer doesn't know is that we have dragons on our side. The guide says we won't reach the pass until tomorrow after-noon. We are hoping you'll catch up with us before then. Dominic alerted the stationmaster at Trey Falls that you were coming and would need a guide. The village is on the south-ern border of the Duke of Trevelyan's land, and apparently the duke is a longtime enemy of the Earl of Freydor. The vil-lagers actually cheered when they heard the news of the earl's death. They are happy to assist us.*

That is good. Thank you, Anton. We'll catch up with you as soon as we can.

Lennie called everyone to gather around so she could report the news.

"Trevelyan?" Roslyn asked, her face lighting up. "I know him! He's an old friend of my father's. Papa used to call him Five."

"Why would he do that?" Terrance asked.

Roslyn grinned. "They were actually in a competition once for my mother's hand. Papa was called Seven. He won, of course. But then Five turned out to be the Duke of Trevelyan's youngest son, and he brought troops to help my father take back the throne that had been stolen from him."

"And now this Five is the duke?" Lennie asked.

Roslyn nodded, her smile fading. "It was very sad. Five's older brother died in a terrible avalanche."

Lennie recalled that Anton had said the duke and Freydor were enemies. "Roslyn, after we reach Trey Falls, we'll head northwest toward Freydor's land. But if you continue north on the King's Way, you could go to the duke's castle, right?"

Roslyn nodded. "I could. I've been there before, so I know the way."

"Is the duke even there?" Terrance asked. "He didn't go to Lourdon for your wedding?"

"He said he was too ill to attend." Roslyn bit her lip. "But I've heard that he hates Freydor, so maybe he didn't want to come."

"I'm worried that we'll be ambushed in that narrow gorge," Lennie explained. "See if you can persuade the duke to send some soldiers."

Roslyn nodded. "I'm sure he will. He was a general for my father's army until he unexpectedly inherited the title."

"Of course, we can't have you traveling alone," Lennie murmured.

"I'll be honored to accompany Her Highness," Terrance offered quickly, then glanced toward Roslyn with pinkened cheeks. "If that is acceptable to you."

"Of course." Roslyn's cheeks turned a matching shade of pink.

"Then it's settled." Lennie quickly faced front so they wouldn't see her smile.

The sun was lowering in the sky when Lennie heard rustling noises behind her. She looked over her shoulder. Bran had wakened to find Father Bertram sleeping next to him. He sat up and flung his cloak back to look at his wound, now healed and free of its bandage.

He glanced up and met Lennie's gaze.

She blinked, then quickly looked away. Unfortunately, her gaze landed on his chest. With heat surging to her cheeks, she turned to face front.

"The sun is setting," he grumbled behind her. "I've been asleep all day?"

"You were feverish." She took a deep breath, then glanced back at him. "Do you feel better now?"

"Aye. A bit lightheaded."

"You haven't eaten all day."

He leaned over Father Bertram and grabbed an apple out of the food basket. "Would you like one?"

"No thank you." She turned back to the road. Soon, she heard him crunch into his apple.

"And how are you today, Lennie?" he asked softly.

Her heart softened just at the sound of him saying her name. And instantly she was swirled back into the memory of being held and kissed. Good goddesses, how was she going to reject this man?

"You look as beautiful as ever," he answered for her.

Oh, stop being so sweet, she thought sadly.

He climbed onto the bench to sit beside her. Glancing at him, she noticed he was moving easily now and had removed his sling. Only the splints and bandage remained on his right forearm. He took another bite from his apple.

"Do you always heal so quickly?" she asked.

"I don't know. I've never crashed before." He lifted his right arm over his head. "I think I'll be able to fly soon."

And fly away, she thought drearily. Once this mission was over, she should never see him again.

"What did I miss while I slept?" He took one last bite from the apple, then tossed the core into the woods.

She told him what was happening with Dominic, and how Roslyn and Terrance were going to seek assistance from the Duke of Trevelyan. "Hopefully we'll arrive at Trey—" She broke off when she heard her father's voice in her head, calling to her.

"Your brother?" Bran whispered.

"My . . . king," she corrected herself, then listened while her parents described the events that had happened along the coast.

With the battles going on here, we couldn't really keep up with what has been happening to you, Gwennore explained.

Lennie repeated what she'd heard from Pendras and Anton and the plans she'd made. Her father asked King Ulfrid, who was nearby, and Ulfrid, whom he called Rupert, confirmed that Trevelyan would rally his troops to help them.

Rupert just told me something interesting, Silas reported. *The reason he sailed north to Freydor's land before the wedding was because he'd received a warning from Trevelyan. The duke had urged Rupert to investigate Freydor. Said the earl was not to be trusted.*

He was right, Lennie replied.

Be careful, Gwennore urged her. *Greer is dangerous.*

Aye, Silas told her. *Make sure Trevelyan is there with some troops before you try anything.*

Don't worry, Your Majesties, Sergei butted in. *I won't let any harm come to your daughter.*

Lennie's hands tightened on the reins. After centuries of

dragon telepathy, a certain etiquette had evolved to afford those participating a semblance of privacy. Even though any dragon could hear, it was considered poor form for a dragon to join a conversation to which he hadn't been invited. Did Sergei already see himself as part of the family? Even her parents were silent, no doubt caught by surprise.

Sergei glanced back at her with a smirk.

He thinks I'm trapped, Lennie thought. *He thinks he's won.* Anger swelled inside her. Knowing that every dragon on Aerthlan would hear her, she made an announcement. *Just so you'll know, Mother and Father—after careful consideration, I have decided I will not accept any offer of marriage.*

Sergei halted his horse with a jerk on the reins, then gave her a fierce look. She gazed back, arching a brow. If he dared to object, she could cite his name, humiliate him before all the dragons, and essentially end his career.

There was a pause while her parents digested this news. No doubt they were wondering what had happened to inspire such a sudden, seemingly random, proclamation.

Of course, my dear, Gwennore agreed with her. *You are still young, and there is plenty of time.*

You mustn't let anyone pressure you into a relationship you don't want, Silas added with a stern tone. *If anyone is foolish enough to attempt that, he will find himself in serious trouble.*

Exactly, Gwennore agreed. *We would never tolerate such rude behavior.*

Sergei's face reddened with rage. While Lennie said her good-byes to her parents, he jerked at his horse's reins and charged down the road.

"What has him so upset?" Bran asked.

"Too much pride," Lennie muttered, then motioned for everyone to gather around. "I have news from King Silas. King Leo arrived with the Tourinian army, and they, along with the other kings, have destroyed a fleet of pirate ships and successfully battled on land with the pirates and Freydor's mercenaries. They've taken over Freydor's castle, and King Brodgar, Queen Gwennore, and the injured Aleksi are remaining there to set things right. Those thugs who survived the battle have fled inland toward the mountains."

"So they're hoping to join up with Greer?" Terrance asked.

"It looks that way," Lennie replied.

"Greer boasted that he had taken over Freydor's gold mine in the mountains," Bran said. "So I assume he has another group of mercenaries there."

"Any idea where this gold mine is located?" Lennie asked Roslyn. Tourin was her country, so she should know.

The princess shrugged. "There are numerous mines all through the mountains. I believe Freydor's is in a mountain close to the Northern Sea. There are some incredibly high and jagged cliffs along the coast where the wind can knock you off your feet. I don't know the way there myself, but Trevelyan should be able to take us."

As they rolled over the summit of another hill, Lennie spotted Sergei in the valley below, crossing a wide bridge over a rushing river.

"That's the Trey River," Roslyn announced. "We should be close to Trey Falls now."

Just in time, Lennie thought, as she glanced toward the setting sun.

"After the Trey River goes south through the mountains, it curves west here to flow toward the Great Western Ocean," Roslyn explained. "The Coastal Road follows it out to the sea. In the mountains, the river cuts through Trevelyan's land, forming the widest valley in the mountains. The King's Way passes through the valley." She lowered her voice to tell Terrance how they would reach the duke's castle.

"So will you tell me why Sergei is upset?" Bran asked in hushed voice.

After a slight hesitation, Lennie admitted, "He doesn't take rejection well."

"You rejected him?"

She winced inwardly at the hopeful look that brightened Bran's handsome face. The poor man was obviously thinking this meant he had a chance with her when, in fact, the situation was impossible. She knew she should explain that here and now, but it was hard to make the words come out.

"Lennie—"

"I shouldn't have kissed you," she blurted out, then looked away from the expression on his face—a mixture of disbelief and distress. "I'm sorry."

"If you wanted to kiss me, and I believe you did, then you shouldn't be sorry."

"It was wrong of me to encourage you in this infatuation that you're—"

"My feelings are quite real."

"How can they be? You've known me for what . . . two days?"

"And five months." His jaw clenched. "I *do* know you."

The poor man was gnashing his teeth just as Father Bertram had predicted. With her heart aching, she shook her head. "You only think you know me because you've imagined me as some sort of angel for five months. But I'm not an angel."

"You are to me." He gave her an exasperated look. "Shall I tell you what I *do* know? I dreamed about you for months, and in that time, while I was torturing myself over Arlo's death and hating myself, you came to represent all that is pure and noble in the world, all that is far beyond my reach. You gave me comfort when I was in pain and hope for a better tomorrow, the hope that someday I could be the kind of honorable man who would be worthy of you."

Tears stung her eyes. She *was* beyond his reach, and she hated it. "It was just a dream, Bran."

"A dream come true. When I met you in person, I saw how brave and beautiful, clever and kind you are. And I knew that all the longing I had felt for you over the past five months had not been in error. My soul had recognized you from the start."

Oh, how this man tugged at her heart. Lennie looked away, blinking back her tears. "I am truly sorry."

He dragged a hand through his hair. "I know you have feelings for me. When we kissed, I could feel your passion—"

"Yes, I am attracted to you. I admit that. But I'm also not good for you. I'm driving you to despair—"

"Only because you're keeping secrets from me." He shifted on the driver's bench to face her. "Tell me what the problem is. We'll find a way. We'll fix it. Together."

She sighed. If only they could. "There are several problems."

"Tell me."

"I am expected to marry a dragon."

He frowned, considering this. "Is that why you have two dragons courting you?" When she nodded, he continued to press her. "Is it a Norveshki custom? Does every girl there dream of growing up to marry a dragon?"

"No. There aren't that many dragons to go around. Anton and Sergei are the only ones available."

"Then why you, Lennie?"

She grimaced. "Mating with a dragon is the only way to ensure that I will give birth to a dragon."

Bran scoffed. "And why is that important? It seems a pathetic reason to marry someone, especially when you don't even like either of your suitors."

It would be pathetic if she wasn't the heir to the throne. She gave him an apologetic look. "I am really sorry. I feel as if I led you on."

"No." He shook his head. "I decided yesterday that I was

going to pursue you. The more I know you, the more I fall in—"

"Please don't—"

"Too late." With a frustrated groan, he dragged a hand through his hair.

Bertram's predictions always came true, Lennie thought.

They had reached the river, and the horses' hooves clattered noisily over the wooden surface of the bridge.

"What?" Bertram mumbled. "What happened?"

Lennie glanced back and saw the elderly priest struggling to sit up. The noise of crossing the bridge must have woken him.

"You were asleep," Bran told him. "We just crossed the Trey River."

"Oh. I've always wanted to see—" His voice broke off suddenly, and Lennie looked back again. The priest's eyes had glazed over as he gazed at the darkening sky.

Sebastian drew his horse near to the wagon. "He's about to make a prediction."

Lennie tensed. *Please, no more deaths.*

"The princess will be betrayed," Bertram said. He blinked and looked around. "What did I say?"

" 'The princess will be betrayed,' " Sebastian repeated.

Lennie's breath caught. Was he referring to her? Or Roslyn? Or one of the other princesses back at Lourdon Palace? She exchanged a worried look with Roslyn.

"What princess are you talking about?" Bran asked.

Bertram shrugged. "The only princess I know is Roslyn."

"I've already been betrayed," Roslyn muttered. "Earl Freydor, remember? Father, do your predictions cover past events, too?"

"No." Bertram slumped with a sad look. "They always refer to the future. And they always come true."

Lennie swallowed hard. Who would betray her?

"Who would betray me?" Roslyn repeated Lennie's own

thoughts. She cast a nervous glance at Terrance, then huffed. "I don't believe it."

Terrance's face flushed. "I would never, Your Highness. I would rather die than—"

"I know that." Roslyn reached a hand toward him, and he grasped it, then kissed it.

It's probably not Roslyn, Lennie thought as she turned to face the road ahead.

They reached another summit, and there, nestled along the river, was the village of Trey Falls. As the last sliver of sun disappeared behind the neighboring hills, lanterns were lit along the village streets and lamps flickered in the windows of homes and storefronts.

It should be a cozy, cheerful sight, Lennie thought, but all she could feel was a growing trepidation. If it wasn't Roslyn who was going to be betrayed, then it was probably her.

Who would dare betray her?

Chapter 16

As the sun set, Kasper pulled back some branches to reveal a hidden cave in the side of the mountain gorge. Pendras figured the Embraced young man was from the highlands of Tourin; he had been in the lead all day and knew exactly where to find this obscure cave.

Greer followed the usual procedure, threatening to kill Prince Reynfrid in order to make Pendras and Zane behave. Soon, the horses were tethered in a nearby grove of trees, hidden by a thick canopy overhead. The three captives were herded into the cave, told to sit down, and fettered once again at one wrist and one ankle. Their chains were purposely tangled together to hinder their movements.

From a leather pouch, Kasper retrieved the hot coal he'd stuffed into a dried cow patty collected from last night's barn. He used this punk to start a small fire. The flames flashed tongues of light over the cave walls and glistened off trickles of water. After Kasper lit two lanterns, he let the fire die down to glowing embers.

Once again the captives were given a crust of bread and some water, while their captors feasted on dried meat, cheese, and wine. And once again, Greer warned them that Kasper's shield made escape impossible. The entire area around the cave had been closed off. Pendras knew the wall would fall when Kasper finally fell asleep, but the way he was chained up with the others would make it nearly impossible for them to move in concert. And, no doubt, the noise of their clanging chains would wake Greer and his cohorts.

"When do we reach the mi—" Roland started, but Greer hushed him, motioning with his head toward the captives.

Pendras figured the older priest was referring to the gold mine he'd heard about from Lennie. She'd received her information from the Raven, who had overheard Greer boasting that he'd taken over Freydor's gold mine. Obviously, Greer was reluctant to discuss his plans where the captives could hear.

With nothing else to do, Roland decided it would be entertaining to harass the prisoners. He tossed a piece of dried beef to Reynfrid, then laughed when it landed in the dirt. "Go ahead, Your Highness. Enjoy!"

Reynfrid gave him a bland look, refusing to play along.

Roland motioned to him, smirking as he talked to his companions. "Look how bloody regal he acts. Lucky bastard is what he is. He gets to stay alive just because he was born a prince."

Greer shrugged. "The dragon has some value, too."

"I suppose." Roland sneered at Pendras, then narrowed his eyes on Zane. "As for you, the only reason to keep you alive is the joy we get from tormenting you."

Reynfrid shook his head at Zane, warning him not to be dragged into Roland's twisted entertainment, but the young man ignored him.

Zane scoffed. "Why should I care what a whoreson like you has to say?"

Pendras exchanged a wary look with Reynfrid. This was not going to go over well.

Sure enough, Roland jumped to his feet, his face flushed with anger. "Oh, I have plenty to say, you asshole. I heard your brother cried like a baby when he was murdered."

Zane went pale, his jaw clenched.

"Isn't that right, Greer?" Roland turned toward their leader. "Did Arlo even put up a fight when you froze him?"

"Shut up!" Zane yelled at him.

Greer shrugged. "He was an easy kill."

Pendras exchanged another look with Reynfrid. They had just witnessed the man confess to murder.

"Enough of your nonsense, Roland." Greer rose to his feet and headed for the mouth of the cave. "I need to take a piss." He wandered outside.

Pendras leaned forward to see how far Greer would go, so he could get an idea where the invisible wall was.

Apparently Roland had not had enough fun. He aimed a sneer at Zane. "I always knew your brother was a weakling."

Zane's chains clanged as he stiffened.

"Lay off him," Pendras warned the obnoxious priest. "Before I melt your face like butter."

"Try it and I kill the precious prince," Roland snarled.

Zane shifted his glare to Pendras. "I don't need your protection. Roland's attacking me with words because he's too big a coward to fight me." He motioned to Roland with his free hand. "Come on, Rolly-poly. Come at me."

Roland hissed in a breath.

Pendras could feel the heat coming off Zane. No doubt one touch from him, and a man would be cooked. Interesting that his Embraced gift was the opposite of Greer's.

"Come on, Roland," Zane taunted him. "Are you afraid I'll make your blood boil?"

Roland snorted. "Tough talk. You'll burn yourself to a crisp before I can even say 'ouch.'"

"Let's give it a try, then." Zane struggled to get to his feet. His fettered ankle yanked at the chain connected to Pendras's wrist.

"Ha!" Roland stuck his thumbs in his belt. "I can knock

you flat from a distance. All I have to do is talk about the fun I had with your sister."

Zane gasped, then his face turned red as his heat surged to a dangerous level. He lurched forward, tugging at the chains connected to Pendras and Reynfrid. "You sick bastard! You molested Vera?"

The Raven and Zane had a sister? Pendras's mind raced. Had she grown up with them at the Monastery of Light? And the damn monks there had molested her? What bastards! Fire swirled in his belly, demanding to be released right in the priest's smirking face.

Roland chuckled. "I heard about you and Bran beating the crap out of Vera's admirers."

Zane's eyes narrowed. "She never mentioned you, or we would have beaten you, too. You sick perverts should die for—"

Roland laughed. "I never touched Vera. She was too old for my taste. Thirteen?" He waved a dismissive hand. "I preferred the younger one. So sweet and innocent. What was her name? Oh, right! Milena."

Reynfrid jerked, his eyes growing wide with alarm.

"She was only nine!" Zane bellowed. He lunged forward, tugging at the chains.

Reynfrid clambered to his feet. "Milena?" His hands fisted as he glowered at the priest. "You piece of shit, what did you do to her?"

Roland looked surprised for a moment, then sniggered. "Oh, that's right. Master Lorne sent Milena to Lourdon Palace to spy for him. I guess you know her?"

Reynfrid froze with a stunned expression.

Roland slapped his leg as he doubled over with laughter. "Oh, this is rich. The fancy prince didn't know he was being spied on."

Reynfrid swallowed hard. "You molested her."

Roland shrugged. "Just following orders. The Master wanted

the girls trained in methods of seduction." When Reynfrid growled low in his throat, Roland grinned. "Why so upset, Your Highness? Did Milena try to seduce you? If she succeeded, you can thank me for educating—"

"I'll kill you," Reynfrid hissed.

"Ha!" Roland smirked. "It looks like she succeeded."

"No, she didn't," Greer said as he stepped inside the cave. "She sent a message to Master Lorne, claiming that she had failed and that the prince was beyond our reach. The Master debated for a while whether she should pay the price for her failure. But I suppose even he was reluctant to snuff his own daughter."

Reynfrid went pale. "You were planning to kill her?"

Greer shrugged. "She was on the list, but not a high priority. Why bother when she's just a useless bitch?"

"I'll kill you both," Reynfrid growled.

"No, you won't," Zane argued. "I'm killing them."

From the fierce way Reynfrid was reacting, Pendras suspected Milena had actually come close to completing her mission. But then, she must have backed out, putting herself at risk in order to save him. If that was the case, she'd been caught in her own trap by falling for the prince. Once Reynfrid settled down, he would realize it, too.

Pendras gave Roland a disgusted look. "Actually, you now have three men who want to kill you. I detest men who abuse women and children."

"Roland." Greer shot him an annoyed look. "Didn't I tell you to stop?"

Roland shrugged. "No harm done."

"You are mistaken." Greer strode toward him. "Stop being such a fool. You just made them harder to control."

"Then let's kill them now!" Roland yelled.

Greer looked them over as if he were considering it.

Pendras had spent most of the day preparing for a situation like this. "You need us. If you're going to take over Tourin, you need the prince. And you need Zane to keep the Raven from coming after you."

Greer's eyes narrowed. "And why would we need you, dragon?"

"Are you interested in taking Norveshka, too?"

Greer scoffed. "Can you deliver it?"

"Perhaps. My sister is—"

"Don't say it," Reynfrid hissed at Pendras.

"My sister is heir to the throne," Pendras announced. "But the throne should belong to me."

"Pendras!" Reynfrid lurched toward him.

"What is he doing?" Zane asked.

Reynfrid grimaced. "I never would have believed this. He's betraying his sister."

Greer stepped closer. "Are you saying you're the Norveshki prince?"

"Aye." Pendras nodded. "I am."

Greer's eyes widened, and Roland let out a hoot of victory. Kasper watched them all with a wary expression as if he wished he were far away.

"For centuries, the crown has always passed to the eldest male dragon of the royal family," Pendras explained. "That is me. Keep us alive, so you can help me take what is mine."

"Dammit, Pendras," Reynfrid growled.

Even Zane glowered at him.

Greer smiled slowly. "From the way the others are reacting, I reckon you're telling the truth. So tell me, Prince, why should I help you take the crown when I would prefer to have it for myself?"

"I can give you jewels and land. You'll be the richest man on Aerthlan. Great wealth always brings great power."

Greer nodded. "I think we'll keep you alive after all, dragon."

*   *   *

As they rode into the village of Trey Falls, Bran was dismayed to see how busy it was. All he wanted was to be alone with Lennie so they could talk, but that didn't appear likely with the large crowd. The main road was already lined with various shops, inns, and taverns, but additional stalls had been set up, jamming up the traffic while the local people hawked homemade cloth, jam, soap, and seeds.

When they reached the main square, the crowd grew even thicker, and Lennie had to inch the wagon slowly toward the posting station.

The stationmaster greeted them, his eyes widening as he looked them over. "I didn't realize there would be so many of you. I'm afraid I only reserved one room. As you can see, all the inns are full."

"The women can take the room," Bran suggested. "The men can bunk down in the stable with the wagon."

The priests and Terrance nodded in agreement, while Sergei stood to the side, scowling.

"Actually," Lennie said as she climbed down from the wagon, "I wasn't planning on spending the night. We need to catch up with our friends who passed by earlier. I heard you could lend us a guide."

The stationmaster shook his head. "Not this late. The terrain is too dangerous to cross in the dark. And this wagon will never make it. We'll set you up with some pack mules and a guide in the morning. For now, I suggest you settle in and enjoy the celebration."

Bran could tell Lennie was disappointed and frustrated. He was, too, when he thought of his younger brother still in danger. "We'll catch up with the others tomorrow."

Roslyn gave her a cheerful smile. "Won't it be lovely to sleep in an actual bed tonight?"

"And have a bath?" Milena added.

"What exactly is being celebrated?" Father Bertram asked.

The stationmaster gestured toward the busy square. "It's a giant seed swap. Say a farmer won a blue ribbon for his excellent cabbage at the fall fair. Everyone will want some of his cabbage seeds now before the planting season." He chuckled. "But if you ask me, it's just an excuse for everyone to get together and party after a long winter of being stuck on their farms."

"It sounds like fun," Roslyn said. "But I think I'll see the falls first. I haven't seen them in ages."

"I've never seen them," Terrance told her.

With a grin, Roslyn took his arm. "Then I will show them to you. Anyone else coming?"

"I'll be along in a few minutes." Lennie grabbed a saddlebag to take to the room. Milena grabbed two more and followed her into the inn.

Bertram and Sebastian decided to go into a nearby tavern for a hot meal. They invited Bran, but he opted to follow Terrance and Roslyn to the falls. Hopefully, Lennie would arrive later, and he'd have a chance to talk to her.

It was a short walk from the village, and as they entered a grove of pine and fir trees, the noise of the crowd faded away and was soon replaced with the sound of crashing water. The scent of the woods was crisp and comforting, the ground spongy and thick with a layer of fallen needles.

There were actually three falls. The path the three of them were following led to the first and highest one. A small group of people was there, gawking at the sight and clambering around on the rocks piled along the river. A few wooden benches lining the bank were damp with the mist generated by the falling water.

After a while, Roslyn led Terrance downriver, following the path to the second falls. Bran held back, waiting for Lennie to arrive.

And he waited. After a while, he ventured deep into the woods to relieve himself. Then he went back to the river to wash his hands. Slowly, he meandered downriver to the second falls. It was only about three feet high, not nearly as spectacular as the first one, so just a few people were there. Roslyn and Terrance were nowhere in sight, but his heart lifted when he spotted Lennie arriving.

She smiled and turned to gaze at the falls.

"Feeling better?" he asked.

She nodded. "Yes. This reminds me of home. We have so many falls and lakes and beautiful mountains in Norveshka. It's my idea of heaven." She took a deep breath. "Even the air is heavenly."

"I'd like to see your country someday."

Her smile faded. "I wish I could show it to you. My father has a cabin that overlooks a glacier. Some of the ice melts in the summer, then refreezes in the winter, forming tubes in the glacier. When the wind blows, it makes the most beautiful, mellow sound that echoes through the mountains. And at night, you can see ribbons of glowing green and purple move like waves across the sky."

"It sounds amazing." The tender look on her face touched his heart. "You love your country."

"Aye." She gave him a sad look. "But it demands so much from me. I'm afraid it will feel more like a prison someday." She turned to wander down the path to the third and last waterfall.

He followed her at a distance, wondering what secrets she was holding onto. She'd opened up a little bit, but her comments had only left him with more questions. How could a beloved home feel like a prison?

As they approached the last falls, the river curved to the left. In the distance, he spotted Terrance and Roslyn sitting on a bench in a grove of trees. Their voices filtered through the woods.

"You never told me why you left Benwick," Roslyn said, turning to face Terrance.

Lennie stopped and motioned for Bran to halt, also. She leaned close to him and whispered, "I want to hear this."

Bran drew her behind a tree, and they peeked around.

Terrance sighed. "Do you remember how every three months, there would be games to see who was best at running, boxing, archery, and swordplay?"

"Yes." Roslyn grinned. "And you always won the archery contest."

Terrance smiled back. "And you won the women's contest."

"I had the best teacher."

"I had the best pupil."

With a grimace, Lennie shuddered, and Bran suppressed a chuckle.

"I was always careful not to use my Embraced power during the games," Terrance continued, "as it would have given me an unfair advantage."

"That's right." Roslyn nodded. "You were always very honorable."

"Thank you. But one summer during the games, while you were home, one of the students lodged a formal complaint against me, claiming I always won because I used my gift to cheat."

Roslyn gasped. "How terrible!"

"There was no way to prove I wasn't using my Embraced power. Nevis believed me, but the students started grumbling and boycotting their archery lessons."

"Oh, how awful for you." Roslyn touched his arm.

"And then, a rumor started that I'd been cheating for years just to impress someone."

"Who could that be?"

Terrance winced. "You. Apparently, a few people had noticed my feelings for you."

"Oh." Roslyn's cheeks turned pink.

"I didn't want to cause any trouble at Benwick, and I certainly didn't want anyone questioning your reputation, so I thought it best to leave."

"Oh, Terrance! Do you have any idea how upset I was when I came back to find you were gone? You should have written to me to let me know where you were."

"I thought about it, but I knew I didn't have a chance with you. Then I heard you were getting married . . ."

"I'm so sorry." Roslyn hung her head. "I was so devastated over losing you that I coped with it in a terrible way."

Terrance nodded. "I had a hard time of it, too."

"Oh, you poor thing. I took up pottery. It seemed to help."

"Really?" Terrance sat up. "I'd like to see some of your work."

Roslyn shrugged. "I still have much to learn."

Lennie whispered to Bran, "She's being modest. Her pottery is beautiful."

"I started a hobby, too," Terrance said. "Whenever I was feeling sad and missing you, I found it relaxing to do something with my hands."

"What do you do?" Roslyn asked.

Terrance hesitated. "I could show you. It's in my breeches. Let me pull it out."

Lennie stiffened and gave Bran a wary look. With a frown, he turned his attention back to Terrance. Unfortunately, he and the princess were sitting with their backs to him, so he couldn't see what was happening.

"Oh, my. It's bigger than I expected," Roslyn murmured. "Can I hold it?"

"Yes." Terrance slid closer to her on the bench.

"It's very smooth," Roslyn commented.

"I spent hours rubbing it," Terrance replied.

With a horrified look, Lennie whispered, "I can't allow Roslyn to fall prey to—"

"Can I blow on it?" Roslyn asked.

With a huff, Lennie marched toward the couple, but Bran pulled her back as a whistling sound carried toward them.

Roslyn laughed. "What a marvelous whistle! You carved this yourself?"

Lennie exchanged an incredulous look with Bran, then they both covered their mouths to keep from making any noise.

"I found that whittling helped the time go by," Terrance told her.

"I love it!" Roslyn held it up, and Bran could finally see the wooden whistle. "You even shaped it like a bird. That was so clever of you, Terrance."

"Would you like to have it?" Terrance asked.

"Oh, yes." Roslyn grinned at him. "I will always treasure it. Thank you."

Her grin faded when she realized how close they were sitting. Suddenly, Terrance leaned forward and gave her a kiss.

He sat back. "Forgive me—"

"Terrance!" Roslyn flung herself at him, and soon, they were lost in a passionate kiss.

"I think it's time for us to go," Bran whispered. He took Lennie's hand and led her through the woods.

"I do hope everything will work out for them."

Bran chuckled. "Just a moment earlier, you were ready to tear them apart."

She winced. "I wasn't sure Terrance was behaving properly."

Bran drew her to a stop. "Oh? What did you think he was doing?"

She scoffed. "Don't ask. No doubt you were thinking the same thing."

"How would I know?" He gave her an innocent look. "I live at a monastery."

"And every woman there wants you." Her eyes narrowed. "Now that I think about it, you certainly knew how to kiss."

"That was not expertise you were feeling. It was all the passion I've been keeping for you in my heart." He stepped closer. "I felt your passion, too."

She put her hands on his chest to stop him. "Bran." Her gaze lowered. "You really need to start wearing a shirt. You'll cause all the women in Trey Falls to suffer heart palpitations."

"Your heart is the only one I'm concerned about." He touched her hair. "I don't want to lose you."

Tears filled her eyes. "I'm not lost. I know how I feel. And even though our situation is impossible, I know I'll never feel this way again."

"Why is it impossible?" He kissed her cheek. "Tell me what is wrong, so I can fix it."

"I wish it was that easy." Her arms slipped around him to hold him tight.

He stroked her hair. "I won't give up on you, Lennie."

With a muffled groan, she buried her face in his chest.

"I knew it!" Sergei yelled as he strode toward them through the woods.

With a gasp, Lennie pulled back.

Bran put an arm around her, keeping her close to his side.

Sergei jabbed a finger at Bran. "That bastard! He's the reason you rejected me."

"He is not!" Lennie stepped toward him. "I told you I'm not marrying anyone."

"You should be mine!" Sergei bellowed. "That rotten bird is not worthy of you, and you know it."

"I will decide who is worthy," Lennie said quietly. "Leave us."

"Is that a royal order, Your Highness?" Sergei smirked when Bran flinched with shock.

Lennie turned pale.

"Now do you understand why you're not worthy?" Sergei snarled at Bran. "The princess has to marry a dragon."

The princess? Bran reached for a tree to keep from stumbling.

"That's enough, Sergei!" Lennie yelled at him. "Leave us."

With one final sneer, Sergei turned on his heel and strode away.

She was a princess? Bran blinked as the woods swirled around him. His fingers dug into the bark of the pine tree as if he needed to ground himself in the reality he'd known before. But there was no escaping this. *A princess.*

"Bran—"

"You're the Norveshki princess?" His voice came out like a croak.

She nodded, then winced at the look on his face.

"You should have told me."

"I-I know." With a grimace, she kicked the toe of her boot against the ground. "I'm sorry."

No wonder she thought their relationship was impossible. Her father, the king, would never accept a raven shifter as a suitable husband for her. "Why didn't you tell me?"

She sighed. "It seemed like the right decision at the time. I didn't know you, but I needed you to work with me so we could rescue our brothers. I knew you'd been raised by the Brotherhood, which wanted to destroy the royal families, so I feared if you knew the truth, you wouldn't trust—"

"But you quickly learned how I felt about you. You had my trust. You should have told me."

"I knew we would part once our brothers were rescued—"

"So a bit of honesty didn't matter?"

She winced.

"What other secrets are you hiding?"

She bit her lip.

There were more secrets. Bran's heart twisted in his chest. And she didn't trust him enough to tell him.

He turned and walked back to the village.

Chapter 17

Bran was in such a daze, he found himself in the village of Trey Falls without remembering how he'd walked back. All he could recall were the words that kept echoing in his head. *A princess. She's a princess.* He stood in the middle of the town square, not sure where to go or what to do. *She's the Norveshki princess.*

That meant her dragon brother, who had been captured with Zane, was the prince. And, since the Norveshki king was always a dragon, her brother was probably heir to the throne. That explained why Lennie was so desperate to save him, desperate enough that she felt justified in keeping secrets.

Bran snorted. Was he trying to find a reason to excuse her? She should have told him the truth. She should have trusted him.

"Why, hello, handsome." A young blond-headed woman sauntered up to him, carrying a tray piled with folded homespun cloth. "You look like you need a shirt. Can I interest you in—"

"Oh, no!" Another woman, a redhead, butted in to show him her tray. "What you need is one of my homemade soaps." She picked up a bar and leaned toward his chest. "Shall I show you how it works?"

Bran stepped back. "No, thank you. I don't have any coin on me."

"Oh, dearie, you can have the soap for free." The redhead winked. "How would you like to get into some hot water?"

The blonde elbowed her. "I saw him first! Aren't you betrothed to my cousin?"

"So?" The redhead huffed. "You're already married!"

"Excuse me." Bran dashed toward the tavern he'd seen the priests enter earlier.

The noise from the crowded dining room was deafening, and all the tables were full. He glanced around, then spotted Father Sebastian waving at him from the back corner. He and Bertram were sitting at a table with two farmers, and from the empty plates in front of them, Bran realized they had finished eating.

Still, with nowhere else to go, Bran figured he'd sit with them for a while and get a bite to eat. As he strode down the aisle, one of the serving girls gawked at him while she was refilling a man's pewter tankard with beer. The man hollered as the beer overflowed onto the table.

"Oh, sorry!" The waitress mopped up the beer with her apron, then winked at Bran as he quickly passed by.

He squeezed onto the bench next to Sebastian and Bertram.

"Ah, there you are, my boy!" Bertram grinned, his eyes almost as red as his cheeks.

Bran noticed the four jugs of beer and the bottle of whiskey on the table next to the empty plates. The older priest was only used to the wine they watered down quite a bit at the monastery.

"Let me introduce you to our new friends." Bertram waved at the two farmers sitting across from them. "This is Ervil and Festus. They grow giant food!"

"The best pumpkins in the world!" one of the farmers boasted as he refilled his tankard with beer. He was a portly fellow with a shiny bald spot at the top of his round pumpkin-shaped head. "I'm Ervil. I won a blue ribbon last fall. My pumpkin was three feet wide!"

Sebastian nodded wisely. "That's a big pumpkin."

"Hear! Hear!" They all clunked their tankards together and took a long drink.

They're completely soused, Bran thought. Not a bad way to be, considering he'd just lost the love of his life. Grabbing an empty tankard, he filled it with beer, then took a long drink.

"You need more than that, Bran," Sebastian declared, then waved at the serving girl. "Bring our friend some beef!"

The girl smiled at Bran. "Coming right up!"

"Speaking of beef..." Ervil motioned toward Bran. "Where's your shirt, son?"

Before Bran could answer, Bertram jumped in. "He broke his arm and couldn't get a shirt over the splint."

Since Bran no longer needed to explain, he took another long drink instead.

"Hmm." Ervil frowned, contemplating the news for a while so he could draw a meaningful conclusion. "That had to hurt."

Bran was about to reply that it had indeed hurt when the other farmer, Festus, raised his hands in the air as if he was about to make a big announcement.

"I broke my toe once."

"I remember that!" Ervil thumped his friend on the back. "Good times."

"Hear! Hear!" They all drank again, and once again, Bran joined in. Then he noticed his tankard was almost empty, so he refilled it.

"Festus grows award-winning cucumbers," Sebastian told Bran.

"That's right!" Festus, a long and lanky old fellow, filled a cup from the whiskey vessel. "Best cucumbers you'll ever find." He tossed the whiskey back, then slammed the cup onto the table.

Bran blinked, surprised the cup had remained intact.

"My blue-ribbon cucumber was thirteen inches long!" Festus shouted.

Sebastian nodded wisely. "That's a long cucumber."

"Hear! Hear!" They all drank some more.

Ervil leaned forward onto his elbows. "Now where were we on our deal?"

Bertram refilled his tankard. "I would love some of your pumpkin seeds, Ervil. Our kitchen garden at the monastery doesn't have any pumpkins."

"A garden without pumpkins is a crime!" Ervil cried.

Bertram nodded sadly. "I agree. But I don't have any seeds to barter with. If you would like to visit the monastery, we could give you some cheese."

"Hmm." Ervil drank more beer. "We don't really need any more cheese."

"I tell you what we need." Festus poured more whiskey into his cup. "Women."

Bertram and Sebastian jerked upright. Bran wondered if this party was about to come to blows. Fortunately, it was three against two. But unfortunately, he was one-handed at the moment and his priestly friends were not as strong as the farmers.

"You're right!" Ervil banged a fist on the table. "We need young women for our sons. The boys want to get married, but all the women around here are already taken."

"Oh, I see." Sebastian turned toward Bertram. "You do have a number of single women at the monastery."

Bertram huffed. "They are not for sale! Those are nice, re- spectable young ladies!"

"You have ladies at the monastery?" Ervil asked.

"Homeless women," Sebastian explained. "Bertram, some

of them might like the idea of having their own home and family."

Bertram frowned. "I feel responsible for them. I can't let them feel pressured into marriages they don't want."

"Oh, no!" Festus waved his hands. "We would never do that!"

"I know what to do," Ervil announced. "We'll send our boys to stay at your monastery for a few weeks—"

"After planting season," Festus interrupted.

"—and then the boys can see if any of your women like them." Ervil's face lit up. "It could end in true love!"

"True love," Bran grumbled.

"Holy Light." Ervil looked surprised. "The boy can talk."

Bran scoffed, then took another drink.

"Hmm." Festus studied him. "I think the lad is having lady problems."

"Oh, no!" Bertram waved a hand dismissively. "Bran is a good boy. He would never—"

"She says there is no future for us." Bran finished his beer.

"I knew it! Lady problems." Festus poured some whiskey into Bran's tankard. "At a time like this, you need the hard stuff."

"Oh, no!" Bertram objected. "Bran's a good boy. He would never drink—"

Bran drank the whiskey and thumped his tankard on the table.

"Oh, dear." Bertram drank more beer.

The waitress set another jug and a plate of roast beef and potatoes in front of Bran. "Here you go, handsome. Is there anything else I can get for you?"

"No, thank you," Bran muttered, hardly looking at her.

With a huff, she strode away.

Ervil made a clucking noise. "Oh, he has it bad when he doesn't even notice Molly."

Festus snickered. "I'll say. She's got a nice set of pumpkins on her. So what is the problem with your young lady?"

Bran took a bite of beef. "She's a bloody princess."

"Oh ho!" Ervil leaned back. "I know exactly what you mean. My daughter is a princess. The other day, after I cut off a slice of bread, I used the same knife to get some jam and spilled some crumbs in the jar. She nearly took my head off!"

Sebastian gazed at Bran, his eyes just a little unfocused. "You mean a real princess?"

"Now, my sister is a real princess," Festus announced. "One time, when I spilled some tea on the table, I mopped it up with one of the doilies she'd made, and she didn't speak to me for three months!"

"Humph!" Ervil commiserated with his friend.

"That wasn't nice," Bertram mumbled.

"I know!" Festus took on an injured look. "That was so rude of her."

"I was referring to you." Bertram pointed at Festus.

"Now, now." Ervil drank more beer. "I'll have you know Festus and I know how to treat women. I've been married forty-three years!"

"Forty-five!" Festus thumped his chest. "Now, young man"—he gazed bleary-eyed at Bran—"if you're having trouble romancing your young lady, you just leave it to us. We'll tell you exactly what you need to have a happy relationship."

Bran scoffed and poured more whiskey into his tankard. If he could ever persuade Lennie to marry him, they'd automatically be happy.

Bertram frowned. "That will not be necessary. Sebastian and I are quite capable of giving Bran sound advice."

"No offense, friend," Ervil said, refilling Bertram's tankard, "but you've never been married. I think this is a job for experts. That's me and Festus."

"That's right." Festus sat up. "So let us begin." He held up two fingers. "First of all, you should know there are two pillars that uphold a happy marriage. One: love. And two: respect."

"Wait a minute," Ervil interrupted. "What about passion? A virile and shirtless young man like this is going to need passion in his life."

"I have plenty of passion," Bran grumbled, then took another bite of food.

"I'm sure you do." Ervil smirked at his friend. "After all, his cucumber is still fresh."

Festus nodded sadly. "You're right. I'd forgotten about that. At my age, the cucumber is . . ."

"Pickled?" Ervil sniggered.

Festus huffed. "I bet yours is, too!"

Ervil's grin faded. "How did you know?"

Festus shrugged, then held up his hand again. With his thumb curled in against his palm, four fingers were extended. "The three pillars of a happy marriage—"

"You're showing four," Bertram told him.

"Oh. Right." Festus's pinky finger wouldn't cooperate, so he used his other hand to fold it down and trap it beneath his thumb. "There. The three pillars of a happy marriage: love, respect, and passion."

"What about trust?" Sebastian asked.

The pinky finger popped up. "Four!" Festus exclaimed. "The four pillars of a happy marriage: love, respect, passion, and trust!"

"She doesn't trust me," Bran mumbled. She was still keeping secrets from him.

Ervil slapped a hand on the table. "No wonder you're having trouble!"

"What about kindness?" Bertram asked.

"The five pillars of a happy marriage!" Festus splayed his hand in the air. "Love, respect, passion, and . . . what was it again?"

"Trust and kindness," Sebastian replied wryly.

"Hmm." Ervil frowned. "I hadn't thought about kindness."

Festus shrugged. "Maybe we should try it sometime."

Ervil nodded. "Maybe that's why Myrtle isn't talking to me right now."

Bran jumped up as a wave of nausea hit. "I think I'm going to be sick."

"I told you he doesn't drink like that," Bertram mumbled. "He's a good boy."

More like a miserable one, Bran thought as he stumbled for the door.

Outside, he breathed deeply of the cool night air.

"Are you all right?" Milena approached him. "You look a little green."

"Where did you come from?"

With a smile, she motioned toward a small building beside the inn. "I just had a lovely soak in the bathhouse."

"Oh." He noticed her braided hair was wet.

She stepped closer and wrinkled her nose. "Have you been drinking?"

He swayed on his feet. "Not as much as Bertram and Sebastian."

"Come on." She took his arm. "Let's get you to the wagon so you can lie down."

Bran let her guide him into the stable. "Milena, you knew, didn't you?"

"Knew what? Oh, there's the wagon."

The stable hands had parked the wagon in the back of the stable and piled the crates and baskets nearby.

Milena opened the backboard, then busied herself spreading out a few bedrolls on the wagon bed. "You should be able to sleep here, using the blankets to stay warm."

Bran leaned against the side of the wagon. "She's a princess."

"Roslyn?"

"No, Lennie."

Milena froze with a blanket in her arms. Wincing, she gave Bran an apologetic look. "How did you find out?"

"Sergei. The bastard wanted me to know I wasn't worthy of her."

"He would," Milena muttered, then shook out the blanket and let it fall on top of the mattress she'd made of bedrolls. "He's the one not worthy of her."

"You think I could be?"

"I was hoping you would be." Milena perched on the end of the wagon. "But I know how it is. I had a similar problem myself."

"What do you mean?" Bran asked, but she merely shrugged and didn't answer. He sat next to her. "Why didn't you tell me?"

"About Princess Lenushka?"

"That's her name?" Bran clenched his teeth. Dammit, he hadn't even known her real name. "You should have warned me."

"She asked me not to."

He scoffed. "I'm your brother! Do you side with royalty now?"

"I don't know!" Milena gave him a pained look. "Do you have any idea how difficult this is for me? I love you and Zane, and I'll do anything to protect you. But I don't give a damn about the Brotherhood. Growing up at the monastery was torture. For all of us." Her eyes filled with tears.

Bran had a sudden terrible suspicion that she might have suffered more than he'd known. "Milena, what . . . ?"

She shook her head. "Queen Brigitta has been good to me. And . . . her children, too."

"You mean Roslyn?"

Milena's cheeks turned pink as she looked away.

Bran's breath caught as a new idea sneaked into his head. He knew Master Lorne had sent his sisters to Ebton and Lourdon Palace not just to spy, but to seduce any man they were ordered to target. Vera had never received such an order because the Eberoni princes, Eric and Dominic, were almost always at Benwick Academy. But had Milena been told to seduce the prince at Lourdon Palace? "Has something happened between you and Reynfrid?"

Milena closed her eyes briefly with a miserable look. "We became good friends, but then he wanted . . ." Her eyes glistened with tears. "I wanted more, too, but I know my place. He's going to inherit the throne someday. There could never be anything between us."

"But you love him?"

She wiped a tear from her cheek. "I don't want to talk about it." She turned toward Bran. "I was watching you and Lenushka. You're so good together. I was hoping it could somehow work out for you, but I'm afraid you're stuck in the same dreadful situation that I—"

"It *will* work," Bran insisted. "Her brother will inherit the throne, so he can father dragon babies. That should leave Lennie free to marry whomever she—"

"Wait a minute," Milena interrupted. "Who told you that?"

Bran shrugged. "No one, but her brother's a dragon—"

"Bran, Princess Lenushka has been named the heir. The crown will be hers."

"What?" Bran stiffened.

"She didn't tell you that?"

He nearly fell over. Why hadn't she told him? Another one of her damned secrets! But it all made sense now. Why she feared her beloved home would become a prison. Why she felt pressured to give birth to a dragon. Why she claimed her country demanded too much of her. She was trapped. And together, they were most likely doomed.

"There you are." Lennie appeared at the entrance of the stable. Her face was pale, her eyes red as if she'd been crying. "I-I was wondering how you were doing."

He dragged a hand through his hair, too distraught to deal with her now, too flustered by the thought that she could be suffering as much as he was. "Why are you here?"

"I wanted to make sure you were all right." She wandered inside, casting an annoyed look at Milena. "But I see you wasted no time finding another woman to console you."

Milena winced.

Bran clenched his jaw. "What business is it of yours? Didn't you say it was impossible for us?"

Lennie stopped with a jerk, her lovely eyes flashing with anger. "Don't assume our situation is not causing me pain. But apparently, I haven't been the only one with secrets. How long have you and Milena—"

"It's not what you think," Milena protested. "I'm—"

"Milena, don't," Bran whispered. "It will put you in danger."

She scoffed. "I've been living with danger for years! I'm sick of it." She slid off the wagon and landed on her feet. "I'm Bran's sister!"

Lennie blinked once. Twice. "What?"

"His sister." Milena shrugged. "Or to be more precise, I'm Zane's older sister. We share the same mother, and our father was Master Lorne."

Lennie looked at her and then Bran. "Then . . . ?"

"Technically, we're cousins," Bran grumbled. "But Arlo was their half brother through their mother, and my half brother through my father, so we've always considered ourselves siblings. I know it's a twisted heritage, but then, Lord Morris and Master Lorne were a pair of sick, twisted brothers."

Milena nodded. "That's the truth."

Lennie gave her a confused look. "Then how did you become a lady-in-waiting to Queen Brigitta?"

Bran grabbed Milena's hand and whispered, "You don't have to say anything."

She gave him a sad look. "I'm tired of the constant worry of being found out. And sick of the lies." She turned toward Lennie and lifted her chin. "Master Lorne sent me to Lourdon Palace to work as a spy."

"*What?*" Roslyn screeched as she appeared at the stable door with Terrance. "Did you just say you're a spy?"

Milena's grip on Bran's hand tightened.

He winced. If this wasn't handled well, his sister could end up facing an execution. "I won't let anything happen to you," he whispered, then raised his voice. "You cannot blame my sister for the circumstances of her birth. She didn't choose to have Master Lorne for a father or to grow up in that hellhole of a monastery. Nor did she choose to become a spy. When the Brotherhood gave one of us a mission, we had to accept it or die."

Roslyn strode toward them. "But she could have told us!"

"I wish I had," Milena confessed. "Your family has always been so good to me."

Roslyn's eyes filled with tears. "We cared about you, and this is how you repay us?"

"She has never betrayed you!" Bran insisted. "Even when you asked her to keep Lennie's royal birthright a secret from *me*, her own brother, she sided with *you*!"

"Bran—" Milena started.

"I will not have you suffer for this!" Bran shouted. "You have suffered enough."

Milena suddenly broke into tears.

Bran pulled her close, and as her shoulders shook with sobs, he had the terrible feeling once again that she'd suffered more than he'd ever known.

Chapter 18

It was an awkward night in their bedchamber, Lennie thought. After she and Roslyn had used the facilities at the bathhouse, they'd had a quick bite to eat, then gone to their room. Milena was already there. She'd made a pallet on the floor by the fireplace.

She motioned toward the one large bed. "Your Highnesses should sleep there."

Roslyn turned away to undress, not speaking to her. Lennie knew, from Roslyn's grumbling over dinner, that her feelings were hurt because Milena had deceived them.

Lennie set a plate of bread and cheese on the floor next to Milena. "I brought this from the tavern. I didn't think you'd eaten."

"Thank you." Milena took a bite of cheese and slanted a wary look at Roslyn. "There is water in the jug on the dressing table if you wish to brush your teeth. I left the saddlebags on the chair."

"Thank you." Lennie undressed, then brushed her teeth after Roslyn. She noted that Milena had barely touched her food. She'd stretched out on her pallet, facing the fire and supposedly sleeping, but Lennie suspected she was only pretending.

In the bed, Roslyn was on her side, her back to everyone as she also pretended to sleep.

Lennie turned down the lantern, and the room dimmed, lit

only by the small fire in the hearth. With a sigh, she climbed into bed. The only sounds were the crackling of the fire and the irregular breathing of those too upset or miserable to sleep.

Lennie's mind seemed determined to keep her miserable, too, as it kept replaying the scene earlier in the woods. Over and over, she recalled the stunned look of disbelief and injury on Bran's face. And over and over, she felt the pangs of guilt. Why had she kept her identity secret? At the time she'd made that terrible decision, it had seemed the right thing to do. She'd known very little about Bran then. She'd considered him a criminal, so she'd had no concern about his feelings.

She hadn't imagined his love and devotion to her. And she would have never dreamed that her heart would be so affected by him. The short time that they'd been together seemed somehow as long as a lifetime. And now that she'd upset him, it hurt much more than she'd ever supposed it would.

But the more cautious side of her feared that her feelings for him had evolved much too quickly. Had she somehow, in her distress over feeling trapped, sought an escape? Had she done as Bran had done the last five months, allowed dreams to give her hope and comfort? Was that all this was: a lovely dream that offered them an escape from a reality too harsh to accept?

But how could a dream hurt this much? The thought of living the rest of her life without Bran was tearing her apart.

To take her mind off it all, she contacted Anton.

Anton, are you there? Give me an update.

Yes, Your Highness, Anton responded right away. *We have made camp beside the path that leads toward the narrow mountain pass. The local guide said the pass is a short journey away. He calls it the Gorge of Great Despair.*

Lovely, Lennie grumbled mentally.

It's infamous for mudslides in the spring, rockslides in the summer, and avalanches in the winter. And if nature doesn't kill you, the bandits will.

Lennie wondered if the local bandits were in league with Greer as the pirates had been along the coast. *Anton, we're stuck here in Trey Falls for the night, but we'll leave at daybreak. Princess Roslyn and Terrance will head north to ask the Duke of Trevelyan for additional troops. Please wait for us before you enter the gorge.*

I'll tell Dominic. He'll be glad to hear reinforcements are on the way.

See you tomorrow. Lennie cut off the communication.

Next to her, Roslyn punched her pillow in an attempt to get comfortable. On the floor, Milena sniffled. No doubt the lady-in-waiting was terrified of what the future held for her now that she'd confessed to being a spy.

"We need to sleep," Lennie said softly. "We each have a long day tomorrow. Roslyn, we will need those Trevelyan troops as quickly as possible."

"I know," she mumbled.

Lennie, can you hear me? Father? Mother?

Pendras! Lennie sat up in bed. "My brother has made contact."

Roslyn and Milena both sat up to look at her.

We're here, Gwennore replied. *It's good to hear from you. Tell us your situation, son,* Silas urged him.

The shield-maker, Kasper, has finally fallen asleep, Pendras reported. *I believe he comes from this area, since he knows it so well.*

How are you? Lennie asked. *And the other captives?*

We're all right. Hungry and tired, but unharmed. We're in a cave by a narrow mountain pass.

Dominic is just behind you, Lennie told her brother. *And we will catch up with him tomorrow. Roslyn and Terrance will bring troops from the Duke of Trevelyan.*

Leo, Rupert, and I are headed your way with the Tourin-

ian army, Silas reported. *To save time, we're taking the northern road along the coast where the land is flat. Rupert says Freydor's gold mine is close to the coast, so once you make it through the pass, you'll reach the mine about the same time that we do.*

Good to hear, Pendras replied.

I'm worried Greer will react poorly when he sees he's outnumbered, Gwennore told them. *Please be careful.*

I know. There was a pause, then Pendras continued, *I've tried to insure our lives here. I—I hate to say this, but I offered to ah . . . betray my sister and help Greer—*

You what? Silas roared.

I'm just pretending! Pendras yelled back. *I'm trying to keep us alive here.*

It was a smart move, Pendras. Lennie defended her brother, although Bertram's prediction flitted through her mind once again. *The princess will be betrayed.* She would never believe her brother capable of such an act, but if, somehow, he was, it would be foolish for him to admit to it in advance.

So who would betray her? Sergei? That would be a huge risk for him, since it could result in execution. Never in the history of Norveshka had a dragon turned on the royal family. Who else? Her heart tightened. Surely not Bran. He was upset with her now, but he'd never knowingly cause her harm. Or would his feelings change once he learned she was the dragon who'd caused him to crash?

Is King Ulfrid nearby? Pendras asked.

Rupert? Yes, Silas replied. *Why?*

One of the villains here, a priest named Roland, was taunting Zane about his sister. Apparently she was sent to work as a lady-in-waiting at—

Milena is here with me, Lennie interrupted, compelled to somehow help the young woman. A captured spy could be executed or imprisoned, but, as far as Lennie could tell, Milena had never caused any harm to the Tourinian royal family. *She was raised in that horrible monastery with Bran and Zane. Her father, Master Lorne, forced her to serve as a spy at Lourdon Palace. She has admitted it voluntarily.*

She's a spy? Silas's voice sounded tense.

Please, Lennie begged. *Before you tell King Ulfrid, let me assure you that Milena is grateful for the kindness the royal families have extended to her. When I asked her to refrain from telling Bran my true identity, she did as I asked, even though Bran is her brother. I am totally convinced she is loyal to us. And she hates the Brotherhood.*

She certainly has good reason to hate them, Pendras added. *While Roland was taunting Zane, the truth came out. Those sick monks at the Brotherhood's monastery were ordered to molest Zane's sisters. Apparently most of the assholes assaulted the older sister, but Roland went after Milena, who was only nine years old at the time.*

Lennie gasped, her gaze moving automatically to Milena. When the lady-in-waiting saw Lennie's expression of horror, she turned pale and started trembling.

Bastard, Silas growled. *I'll kill him.*

You'll have to wait in line, Pendras told his father. *Zane, Reynfrid, and I have all vowed to kill him.*

"Do the kings know I'm a spy now?" Milena whispered in a shaky voice from her pallet on the floor. "Do . . . do they want to kill me?"

"No!" Lennie scrambled off the bed and hurried over to Milena. "They want to kill Roland."

Milena gasped, then pulled her knees up to her chest and covered her face. "I didn't want anyone to know . . ."

Lennie wrapped her arms around her. "I'm so sorry."

"What is it?" Roslyn climbed out of bed. "What's going on?"

"I'll explain later," Lennie whispered.

"It was part of our training," Milena mumbled, her face still hidden. "My father ordered them to . . ." She shuddered.

Her own father was behind such abuse? "I'm glad he's dead," Lennie growled.

"Vera had it the worst," Milena mumbled. "There must have been eight monks molesting her."

Roslyn gasped, then fell to her knees beside them.

"Master Lorne forbade them to actually rape us. He wanted us both experienced and virginal, so he could use us later." Milena wiped her cheeks as tears rolled down her face. "Vera actually encouraged the monks to go after her. At first, I was appalled, but then I realized she was doing it to keep me safe."

"Oh, dear Light," Roslyn whispered.

Milena sniffed. "At first it worked, but then Roland . . ."

"I'll kill him," Roslyn hissed.

"You'll be number six on the waiting list." Lennie rubbed Milena's back. "I swear I won't let anyone hurt you again. If you get in trouble at Lourdon Palace for spying, I'll shift and fly you straight to Norveshka. You'll have a home with me as long as you want."

"I won't let anything happen to her, either!" Roslyn exclaimed.

Milena lifted her head to gaze at them both. "Thank you. I know I don't deserve your kindness after deceiving you."

"You were forced to spy." Lennie patted her on the shoulder. "If you had refused, the Brotherhood would have killed you."

"Oh, Milena," Roslyn cried, embracing her. "It must have been so hard for you."

Milena took a deep breath, then let it out slowly. "I'm relieved I don't have to keep secrets anymore."

Lennie winced. She still had one big secret she was keeping from Bran, but she was afraid if she told him now, he would give up on her completely.

Lennie, her father called out to her. *You say Milena is with you?*

Aye, she is.

I have told Rupert what happened. At first, the news of Milena's spying upset him, but when he heard the whole story, he has vowed, as we all have, to kill Roland. He wants you to assure Lady Milena that she is considered a member of his royal household, so she is under his protection. No harm will come to her.

I'll tell her, Lennie replied. *Thank you.* She repeated Rupert's announcement, and Milena fell back onto the pallet with tears in her eyes.

Roslyn took her hand. "There, you see? Everything will be fine."

Milena nodded, then glanced at Lennie. "How did you find out about Roland?"

"Pendras told us." Lennie winced. "I'm afraid Roland was bragging about what he'd done, so he could torment your brother."

With a groan, Milena turned her head to look at the fire. "Poor Zane. It must have upset him—" She gasped and sat up. "Then Reynfrid knows?"

Lennie nodded. "He's one of many who has vowed to kill Roland."

"Oh, no!" Milena fell back and curled into a ball. "Oh, dear Light, how can I ever face him again?"

"You have no reason to be ashamed!" Lennie said.

"Exactly!" Roslyn agreed. She patted Milena on the shoulder. "Do you care for my brother?"

Milena nodded. "I do, but I know I'm not worthy."

"Stop that." Roslyn thumped her gently. "I know for a fact that Reynfrid cares about you."

Milena sighed. "It is impossible for us. I'm not just an orphan with no money or property, I'm the niece of Lord Morris, a member of the Circle of Five, and the daughter of Master Lorne, who also tried to take over the world with the Brotherhood of the Sun. No one will ever accept me—"

"I do!" Roslyn cried.

Milena gave her a sad smile. "You are a sweetheart, Your Highness. Most courtiers are not. Your parents will not want to invite civil strife with the nobility."

Roslyn bit her lip. "I'm not going to give up on you. I'll try to convince my parents."

Milena snorted. "Don't say anything to them. We don't know yet if Reynfrid wants anything to do with me." She frowned. "He may have been disgusted by the things Roland admitted."

"No." Roslyn shook her head. "Reynfrid will be sympathetic."

Milena winced. "I will not accept him if all he feels for me is pity."

She wants true love, Lennie thought with a sigh. But it would not be easy for Milena and Reynfrid. Or Roslyn and Terrance. Or herself and Bran. All the reasons that would turn the nobility against Milena applied to Bran as well. His relationship to Lord Morris and Master Lorne would doom him. His kidnapping of Queen Luciana and Princess Eviana of Eberon would condemn him. He was not a dragon; nor could he father one. He wasn't even a Norveshki. He would never be accepted as king. The country would reject him. And her.

She swallowed hard as she realized the full extent of her predicament. If she refused to give up Bran, she would lose the crown.

At dawn, Lennie said farewell to Roslyn and Terrance as they mounted their horses. The two charged north on the King's Way, headed to the Duke of Trevelyan's castle.

The stable hands had packed the party's food and some of their weapons onto a few spare horses. The rest of their supplies had to be left behind. Lennie was more interested in speed than comfort at this point. They absolutely had to catch up with Dominic today.

When Bran and the two priests emerged from the stable, she noted how bleary-eyed Father Bertram was. He had obviously imbibed too much the night before. Bran and Father Sebastian had damp hair and were freshly shaved, so she assumed they'd risen early to go to the bathhouse. Bran had removed the bandage from his forearm and was now wearing a shirt beneath his cape. He glanced at her briefly with a sad look, then busied himself with the horses. His right arm seemed to be healed, though she wasn't sure if he would be able to fly.

She also wasn't sure what to say to Bran, so she approached Father Bertram, instead, as he leaned wearily against his short-legged horse, Daffy. "Father, you could stay here and rest, if you prefer. The next few days could be dangerous."

"We are determined to help free Zane," Bertram told her.

Sebastian agreed, then lowered his voice. "Bran told us last night that you know the truth about Milena. We are gravely concerned for her safety."

Lennie smiled. "No need to worry. When I was in contact with King Silas last night, he passed the news on to King Ulfrid, and he has assured Milena that no harm will come to her."

"Oh, the Light be praised!" Bertram exclaimed. "What wonderful news!" He rushed over to tell Bran.

Lennie's smile faded as she realized Bran and the priests didn't know what Roland had done. "Father Sebastian, I'm afraid there is more to Milena's story. It is very personal, so I am reluctant to tell you. Zane already knows, though, so you will learn of it eventually."

"Are you referring to Roland?" Sebastian asked quietly.

Lennie blinked. "Then you know?"

Sebastian winced. "Not exactly, but I guessed when I saw

how Milena reacted to his name. I know what happened to the older sister, Vera."

"Where is she?"

"Can you keep a secret?" Sebastian snorted. "I'm sure you can. Is it true you are the Norveshki princess?"

Lennie nodded, realizing the clever priest was trying to change the subject to protect Vera. "Is Vera a spy, too?"

Sebastian hesitated, then said, "I can assure you that she is loyal to the crown she serves. And speaking of crowns, are you really inheriting the Norveshki one?"

"Aye."

The priest frowned. "You don't look very happy about it. How do you feel about Bran?"

Lennie sighed. "I'm not sure."

"He's sure about you."

She glanced at Bran, and her heart tightened. He was smiling, relieved by the good news Bertram had told him. How could she give him up? How could she give up the throne her parents wanted her to have?

"Good morning," Milena said as she approached, carrying her saddlebag.

"Are we all here?" Lennie looked around. The guide was ready to go. Her heart skipped a beat when she realized Sergei was missing. *The princess will be betrayed.*

She didn't want to believe it. *Sergei, where are you?*

Your Highness, he grumbled back. *I am scouting the area you will be traveling through to make sure it is safe.*

She hadn't ordered him to do that, but she didn't want to argue with him. *Very well. Thank you.*

She mounted her horse and nodded toward the guide, a fellow named Travis. "Let's go."

They took off at a brisk pace, crossing the countryside, skirting bogs and following mountain streams, swollen and dangerous with snowmelt. The mountains grew higher, and with their path now narrow and strewn with fallen rocks, they were forced to slow down. By noon, they reached the road that Dominic was on and were able to pick up speed.

She spotted Sergei ahead. After he noted their position, he flew on to catch up with Dominic.

Anton, she called to him. *Sergei should be there soon.*

Good, Anton replied. *We have arrived at the entrance to the narrow gorge.*

Wait there. We're on our way. Send Quentin to fly west to see if Trevelyan's troops are coming.

Quentin flew off an hour ago to check on Greer's progress through the mountain pass. I'll fly over to look for the troops.

All right. Thank you, Anton.

By late afternoon, they reached Dominic and his nine men. They had set up camp close to the entrance of the gorge. It was a small meadow, surrounded by trees and intersected by a small creek that emerged from the narrow canyon.

"This is Prince Dominic," Lennie said, introducing him to the others in her group. "He's a colonel in the Eberoni army and future Lord Protector of the Realm."

Dominic had spent the time wisely while he'd waited for Lennie to catch up. He and his men had cut down numerous thin saplings, then lashed them together with rope. On top of these raft-like structures, they attached the few shields they had. The structures were designed to provide them overhead protection from any arrows or spears shot into the gorge as they passed through.

"Excellent." Lennie greeted Dominic with an embrace.

Dominic smiled. "With these barriers, along with the dragons and Trevelyan's troops, we should be able to get through." His smile faded when he spotted Bran. "Is that the Raven?"

Before Lennie could answer, Dominic whipped out a dagger and dashed toward Bran.

"You bastard!" Dominic seized Bran by his cloak and pointed the dagger at him.

Bran stiffened but made no move to defend himself.

Lennie's heart twisted as she ran toward them.

"What are you doing?" Bertram nearly fell off his little horse in his haste to reach Bran's side.

Milena and Sebastian both gasped and hurried toward them as well.

"I've been looking for you for months," Dominic growled. "You kidnapped my mother and my sister."

Bran nodded with a resigned look. "That is true."

Dominic moved his blade closer to Bran's throat. "Then you will die today."

Chapter 19

"Stop!" Lennie seized hold of Dominic's arm.

He gave her an incredulous look. "What are you doing? This man kidnapped your best friend."

Lennie wrenched the dagger from Dominic's hand while he was still too surprised to struggle with her. "He also helped Quentin save her." As she dropped the blade to the ground, she noted Bran watching her with a mixture of pride and love. Her heart warmed at the sign that he still cared for her.

Dominic kept his grip on Bran's cloak. "He admitted to the kidnappings. I'm hauling him back to Eberon to stand trial."

"No!" Father Bertram grabbed onto Bran from behind and pulled as if he were playing tug-of-war, with Bran as the rope.

"Both of you release him," Lennie ordered.

Dominic shot her a furious look, then shoved Bran back with a mighty push. Bran managed to stay on his feet, but Bertram tumbled over.

"Dominic." Lennie frowned at him. "There's no need to—"

"The Raven is a criminal," Dominic growled. "And those who have given him aid are also guilty."

As Bran helped Bertram back onto his feet, Father Sebastian quickly introduced himself as the head priest of Lourdon Cathedral, working for the Tourinian royal family.

"I can vouch for Bran, Your Highness," Sebastian assured the Eberoni prince. "There is more to the story than you know."

Dominic scoffed. "Not enough to justify his crimes."

Lennie had already heard how Eviana's kidnapping had taken place, but she was curious about what had happened to Eviana's mother. "Bran, can you tell us what happened with the queen?"

He adjusted his cloak, then gave Dominic an apologetic look. "I never intended any harm to come to your mother. I planned to protect her until I could find a way to free her."

With a snort, Dominic picked up his dagger and examined the blade as if he were still contemplating using it. "You expect me to believe your nonsense when you were the one who kidnapped her?"

"My brother Arlo was tasked with the kidnapping of Princess Eviana. Failure of his mission meant death. I helped him in order to keep him alive. We drugged everyone on the caravan headed south, believing the princess was in the covered wagon. When we entered the wagon, we found the unconscious queen and a young woman who was not the princess."

Lennie nodded. That had been Faith, who had volunteered to pretend to be Eviana.

"Greer followed us into the covered wagon," Bran continued, "and when he saw the queen, he drew his sword, ready to kill her on the spot."

Dominic hissed in a breath.

"I stopped him. Greer argued that we needed to kill the royal families anyway, so he should go ahead and get started." Bran sighed. "I couldn't bear to see an innocent woman slain."

"How decent of you," Dominic hissed.

"I had to come up with a reason to keep her alive that would convince Greer." Bran hesitated, then admitted, "I suggested we take the queen hostage, so we could use her to force the princess to comply with our demands, once we captured her."

"So you planned to torture my mother?" Dominic growled.

"I was making stuff up to keep her alive," Bran insisted. "And I was trying to keep Arlo safe, too."

Lennie stepped close to Dominic and whispered, "His brother didn't survive the night. Greer froze him."

Dominic winced, then turned to Bran. "You lost your brother?"

Bran nodded with a pained look. "I failed him."

"It was Greer's fault," Bertram muttered, patting Bran on the shoulder.

"Continue," Dominic ordered, his tone softer now.

"After I made sure the princess was safe, I flew back to the monastery, intending to rescue the queen. But Quentin and a dragon arrived to save her. So I shifted and rescued my youngest brother, Zane. We have spent the last five months hunting for Greer to avenge our brother's death."

Lennie took a deep breath, her heart aching for Bran. The poor man had been mistakenly blamed for everything, and yet, he blamed himself. If only he could be happy now, but she feared their situation would only bring him more misery.

"So you see, Your Highness," Sebastian told Dominic, "we're on the same side now. We all want to capture Greer and rescue the three captives."

Bran nodded. "I will do everything in my power to help you. I cannot bear to lose another brother."

Dominic studied him, then jabbed the dagger back into its sheath. "Fine. But when this is all over, my father will want a word with you. For now, you and your friends will follow my orders. Understood?"

"Of course," Father Sebastian assured him.

Lennie was relieved this bit of drama was over, but then realized there could be another problem. "Where is Sergei?"

"He was here," Dominic replied. "I sent him off with our guide to a local farm, so they could buy a highland cow. One with big horns." When Lennie raised her eyebrows, he gave her a small smile. "I have a plan."

Lennie wondered what it could be as Dominic turned his attention to his men. Soon they were building a campfire and skinning a few rabbits they had tracked and killed.

Along with Milena and Roslyn, Lennie unpacked the food they had brought and arranged it in bowls close to the fire, where the rabbits were now roasting. With the sun descending toward the horizon, they settled around the fire to eat bread and cheese while they waited for the rabbits to be done.

Lennie sat next to Dominic so they could discuss plans. When he told her what he intended to do that night, she smiled.

"My father used that same trick once in the Norveshki mountains to get rid of a gang of thieves."

Dominic nodded. "Ah, here's the cow."

The guide and Sergei led a docile, shaggy cow into the camp, then tied it to a tree.

"Excellent," Dominic told the two men. "Come and eat. As soon as it gets dark, we'll put the plan into action."

Lennie glanced up as an eagle swooped by overhead. "Quentin's back."

Quentin dressed behind some trees, then joined them at the campfire. "Greer and his prisoners are almost through the gorge. When I left, they were still traveling north. At the end of the gorge, there's a large group of armed thugs waiting for them. And there are more thugs stationed along the western rim, waiting to ambush us once we pass through."

"Could you see the captives?" Lennie asked. "Were they all right?"

"Yes," Quentin replied as he sat next to a soldier. "In fact, Pendras spotted me and gave me a nod."

Anton arrived, and after he had shifted and dressed, he dashed toward them with an excited grin. "Trevelyan has sent four troops! I saw Roslyn and Terrance among them, and it looks like the duke himself is leading the charge. They should reach the eastern rim of the gorge by midmorning."

They divided up the roasted rabbits and ate while the sun dipped behind the summit of the mountains to the west. Only a nimbus of pink and gold remained. As darkness fell, the air chilled.

Dominic added more wood to the fire, then explained his plans for the next day. "Tomorrow morning, my soldiers and I will enter the gorge."

"What about us?" Father Sebastian asked, motioning to himself, Bertram, and Milena. "We need to go, too."

"The gorge will be too dangerous for you." When they started to protest, Dominic raised a hand. "Let me explain. The guides have told me of a path that leads up to the eastern rim. The priests and the women will hike up that path with the guides. Once you reach the top, you can join Trevelyan and his troops. You'll be safe with them. From there, you can all travel north and meet us on more level ground at the other end of the gorge."

"I should stay with you," Lennie told Dominic quietly. She knew he was in charge, since he was a colonel, but she still intended to participate. "I know how to fight."

He leaned close and whispered, "I need you more as a dragon, and the gorge will be too narrow for you to fly in. You should be on the rim, where you can attack from above."

She nodded. "All right." She glanced across the flames of the campfire and noticed Bran watching her with a worried look.

"If the gorge is that dangerous, why should anyone go through it?" Sebastian asked. "Why don't we all go up to the eastern rim?"

Dominic smiled. "A good question. Those of us in the gorge will be acting as bait. I want the brigands to attack, so we'll know where they are."

"But that's too dangerous!" Bertram looked horrified.

Dominic shrugged. "That is the nature of war. We'll have the shields we made for protection. I'm counting on the dragons and Trevelyan's troops to destroy all the brigands along the gorge. That way, by the time we reach Greer, he'll have far fewer men to protect him. He'll be easier to defeat, and it will be easier to rescue the captives."

"I believe Greer is headed for Freydor's gold mine," Bran said.

Dominic snorted. "All the gold in the world won't help him once we arrive with Trevelyan's troops and meet up with the kings and the Tourinian army."

Lennie frowned. Once Greer realized how hopeless his situation was, would he take out his anger on the captives before they could be rescued? If Kasper kept the shield up, Greer could do anything he wanted inside their bubble, while an entire army remained helpless to stop him.

As the last hint of sunlight faded away, Dominic rose to his feet. "It's time to get started. The brigands will be watching tonight to see if we try passing through the gorge in the dark. I plan to get rid of as many as possible now, so we'll have a better chance of surviving tomorrow. Is the cow ready?"

"Aye, Colonel," one of his men replied. The soldiers had fastened a burning torch to each end of the cow's horns. The cow was agitated with the fire so close to him, so the soldiers were holding it tightly.

"You're using the poor cow to incite an attack?" Bertram asked.

"Does anyone else want to volunteer to walk through the gorge with a torch?" Dominic asked. "Once the brigands spot the torches, they'll bombard the area with arrows and spears. That'll give away their position, and the dragons, Sergei and Anton, will breathe fire on them."

"Poor cow," Bertram grumbled.

Dominic sighed. "I know, but it is the best way to get the brigands to expose themselves. Obviously, it will be dangerous for the cow and whoever leads him. I will do it, myself."

"Colonel!" his men objected, but Dominic hushed them with a raised hand.

"They have a point," Lennie told him quietly. "You're too valuable to put yourself at risk."

"I'll do it," Bran offered, rising to his feet.

Lennie's heart tightened.

Dominic narrowed his eyes. "You?"

"Bran, no." Bertram tugged on his cloak.

"All I have to do is get the cow to move through the gorge, right?" Bran asked. "I can do it."

"But why would you?" Dominic asked.

"I told you I would do everything in my power to help you, so I am keeping my word." He shrugged. "Besides, Lennie is right. You're a prince, an Eberoni colonel. You're needed. Consider this my apology for the suffering I caused your mother and sister."

Lennie's heart twisted. Did Bran think he wasn't needed? Why did he keep trying to save everyone but himself? Tears came to her eyes when she realized how selfless and noble he was. He was the most beautiful man she'd ever known.

But while he took care of everyone, who was there to look out for him? Who would love him the way he deserved?

"Very well." Dominic gave Bran a curt nod. "Good luck to you."

As Bran strode over to take the cow's lead, Milena and the two priests ran after him, begging him to be careful.

Lennie's heart pounded. She had to protect him. "No! I'll do it."

Bran spun around to stare at her.

"Lennie." Dominic grabbed hold of her arm. "You're the crown princess. You can't."

A tear rolled down her cheek. *But I can't see Bran in danger.*

Bran's gaze grew intense with emotion. "You mustn't put yourself at risk, Your Highness. I will return safely."

She blinked away her tears. "You have to. I'm counting on you."

"Of course he'll be fine." Bertram embraced him, then patted him on the shoulder. "Try to save the cow, too."

Sebastian snorted. "Have you forgotten where your favorite beef pies come from?"

Milena gave Bran a tearful hug, then walked beside him as he led the cow toward the gorge. Two large boulders marked the narrow entrance, barely wide enough for the cow's long horns to pass through.

The two dragon shifters, Anton and Sergei, strode toward the woods to undress. At the edge of the forest, Sergei glanced back at Bran, and his mouth twisted with disdain.

Lennie's breath caught. If Sergei wanted to be rid of Bran, this mission would give him the perfect opportunity. Her heart thudded in her chest as she watched Bran and the cow enter the Gorge of Great Despair. The only way to make sure he was safe was for her to shift and watch over him.

She waited until the two dragons took off. Then she approached Milena, who was hovering by the entrance to the gorge.

"Milena, will you come with me into the woods? We'll pretend we need to relieve ourselves."

"It won't be pretense." Milena lit a small torch, then used it to light their way into the dark woods. She listened as Lennie told her what she suspected and how she planned to stop it. "I wish I could go with you."

Lennie held the torch while Milena went behind a bush to relieve herself. "I hope my suspicions are wrong."

"Actually, I fear you are right," Milena replied. "If Sergei was convinced that he would be the next king, then having that hope suddenly stripped away would enrage him. From what I have seen of his character, he will not handle that rage well. He will lash out. He can't attack you because he needs you. Bran will be the one he targets."

Lennie handed the torch back to Milena. "You're good at reading people."

She shrugged. "I had to learn to be very observant to survive."

Lennie nodded. "Perhaps so, but I can see why Queen Brigitta values you, and why Reynfrid fell for you."

Milena gave her a sad smile. "I love them, too."

Lennie pulled off her boots. "If Dominic asks where I am, tell him I simply wanted to make sure tonight's mission was going as planned. I don't want to accuse Sergei of anything prematurely in case he turns out to be innocent." She finished undressing and folded her clothes in a neat stack on top of a boulder.

"Good luck," Milena told her as Lennie strode into a nearby grassy glade.

Lennie gave her a salute, then shifted. She took off, flying into the starry sky. In the light of the two moons, she spotted Sergei and Anton in the distance. They were weaving back and forth over the canyon, while the torch lights below in the ravine moved slowly northward. She landed on the eastern rim where she could watch.

It seemed ridiculous now that she'd questioned her feelings last night. Tonight, when Bran had volunteered to put himself in danger, she'd realized her mistake. This was not a dream, nor an attempt to escape her destiny. She had fallen in love. Whether there was a future for her and Bran, she didn't know, but she knew now without a doubt that she would always love him.

And tonight, she would make sure he survived.

"Ouch." Bran muttered a curse as his foot rammed into another small boulder. Once again, he wished he had his boots. The sandals were not great for mountain hiking, particularly in the dark.

He would be able to see better if he wasn't trying to distance himself from the torches, but staying close to the light was asking for trouble.

"Come on, Nellie." He gave the rope another tug when the cow he'd named a minute ago stopped again to munch on a patch of grass growing next to the creek. Nellie seemed to believe they were on a gastronomical tour instead of a suicide mission. Every bit of grass, every scraggly bush had to be examined, then devoured.

"I suppose you deserve a last meal," Bran grumbled. He hoped he hadn't eaten his last dinner. He glanced up, but the canyon rims were too high, and it was too dark to see anything.

To his right was the creek, gurgling over numerous fallen rocks. Beyond it lay about thirty inches of rocks and boulders, then a sheer wall that extended up beyond his sight to end with the eastern rim. To his left, more rocks. The wall curved in and out where parts of the western rim had caved in, leaving piles of rubble.

Every now and then, big boulders jutted out above his head, creating a shelter underneath. He noted these, for they could offer him protection once the arrows and spears started raining down.

Time crept along slowly. Lennie's face kept coming to mind, the way she'd looked when he'd kissed her the other night, all breathless with passion, and the way she'd looked at him tonight before he'd headed into the gorge. There had been fear in her eyes. Desperation. She'd even offered to go in his stead.

She did care for him. He knew it. If he survived tonight, he would make sure she knew how much he loved her.

A slight whistling sound came from overhead, and he yanked at the rope, trying to pull Nellie up against the wall. The arrow was faster and struck the cow's shoulder. Nellie bellowed, then bucked, nearly kicking Bran with her hooves.

He let go of the rope and plastered himself against the canyon wall beneath an overhang. More arrows zinged down, a few hitting Nellie and others thudding into the ground.

The sky suddenly lit up as bursts of fire shot down. Screams rent the air. The arrows stopped, and Nellie lumbered to the side of the creek. As she dipped her head to drink, one of the torches slipped into the water and the flame sizzled out.

Bran emerged slowly from the overhang and looked up. Anton and Sergei had set the western rim ablaze. "We're safe now, Nellie."

Thanks to Nellie's thick hairy coat, only three arrows had penetrated it, and two were shallow enough that he was able to pull them out with the cow hardly seeming to notice. The first one, which had hit her shoulder, was a problem.

He took hold of the lead. "Let's get you back to the camp. Maybe they can save you." Or they might decide to eat Nellie to celebrate the success of the mission, but he didn't mention that.

Suddenly, the sky lit up. Bran glanced up just as a column of fire shot down. He leaped to the side, feeling the heat of the flames as they engulfed the cow.

Damn. He plastered himself against the wall as a second burst of fire shot down. *Sergei.* The bastard was trying to kill him.

With a mournful cry, the cow collapsed into the creek. It

was on fire and the few inches of water in the creek would not be enough to save the poor animal.

Bran stripped and shifted, figuring a black raven would be harder to spot in the ravine. He flew several yards down the gorge, then stopped beneath another overhang when a shot of pain coursed down his wing. He wasn't ready for flight yet. He'd have to make it back to camp in human form.

Chapter 20

Cease your fire! Lennie yelled mentally at Sergei as she soared toward him. The bastard had done it! *You cannot kill an innocent man!*

I'm doing it for you! Sergei shouted back. *The Raven is endangering you, endangering our country!*

The only thing in danger is your plan to be king, Lennie growled back.

I am your only choice! Sergei insisted.

Not true, Anton argued. *I always knew Her Highness would end up with me. I only had to wait for you to show everyone what an ass you are.*

The crown will be mine! Sergei aimed a burst of fire at Anton, but the dragon swerved to miss it.

You dare attack me? Anton hissed.

What the hell is going on? Silas demanded.

I have rejected Sergei's suit, Lennie responded. *He has reacted with rage and violence.*

I have every right to be enraged! Sergei shouted. *Your Majesty, you don't know what's been going on here. The princess has shirked her royal duty and has thrown herself at a lowly—*

Enough! Silas growled. *It is obvious you will not give my daughter the kind of support she deserves. She was right to reject you. Be prepared to defend your actions in court.*

Sergei let out another angry burst of fire, then flew off.

Shall I follow him? Anton asked.

No, Lennie replied. *We need you to provide protection for Dominic and his men tomorrow. Let's go back to camp. Father, I'll explain everything later.*

Very well, Silas grumbled. *I'll see you soon.*

No doubt her father was upset that one of his dragons had attacked another. She couldn't recall such a thing ever happening before. It was a crime so unheard of that there wasn't even a set punishment for it. But obviously, Sergei would be punished.

But then she recalled how quickly her father had defended her even though he didn't know what had transpired. That was the kind of love she was accustomed to, the kind she craved. And the kind she knew she would receive from Bran.

Was he all right? She circled around the gorge, searching for him. There was a fire below, and the scent of burnt hair and beef wafted toward her. She couldn't see Bran anywhere. *Goddesses, please keep him safe.*

The western rim was littered with charred bodies. There would be no more arrows shot into the gorge tonight. If Bran had escaped the arrows and Sergei's blast of fire, he would eventually make it back. She had to believe in him. And goddesses help her, she wanted to believe in their love.

She landed back in the grassy glade and shifted. After locating the clothes she'd left on the boulder, she dressed and quickly returned to camp. Anton was already there and had reported the success of the mission. Dominic and the soldiers were happy. Apparently Anton had refrained from admitting what Sergei had done.

Milena and the priests were gathered around the entrance of the gorge, their expressions taut with worry. Milena was holding a torch to act as a beacon for Bran.

"What happened?" Sebastian asked as Lennie approached.

"Exactly what I suspected." She lowered her voice. "Sergei aimed a blast of fire into the gorge."

They gasped.

"And Bran?" Milena asked.

"I don't know." Lennie gazed into the gorge, but with Milena's torch, she could see only a few feet inside.

"We must pray," Bertram murmured, making the sign of the sun with his hands.

Dominic wandered over to join them. "Any sign of the Raven?"

"Not yet." Milena shot the prince an annoyed look.

Lennie drew Dominic aside and told him what Sergei had done.

"Damn." Dominic grimaced. "Do you think he'll betray us?"

The princess will be betrayed. Bertram's prediction flitted through Lennie's mind. "I'm afraid it's very possible."

Dominic hissed in a breath. "If it happens, we'll deal with it. But I'm going to need your dragon more than ever tomorrow. You and Anton can breathe fire on any new thugs Greer sends to attack us."

Lennie nodded. "All right."

"Bran!" Milena shouted.

Lennie ran back to the boulders that marked the entrance. Sebastian pulled Bran through, straight into his and Bertram's arms. Then Milena handed the torch to Lennie and joined the group hug.

"We were so worried!" Milena cried.

"Is she the Raven's wom—" Dominic started, but Lennie interrupted him.

"She's his sister." Lennie's eyes met Bran's as the priests released him. "*I'm* his woman."

His gaze flared with heat.

"You and the Raven?" Dominic's voice sounded shocked.

"Why not?" Milena asked him, her chin lifted in defiance. "My brother is the eldest son of an earl."

Dominic snorted. "You mean the traitor Lord Morris?"

Lennie ignored them and moved closer to Bran. His shirt was unbuttoned and hanging loose beneath his cloak. His chest, as usual, was magnificent. "Did you shift?"

He nodded. "Yes, but I wasn't able to fly very far." He tilted his head. "Do you know what happened?"

"Yes." She took his hand. "Sergei attacked you and Anton. He flew away."

Bran squeezed her hand, then gave Bertram an apologetic look. "I'm sorry, Father. I wasn't able to save Nellie."

Bertram nodded with tears in his eyes. "We're just grateful to have you back, son."

Lennie smiled. "You named the cow?"

Bran smiled back, still holding her hand. "When can we talk?"

Talk? She wanted more than that. Leaning close to him, she whispered, "Later. When we can have some privacy."

His voice was soft against her ear. "I'll be ready."

A surge of desire shot from her heart to her woman's core. She wanted this beautiful man. No matter what the future held for them, she wanted him. Tonight.

When Bran heard the priests on either side of him softly snoring, he sat up. The campsite was quiet, the fire still burning to give them warmth. The soldiers were taking turns guarding the camp, and apparently whoever was guarding also had the job of feeding logs to the fire.

Bran put on his sandals, then rose slowly to his feet, making sure not to wake Bertram or Sebastian. He walked past the fire to where Milena and Lennie were sleeping. Or pretending to sleep. When he paused beside them, Lennie's eyes opened and she smiled.

"What are you doing?" the soldier on guard duty asked.

Bran pointed to the woods. "Nature calls."

The guard nodded wearily as he trudged around the perimeter of the camp. "Don't venture off too far. There could be brigands or wild animals."

Bran headed into the woods. He relieved himself, then waited. It was chilly away from the fire, so he wrapped his cloak tightly around him.

After a while, he saw a light coming through the woods. A torch.

"Bran?" Lennie called softly.

"Here." He approached her. She'd been smart. Not only did she have a lit torch in one hand, but she was wrapped in a blanket.

She looked around, then motioned with her head. "This way."

He followed her into a glade where the twin moons shone down, glinting silver on the grass. She jabbed the torch into the ground, then turned to face him.

Her white-blond hair fairly glowed in the moonlight, and her skin was radiant.

"You look like an angel," he murmured.

She winced. "I'm not. In fact, I need to confess—"

"I already know." He figured she was referring to being the heir to the Norveshki throne. "Milena told me."

Lennie's eyes widened. "It doesn't bother you?"

"I'm concerned, of course." He dragged a hand through his hair. "I know a great deal is expected of you, and I don't want to cause you any trouble."

Her eyes softened with a loving look. "That is so like you. You're more worried about me than yourself."

"You have a great destiny before you. Someday, you'll be queen." He smiled. "And a wonderful one, I have no doubt." He stepped toward her. "I want to assure you now that you will always have my full support. I have no desire to be a king, Lenushka. All I ever wanted was you."

Her eyes glistened with tears. "Bran."

"I know it might not be possible, but the only title I desire with you is 'husband.' Whether that can happen or not, it will not affect the way I feel about you. I love you. And I always will."

She ran toward him and threw her arms around his neck. "I love you, too."

His angel. He held her tight, rubbing his jaw against her beautiful, soft hair.

She pulled back, and her blanket tumbled to the ground unheeded. "Kiss me." She blinked. "I meant that as a request, not a royal command."

He grinned. "This is a kiss for the princess." He pressed his lips against her brow. "And this is for my daring and darling Lenushka." He wrapped a hand around the back of her head and kissed her slowly and thoroughly.

She melted against him, her hands sliding beneath his cloak to hold him tight. "Bran . . ."

"Hmm?" He trailed kisses down her neck.

"Why on Aerthlan is your shirt buttoned?"

He smiled against her neck. "Because it's chilly."

"You feel very warm to me." She began to unbutton his shirt.

"Lennie."

She glanced up at him with a shy look. "Yes?"

"Do you know what you're doing?"

She shrugged. "I've seen your chest before."

"I'm not sure if it's wise for us to undress."

Her hands stilled. "You don't . . . want me?"

"Oh, I do. But once the clothes start coming off, it will be hard to stop."

She laid a palm against his bare chest. "Do we have to stop?" She glanced at him, frowning. "Is it because you're a priest?"

He shook his head. "I took an oath for five years when I turned nineteen."

"And now you're . . . ?"

"Twenty-four."

She grinned. "Time's up!"

He chuckled.

She finished unbuttoning his shirt. "Of course, as a priest, you may be as inexperienced as I am, but I'm sure we'll figure it out."

His smile faded. "I'm not a virgin."

"What?" She gave him a shocked look. "And Bertram's always saying what a good boy you are. Well, I—"

"Don't tell him."

She scoffed. "Will you tell me? Or is it so lurid, I'll be traumatized for life?"

He winced. "It's more pathetic than lurid. When I was seventeen, a new maid came to work at the monastery. She begged me to come to her room one night, saying there was a rat in there, and she was terrified. But when I went in, carrying a trap, I discovered a bigger trap waiting for me. She bolted the door and threw off her clothes."

"So *she* was the rat!" Lennie huffed. "I suppose she got your cheese?"

He shrugged. "I was young and curious. And flattered, thinking that she wanted me."

"I should have known," Lennie grumbled. "Any man as gorgeous as you is bound to have women throwing themselves at him. So how many rats have jumped onto your ship?"

"She was the only one."

Lennie's eyes narrowed. "So whenever you landed in a village and shifted, the women didn't rush at you?"

He gave her an incredulous look. "I never shifted in public. It would have made the children scream and the village men want to kill me."

Lennie sighed. "I suppose that's true."

"Besides, it wasn't as if the maid actually wanted me. I became suspicious the next day when I checked a calendar to see when the Spring Embrace would occur. I was worried because I knew Zane would be turning ten, and the monks would start flogging him. When I counted how much time he had left, it was nine months."

"Oh. The lady rat wanted to have an Embraced child?"

Bran nodded. "Master Lorne had arranged the whole affair. Apparently, he was no longer capable of fathering children, so he thought he would use me. The maid kept trying to entice me for the rest of that week, but I stayed away. I didn't want to father a child that the Brotherhood would use. Or whip. When I refused to cooperate, the master sent the girl away."

Lennie smoothed her hand on his chest. "I'm sorry. That was a terrible thing he did to you. And the girl."

"Actually, I rather enjoyed it at the time."

"Ha!" She gave him a light thump. "This is not the time for honesty."

"In that case, I loathed every minute of it."

"That's better."

He grabbed her hand and kissed it. "After that, I vowed that I would only make love to a woman I truly loved."

"That would be me."

"Aye." He pulled her close and kissed her once again. She responded eagerly, even opening her mouth to let his tongue explore.

"Bran." She drew back, breathless. "I-I'm not sure what's happening to me, but I want . . . something. I want you."

Desire and longing nearly overwhelmed him, and he pulled her close. "I want you, too. But I don't think I have the right to take you."

"Bran—"

"I'm serious." He rubbed a hand down her back. "Your parents, your nobles and fellow countrymen—they will all find me hard to accept. If I behave without honor now, it will

give them more reason to reject me. I want you, believe me."
He pressed her hips against him so she could feel how hard
he was. She responded with a small gasp.

He kissed her brow. "If I go too far tonight, I could end up
losing you."

She rested her head against his chest. "I shouldn't be angry
with you for being noble. It's one of the reasons I love you."

He planted another kiss on top of her head, then nuzzled
his cheek against her soft hair. "A little kissing would be all
right, I suppose."

"And touching?" She dragged her fingertips along his
back, gently caressing the scars. "I want to kiss all your scars.
I would erase all your bad memories if I could."

"Leave them be. They make me what I am." He explored
the adorable little pointed tip of her ear. "Besides, we should
look to the future, not the past."

Her hands stilled. "But we should enjoy the present. Sergei
once bragged to me that there were ways he could give me
pleasure without—"

"That bastard."

She looked up at Bran and smiled. "Jealous?"

"Hell, yes."

"Would you happen to know anything about those
methods?"

Hell, no. But he could figure them out. "Of course." He
sat her down on the nearby boulder. "First we'll take off your
boots."

Her mouth twitched. "How exciting."

"Trust me." He gave one a tug and it came off. Then he
tickled her instep and kissed her toes.

She laughed. "That's supposed to bring me pleasure?"

"You're giggling, aren't you?"

She shrugged, still smiling.

He removed her other boot, then smoothed the blanket out on the ground. "Come here." He stretched out a hand to her. "That's a request, not a royal command."

With a snort, she plopped down beside him.

His mouth twitched. "How romantic."

"Oh, I know. I should be . . . alluring, right?" She stretched out beside him, lifting her arms above her head. "Take me, big boy."

He nearly choked, trying not to laugh. By the Light, life with Lennie would be filled with joy.

She grinned. "That was a request, not a royal command."

"I understand." He began to unbutton her green uniform jacket. Her grin faded, and his heart began to pound. This was definitely asking for trouble. But right now, he wanted as much trouble as he could get.

He opened her military-style jacket to reveal a lacy camisole underneath. That was his Lennie. He'd never met a woman both so strong and feminine at the same time. He gave the green ribbon at the top of her camisole a tug and it came free. The buttons were tiny, and his hands were trembling, but he managed.

Her chest was expanding rapidly now with each breath. "Go on," she whispered.

He peeled back the sheer cotton fabric to reveal her breasts. Moonlight gleamed off her creamy pale skin, and her nipples pebbled, exposed to the chilly air.

She shivered when he touched her, running his fingertips around the curve of each breast. He rubbed one nipple, then plucked gently at the hardened tip. "Oh, goddesses," she whispered.

He fondled the other nipple, then leaned over to draw the first one into his mouth.

With a moan, she grabbed hold of his head. She was feeling pleasure now—he could feel the thrumming tension in her body and hear the panting of her breath. But how could he push her over the edge into that state of oblivion he'd once experienced? And how could he keep himself from losing his seed?

He kissed her other nipple, sucking at it while she began to squirm beneath him. She clutched at his shoulders and wrapped a leg around him, instinctively drawing him close.

"Lennie." He pulled at the drawstring that held up her breeches. "If you want me to stop, say so."

"Don't stop."

He loosened the waist, then drew the breeches down her long, beautiful legs. Smoothing a hand up her legs, he reached her smallclothes, then rested his hand on the soft mound between her legs.

She gasped and tensed her legs.

"Do you want me to touch you?"

She hesitated just a moment, then let her legs go limp. "Yes."

He rubbed gently at the mound, then with a groan, she spread her legs. When he slipped his fingers along her core, he could feel the dampness of the cloth covering her.

A surge of lust ripped through him. He unbuttoned her smallclothes and dragged them off. Then he nudged her legs farther apart, settling himself between them. His manhood was so swollen now, he ached for release. But dammit, he would see her undone first.

He explored her thoroughly with his fingers, studying her to see which exact spots made her jolt. *There.* This was it.

She cried out, planting her feet on the ground to grind herself against his hand. Moisture soaked his fingers, and the scent drew him in. He leaned down and licked her so he could have a taste.

With a cry, she shattered.

With a groan, he yanked down his breeches and emptied his seed on the grass beside them.

"Bran." She reached for him, and he collapsed beside her, drawing her into his arms.

"Oh, my." She breathed hard. "Is it always like this?"

"No." He buried his face in her neck. "With us, it will only get better."

"Dear goddesses, that might kill us."

Chapter 21

The next morning, Lennie couldn't steal a glimpse at Bran without a blush heating her cheeks and her mouth curling into a silly grin. Even worse, he was reacting the same way. After a few silent exchanges like that over breakfast, they were receiving suspicious looks from Milena and Sebastian.

Good goddesses, at this rate it was going to be obvious they had become lovers. So Lennie turned away, attempting to ignore Bran altogether. It didn't work, for whenever she heard his voice, heat rushed to her face and other parts of her body that were longing for a replay of last night's glorious adventure.

As Dominic readied his horse, she approached to tell him that Pendras had contacted her in the wee hours of the morning. Luckily her brother hadn't interrupted her when she'd been cavorting in the grassy glade with Bran.

"What did Pen say?" Dominic asked. Since he and Pendras were best friends, they tended to call each other Pen and Dom when they were being polite to each other, which was rare. Most of the time, they enjoyed tormenting each other with rude or silly names.

"They made it through the gorge, met up with a large group of ruffians, and set up camp," Lennie reported. "A few hours later a survivor from last night's battle reached them and told Greer what had happened. He was livid and promptly ordered the ruffians to slaughter us all today."

Dominic snorted. "Typical villain response. Did he claim the river would flow with blood?"

"Probably."

Dominic smirked. "He doesn't know about Trevelyan, does he?"

"No, there was no mention of the duke."

"Then he's in for a rude surprise." Dominic squared his broad shoulders. "Let them come. We'll be ready for them, and the more we kill today, the better."

Lennie nodded. "Even so, I think you should take only a few soldiers through the gorge, and let the others go with us up to the rim. You will be sitting ducks at the bottom of the ravine, too easy to target."

Dominic considered her suggestion a moment, then agreed that he didn't want to lose any more men. "We have three raft-like shields made. We call them turtle shells. They can be handled by two men apiece, so we need only six men. I'll send the rest with you." He pointed toward one of the guides. "Travis claims the path to the eastern rim winds back and forth but has a gentle enough incline that you can take the horses. You should get started right away."

"Aye, Colonel." Lennie gave him a salute, then strode over to Milena and the priests to make sure they were ready to go.

As they finished packing their saddlebags, Bran wandered over to her. She could tell, by the way he kept biting his lip, that he was trying not to smile. But his brown eyes were warm and full of love.

"Are you coming with us?" she asked.

He shook his head. "I offered to go with Dominic."

She winced. "Pendras told me that Greer has sent a large group to attack. Please be careful." She grazed his hand with her own, and he quickly grabbed hold and gave her fingers a squeeze before letting go.

"You, too." He held her horse steady while she mounted, then handed her the reins. "I'll see you on the other side of the gorge."

With a parting smile, she steered her horse toward the path where the mounted guides and five soldiers were waiting. "Let's go!"

The two guides and three of the soldiers took the lead. Lennie followed them with Bertram, Milena, and Father Sebastian behind her, and then the last two soldiers in the rear.

As the path wound higher and higher up the side of a mountain, she could glance down and see Bran and the others proceeding through the gorge on horseback with the shields ready. Quentin was in eagle form, flying ahead so he could alert them whenever he spotted the enemy. Anton had flown over to Trevelyan's troops so he could serve as a communication link between Lennie and the duke.

Eventually, the path Lennie was on skirted around to the far side of the mountain. She could no longer see Bran or Dominic, but the view was spectacular, reminding her of the mountains back home. The path climbed slowly until they emerged on a high grassy plain that extended northward for miles. To their left was the cliff, although the path never ventured too close. To their right, the high plain was interrupted far in the distance by mountain peaks, topped with snow. All of this land belonged to the Duke of Trevelyan.

They stopped to rest for a moment, and Lennie strode toward the rim for a peek into the gorge. There, far below, she spotted Bran and the soldiers. The section they were passing through was so narrow, they had to ride in single file. Across the gorge, on the western rim, she spotted vultures circling. The grass was blackened from dragon fire and littered with the charred bodies of last night's skirmish.

After another hour of riding, they spotted the banners and

mounted soldiers of the duke's small army. He had set up camp about half a mile from the rim.

Terrance and Roslyn rode over to join Lennie's group, then escorted them to the duke.

Lennie dismounted and approached the middle-aged man. His hair had more gray than blond, but his eyes were still a sharp blue. "Your Grace, I'm Princess Lenushka of Norveshka."

"A pleasure to meet you." He shook her hand with a strong grip, then pulled a young man forward. "Your Highness, may I introduce my son and heir, Lord Rupert."

"Rupert?" Lennie glanced at the handsome young man, who appeared to be about her age.

Trevelyan chuckled. "Yes, I named him after my dear friend, Rupert, who is King Ulfrid, of course. The king is Rupert's godfather. And Rupert will be inheriting quite a large estate with three castles and a silver mine."

Rupert gave her a quick bow, then muttered to his father, "No need to be so obvious, Pa."

The duke appeared a little embarrassed, so Lennie smiled at him. "You must be very proud. Thank you for coming to our assistance so quickly."

Trevelyan huffed. "I always sensed that Freydor was trouble. And Ulfrid knows he can always count on me." He glanced toward the gorge. "Any sign of the traitors yet?"

"Not yet." Lennie motioned to Anton, who was standing nearby. "Can you look for them? I'll join you soon."

Anton saluted, then slipped behind a few horses to undress and shift.

The duke cleared his throat. "Anton was telling me you'll inherit the Norveshki throne?"

"Yes."

Trevelyan nudged his son closer. "I'll go check the rim now." He mounted up and charged off with a handful of soldiers.

"Sorry about that." Rupert gave her an apologetic smile. "Father tried to match me up with Princess Roslyn last night, but she declared herself already taken."

"That is true." With a grin, Roslyn grabbed Terrance's arm.

"Actually, I'm taken, too," Lennie announced.

"By one of the dragons?" Roslyn asked.

Lennie shook her head. "The Raven." While Roslyn gasped, Milena and the priests exchanged smiles.

"I thought you wanted to kill him just a few days ago!" Roslyn exclaimed.

"That sounds like an interesting story," Rupert said, his blue eyes twinkling with humor.

Lennie looked over the handsome young man. "Actually, Roslyn and I have a few single cousins who happen to be princesses, in case you're interested."

With a laugh, he raised his hands. "I'm in no hurry." He turned to greet Milena and the priests. "If you're hungry, go over to the campfire, and they'll give you something to eat."

As the priests and Milena headed toward the campfire, Anton contacted Lennie.

I have spotted the new group of ruffians, he reported. *They're on the western rim about a mile north of the duke's camp. Dominic and his group are about a mile and a half away.*

On my way, Lennie told him. She gave Rupert and Terrance the location of Greer's men, then Rupert shouted out the order for the troops to mount up. Within minutes, Terrance, Rupert, the duke, and four troops were charging north to attack.

The battle was imminent, so Lennie needed to shift right away. With no trees in sight, she'd have to ask Roslyn, Milena, and two of the female cooks to help her.

As she gathered up four blankets, she told the priests, "By the way, I'm not just a princess. I'm a dragon."

"What?" Bertram blinked.

Sebastian's eyes widened with shock.

"And I need to shift now." She handed out the blankets to the four women.

They held up the blankets to form a small space. Inside this shelter, Lennie stripped and shifted. Roslyn and Milena jumped back, knowing that her body would suddenly expand, but the cooks were caught off guard and fell back on their rumps with a gasp.

"Holy Light!" One of the cooks scrambled to her feet. "She really is a dragon!"

Bertram gasped and stumbled back. Sebastian caught him, then shot Lennie an annoyed look.

"I always knew she was hiding something," Sebastian grumbled. "But I never imagined it was this!"

"Bran is smitten with a dragon woman?" Bertram asked, his face stunned as he looked Lennie over.

Sebastian scowled at Milena. "You knew about this, didn't you?"

Milena sighed as she folded up the blanket she was holding. She gave Lennie a wry look. "Keep Bran safe for us, will you?"

Lennie nodded. Everyone moved back to give her room to extend her wings. With a mighty flap and push from her legs, she took off.

A massive war cry roared down the gorge, and Bran and the others looked up. Arrows shot across from the eastern rim. Trevelyan's troops were attacking. An answering volley of arrows from the western rim suddenly halted in midair and fell into the ravine.

"What the hell?" Dominic stopped his horse to watch.

"That's Terrance," Bran explained.

"The one who used to teach archery at Benwick?" Dominic asked. "I thought he could only control the trajectory of his own arrows."

"His powers improved while he was at the monastery." Bran understood now why Terrance had spent so many hours honing his Embraced gift. He'd been trying to take his mind off Roslyn's engagement to another man.

The soldiers exclaimed when another volley from Greer's men fell harmlessly into the ravine.

"Damn," Dominic whispered. "The man can defeat an army single-handedly. He should be a general. Or the Lord Protector of Tourin."

"You should tell that to King Ulfrid," Bran suggested. "It would help Terrance and Roslyn. They've fallen in love."

Dominic glanced back at Bran with an incredulous look. "Just how many romances were happening during your journey north?" He shook his head. "Never mind. Let's keep going."

They increased their speed through the gorge while the battle continued overhead. Bran spotted Anton flying across the gorge to shoot fire down on the ruffians. Screams filled the air.

The ruffians retaliated, shooting arrows at Anton. He zoomed straight up into the air to escape being hit. Once again, Terrance halted the arrows and let them fall.

A second dragon crossed the gorge, raining fire down on Greer's men. Was Sergei back? Bran wondered, then noticed the smaller size of the dragon. The pinkish belly. *Damn!* It was the runt! The damned dragon who had made him crash had returned.

"Shields up!" Dominic ordered as they neared the area where the battle was happening.

Bran, riding right behind Dominic, was sharing a turtle shell with him. With their left wrists slipped into leather straps, they lifted their arms to hold the shields over their heads. They would be safe from any arrows shot down at them, but they could no longer see what was happening above them.

They rode around a slight bend, and the path widened. Large overhanging rocks lined the left-hand side of the gorge. One of the rocks had a deep shadow underneath—the entrance to a cave, Bran thought.

Just as they drew near, a horde of ruffians streamed out, screaming and wielding battle-axes. Instinctively, Dominic and Bran both lowered the shield to protect their left flank. The four soldiers behind them dismounted, then forced their way forward, using their shields to push back the attackers so they could join Dominic. Together, they formed a wall around their group. They struggled to keep the turtle shell in place while the enemy pounded on them with axes. Beneath the wall, they managed to slice legs with their swords. And in the sliver of space between the shields, they jabbed at the foe.

"Keep it up!" Dominic ordered.

Bran grunted as a battle-axe slammed into the shield right in front of his face. They were making slow progress wounding the ruffians, but they were so outnumbered, he wasn't sure how long they could hold out.

A screech sounded overhead. The smaller dragon swooped into the gorge, narrowly avoiding scraping the walls with its wings. With a well-aimed burst of fire, it incinerated the ruffians. They screamed, rolling about on the ground or running upstream to throw themselves into the creek.

A sudden silence surrounded them, broken only by the sound of their own erratic breathing and a few moans from the enemy.

"Lower the shields," Dominic ordered.

His soldiers made quick work of kicking their way through the bodies and skewering any enemy who was still alive.

Bran glanced up. The battle overhead seemed to be over, too. He spotted the two dragons, flying about, searching for any escapees that could be blasted with fire.

"It's over," Dominic announced. "Let's get going."

"My horse didn't make it," one of the soldiers reported.

"You can use my horse," Bran offered. "I'll fly up and join the troops on the rim."

"Very well." Dominic nodded at him. "You're all right, Raven."

Bran snorted. If only he could get Lennie's father to agree with that assessment. He quickly shed his clothes. "Could you take my clothes, so I'll have something to wear later?"

One of the soldiers waited behind as the others started off, slowly picking their way around the dead bodies. Bran stuffed his clothes into the soldier's saddlebags, then the man rode off to join the others.

Bran shifted, then stretched out his wings. A little twinge in his right wing, but after a few flaps, the tightness went away. He flew at a steady pace, rising higher and higher until he reached the top. The western rim was littered with dead bodies. On the eastern rim, only a bit of flattened grass showed that anyone had ever been there. Most of the troops were headed north with Anton flying overhead. A few men had remained behind to dismantle the campsite.

At the camp, Bran spotted Milena, Roslyn, Terrance, and the priests. The pink-bellied dragon landed next to them.

At last, Bran thought. He wanted a word with the blasted dragon who had tracked him like a criminal, caused him to crash, and broken his arm. But the dragon had also saved them in the gorge. Being a runt had come in handy. He'd just managed to fit between the rock walls. Actually, now that Bran thought about it, the runt had displayed some remarkable skill.

He still deserved a slap in the face, though. If Bran hadn't been incapacitated by the dragon, he could have saved Zane.

As he flew near the campsite, he saw something strange. Milena, Roslyn, and two other women had set a pile of clothes in front of the dragon, then surrounded it with stretched-out blankets.

The dragon's long tail was still visible, sticking out beyond the blankets. Suddenly it shrank and disappeared. The four women closed in, forming a cocoon.

Bran landed. His right arm twinged again as he folded his wings. He'd probably flown enough for the day.

The women lowered the blankets and started folding them up.

In the center was a woman, her back to Bran.

His heart lurched. He recognized that green uniform and the long white-blond hair she was quickly braiding.

Lennie.

She turned and spotted him. "Bran." She smiled. "Is that you?"

He stumbled back, tripping over his own bird legs to collapse in an awkward lump. *Lennie.* His Lennie was a dragon.

She'd been the one who had chased him down. She'd made him crash. She'd broken his arm.

And she'd never told him.

She'd let him kiss her and make love to her without telling him.

"Bran?" Lennie stepped toward him, her smile fading.

He shook his head, his feathers ruffling. What a fool he had been. He should have known. But he'd never heard of a female dragon before. Now he could understand why she was going to inherit the throne. Now he understood why he'd suspected she was still keeping secrets.

She had been.

"Bran." Lennie dropped to her knees so they were eye to eye. "I thought you knew. You said Milena told—" She turned to Milena. "You didn't tell him I was a dragon?"

Milena shook her head. "I told him you were the heiress."

Lennie closed her eyes with a pained look, then turned back to Bran. "I'm sorry. I was going to tell you."

A surge of anger shot through him. Why hadn't she been

honest with him? Why didn't she trust him? How could she claim to love him while keeping something so important a secret?

He thrust his wings out, ignoring the twinge in the right one, and took off, flying north.

He still had to save Zane. And kill Greer.

Chapter 22

Lennie remained hunched on the ground, her heart sinking as she watched Bran fly away.

Roslyn kneeled beside her, wrapping an arm around her shoulders. "It'll be all right. I'm sure of it."

She didn't sound very sure, Lennie thought. "I should have told him. I was going to last night, but . . ." What a fool she'd been. She should have made sure Bran knew everything before throwing herself at him.

Tears stung her eyes. "I can't bear to lose him."

"You won't!" Roslyn cried. She looked at Terrance and her bottom lip quivered. "I know what you mean. I'm afraid, too."

Terrance strode up to Roslyn, then lifted her to her feet. "Now that I've found you, I'll never let you go."

"I won't, either!" Roslyn wrapped her arms around him.

Lennie blinked back her tears as she stood up. "I won't give up on Bran." She just hoped he hadn't given up on her. He was still flying away, now hardly more than a black dot in the distant sky.

Sebastian sighed. "Deceptions and lies always come back to harm you." He winced. "I don't mean to sound insensitive. I'm sure Bran's feelings for you haven't changed. He's simply in shock right now."

"By the Light, I'm still in shock!" Bertram exclaimed. "A female dragon! Who would ever believe that?"

"You must be the first of your kind," Sebastian added, and Lennie nodded.

"My father is a dragon, of course, and my mother's father was a dragon from the Tolenko clan," Lennie explained. "So we believe there was enough dragon blood from both parents to cause me to be a shifter." But whether she could have dragon children was unknown. That was why the nobles had insisted she marry a dragon. They wanted to make sure future rulers would always be dragons.

"It's a blessing," Terrance said as he continued to hold onto Roslyn. "Princess Lenushka shifts into a smaller dragon. When Bran and the others were attacked, she was able to fit into the gorge to defeat the attackers."

"She did?" Sebastian asked, his eyes widening.

Lennie shrugged. "I'm a trained soldier."

"I was at the rim, so I saw the whole thing," Terrance claimed. "Some ruffians were hiding in a cave, and when Bran's group came along, they attacked. Bran and the others were terribly outnumbered, and they might not have survived if Princess Lenushka hadn't flown down, breathing fire."

"Oh, thank you!" Milena ran up to Lennie and embraced her.

"The Light be praised!" Bertram grinned. "Thank you, my dear."

Sebastian smiled at her. "All will be well. Once Bran recovers from his shock, he'll remember you saved their lives."

Lennie hoped so. Right now, Bran was probably remembering how she'd made him crash and break his arm. She motioned toward Terrance. "He's being too modest to mention it, but Terrance could have defeated the enemy single-handedly."

"Really?" Roslyn gazed up at him with wonder in her eyes.

With a blush, Terrance shrugged. "I've been working on my gift to increase its power."

Lennie smiled. "Everyone there saw it. I'm sure Trevelyan will tell King Ulfrid what you did."

"Yes!" Roslyn clapped her hands together.

Lennie strode toward her horse. "We had better go if we're going to catch up with the duke."

They all mounted up and charged north.

As they rode, a thought repeated itself over and over in Lennie's mind. *Don't give up on me, Bran.*

He could never give up on her, Bran realized as the shock of seeing Lennie's dragon form wore off. The whole time he'd been flying north, he'd replayed everything she'd ever said to him. Back at the monastery, she'd apologized for the pain and suffering he'd gone through when he'd broken his arm. And then she'd tried to make him as comfortable as possible in the wagon.

It was true she had chased him in dragon form, but when he thought about it, she had seen him as a criminal, guilty of kidnapping the Eberoni queen and princess. She'd believed him the new master of the Brotherhood.

Hell, it was true he'd carried out the kidnappings. It was also true that he'd called himself the Brotherhood's new leader while he'd traveled about. It had been the best way to convince other priests to give up on the Brotherhood's insane quest to take over the world.

Could he really blame her for his crash and broken arm? He could have stopped flying. He'd chosen not to.

Was he making excuses for her now? He snorted. So what if he was? They'd both made mistakes. If they loved each other, they would remain true to each other.

He did love her. And he believed she loved him. She'd given herself to him last night. That had to mean she trusted him. And she'd thought he already knew she was a dragon.

She hadn't hesitated to save him and the others in the gorge.

Damn! He shouldn't have left her.

He circled around, then noticed for the first time how far he'd gone. He'd passed Trevelyan's troops. Lennie and her companions were bringing up the rear. They had all reached the northern end of the gorge.

His heart pounding, he realized they were now on Frey-dor's land. Greer couldn't be that far away. With his superior vision, Bran spotted an eagle ahead in the distance. It was Quentin, following a small group on horseback.

Zane. Lennie's brother, Pendras, was there, too. And Reynfrid, the prince whom his sister loved.

Now that he'd actually spotted Zane, Bran decided to continue north. His right wing was starting to ache, so he glided as much as he could.

After about an hour, he caught up with Quentin, who had been flying at a slower pace to remain unnoticed behind Greer's group. Quentin acknowledged him with a squawk. No one in Greer's group glanced back. Apparently, they couldn't hear through the invisible wall.

The farther north they traveled, the more barren the mountains became. The air was decidedly colder and the wind stronger. It was a constant wind, Bran realized, and it was coming off the North Sea, which meant they were getting close to the northern coast. Centuries of wind had worn these mountains down so that the peaks were no longer high and jagged, but more dome-shaped. Even the few scraggly pine trees were bent over to the south.

His wing ached more as he struggled to fly against the wind. Even Quentin, with his powerful eight-foot wingspan, had to weave back and forth.

Bran could now see the six men in Greer's group below. The three captives were on horseback, their hands tied to the saddle horns. Dressed for Lourdon in the south, they were now shivering from the cold. Luckily, the shield surrounding them seemed to be providing a shelter from the wind. Their hair was not being blown about.

Greer and his two companions were wearing heavy, hooded cloaks. They veered left, taking the group into a shallow ravine. Their pace slowed as they weaved around fallen boulders and rocks. Bran dipped down, using the ravine wall to the north as a shield against the wind.

Another half an hour passed, then the ravine suddenly turned north, ending at a grassy meadow. Bran flew higher, once again buffeted by the strong winds. Quentin was circling high above the meadow. As Bran ascended, he saw that the meadow ended abruptly with high, treacherous cliffs. They had reached the northern coast.

Below, where the ravine ended at the foot of a mountain, there was a large opening to a cave and a huddle of wooden shacks built on one side. Workers, dressed in rags much too light for the cold winds, were filing out of the cave, carrying leather bags on their backs. The bags were obviously heavy, judging by how bent over the workers were.

After they emptied their bags into a large wooden trough, the workers were shoved by overseers back to the gaping hole in the mountain. Any laborer who moved too slowly was lashed with a whip.

This was the gold mine that Greer had stolen from Freydor. And as far as Bran could tell, the laborers were being treated like slaves.

The overseers and a group of about a hundred ruffians gave Greer a cheer when he arrived. They strode toward him but halted when one of them stubbed a toe on the invisible shield.

The air shimmered around Greer and his group, and then the overseers were able to approach. Their loud voices carried over the wind. And Greer's hood was blown off his head. The shield had to be down.

Bran spotted an outcropping of rocks above the gold mine that formed a hidden ledge big enough to stand on. He landed there and shifted, then peered through the rocks at the scene below.

Zane looked all right. Pissed, but safe. Pendras had to be the one with black hair and an oily bib tied around his neck to keep him from breathing fire. Reynfrid was eyeing the overseers with rage in his eyes. No doubt he hated seeing his people treated like slaves.

As the wind blew the hoods off the heads of Greer's companions, Bran recognized Roland. He was middle-aged and heavyset with lumpy jowls and beady eyes. The third priest was a young man, slim with a hounded, miserable look on his face. That had to be Kasper, the shield-maker. He wasn't watching Greer. His gaze was glued to the mouth of the cave as if he were searching for someone.

Bran moved down the ledge to get a better view. *Ouch.* He'd stepped barefoot onto a small pinecone. As he looked around, he noticed a few pine trees had managed to take root in the mountainside, emerging from the rocks and then bending up toward the sky. They had dropped cones all over the ledge and nearby rocks.

He scooped up a few, then tossed one down close to Zane. His brother glanced up, his eyes widening as he spotted Bran behind the rocks. Bran put a finger against his lips to warn him to stay quiet, and Zane rolled his eyes as if to say he wasn't an idiot.

"Take our prisoners inside," Greer ordered.

A group of about twenty ruffians surrounded the captives. Keeping numerous swords pointed at the three men, the ruffians untied them and marched them into the cave. Kasper started to follow them, but Greer stopped him.

"Stay here and put up the shield," Greer growled.

With his shoulders slumped, Kasper did as he was told. The air shimmered, and their voices were cut off. Bran figured Greer didn't want any of the laborers to hear him making plans with his small army. But as he watched the shield go up, something caught his attention. Could it be . . . ?

He tossed down another cone. It bounced off but caused a series of waves to undulate across the shield's invisible surface, much like a stone being thrown into a still pond.

As the waves spread across the shield, one small area remained untouched. He hadn't imagined it.

Quentin landed beside him and shifted. "Damn, it's cold," he hissed, wrapping his arms around himself. "I'm assuming they can't hear us with their wall up."

"No. Tell me what you see." Bran dropped another cone.

Quentin watched with his eagle eyes; then his brows lifted. "A weakness in the shield?"

Bran nodded. "A small hole." He dropped another pinecone. "It appears to be right above Kasper's head."

"Kasper?" Quentin asked. "The young priest?"

"Aye. He's the shield-maker. Pendras has been able to pass information on to Lennie at night when Kasper falls asleep."

Quentin studied the young man. "He doesn't look at all happy."

"No. I wonder if he projects the shield outward from himself? And that leaves a gap right above him?"

"Maybe. Let's give it a test." Quentin shifted, then grabbed a pinecone with his talons. He took off, flying toward the coast as if he had no interest in the men below, then he circled back toward the mountain. As he passed over Kasper, he dropped the cone.

It fell straight through, bonking the young man on the head before falling to the ground.

Kasper looked up with a surprised expression. Then he noticed the eagle landing amongst the rocks on the mountainside. His eyes narrowed.

Hidden behind rocks, Bran peered through a narrow hole. Kasper glanced at Greer, then at the mouth of the cave. He remained still, frowning, but saying nothing.

"Interesting," Bran muttered.

Quentin, still in eagle form, perched in plain sight, tilted his head, watching Kasper. Then he dropped back onto the hidden ledge and shifted. "I see two possibilities. One, he's loyal to Greer but is afraid to admit there's a hole in the shield. Or two, he's not admitting it because he's not really on Greer's side."

Bran nodded. "Greer could be forcing him."

Quentin sighed. "I'm not sure if this is going to help. The hole looks too small for me to get through."

"Too small for an eagle, but not for a raven."

Quentin gave him a worried look. "Don't do it now. If you make it through, you'll be trapped inside the bubble, unarmed and surrounded by a hundred men with weapons."

"I know. But once the others arrive, I could do it and make Kasper drop the shield. Then our troops could attack."

Quentin nodded. "Then that's the plan. I'll fly west to alert the kings and the Tourinian army. You fly back to Dominic and the duke. Together, we can lead the two factions here. We should try to arrive at the same time."

"Tomorrow. Noon?" Bran suggested.

Quentin agreed, and they both shifted and flew off.

Inside the cave, a now-dressed Pendras noted that the group of ruffians handling him, Reynfrid, and Zane were a careless, lazy bunch. A bunch of bullies who were more interested in insulting him and harassing the workers than doing their jobs properly.

They shoved a few laborers out of the way and kicked them for the fun of it before corralling Pendras and his companions beside a far wall. He was seriously considering punching one of them and starting a fight. But he and his two companions were grossly outnumbered, and he wasn't sure the laborers would jump in to help. They might have been cowed by too much abuse.

More laborers filed into the cavern from the dark hole that was the entrance to the mine. They were accompanied by a young boy and even younger girl, dressed in filthy rags and carrying torches to light the way for the miners.

"*You force children to labor in the mines?*" Reynfrid roared, and clobbered one of the ruffians.

Several of his cohorts retaliated, punching Reynfrid in the nose and knocking him down.

"Stop!" Pendras shoved the ruffians back, and they attacked him.

Then two howled in pain. Zane had grasped two of the assholes and was cooking them alive with his Embraced power. The others pulled the injured away, then brandished their swords.

"Back up against the wall before we kill you!" one of them sneered.

Pendras and his companions backed up. Reynfrid had blood dripping from his nose, and Zane was flushed with the heat he had generated.

A handcuff was snapped around Pendras's left wrist, then a long chain connected it to Reynfrid's wrist, and then Zane's. The ruffians did the same thing with a shackle around each of their ankles. With one last shove, the louts turned and stalked out of the cave. Only one remained by the entrance, and he soon became bored enough to entertain himself by harassing the laborers as they carried their loads of ore outside.

Pendras and his companions huddled together so they could whisper.

"They're enslaving my people," Reynfrid growled. "And children. I will not tolerate this."

Zane nodded. "The bastards should all die."

Reynfrid gave him an approving look. "I like the way you think. Thanks for helping us out."

"Did you see the eagle?" Pendras asked. "Quentin knows we're here. He'll bring the forces."

"My brother, the Raven, was here, too," Zane whispered.

"They're working together?" Reynfrid asked.

Zane nodded. "We should, too."

Reynfrid smiled at him. "Of course."

"Just let me be the one to kill Greer," Zane grumbled. "The bastard killed my brother."

Reynfrid's smile faded into a grimace. "I'm going after Roland."

Zane stiffened. "I should do it. Milena's my sister—"

"And, if I have my way, she'll be my wife," Reynfrid interrupted.

The guard glanced over at them, and they all grew quiet.

Reynfrid's hands curled into fists as he watched the two children bring out more laborers from the mine.

Kasper rushed inside as the two children approached. With a gasp, they dropped their torches and ran to him. With tears in his eyes, he drew them close.

"I've been so worried about you." Kasper hunched down to examine them both. "Are you all right?"

"Hey!" the guard at the entrance yelled at Kasper. "Get your brother and sister back to work!"

Kasper rose to his feet. "I agreed to cooperate if you kept them alive, but you're working them to death!"

The guard snorted. "The brats have it easy. All they do is walk around with torches."

The little girl tugged on Kasper's arm. "We're all right. When the bad men were mean to us, the good men hit them." She pointed at Pendras and his companions.

Kasper gave them a wary look, then herded his siblings outside. "Let's find you some food."

Pendras exchanged a look with his companions. It was obvious now that Kasper was being coerced into using his power for Greer. Once the troops arrived and Kasper saw the opportunity to escape with his siblings, he would probably take it.

"Lazy brats," the guard grumbled. "Hey, you!" he yelled at two laborers emerging from the mine. "After you unload your ore, come back and pick up those torches."

With the guard busy making sure the laborers did everything he ordered, Pendras whispered to his companions. "Later tonight, I'll pull off this oily rag and melt the chain off my handcuff. Yours, too. Then, if we hold the chain in our hands, they will still believe we are constrained."

"We'll still be connected by our ankles," Reynfrid said.

"I can use my heat to weaken the chains," Zane offered.

"Good." Pendras nodded. "Every night when Kasper fell asleep and let the shield drop, I was able to contact my sister and father. The kings are bringing an army from the west. Dominic, my sister, and the Duke of Trevelyan are bringing troops from the east."

Reynfrid snorted. "Now you tell us?"

Pendras shrugged. "I didn't have a chance before."

"And all that nonsense about betraying Lennie?" Reynfrid asked.

"Just bullshit to keep us safe." Pendras gave him a wry look. "You should have known."

Reynfrid's mouth curled up. "I did. The minute you insisted Greer keep us alive."

"Did you ever hear anything about my brother?" Zane asked.

Pendras nodded. "Bran has been traveling with my sister and Princess Roslyn, Terrance, and Lady Milena."

"Milena's coming here?" Reynfrid asked.

"Aye," Pendras answered. "And two priests came along, insisting they must help rescue Zane."

Zane's mouth dropped open.

"Once the troops arrive and Greer realizes he's outnumbered, he'll be frantic," Pendras said. "And when all hell breaks loose, we'll make our move."

Chapter 23

B ran's wing was throbbing in pain by the time he sighted the duke's troops. As he neared Dominic, the colonel spotted him and called for a halt. The soldier who had taken his clothes earlier in the gorge pulled them out of his saddlebags and handed them to Bran after he landed.

Dominic, Trevelyan, and his son, Rupert, gathered around Bran. While he dressed, he told them everything that had happened.

"Let's keep moving," Dominic declared. "We should set up camp about a mile from the gold mine, if possible. Then we'll be ready to attack tomorrow."

"Our best route is to continue north to the coastal plain, where the land is flat." The duke glanced at the sun. "We have a few hours of sunlight left."

"Mount up!" Dominic ordered. Those who had ventured off to relieve themselves ran back.

Rubbing his aching right arm, Bran looked around for a horse.

"Are you in pain?"

He spun around to find Lennie behind him.

She gave his arm a worried look. "I'm afraid you've been flying too much."

"I'll be all right."

Her frown deepened. "I heard everything you said."

He winced. "Then you saw me getting dressed."

She waved a dismissive hand. "I've seen you naked before." She bit her lip. "When I made you crash."

"Ah."

"That's when I saw the scars on your back. It made me furious that you'd been treated like that."

"Lennie . . ."

"I'm sorry," she said at the same time that he said it. She shook her head. "You have nothing to be sorry about."

"I left you." Bran stepped toward her. "I shouldn't have done that."

"I should have been honest from the beginning."

"Oh, Lennie." He embraced her, wincing as a jolt of pain shot through his right arm.

"We're going!" Dominic shouted at them.

"He's injured," Lennie told the colonel. "He needs to rest."

Dominic nodded. "See if there's room in one of the duke's supply wagons."

"This way." Lennie led him to the back of the caravan.

He climbed into a wagon with foodstuffs; then, to his surprise, Lennie climbed in with him. "What are you doing?"

"I'm going to feed you and look after you." As the wagon moved forward, she rummaged in a basket and found some bread and dried beef. "Are you really planning on diving into the hole in the shield?"

Bran nodded while he chewed.

Lennie winced. "If Kasper doesn't drop the shield, you'll be trapped."

"I think he'll drop it."

Lennie scoffed. "It's too dangerous."

He shrugged his left shoulder, since his right one was aching.

Lennie rearranged some baskets to give him room to lie down. "I'm not going to lose you, Bran. Tomorrow, I'll be right behind you."

He smiled. "My own personal dragon bodyguard?"

"Yes." She gave him a shy look. "Are you all right with me being a dragon?"

He took her hand. "Are you all right with me being a fool?"

She snorted. "You're not a fool. At least, not any more so than me."

"Then we make the perfect couple."

She gave him a sad smile. "I think so, but convincing my father may not be easy."

He squeezed her hand. "We'll make it. Together."

That night, the cave was lit by just a few torches. It was so dark, Pendras couldn't see the two guards by the entrance. But that also meant they couldn't see him.

Lennie? he called, but there was no answer. Kasper must have put the shield up in the cave, probably to protect himself and his siblings.

With his free hand, Pendras pulled the oily cloth from his chin and neck and tossed it aside. When he heard the guards snoring, he went to work. After extending the chain connected to his handcuff, he pursed his lips and blew a narrow stream of fire. By the light of the fire, he could see exactly where to aim the heat.

No one seemed to notice what looked like an extra torch in the cave. He kept at it till the chain link turned red with heat. With a yank on the chain, his hand broke free.

He heard a slight rustling of chains. That had to be Zane working on the ankle cuffs. Reynfrid tapped him with his cuffed hand; then Pendras located the chain so he could break it, too.

It seemed like an eternity later, but they were eventually all free.

Lennie? He tried once again.

Pendras, how are you? Lennie asked.

We're fine, Pendras replied. Kasper must have fallen asleep. *I saw Quentin and Bran earlier.*

Quentin is here with me, Silas responded. *We're camped two miles west of you.*

We're a mile to the east, Lennie reported. *We're planning on a two-pronged attack at noon.*

We'll be ready, Pendras replied.

Get some rest, Silas ordered. *See you tomorrow.*

Pendras whispered the news to his companions, and then they settled onto the hard, cold ground to attempt to sleep.

The next morning, as sunlight crept into the cave, Pendras and his companions sat up, carefully arranging the chains to make it look as if they were still shackled at the ankles. They each held the end of a chain in their right hand to hide the fact that they were free.

When some bread was thrown in their direction, they ate it quietly with their left hands.

Pendras overheard the guards talking at the cave entrance. Apparently, Greer had no idea that the kings were nearby with an army. Or that the Duke of Trevelyan had brought troops. Greer was angry this morning, believing that the ruffians he had sent to destroy Dominic and Bran in the gorge had deserted him, since they had failed to return. The arrogant fool never imagined that they could all be dead.

The guards chuckled when they discussed the possibility that Dominic and his puny group of soldiers might have survived and might show up at the gold mine. Greer's army numbered over a hundred, so it would be a slaughter. Then the guards aimed a sneer at the captives as if to remind them that they might also die today.

Other than that, the day was apparently proceeding as normal. The laborers were sent back into the mine, and after an hour or so, some began filing out with backpacks filled with ore.

Pendras and his companions were largely ignored and forgotten. They took advantage of the situation by taking turns to stand up and stretch their muscles, so they would be ready for action.

The sunlight grew brighter outside as they waited for noon. They whispered some plans and waited.

Finally. Shouts rang outside, and the ruffians immediately panicked, running about and screeching.

"Bring the hostages!" Greer screamed.

A dozen of the oafs rushed inside the cave, desperation on their faces as they grabbed Pendras, Reynfrid, and Zane. In the general chaos, they didn't notice that the ankle chains were no longer connected. Pendras and his companions kept a tight grip on the chains in their hands.

Pendras blinked as they emerged into the bright sunlight.

"Hurry!" Greer shouted. "Bring them close. Kasper, put up the shield!"

The shield went up. Pendras and his companions were shoved to the front, and there, three bastards grabbed them from behind and pressed daggers against their necks.

At least now that he was in front, Pendras could see what was happening. To the left was the Tourinian army. Silas and Ulfrid called a halt. The two fathers looked grim, no doubt enraged at the sight of their sons about to have their throats slit. Along with the army, there were four dragons circling overhead. No wonder Greer and his cohorts had panicked.

To the right was another army, about half the size, with two dragons. Anton and Lennie. Pendras wondered what had happened to Sergei. Dominic was in the front, calling a halt. Over by the wooden shacks outside the shield, two ruffians were holding Kasper's siblings. The little girl was crying. The little boy's chin was quivering, but he was trying to look brave in spite of the man's beefy hand encircling his neck.

An eagle circled overhead. Quentin. He was ducking and

diving, trying to draw everyone's attention, Pendras thought, though he spotted the Raven coming in from the far right.

Suddenly, the Raven shot through the shield, knocking hard against Kasper's head. As Kasper screamed and fell down, everyone turned to watch.

"Now!" Pendras shouted. He, Reynfrid, and Zane shoved the daggers away from their throats and twisted, using their iron cuffs to clobber the men who held them.

The Raven shifted on top of Kasper, grabbing him and holding him down. "Drop the shield!"

Close by, Pendras and his fellow captives continued to knock down the enemy and steal their swords.

"Save my brother and sister!" Kasper yelled as he dropped the shield.

Pendras and Reynfrid, each with multiple swords secured under their belts, ran for the little boy and girl. The two ruffians backed away, dragging the children with them.

Anton flew toward them, shooting fire into the air. The two men screeched and ran away, leaving the children behind. Pendras aimed a burst of fire at the two men, and they went down in flames.

Reynfrid gathered up the children as Kasper ran toward them.

"Take them into the cave with the laborers and put up the shield," Reynfrid ordered. "Stay there until it's safe to come out."

"Yes, Your Highness." Kasper picked up his little sister and took his brother's hand. "Thank you." He ran for the cave with his brother beside him.

An angry dragon screech caught Pendras's attention. Lennie was upset as she circled overhead. Bran was in trouble, unarmed with three ruffians surrounding him. Lennie shot down a column of fire, killing two. While the third one was distracted, Zane grabbed hold of him and released his power. The man screamed, his blood boiling until he collapsed dead. With the three attackers down, Bran grabbed a sword from the first one, while Pendras and Reynfrid took the other two.

The steady beat of war drums began as the Tourinian army started to advance. To the east, Dominic's and Trevelyan's troops joined in, banging their swords against their shields in time with the drums as they moved forward.

"Around me!" Greer screamed. "Protect me!"

The remaining force of more than ninety men rushed to form a circle around Greer and Roland.

"Are you going to die for those bastards?" Pendras shouted at Greer's followers. "You're outnumbered, and your shield is gone! Surrender now if you want to live."

The men began muttering to each other.

"Hold your positions!" Greer hollered. "I'll pay you double!"

"All the gold in the world will not get you out of this, Greer!" Bran yelled. "You're dying today!"

"Don't believe them!" Greer shouted at his men. "I have power. I can blow the armies off the cliff!"

Meanwhile, the armies continued to advance—a slow, ominous march in time to the steady beat of drums. Six dragons circled overhead. The ruffians glanced about nervously, their mutterings growing more frantic.

"I want Roland!" Reynfrid shouted. "Send him out!"

"No!" Roland cowered behind Greer.

Pendras shot a blast, setting one of the thugs on fire. With a screech, he fell to the ground. Greer's men stumbled back, nearly tripping over one another.

"I can do this all day!" Pendras stalked around the group. "Who wants to be next?"

Above them, Anton breathed fire on another lout. As the man rolled on the ground screaming, the others grew more panicked.

"We'll keep picking you off until you give us Roland!" Pendras shouted.

"No!" Roland screeched as the men thrust him forward. "Greer, help me!"

Greer was silent as his men ejected Roland from the circle.

"Give him a sword," Reynfrid ordered. "I won't kill an unarmed man."

Bran tossed his sword at Roland's feet, and the priest quickly picked it up.

"Stay away from me!" Roland swung the sword back and forth wildly.

Reynfrid advanced, his sword pointed at the priest. "This is for what you did to Milena."

"What?" Bran looked shocked. "What did he . . . ? That bastard!" With rage in his eyes, Bran tried to grab Pendras's sword.

"Let Reynfrid take care of it," Pendras said quietly.

"She's my sister!" Bran cried, then ran over to Zane. "Is it true?"

Zane nodded. "Roland molested her."

"I was just following orders!" Roland cried. "Greer, help me!"

Greer backed away toward the cliff, taking his group of bodyguards with him.

Reynfrid lunged, knocking the sword out of Roland's hand. Roland screeched, jumping back so fast he stumbled and fell.

"For Milena!" Reynfrid shouted and rammed his sword into Roland's chest.

A volley of arrows came from both armies, and about a third of Greer's bodyguards fell. The dragons flew overhead, breathing fire, and another third fell. The remaining ones ran, and the dragons chased them. Some tried to escape into the mine, but Kasper had the shield across the entrance to the cave. Others tried to run into the ravine, but the dragons hunted them down.

Bran watched the battle in a daze, still stunned by the news that Roland had molested Milena. He shook himself. Roland was dead. Now it was time to kill Greer.

Greer was alone, deserted by his men. Pendras and his group charged toward him. Greer waved his arm, knocking Pendras and Reynfrid back with a burst of cold air. Zane, his face flushed with heat, had turned on his powers to the point that the cold air had no effect on him. Impervious, he pushed through the blasts of cold air until he was close enough to stab Greer with his sword.

Wincing in pain, Greer grabbed onto Zane's neck. "You bastard. I'll take you with me." He activated his freezing power while Zane countered with more heat.

Ice crystals formed on Greer's skin as he tried to freeze Zane to death, while Zane turned dark red with heat.

"Stop it, Zane!" Bran ran toward them. "Stop before it kills you!" He tried grabbing onto his brother but the heat burned his hands. Circling behind Greer, Bran looped an arm around the man's neck to pull him back. He winced in pain as the freezing cold enveloped him.

Pendras stopped in front of the struggling men. "Both of you let go! I'll breathe fire on him to kill him!"

Greer responded by waving a hand and blasting cold air at Pendras to knock him back.

Zane sagged on his feet, about to lose consciousness from the heat he was producing.

"Stop!" Bran seized hold of Greer's cloak with one hand, then with his other, he pulled Zane's dagger out, wincing at the heat of it. He plunged the blade into Greer's side.

With a cry, Greer waved his arm at Bran, blasting him with cold air. As Bran went flying back, he held tight with both hands to Greer's cloak.

Zane screamed as Bran flew back over the cliff, taking Greer with him.

Even as Bran tumbled through the air, he shifted. His right wing seized up in pain, but he frantically tried to flap his wings, desperate to avoid the rocks below.

Greer landed with a thud, and blood seeped from his head and wounds.

Bran struggled to fly, but the wind was tossing him back toward the cliff. He caught himself, planting his talons against the sheer cliff, then pushed off. Again he tried to fly, but his right wing was not working.

A screech sounded overhead, and a small dragon with a pink belly zoomed toward him and scooped him up.

Thank the Light the love of his life was a dragon.

Chapter 24

Lennie flew back to Trevelyan's campsite with the Raven held tightly against her chest. The camp was mostly bare, just a few servants and cooks gathered around the campfires with five wagons parked nearby, and a few spare horses grazing on grass.

She hovered over the wagon where Bran had rested the day before and slept last night. His clothes were still there, along with a few blankets.

Carefully, she deposited him on the blanket. After he shifted, she did, too, landing neatly beside him.

"Lennie." He tossed a blanket around her, wincing as pain shot through his injured arm. "People will see you."

She glanced back at the servants and cooks, who were watching with their mouths dropped open, then drew the blanket tighter around her shoulders. "Oh, well. This is the way it is for us shifters. We get used to nudity."

"I don't like men gawking at you."

She snorted. "It seems rather trivial after almost losing you." She turned back to him and realized he was naked, too. And lying right in front of her. She blinked.

"Lennie? What are you looking at?"

"Hmm?"

"I thought you were used to nudity?"

"Who, me?"

"Lennie. I'm up here." He motioned to his face.

"Oh?" She lifted her gaze, her cheeks growing warm. "Well, I'm simply looking you over to make sure you're all right. You scared me to death, you know. Don't ever do that again!"

His mouth twitched. "Is that a royal command?"

"Yes." Her gaze drifted back to the most interesting part of his naked body. Goodness. When Anton had stripped in front of her when he was fifteen, he hadn't looked nearly this impressive.

"Staring has consequences, Lennie."

"What consequences?"

He gave her a wry look. "I thought you said you'd seen me naked before?"

"Only from the back." She glanced down at his groin once again. "This is rather new for me."

A servant by the campfire cleared his throat. "Miss— Your Highness? Can you tell us the outcome of the battle?"

Bran quickly threw a blanket over himself.

Lennie glanced back and smiled. "The battle is over. Greer is dead, and the captives have been rescued."

The servants exchanged incredulous glances.

"That quickly?" the male servant asked.

"Were any of our people injured?" a female cook asked.

"No, I don't believe so," Lennie replied. "They should be returning in a little while."

"Oh!" The cook pressed a hand to her chest. "We should start cooking! They'll want to celebrate."

As they busied themselves building a series of cooking fires, Lennie turned back to Bran.

"We should go back," he murmured. "Zane could be injured. I've always been afraid he would boil himself to death."

Lennie nodded. "Let's get dressed." She handed him his smallclothes, and he pulled back the blanket to put them on.

He winced again at the pain. "I think I sprained my arm. Or pulled a muscle."

"I'll help you." She dragged the smallclothes up his legs, then stopped, staring at him once again. "Am I imagining this or are you even bigger?"

"I told you staring had consequences." He laid back and lifted his hips so she could pull the smallclothes up to his hips.

"I must say . . ." She fastened the button at his waist. "I'm growing increasingly curious. And anxious."

His mouth twitched. "This is not the time, Lennie."

"I know." She helped him put on his breeches. "But when everything is done, and your arm is healed, we should fly to my father's cabin, where we can be alone."

"I'd love to." He lifted his hips again so she could pull the breeches up. "But only if your parents approve of us."

Lennie winced. That would be the difficult part.

Bran stood up and stretched a blanket out behind her. "Now you can get dressed."

She smiled, enjoying the way he kept trying to protect her from prying eyes. Except his own. There was a definite gleam in his gaze as he watched her dress. After she pulled on her boots, she helped him with his shirt and cape.

"Let's go." She jumped down from the wagon and strode toward a saddled horse.

He mounted another horse, and together, they rode back to the gold mine.

It was a much different scene now. King Ulfrid and Reynfrid were busy interviewing the laborers. Quite a few had been dragged off farms on Freydor's land and forced to work in the mines. Ulfrid promised to return them home, but first they were being fed and given any spare clothes and blankets that could be found.

Some of the laborers had no home, so Ulfrid decided to

take them to the nearest castle on Freydor's land. Because Freydor was a traitor, his land and possessions would revert to the crown, so Ulfrid was free to use the castles as he wished.

Bertram suggested establishing a second Monastery of Mercy in the north, where the homeless could find shelter and training for employment. Ulfrid liked the idea and promised to hand over one of Freydor's farms for Bertram to use.

Half of the Tourinian army was sent back to secure the rest of Freydor's holdings. The other half took the shovels from the mine to dig large holes to bury the dead.

Lennie and Bran found Zane in one of the wooden shacks. Sebastian had deposited him on a narrow bed, and he and Milena were taking care of him, keeping him cool with wet cloths.

Bran sat beside him. "Zane, can you hear me?"

Zane thrashed, shaking his head. "Bran. Over the cliff. I lost Bran."

"No!" Bran grabbed his hand. "I'm here. Zane, I'm all right."

"Bran?" Zane opened his eyes and stared at him. "Are we dead?"

"No." Bran smiled at him. "We're alive."

"And the Brotherhood is over." Milena smiled at them.

Reynfrid stepped inside the shack. "How is Zane?"

"He'll be all right," Lennie told him.

"That's good." Reynfrid glanced at Milena, who blushed and looked away.

Reynfrid shifted his feet, then said to her, "I was surprised that you came all this way."

Milena shrugged. "I was worried about Zane."

"I see." Reynfrid hesitated, frowning. "Only Zane?"

"Well." Milena's cheeks turned a brighter pink. "I was concerned for you and Pendras, of course."

"Me?"

"Yes."

"Milena."

"Yes?"

"I . . . I killed him."

She turned away, covering her mouth.

"You should never be ashamed," Reynfrid insisted. "He's gone. He can never hurt you again."

"But I am ashamed." Milena turned toward him with tears in her eyes. "I was a spy. I deceived you."

"How? Were you lying to me every time we talked in the garden?"

"No."

"Were you only pretending to like me?"

"No!"

"Milena, you have my heart. You always have."

Tears rolled down her face.

"Come here." Reynfrid extended his arms to her, and she ran into his embrace.

Lennie exchanged a grin with Bran.

Pendras peeked into the cabin. "Our fathers want to see us."

Lennie's grin faded.

Pendras led the way to where Kings Ulfrid, Silas, and Leo were gathered by the mouth of the cave. Dominic and Quentin were already with them, deep in conversation. Terrance and Roslyn stood nearby, looking nervous.

Reynfrid took Milena's hand as he walked with her. Her face was pale with apprehension.

Lennie felt the same way as she approached with Bran.

They stopped in front of the kings, and the women curtsied. The men bowed their heads.

"Excellent work, son!" Leo slapped a gloved hand on Dominic's back. "It's good to see the princes safe and sound."

Pendras and Reynfrid bowed their heads. "Thank you."

Leo chuckled. "No, we thank you! You did most of the work. We sat back and enjoyed the show."

"Indeed," Ulfrid agreed, looking over the entire group. "Between you and the dragons, we had very little to do."

"Your presence here was a powerful force of intimidation," Reynfrid said. "It set Greer and his cohorts into a panic, and we were able to take advantage of it."

Ulfrid nodded, his eyes narrowing as he noticed his son holding Lady Milena's hand.

Lennie motioned to Terrance. "We won the battle yesterday at the Gorge of Great Despair mainly due to Terrance and his incredible gift."

Silas glanced at the young man. "You're Embraced?"

Before Terrance could answer, Roslyn butted in. "Terrance is amazing! He can control where arrows go, anyone's arrows, massive numbers of arrows all at once. He saved us from the highwaymen, and he won the battle yesterday single-handedly."

"Really?" Ulfrid asked, frowning once again as he noticed his daughter holding Terrance's hand. "I don't believe we have met."

"I was raised on the Isle of Secrets with Quentin," Terrance explained. "I'm originally from Tourin, but when I returned here, I found my parents had passed away. I went to Benwick Academy and eventually became the archery instructor there."

"He's the best archer in the world!" Roslyn exclaimed.

There was an awkward pause as Ulfrid and Silas looked their children over.

"Father." Reynfrid lifted his chin. "I have decided to marry Lady Milena."

Milena gasped.

Ulfrid blinked. "What?"

Lennie grabbed onto Bran's hand. "I've decided to marry Bran."

"*What?*" Silas shouted.

"And I want to marry Terrance!" Roslyn cried.

"*What?*" Ulfrid exchanged an incredulous look with Silas.

Silas dragged a hand through his hair. "We leave our children on their own for less than a week and this happens?"

Leo snorted, then gave Dominic a wary glance. "Don't tell me you've found someone."

"Not me!" Dominic raised his hands.

"Me, either," Pendras added.

"Thank the Light for small mercies," Silas muttered.

"This is all too sudden," Ulfrid muttered.

"I have been in love with Milena for months," Reynfrid insisted.

Ulfrid sighed. "She was a spy." He glanced at her. "Though I am totally prepared to forgive you, given the circumstances."

"Thank you, Your Majesty." Milena bowed her head. "I know I am not worthy—"

"Do you love me, Milena?" Reynfrid asked.

She blinked back tears. "Of course, but—"

"That's all I need to know," Reynfrid announced.

Ulfrid frowned. "We should think about this." He turned to Roslyn. "You were supposed to marry someone else just a few days ago. Thank the Light you didn't, but still—"

"I have loved Terrance for years," Roslyn declared. "All the time I was at Benwick."

Terrance bowed his head. "I know I am not worthy—"

"Stop that!" Roslyn exclaimed. Her eyes glimmered with tears. "I am the one who isn't worthy. I almost married a traitor who was planning on killing us all!"

"How could you have known he was so evil?" Terrance wrapped an arm around her shoulders. "You should never apologize for being someone who tries to see the best in others."

Ulfrid drew in a deep breath, then let it out. "All right."

"We can get married?" Roslyn asked.

"No!" Ulfrid glowered at his children. "Let me finish. The four of you are coming back with me on my ship. You'll remain at Lourdon Palace while your mother and I consider the situation and come to a decision. We'll need to become better acquainted with Terrance and Milena."

While all this was happening, Silas had been scowling at Bran, which was making Lennie increasingly nervous.

"My turn," Silas grumbled. "You can't give me the excuse that you've been in love for years. You just met a few days ago."

Lennie cleared her throat. "Bran met me five months ago."

Bran nodded. "The night the Eberoni queen was kidnapped." He bowed to King Leo. "My sincere apologies to you and your wife."

With a low growl, Leo crossed his arms. "Shall I kill him for you, Silas?"

"No!" Lennie stepped in front of Bran.

Leo snorted. "Dominic explained what happened, but I have to agree with Silas. This has all happened much too quickly. I'm not sure this Raven can be trusted."

"How can you say that?" Lennie protested. "He risked his life today to break the shield. And then he nearly died while trying to kill Greer."

"That's true," Dominic agreed. "I wanted to hate the Raven, but he's proved himself loyal and brave."

Quentin nodded. "I'll vouch for him, too."

Leo huffed.

Silas frowned. "And you claim to love each other?"

"Yes," Lennie and Bran answered at the same time, then smiled at each other.

"In that case, your feelings will survive a short delay," Silas announced. "I propose you wait three months. Then we'll see—"

"That's too long," Lennie protested. "Three weeks."

Silas snorted. "Six weeks. That's final."

Bran bowed his head. "Yes, Your Majesty."

Silas eyed him carefully. "As one of the Brotherhood, you wanted to rule the world. You'll forgive me for being suspicious when you want to marry the princess who will inherit the Norveshki throne."

"I have no interest in being king, Your Majesty," Bran insisted.

"So you say." Silas narrowed his eyes. "How much do you love her? What if I tell you that your marriage to my daughter will cause her to lose the throne?"

Bran stiffened.

"Papa—" Lennie began, but he lifted a hand to hush her.

"What do you say, Bran?"

His face pale, Bran stepped back, releasing Lennie's hand. "I would never get in the way of her destiny."

"Bran!" Lennie cried.

He shook his head. "Lennie, I will always love you. Even if I cannot have you, I will still love you. And wish the best for you."

"Stop it!" Lennie grabbed his hand. "We'll figure out a way." She glanced at her father. "We have six weeks, right? We'll make it work." She turned back to Bran. "I'm not giving up on you. Ever."

He squeezed her hand. "We'll make it work."

Silas scoffed. "I'm going back to Lourdon on Ulfrid's ship, where my wife is waiting. You, Bran, will come with me. Along with your brother and the priests."

"And me?" Lennie asked.

"No." Silas frowned at her. "You and your brother are flying home to Draven Castle now."

Lennie's heart sank. She turned to Bran. "I'll see you in six weeks?"

"Aye. Safe travels."

She nodded as tears stung her eyes. "I'll miss you."

He squeezed her hand. "Me, too."

"Get some rest so your arm will heal. We have a date at my father's cabin, remember?"

He nodded, then kissed her hand.

Blinking back the tears, she stepped into the cave to strip. After shifting, she lumbered back out. Pendras had already shifted and was waiting for her.

With one last look at Bran, she took off. Pendras joined her, and together, they flew home to Norveshka.

Chapter 25

The next day, Lennie rested after the long flight, lying in bed feeling morose. But when she joined Pendras for dinner, she realized how close she had come to losing her brother and suddenly felt elated. Her mission had been a success! She'd saved her brother and Reynfrid. She'd even helped Bran save his brother, Zane. Greer had been killed, along with Roland. The Brotherhood of the Sun was utterly destroyed. The Kingdoms were no longer threatened, her friends and family were safe, and peace would once again rule over Aerthlan.

She wouldn't lose Bran, she reminded herself as she sipped some wine.

"I wonder what happened to Sergei," Pendras muttered as he cut into a thick steak.

Lennie winced. She'd forgotten about her would-be suitor. "Have you tried contacting him?"

"Yes, but no answer."

"I don't think he'll be back." Lennie grabbed a roll from the basket and broke it in two. "At the gorge, he breathed fire on Bran, trying to kill him."

"What?" Pendras stopped with a fork halfway to his mouth.

"It's true. And then he even shot some fire at Anton."

Pendras slammed down his fork. "That bastard. No wonder he's disappeared."

Lennie nodded as she buttered her bread. "I suppose if he went to trial, he would be banished. He's saving us the trouble."

"A rogue dragon." Pendras stuffed the bite of steak into his mouth. "That could be dangerous."

Lennie thought back to Father Bertram's words that a princess would be betrayed. She hoped Sergei's betrayal was over, and that he wouldn't cause any trouble in the future.

Pendras wrinkled his nose in disgust. "And to think that bastard wanted to marry you."

"He wasn't interested in me, really. It was the throne he wanted."

Pendras studied her as he chewed. "What about Anton? Could you see yourself marrying him?"

Lennie shook her head. "He's a good man, but he's a follower, not a leader."

"True." Pendras sliced off another piece of steak. "By the Light, I've been eating all day. They nearly starved me to death."

"I'm sorry." Lennie munched on her bread.

"You're serious about the Raven?" Pendras asked, stuffing more meat into his mouth.

"Very much so." Lennie sliced off a piece of steak.

"Father is right, you know. The nobles will throw a fit."

"They needn't be afraid of Bran. He doesn't want to be king." Lennie eyed her brother. "When you told Greer you'd been cheated of the throne—"

"Lennie, I was making it up. I've always been proud of you for being the first female dragon."

"I know that, and believe me, I really appreciate your support. But we both know, Pendras, you're a bigger dragon than me, and a stronger warrior."

He shrugged. "So that's why I'll be general and Lord Protector of the Realm." He took another bite. "I'm fine with that, Lennie. As long as I can keep Norveshka safe, I'm happy."

An inkling of an idea came to Lennie's mind. "Of all the dragons I know, you would make the best king. After father, of course."

Pendras stopped chewing. "What are you saying?"

Lennie sat back. "You should be the next king."

Pendras's eyes widened. "Are you giving up the throne? Our parents will be furious—"

"No. I'll be queen. But you'll be king."

"Are you kidding?"

"No. Pendras, we have always gotten along. We can do it. Our parents share the throne without a problem. We can, too."

"There's never been a brother-sister reign before."

"There's never been a female dragon before," Lennie countered. "I think it's the perfect solution. And it will enable us both to marry whomever we please."

Pendras snorted. "I have a feeling this idea was motivated more by your love for Bran than me."

Lennie smiled. "Perhaps."

Pendras rolled his eyes. "And how do we decide who inherits after us? We could both have families someday."

Lennie considered that question for a moment. "The tradition is for a male dragon to be king. So, the first male dragon shifter will inherit, whether he's your son or mine."

Pendras raised an eyebrow. "Any son of mine will definitely be a dragon. But if you marry the Raven—"

"There's no way of knowing what will happen," Lennie finished. "I'm fine with that. Any child I have with Bran will be greatly loved."

"All right. Let's do it." Pendras grinned. "You'll have to convince our parents."

Lennie nodded. "Don't worry. I have the perfect argument."

"What is it?"

Lennie smiled. "I'll tell them that by sharing the throne, you and I will each have the chance to experience the same sort of happy and loving marriage that they enjoy."

Pendras hissed in a breath. "Oh, a shot straight to the heart."

Lennie nodded. "They won't be able to refuse."

A week later, when Silas and Gwennore finally arrived, Lennie's theory proved correct.

Gwennore agreed right away.

Silas frowned at Lennie. "You're doing this so you can marry that Raven, aren't you?"

"He's the only one I want," Lennie confessed.

Gwennore smiled. "I got to know him on the way back to Lourdon. He seems quite wonderful. And extremely handsome."

Silas shot her an annoyed look.

"Though not nearly as handsome as you." Gwennore's eyes twinkled with humor as she touched her husband's arm.

"That's more like it," Silas muttered, taking his wife's hand in his.

"I find it quite logical that our daughter would be attracted to a very sweet and handsome man," Gwennore continued. "After all, she acquired her taste by growing up with a sweet and handsome father and brother."

Silas's mouth twitched. "And she acquired her clever mind from her mother."

"And her naughty sense of humor from her father," Gwennore added.

"Enough," Lennie muttered. "I'm going to lose my breakfast."

Silas chuckled. "I thought you wanted a marriage like ours!"

Lennie grinned. She certainly did.

* * *

It had taken a week to return to the monastery. The second week, Bran rested his arm and moped about, feeling depressed. He'd done his best on the trip back to Lourdon. He'd answered all the questions the kings had thrown at him. He'd apologized to Queen Luciana. He'd been as honest and polite as he could. He'd even attempted to impress Silas with his ability to speak the Norveshki language. Actually, he knew all four Aerthlan languages, but Silas had merely grumbled that Bran had learned them so he and the Brotherhood could take over the world.

Sebastian and Bertram had spoken up for him. Even Quentin, Eviana, and Dominic had.

King Leo seemed ready to forgive and forget, but Silas had remained grumpy to the end. Bran had no idea if the grouchy old dragon would ever accept him.

Maybe Lennie would have better luck persuading her father. Or maybe Lennie would realize her future as queen was more important than her feelings for a bird.

Zane was feeling much better. Bran knew his brother was talking to Bertram about him. The two of them were worried.

Yes, he was lovesick. It was more than that, though. He'd lived for revenge the last five months. With Greer and the Brotherhood dead, he wasn't sure what to do with himself now. For years, he'd been a spy, but those skills were no longer needed.

The person he admired the most in the world was Bertram. Could he continue Bertram's work in Norveshka? Would he even be living in that country?

After the second week, a letter arrived from Sebastian. Bertram ripped it open and quickly read. "Yes! We must go to Lourdon immediately!"

"What's wrong?" Bran reached for the letter, but Bertram stuffed it into his robe.

"Saddle the horses!" Bertram hurried toward the barn. "I must get Daffy ready."

Soon, Bertram, Zane, and Bran were riding to Lourdon. The priest refused to explain their mission. He would only say that they were to meet Father Sebastian in Lourdon Cathedral.

"Is someone getting married?" Zane asked.

"No, no." Bertram waved a dismissive hand.

"It wouldn't surprise me," Zane grumbled. "Terrance stayed behind at the palace so he could become the new captain of the guard. He and Princess Roslyn look plenty eager to be married."

Bertram smiled. "I expect we'll hear of their engagement soon. And your sister with the prince."

Someone should be happy, Bran thought.

When they arrived at Lourdon Cathedral, he was surprised to see an expensive coach parked outside. They tied off their horses and went inside.

Bertram knocked on Sebastian's office door. "We're here!" He glanced back at Bran. "Prepare yourself."

"For what?" Bran asked as Sebastian opened the door.

"Come in." Sebastian ushered them inside.

Bran stopped short when he saw an old man sitting by the fire. A young woman stood nearby, clutching her hands nervously.

"Oh, my!" Bertram exclaimed as he looked at the young woman. "You look so much like Beatrice."

"I've been told that." She smiled. "I'm Lady Belinda."

Beatrice? Bran thought as he bowed his head to the young lady. Wasn't that the name of his mother?

The old man leaned on a cane as he rose to his feet. He stood tall, his black hair streaked with gray, his brown eyes carefully studying Bran. "You're Bran Morris?"

"Aye." Bran's gaze shifted back and forth from the old

man to the young woman. She appeared delighted, but the man looked distraught. "Can I help you?"

The man looked away with tears in his eyes.

"This is the Duke of Southwood," Sebastian explained. "I took the liberty of visiting him a few days ago."

"Your Grace." Bran bowed his head, and Zane followed suit.

The duke took a deep breath. "You are the answer to a prayer that has gone unheard for years." He took a step toward Bran. "Beatrice was my sister. Your mother."

Bran's thoughts swirled. He had family?

"Holy Light," Zane whispered.

The duke motioned toward the young woman. "My daughter, Belinda."

She grinned. "Your cousin!"

Bran stiffened with shock. He glanced at Bertram. Was this really happening?

"It's true, my boy," Bertram whispered. "This is your family."

Bran looked them over. "But . . ." A sudden surge of anger ripped through him. All the time he'd been suffering at that hellhole of a monastery, where had this so-called family been? "Where have you been?"

The Duke of Southwood slumped over, placing a hand over his heart.

"Papa!" Belinda helped him back to the chair. "He's not well. This is upsetting him."

"It's upsetting *me*," Bran growled. "Do you have any idea what my brothers and I went through?"

"Yes!" the duke cried. "Sebastian told me. A few days ago. I'm so sorry. I tried to find you years ago. Bertram told me where you were. I sent a letter to the monastery. Then a letter came back from Master Lorne. He said you were dead."

Bran flinched.

"Holy crap," Zane whispered.

The duke shook his head. "He even sent a death certificate. I should have gone there and checked, though. I'm so sorry."

"I should have checked, too," Bertram said with tears running down his face.

Bran took a deep breath. So this was why Father Bertram had not attempted to contact him all those years. "This will take some getting used to."

"You should come live with us," Lady Belinda suggested. "And your brother, too."

Zane lifted his hands. "I'm not actually related to you. My father was that lying bastard Master Lorne, and my mother was someone else. Bran is actually my cousin."

Belinda shrugged. "Any cousin of my cousin is a cousin of mine. You are both welcome to live with us." When Bran hesitated, she gave him a pleading look. "Please. You have no idea how lonesome the castle has become. Ever since . . ." She turned away, her eyes glimmering with tears.

"My son, Benjamin, died four years ago in a boating accident," the duke confessed. With a sad smile, he looked at Bran. "You, dear boy, are my heir."

Bran blinked.

"Damn," Zane muttered.

"Language," Bertram whispered.

"Please come and live with us," Belinda asked once again.

"I know nothing about being a duke," Bran said.

The Duke of Southwood smiled. "You remind me of my Uncle Bran. He was always just that honest."

Bran looked at his brother. "Will you come with me?"

Zane shrugged. "Why not? I don't have anywhere else to go."

Bertram huffed. "You always have a home with me."

Zane grinned. "I know, but I don't want to be a priest." He glanced at Belinda. "My Lady, we have two sisters, too."

Belinda's face lit up. "Wonderful! They must come live with us, too."

"One is in Ebton," Sebastian explained. "And the other is a lady-in-waiting to Queen Brigitta."

Belinda gasped. "How exciting!"

Zane scoffed. "You think that's exciting, wait till you hear about her upcoming engagement to Prince Reynfrid."

"That's not certain yet," Bran warned his brother.

"Your sister and Prince Reynfrid?" The duke's face brightened. "Why, of course, your sister must be a member of our family. Perhaps I can put a word in for her? Maybe a dowry?"

"What a wonderful idea!" Belinda clapped her hands together.

Bran couldn't help but smile. No doubt the duke was thrilled at the idea of becoming a father-in-law of sorts to the future king.

"And that's not all," Zane boasted. "Bran here might be marrying the future queen of Norveshka!"

"Enough," Bran hissed at his brother. "That is not certain, either."

The duke grinned, now looking five years younger than when they'd first entered the room. "Oh, my! Life is certainly becoming exciting."

"I have to be honest," Bran insisted. "These marriages are not confirmed."

"I understand." The duke nodded. "But as the head of the family, it is my duty to help smooth these things over. Perhaps it will help that you now have a title. You are the Baron of Blackwood."

"Holy crap!" Zane exclaimed again.

"Language," Bran mumbled. Would his newfound family and title be enough to make King Silas accept him?

Chapter 26

Four weeks later . . .

Lennie urged her horse into a gallop as she charged toward the Monastery of Mercy. Her heart pounded. Soon she would see Bran!

"Not so fast!" Gwennore shouted as she tried to keep up.

The four guards with them spread out to provide protection. Ever since Pendras's kidnapping, Lennie's father had insisted on extra guards for the entire family.

Lennie had waited not so patiently for the six weeks to pass. About a week ago, she'd received an invitation. A double engagement party at Lourdon Palace. So Reynfrid and Roslyn had managed to convince their parents to let them marry the ones they loved. Lennie was delighted for them, but wondered how long it would take for her father to give in.

Soon after the invitation had arrived, another one had followed. Some fellow called Baron Blackwood was asking to meet her in the library at Lourdon Palace. She'd promptly thrown the letter into the rubbish bin. Now that she'd formally rejected Sergei and Anton, suitors were popping out of the woodwork.

Bran was the only one she wanted. And soon she would see him.

Her brother and father had opted to fly all the way to

Lourdon Palace. But Lennie had wanted to stop on the way so she could see Bran at the monastery. She and her mother had taken the royal barge down the Norva River. They'd stopped at a ferry near the monastery, then had rented horses for the rest of the journey.

As she rode past the barn and the kitchen garden, she noted Joanna and the other young ladies working alongside some men she'd never seen before. At the gate, she stopped and dismounted. After handing her reins to one of the guards, she dashed into the monastery.

"Bran!" she called out.

Bertram peered out from the dining hall. "Oh, Your Highness." He strode outside to meet them. "What a pleasure to see you."

"Where's Bran?"

"He's—oh." Bertram smiled at Gwennore. "I believe we met on Ulfrid's ship, but I can't recall."

"My mother, Queen Gwennore." Lennie made a quick introduction. "This is Father Bertram."

Gwennore shook his hand. "I've heard so much about you"—she looked around—"and your monastery. Is it true you will accept anyone without a home?"

"Yes," Bertram replied proudly. "That is why we have so many young women here. But maybe not for long! Ervil and Festus, from the village of Trey Falls, have sent their sons."

"I would like to do something like this in Norveshka," Gwennore continued.

"Where is Bran?" Lennie asked again.

"Oh, he's not here." Bertram waved a hand vaguely.

Lennie's heart clenched. "He left? Did he say where he was going?"

"Oh, he's . . . not far from Lourdon Palace. I suspect you'll see him there. Zane is with him, too. Did you hear that Milena and Roslyn have gotten engaged?"

"Yes," Lennie replied impatiently. "We're on our way to the engagement party."

"Well then, you should get going." Bertram paused. "Unless you would like refreshments first."

"I would love a cup of tea," Gwennore said, smiling. "And I would love to hear more about the monastery."

"Mother!" Lennie almost screamed with frustration.

"Don't worry." Gwennore took her arm and led her into the dining hall. "I'm sure you'll see Bran at the engagement party. After all, Milena is his sister."

Lennie gritted her teeth and attempted to drink some tea.

Finally, they left and she raced her horse back to the barge. She was pacing up and down the deck by the time her mother and the guards arrived.

The time crept by as the barge moved slowly downriver to the pier just south of Lourdon. There, they were welcomed by a few soldiers from a nearby castle. Apparently, they were on the Duke of Southwood's land, and he was inviting them to tea at his home.

"Not more tea," Lennie muttered. "I'm sorry, but we're expected at the palace right away."

The duke had made some horses available for them, and they rode the short distance to Lourdon.

At Lourdon Palace, Lennie was shown to a guestroom. She was freshening herself up and considering a visit to Roslyn when there was a knock at the door. Her heart lurched. Was it Bran?

She ran to the door. It was just her luggage. After the servants left, she considered putting on a pretty gown. Bran had never actually seen her in a gown.

There was another knock, and she dashed to the door. A letter for her. "Thank you." She closed the door and tore open the envelope.

Another invitation to meet Baron Blackwood? He was waiting in the library? Ha! She tossed it aside.

Roslyn's bedchamber was nearby, so she went there and knocked on the door.

"There you are!" Roslyn dragged her inside, laughing. "We've been waiting for you."

Once again, all the girl cousins were there, and Lennie went down the line, exchanging hugs with Eviana, Julia, Faith, Kendall, and Glenda.

They were all laughing and holding scissors in their hands.

"We've been having a cutting party," Faith announced.

"What's that?" Lennie turned to examine the six dressmaker dummies that had displayed the six horrid bridesmaid gowns. On the floor lay heaps of lace, fringe, and ruffles. The six birds that had been on the gowns were now hanging from the chandelier.

"Don't you love it?" Roslyn gave one of the birds a push, and all six flew in a circle. "I'm thinking of giving it to Eviana's baby."

Eviana shook her head. "You'll give the poor thing nightmares."

"Speaking of nightmares," Julia said. "What do you think of the gowns now?"

Stripped of all the glitter and frills, the gowns now had a simple beauty to them. "I like them," Lennie said. "But please, don't make me wear the pink one."

Roslyn laughed. "Then can I have it? I'd love to wear it to the party."

Kendall pointed to the green one. "I think you should take this one, Lennie. It would look perfect with your eyes."

Soon, they had Lennie dressed and her hair piled artfully on her head.

"Oh, you look like a princess," Glenda teased, and they all laughed.

A knock sounded on the door, and Milena sauntered in. "Oh, my goodness, those gowns look so much better!"

Roslyn sighed. "I knew they didn't look right, but when I

tried to fix them, I kept adding more stuff. I should have realized that sometimes less is more."

Milena smiled. "Lennie, you look lovely. I was given this letter to pass on to you."

"Is it from Bran?" Lennie ripped it open. "Not Baron Blackwood again! What is this man's problem?"

"Lennie, he's been waiting for you in the library for an hour," Milena said.

"I'm not interested!" Lennie huffed. "Milena, you of all people should know that. I only want Bran."

Roslyn covered her mouth as she choked with laughter.

"What's so amusing?" Lennie grumbled. "Do you know, I went all the way to the monastery, and Bran wasn't there."

There was a knock at the door, and Milena rushed to open it. "Oh, Your Majesty, come in." She glanced into the hallway and grinned.

Lennie's father marched in and frowned at her. "I see you finally made it to the palace. But instead of meeting your suitor as he requested, you're here having a party."

"What suitor?" Lennie asked.

"Baron Blackwood," Silas muttered. "The man got tired of waiting—"

"Well, good," Lennie grumbled. "I don't want to see him."

"—and so, he came to see me," Silas continued. "He has formally asked for your hand, and you'll be relieved to know that I have accepted."

"*What?*" Lennie screeched.

"Oh, how wonderful!" Roslyn clapped her hands, and everyone cheered.

Lennie huffed. "I'll never marry that Baron—"

"Baron Blackwood." Silas motioned for the man to enter.

A handsome, well-dressed young man marched in.

Lennie blinked. "Bran?"

"Baron Blackwood at your service." He bowed.

"What?" Lennie looked askance at him.

Milena grinned. "Bran is the future Duke of Southwood."

"Excuse me?" Lennie asked.

Her father grinned. "I want you to know that I was prepared to accept him before I learned of this latest development."

"Thank you, Your Majesty." Bran bowed his head, then went down on one knee to offer Lennie a ring. "This was my mother's ring. I hope you will accept it. And me."

"Bran, I accepted you weeks ago." Lennie took the ring, then swatted him on the shoulder. "You should have told me!"

Grinning, he rose to his feet. "Are you angry with me?"

"Yes." She reconsidered. "No." She grabbed his fancy jacket and pulled him close for a kiss.

The cousins and Milena cheered.

"We should have a triple engagement party!" Roslyn exclaimed.

Lennie wrapped her arms around Bran's neck and whispered in his ear. "We should go on our date to the mountain cabin soon."

"Definitely." He kissed her cheek. "My arm is all healed now."

"No more falling and crashing," she told him.

"A Raven only falls once."

She smiled. "And when a dragon falls, it's forever."

Don't miss the first in the Embraced by Magic series, available now!

HOW TO LOVE YOUR ELF

Embraced by Magic

New York Times and *USA Today* bestselling author Kerrelyn Sparks

Raised in isolation on the magic-shrouded Isle of the Moon, five girls became five sisters. Now women, they are ready to claim their places in the world—and perhaps change it forever . . .

FLAME AND FORTUNE

Sorcha knew the mission was dangerous. Leaving the safe grounds of her brother's kingdom and parlaying with the elves across their border . . . well, treachery seemed at least as likely as true peace. But to support her sister, Sorcha would brave far more than the underhanded ways of the elves. Or so she thought, before she was taken hostage.

Of course, her captors didn't count on her particular abilities—or on the help of the Woodsman, the mysterious thief who made his home in the forest. He saw the battle from the trees, saw the soldier attacking against incredible odds to save a comrade—and then saw the valiant fighter revealed as Princess Sorcha of Norveshka. He can't tell if he wants to kidnap her or kiss her. But despite Sorcha's stubbornness, his inconvenient honor, and a rebellion on the cusp of full war, something burns between them that neither can let go . . .

Visit our website at
KensingtonBooks.com
to sign up for our newsletters, read
more from your favorite authors, see
books by series, view reading group
guides, and more!

Become a Part of Our
Between the Chapters Book Club
Community and Join the Conversation

Betweenthechapters.net

Submit your book review for a chance to win exclusive
Between the Chapters swag you can't get anywhere else!
https://www.kensingtonbooks.com/pages/review/